HEATWAVE AND CRAZY BIRDS

HEATWAVE AND CRAZY BIRDS

GABRIELA AVIGUR-ROTEM

TRANSLATED BY DALYA BILU

DALKEY ARCHIVE PRESS
CHAMPAIGN • DUBLIN • LONDON

Originally published in Hebrew as *Chamsin Ve-Tziporim Meshugaot* by Keshet, Tel Aviv, 2001
Copyright © 2001 by Gabriela Avigur-Rotem
Worldwide translation copyright © by the Institute for the Translation of Hebrew Literature
First edition, 2011

Library of Congress Cataloging-in-Publication Data

Avigur-Rotem, Gavri'elah, 1946-
[Hamsin ve-tsiporim meshuga'ot. English]
Heatwave and crazy birds / Gabriela Avigur-Rotem ; translated by Dalya Bilu. -- 1st ed.
    p. cm.
"Originally published in Hebrew as Chamsin Ve-Tziporim Meshugaot by Keshet, Tel Aviv, 2001."
ISBN 978-1-56478-643-2 (pbk. : alk. paper)
I. Bilu, Dalya. II. Title.
PJ5054.A9124H3613 2011
892.4'36--dc22
                        2011012928

Partially funded by the University of Illinois at Urbana-Champaign and by a grant from the Illinois
Arts Council, a state agency

The Hebrew Literature Series is published in collaboration with the Institute for the Translation of
Hebrew Literature and sponsored by the Office of Cultural Affairs, Consulate General of Israel in
New York

www.dalkeyarchive.com

Cover: design and composition by Danielle Dutton, illustration by Nicholas Motte
Printed on permanent/durable acid-free paper and bound in the United States of America

STORKS

If you were God, we once had a game, if you were God, what would you do?
  No more calligraphy lessons—
  And no arithmetic. Ever—
  And for all the Arabs to be dead—
  And for all the people from the Holocaust to be alive—
  Then from the War of Independence too—
  Them too—
  And from Trumpeldor—
  Them too—
  And from Judah's Maccabees and from Bar Kokhba—
  But that was ages and ages ago—
  But if you're God—
  If you were God you couldn't make a stone too heavy for you to lift—
that's me, quoting you, confusing them and confused for a minute myself,
left? Right? "But you were born here!" "No." "Didn't you grow up here?"
But they've torn things down here, sold, built, enlarged, they haven't left
a stone in its place except for your house which is suddenly here, it must
be—it is!—but no—those trees, the thicket—let me out for a minute—this
huge ficus tree wasn't here, it was, but not like this, a green lion tree with
its leafy maw open to devour the house humped into the ground, ready to
turn into archaeology—"Well? Is this it?" I turn around. Of course. The
blue gate's open, how did I walk through it without noticing—"This is it."
"A real monster!" "The house?" "That tree! Its roots have probably raised

half the floor!" The lawyer rustles in my wake—dry leaves whispering up to his ankles—where are the paving stones, one step instead of two at the entrance—"You won't get anything for the house," he sneezes, "but the land's worth a fortune—" "Allow me—" I extricate the wrong key from the keyhole, find the yellow one, stick it in, and turn once hard and once soft and one last half turn and then I turn around. The ficus. It's grown a muscular trunk, gray elephant-hide, and a mighty almost black crest. Nothing grows below it and behind it and its roots run into the house—

"Are you going in?" This isn't how I imagined my entry. Hundreds of times I surprised you, entering without a sound, touching your shoulder, hundreds of times I returned, the path was swept free even of dust, after the burning light outside the inside is always damp and dim as a cave, the opening door swings shut again as if pushed by a gentle hand; behind it, on the wall, padded parkas swell in the dark. "What a smell! Open a window!" The Law comes up behind me, "It should be here, in the living room—" I grope for the switch on the right behind the arms of the coats, a sickly light trembles in a glass pear. "This is the entrance hall," I conduct a guided tour of your house, "and this is the living room—" The switch on the left. Only two globes light up in the chandelier you made out of an old cart wheel here on the porch with Nahum and me watching. It was cold, and the smell of moldy leaves rose from the garden. This is the invention that changed the world, you growled, bowed over the wires, electricity, Nahum was sure, but you raised pale eyes to him; when you were angry they glittered like a broken sea. The wheel! you snapped in that voice of yours, almost like the crack of a whip. Nahum swallowed and said nothing. The wheel—what kind of invention is that! I snorted. I was protected. You raised your eyes again. This time you grinned: What-would-we-do-without-you-Goddess-Anat— Is she still here? Yes, still here, in the Biedermeier; "Daylight robbery, no less—" the Law whistles softly at your collection—clay lamps, seals, bronze and silver coins, a broken-armed Aphrodite, an iron Anat dimpled with rust—"Why ask for trouble?" says the Law, mentioning article 12, "write a nice letter to . . ." And now he sees too. "There it is." I point to the pyxis behind the curved glass—"Are you sure?" A squat clay pot, heavy-lidded, the handle of the lid a centaur's head and torso. "This is the only pyxis—" "Let's have a look," he suggests.

The library starts at the skirting tiles and ends at the ceiling, in its center the same rectangular wooden box, behind its closed lid is there still a double row of bottles of "medicinal" brandy, sherry, Slivovitz, and above them on a narrow glass shelf a platoon of thick-bottomed glasses multiplied in the mirror behind them, in the mirrors at the sides, into an entire battalion of squat greenish-glass dwarves, with you among them, pouring me a cognac, fuming with anger. What were you doing, trying to be Houdini? I was sitting in this armchair—"Come on, let's have a look," the lawyer doesn't dare open the glass door himself, but I go on sitting in the very same armchair, exhausted, outside shouts, calls, running footsteps, *Loya! Lo-ya! Where are you?* The *Here I am—cock-a-doodle-do!* dies in my throat and you hand me the glass—drink!—answer for me—she's here! The aroma is strong and sharp, warming, what's Houdini, I cough, who, you correct me, annoyed, almost insulted that I don't know, how come I still don't know, I'm old enough to read, after all, I'm here, I try my voice and they all come running in, Bilu and Ora and Elhanan and Yosefa and Adriana and Yossi and Dina, she's here, she's here—the lawyer turns on his heel. "You can look at it afterwards," he gives in, "and let me know— shii . . ." He trips over a row of projecting floor tiles. "It's that ficus! You'll need a bulldozer to uproot it." I jump up—Advocate Betzer!—cross the room, open the front door. The padded jackets resist softly. "Mr. Betzer, thank you very much—" I talk to him like an obstinate passenger, but he's inquisitive, snoopy, soft and panting as a spaniel in summer, peeping into the passage leading to the bathroom, the bedrooms, trying the doors, all of them locked. "I'll manage on my own—" I lean against the open door, the parkas crushed behind it. "And let me know!" I follow him outside into boiling light beyond the ficus, into what was once a garden and is now thorns and bald patches. "Look how much land!" He stands between the palms; the trunks are gray, straight, almost too slender for their height, their crests ragged but their fringes bristly, turning into black knives in the light. From the palms stretch clay-colored furrows, at the end—the orange grove, dark, dense, and tangled, the light touching only the tips of the treetops with the tips of its fingernails. "This is the rented plot," Advocate Betzer informs me as if I didn't know, "and there's the orange grove—"

It's hot. Humid. I turn to the gate, at its left the cypress tree—you planted two, but only this one took, how tall it's grown, the bougainvillea from the hedge twines around its trunk, flowering with orange-purple butterflies, but in the steamy air everything is black and white—"The orange grove's a lost cause," the lawyer's sweltering in the heat but nevertheless feels obliged. "Lost?" "It's dry as a bone; in any case, no sane person hangs onto a citrus grove these days, but listen to me; don't sell it until Passover—" "Why?" I ask although I know he'll say: because of the prices—but he surprises me: "Because of the smell . . . the smell . . . The smell of the orange groves before Passover—how long haven't you been here?"

A long time.

Very long.

Quarter of a century. More—

The kitchen on the right. Like ours: beige marble with orange veins. Wooden cabinets painted cream. Three rows of white tiles above them a window and screen clogged with grease and dust, but it too opens, and the outside view is filled by the pomegranate tree.

The keys are waiting in the fuse box. On to the toilet: still painted pale green, waist-high, and smelling of the Sick Fund clinic. The water in the toilet bowl is brown, as if it's grown rusty in the course of time. I pull the cord. It gurgles, bubbles, and suddenly thunders in a gray deluge from the heights of the tank. I lower the lid and sit down to wait; for a moment it seems that yes, now-now-now, the big butterfly is coming back to my throat, to flutter between my ribs, to tickle the soles of my feet as it always did when I hid in very small places, where it was sometimes a butterfly and sometimes a rare green soda pop that left, after half an hour of sweetness, a bitter seltzer water in my feet. And sometimes inside a crate made of planks and gaps that drew hot stripes of sun on me or a cardboard box that served briefly as a puppy's kennel until it grew up or ran away or got run over, but the smell, a dense smell of kindness and milk and wisps of warm fur—or in a dark blue chest with copper-clad corners, half winter clothes and half vapors of their breath—naphthalene and damp felt and thick mud and thin rain, a sad, European smell, so different from the fragrance of the oranges in their softly whispering silky tissue paper, from the smell of dusty pines roasted in the sun—the smell encloses me like the shell of a peanut, kindling a wild, hurrahing exultation, I'm going away and they're looking for me outside, it always comes with them looking for me outside, calling me, arguing, is she here? No, not here, no one could hide in here, Loya could, not even Loya, were you trying to be Houdini?

I stand up. Your toilet is small, but the ceiling is high, the space bright, the window open, the heatwave already here.

Here's the door to Nahum's room, opposite it—to yours, is the double bed still in a storm of pillows and blankets as if a battle had raged there till dawn?—and the living room again, the same couch, the same two arm-chairs opposite it, stiff, covered with matte-green upholstery, back in fash-ion after a quarter of a century, the low rectangular Formica table too, and the Biedermeier in the corner, an uncle from another opera, and the pyxis inside it. What to do with you, give me a sign. I'm here. Not in longings, not in dreams. I can touch, rummage, burrow—

But not yet. Tonight I'll sleep here, in the living room. I pull out the drawer with the bedclothes under the couch—heavy, sour cotton sheets, splattered with rust—outside, outside, to the washing lines—yes, they're still here, sagging deeper in the middle—the afternoon sun will toast the sheets—tonight I'll sleep on sheets crisp with heat—

If I sleep. The couch is bulging, resistant, the upholstery scratchy, the guest couch you called it, no wonder no guest ever slept there—

A cat, you're an alley cat, Jean-Jacques intended a compliment, you always fall on your feet, he said, eat everything—plastic, nylon, tin—fall asleep anywhere, anyhow, so why not here and now? The sheets creak, the back of the couch curves, projects outwards, and I can never fall asleep with my back to the room, certainly not now; the darkness rustles, breathes, scratches to get out—

What made me stay to sleep. There may be snakes here. Scorpions. Rats. Did I bother to check?

Balzac, a sleepless passenger once told me on a flight to Paris, Balzac had a round bed with black silk sheets. Oho, we spoke Frenchified Hebrew, he probably slept very well, Monsieur Balzac! Oh non-non-non-non! The passenger protested, Monsieur Balzac never slept at night! What did Monsieur Balzac do at night? He drank coffee and wrote novels and shortened his life.

He was the kind of person who was sure the one plane he was flying on—no matter how seldom he flew—would fall and crash: you can see those types sitting next to the window with taut necks, counting the screws on the wing, changing color whenever the plane changes direction. On transatlantic flights they lie with their eyes closed in order to cheat their fear, change position, get up to go to the toilet, go up to the flight attendants, ask for tea, mineral water, something for heartburn, migraine, nausea. Over the ocean they are convinced that we are about to fall into the water with a mighty splashshsh. Fists of water will crumple the plane like an empty tin can. And then—the silver fishes will come and nibble their cheeks, the tips of their noses, their ears, leaving only skeletons wrapped in tattered clothes floating in the body of the mangled plane; and afterwards snails will screw themselves into the cavities of their nostrils; eels will coil around their skulls like living turbans; an octopus will tap on their ribs with a groping arm, and a black clam will squeeze under what was once their tongue—Actually a very beautiful death, I smiled at Jean-Jacques who talked and talked—only the first moments are hard—a plane is much safer than a car, safer than a child's scooter—I promised him the next day during that meal in the Latin Quarter, but he didn't believe me; it isn't natural, it isn't human, it isn't normal, to fly. What do I lack for up there, I tried to persuade him in vain, protected from cold, from heat, from big spaces, from bad surprises—

I didn't sleep all night, but the stripes of outside between the stripes of shutter are already milky-gray and I've been listening who knows how long to the birds sewing rapid sound-stitches into what remains of the darkness; there's something piercing about them and something glittering—

I go out barefoot, disheveled, smelling of sleeplessness, but who cares: all around there isn't a soul but me. And the trees. And the earth. And the birds. One of them giving voice to a tart-sweet burgundy warble like plum compote, that's it there, the very black one, and here's another one, but much more faded, maybe it's old, maybe ill, and here's another one, pale gray with a black hangman's hood and a lemony stomach, it barks and another one comes and another one, what's happened to the birds, have a bunch of new immigrants arrived or what, I remember sparrows on the road after the rain, a hoopoe bird out of a book—but here's one, I swear, an honest-to-goodness hoopoe bird with a pick on her head digging in the grass with a brisk staccato, and now the black one lands next to her, dressed like a Mafia boss for a funeral, his beak is orange and his voice clear and Italian, and who's that tiny little one, changing colors in the light like an iridescent chip of peacock—the birds have run wild here like everything else: the ficus, the bougainvillea, the conch grass, the drains— should I hurry to the phone, to summon a plumber, a gardener, a renovator without delay? But what's the rush, it's only me here, no emergency, no safety belts needed, smoking permitted—

Nahum's room is locked. Your room is locked. Every keyhole like a little girl cut out of darkness; a giant head attached without a neck to a widening dress, without arms, without legs, signaling cold-cold-cold—but I'll open anyway—who can tell me not to—I'll open and see what there is to see.

Not today.

Today I'll go and buy myself a pair of "biblical" sandals, if they still sell them here in the shopping center. My hair's electric, my fingers swollen stiff, even through my sunglasses the light's like a blowtorch—and the center. Where's the center. The center's moved. I walk, stray into a new area, return, try again, suddenly find the row of eucalyptuses, huger than then, underneath them we would argue and peel away the bark until their real skin was revealed, smooth, pinky-white, feminine, or break leaf daggers in hands filling with a light green smell, and when does the paved plaza date from, the ugly fountain—cement painted sky blue—and what's happened to the public meeting hall—it's grown taller, sprung a second story, a double entrance, glass doors and stairs instead of the falafel stall and the great cauldron of *corn-on-the-cob piping hot corn-on-the-cob* in a voice roasted hoarse, serving me only for free after the movie because I was the one who turned the reel with the translation-on-the-side until the Cinemascope-in-spectacular-Technicolor arrived with the Hebrew-translation-in-the-body-of-the-movie—

"Is this the meeting hall?" I inquire of a dark suit with a James Bond briefcase hurrying by, "*Matnas*," he throws at me, the Youth, Sport, and Culture Center, no further elaboration, he's already gone, but behind the old meeting hall to my surprise I meet the same smell of tasteless boiled chicken, groats, and grated carrots—a punishment from which only I was exempt, because for lunch I bought falafel and a popsicle that broke in my mouth and ran sticky down my little finger until it reached the strap of the watch I wore from the age of seven so that I would know exactly when the bus arrived and run home from wherever I was to spare my father anxiety—Eating that food will give you an ulcer, Ora's mother promised me problems with my spleen, liver, gall bladder—Yes, yes, you're young now, you can afford to eat gravel and drink acid, but when you get older . . . Where are you now, Ora's mother? Six feet under, I'll bet. And I'm still here, you see? Going to buy myself sandals for a month, a waste, right, so what, what's life if not a terrible, wonderful waste, nobody gets a second chance, who says so, I had one, why had, have, a house and an orange grove that will let me live another thirty years of irresponsibility; I haven't been to China yet. I haven't walked along the Great Wall, I haven't toured the Forbidden City, I haven't dipped my hand in the silky river lapping the toes of the Guilin Mountains—where's the new center? I cut short an argument between two children, one pointing left, the other snickering, he's pulling your leg! I decide to believe the first one, walk along the new, clean street, on either side little gardens severely trimmed and spotless white villas with honey-colored shutters and humming air conditioners flashing drops of water in the sun. And here's the center: a colossal cube of pale marble, inside a neon-lit space crowded with boutiques and dried-up air smelling of French fries and linoleum. In Rome, Chic, and Parade, young dyed-blonde gum-chewing sales girls shrug their shoulders—"What'd'ya say your size is?"—send me to the children's shoes. Only in Garfield do I find sandals. Jeans colored. Brown leather, biblical? Where've you been living, Miss—

I skip the supermarket. For bread, cheese, and canned goods I'll look for the grocery, if it still exists here somewhere, I ask a woman who looks quite ancient and discover that what was once Rasco Housing Development C is no more, it's been replaced by Pinewoods Residential Estates, the developers wanted to sell, today everything's money, and who'd live in Rasco Housing C these days, so they changed the names of all the streets while they were about it, a young man, apparently her son, joins us on the way to the exit gate, "When I was small," he grins, "it was all names you had to look up in the encyclopedia: KaKaL, TARSAT, MALAL, YALAG— if you're looking for them you can forget it—" "What did they change them to?" I ask. "Into flowers and plants," says the son, putting the plastic shopping bags into the boot of the car, "green's in now, it's all the rage—Kalanit, Koranit, Hamanit, Hartzit—"

Only now I notice: on every corner a street name in white on pastoral green, a veritable garden of herbs and flowers, Rakefet crossing Hartzit, Nurit turning into Koranit—just a minute, isn't this the street where the grocer's shop was? Yes, here it is, almost buried under the ficus trees, but definitely it, even the sign, Morgenstern's Grocery with Mrs.-Morgenstern-the-Grocer's as short and sour as ever. I stop on the threshold, hold my breath, now she'll raise her eyes, she raises them over reading glasses, that's new, she looks at me, waits, I wait, my heart in my throat, but she doesn't recognize me, "Nu, what you wants?" she asks in the same Hebrew, in the same potsherd voice. "Black bread—and milk—and white cheese—" "Nu, that you takes alone," she jerks her three chins from side to side of her kingdom—"Do you have a plastic bag?" She pulls one out from under the counter with demonstrative reluctance—"Why you not to bring basket? Here isn't supermarket!" She watches me. "You wants eggs? This fresh from farm—comes today!" I take half a dozen and approach the counter. She does her calculations with her breath coming in slow grunts, as if she is about to fall asleep and start snoring—a quarter of a century has passed and she hasn't changed—still writing with May-He-Rest-in-Peace's flat carpenter's pencil—she hands me the bill, I pay, smile, try—"Shalom, Missus Morgenstern"—"Shalom," she grunts, not recognizing, not taking the hint, when I'm half out of the door she aims at my back, "You don't want newsespapers? We have all! All newses in country, evenings, Hebrews, Hungarian too—" "I don't read newspapers," I catch a glimpse of the shocked anger on her face before I finally leave and hear her wishing that I break my bones in Yiddish. Shkorifinshtshicha we called her, I suddenly remember, after the spiteful neighbor woman in Bialik's story, because of her voice, and her Yiddish, and the blue number on her arm.

Early in the evening I open the double shutter doors to the porch. The balustrade is high and wide, inviting watermelon seeds set out to dry on a bed of coarse salt, shining like diamonds in the sun. The sunset flames behind the hammered black filigree of the jacaranda leaves. Once there was a hammock here to lie on under the soft, mesmerizing drift of lilac blossoms, but when, when do they bloom, when do the flowers fall in that quiet drift, maybe I'll stay till then, maybe I'll buy a hammock, tie it up, lie on it like then, and the flowers—nonsense. *Venimus vidimus iimus*, Davidi: we came, we saw, we left. I'll rummage around here a bit, sort out what I find, perhaps I'll take something, and I'll sell all the rest. I'm only here till then. With limited liability. Even the grocer's isn't in Absalom the Fourteenth street any more—Elhanan's father overheard, chuckled, corrected, explained, Absalom Feinberg, the Lord avenge his blood,—but in Koranit Lane. What's Koranit when it's at home? According to the plant guide I find on the bookshelves, a common narrow-leafed subshrub, an aromatic herb, Thymus in Latin, its full name in Hebrew is *Koranit Mekurkefet*—scalped? Like the title of a book about Red Indians by Karl May or the name of that movie I wasn't allowed to do the translation-on-the-side for, a movie for adults only, sixteen and over and how old was I then and what was the name of the movie: *Hashoshana Hamekurkefet*? The Scalped Rose? I return to the porch, the sky is already deep blue, the sunset gone in a flash, ten pink minutes and cut—how could I forget, the movie was called "The Rose Tattoo." Do you know what a tattoo is at all? You asked me, perhaps trying to soften the blow perhaps to explain the prohibition, and I replied, sure I do, it's writing in ink that doesn't come off like the number on Mrs.-Morgenstern-the-grocer's and Hasia Horovitz's arm—Professor Kaplan, take the pest away from here! You say in that darkening voice, and Daddy doesn't have to hurry me up, I'm out of the house already, hearing you shout inside.

Almost every fine Saturday you and Daddy, Nahum and me, an odd family, on the way there—you two in the cabin, us among the ropes, black rubber baskets, brushes, spade, pick, axe, lanterns, etc. in the back, bumping along in clouds of dust, driving for hours, stopping with a jolt next to a hill or tell, Daddy stretching his legs, you rubbing your hands, and Nahum and I exchanging looks; just a hill, a plain ordinary hill. A few stones—thorns—the things you find are always dusty, even the coins, and the sun's always burning and soon it's hot, very hot, even when it's almost on the beach or not far from it and a salty wind's blowing—even then—the sun's like fire and Nahum and I shake a sieve between us and discover one corroded coin, and you get excited—treasure!—what treasure, where treasure, treasure's buried in ironclad chests in the heart of a dripping rainforest, between heavy garlands of orchids and anacondas, answering the probing beam of the flashlight with a spectacular burst of starry light—

And with you two it's always sun, thorns, dust, and stones, but sometimes everything cracks—Ota! A bunker! You ask for a pick, rope, flashlight—tear open, almost without help, a hole in the glaring heat, call us from the belly of the earth in an echoing voice to come and see, but careful, be careful, Loya, only my patience has run out, I jump, slide, slither into the cool darkness dense with the smell of stone that hasn't seen the sun for centuries, here, here there was a bunker! You enthuse, the beam of your flashlight wavering on enormous clay jars, here they kept oil or dried figs, Ali Baba and the forty thieves, I announce, but you take no notice, tap gingerly on the jars, try to shift them, who dug it, when, why, you and Daddy are already arguing, look here, they kept pigeons here, it's a columbarium, you glide your flashlight to another dark annex, rows of identical little niches, one below the other, even when Daddy adds his flashlight to yours the darkness gathered in each little niche is not diluted, it stares out at us from scores of eyes. Pigeons? Under the earth? You must be joking, pigeons fly, yes, you agree, and come back with messages tied to their legs, it was their I.S.—Information Service in the "Hagana," Nahum knows, and I peek at Daddy to see if this is really a possibility, hard to tell anything from the expression on his face, only his voice betrays scholarly reservations, they buried the dead here—How? Your roar explodes inside the bunker, but Daddy is not deterred, they burned them, and put the ashes in little boxes, and Nahum and I are already moving away from their argument, our small flashlights casting a pale liquid light on the walls, look, there's another opening here, and I crawl in, maybe I'll be like little Maria de Sautuola, discover prehistoric bison on the ceiling of the cave, Loya, Loya no! They stop arguing at once, hurry up, but I'm already on my belly, the stone is smooth, cool, enclosing me like two slices of bread sandwiching a piece of cheese, wait Loya wait, but I go on, I can already get on all fours, stand erect, stretch out my arms, everything is pitch black except for the circle of light you send in and the voices, yours, Daddy's, in great alarm: Loya? Loya?

The darkness passes me coach after coach after coach after coach—a slow, continuous, steaming train. Take your time, Hedva advised me before the flight, and I try, slowly and deliberately, the way we once left raspberry drops to melt in our mouths. The night here is full of sounds: the dry hovering of fragile wings, a sudden flutter of light, a hiccup of water in the throat of the sink, the slow snap of old furniture. How can I possibly fall asleep? I switch on the light. Look for a book. Here's a book about birds. In the introduction it says there are different kinds. Sedentary and migratory. If you have wings—you always have options. You wake up one morning and say—I'm hot, I'm cold, I don't like it here, I'll spread my wings, I'll leave, I'll migrate, I'll be back when this disagreeable season agrees to change, I'll return with the squills, with the chrysanthemums—and here's a hoopoe bird: its scientific name sounds like a dance troupe from Africa—*Upupa epops*—but to me she looks like a Polish yenta who lives in a house full of unopened chocolate boxes and crocheted doilies on the backs of all the chairs; in the mornings she pecks at the grass with the same expression of disdain as her double lifts the edge of the damp wrapping paper from a block of white cheese in the grocery store, lowering her red-tipped nose to sniff, looks at me with one suspicious eye, and then the other, and suddenly spreads her wings with their convict stripes—flies two meters and lands with her crest spread like a fan semitransparent in the light. Sleep seems impossible. I've switched off the light, and now I toss and turn, get up, open the shutters, from the garden a damp, throaty, continuous croaking rises, the curved glass of the Biedermeier distorts the light of the street lamp into crooked stripes of silvery gray—I give up, sit down on the armchair, pick up my legs and hug them to me, and thus, shrouded in a sheet, I wait for morning—but the moment when the night between the shutter slats turns into day is impossible to pin down, like the moment of takeoff, which you discover only after the plane gains altitude, like love, which you only recognize after it has scratched—

"Did I wake you?" It's the lawyer at half past six in the morning, working like a lunatic, "I wanted to talk to you before the holidays begin . . . what did you decide? Just a minute, there's someone on the line, no don't hang up, it might be that buyer I told you about—the deal of a lifetime—what?— just a minute—what? You don't want me to send him in the meantime? Are you sure? Okay, then, let me know. But before the holiday—what holiday? Rosh Hashanah, the New Year, what's the matter with you—"

The new center is packed with people—where were they all a week ago— loaded shopping carts, lines, sales attendants offering tastes of wine, soup, apple-flavored honey—but I hug the electric fan I bought with both hands and contemplate the line from the side: strangers, strangers, strangers look right through me, not one familiar face, not one who coughs or clears his throat to catch my attention, to ask for water, coffee, a newspaper, ear- phones —nobody needs me. Wonderful. Terrible. I can do whatever I want. Wonderful. What do I want?

Street, pavement, parking lot, "clothed in cement and concrete" just as in Nathan Alterman's 1936 song, here and there a trim moustache of lawn, only back in your yard can the powdery soil still be felt, pushing up be- tween my toes. Under this earth, you promised, are great treasures, cities, forts, walls one on top of the other, compressed layer by layer, even here, in Rasco C, you hear? You would stamp, raising dust, squat, cock an ear like an American Indian listening for a train, and whenever a bulldozer or tractor arrived to dig foundations or expose underground pipes you would race outside and shout and wave your arms and climb onto the treads and struggle with the astonished, mustachioed tractor driver in his round blue cloth hat—and once Ora's mother stood next to me, panting, righteous, af- ter hurrying back from the council offices, I phoned the police—they're on their way—who does he think he is—and then she noticed me and seized me in a vice-like grip, and you, Loyinka, are coming with me, but I slipped out of her grip and ran to the edge of the neighborhood, to our bunker. How could you not have guessed, not have found out all those years. Next to Nahmani's orange grove, in the old shipping crate. We hoarded candles there, rags, nails, empty bottles, matches, if the Nazis came, if the Arabs came to throw women and children into the sea, we were ready. Elhanan drilled us in throwing Molotov cocktails like in the Russian movies where there was always an amazing blond giant who threw a burning bottle at a tank before he was shot and fell on his back with his clear eyes open to the sky.

What is it this time, you would grumble, grumble and give me matches, potatoes, half a bottle of oil, what do you need it for—but you wouldn't wait for an answer, accompanying your giving with a kind of angry affection, and perhaps that's why the catch-me-if-you-cans, the treasure-hunters, the hide-and-seekers, would so often land up at your house, and I too, of course, come bursting in, panting, running, *Hannibal ad portas?* you ask, is Hannibal at the gate? but only if I'm alone, careful not to embarrass me, did you save, did you keep the four volumes of Mommsen for me too: small, dark green, emblazoned with a gold she-wolf suckling a cub-sized Romulus and Remus—in one of the volumes against a black background the thick-necked head of Hamilcar, his eyes empty and an extra head sculpted on his helmet, and on the page opposite him a slender, sensitive, sour-faced Hannibal, frowning brow over eyes I could swear were between blue and gray—

Hannibal was one of us without a shadow of a doubt, it's in the Bible, not him, but his fathers' fathers' fathers, Hiram king of Tyre, Jezebel daughter of Ethbaal king of Sidon, of whom nothing was left but her feet and the palms of her hands and the beautiful head a kneeling woman turns to the viewer in Gustave Doré's illustration, they threw her to the dogs, but her sons—Jehoram and Ahaziah—ruled over Israel, and her daughter, Athaliah, married the king of Judah: Didn't they teach you that in school?

This same Jezebel was the aunt of Mutton the king of Tyre, whose daughter Elissa, or Elissar, otherwise known as Dido—"the fugitive"? Right, the fugitive who escaped from Tyre and founded Karthadshat, in other words Carthago or Carthage, the motherland of Hamilcar and Hasdrubal and Hannibal—the Carthaginians refused to hand him over to the Romans! Your voice rises—and the Second Punic War broke out! The one with the elephants? You shake your head and I understand that this is no time for elephants, thirty-seven elephants Hannibal took to cross the Alps, and you had a story about each of them—We're the only ones who hand people over!—your voice boils, and I know that "we're the only ones" spells bad news, hope that somebody will come—Nahum, Ora, Adriana, Bilu, even Hasia Horovitz with a newspaper-padded string bag inside which jars of compote and jam and horseradish bump into each other with a soft rattling sound, *Timeo Danaos* you hum in a kind of synagogue singsong and wink, *I fear the Greeks*, knowing that I know these were the words of Laocoön to the Trojans on seeing the wooden horse, hinting to me to stay as if you're afraid of getting involved with Shlomi's mother (with Shlomi's mother?) who's as pale and glum as *palacinky*—no, I would shrug my shoulders at almost every holiday meal, and she would press me anyway, eat, eat, you thin, you needs lot of strength, and Shlomi wants to bury himself under the tablecloth, his thin, very sunburned father sits at the table in a blue workman's undershirt, eats rapidly, everything on his plate, and then smokes a cigarette and doesn't say a word, and Shlomi talks to him in fluent Yiddish like some old man from the Diaspora, wearing glasses and trailing behind me like a tail—

The dark is hot and full of grunts. The couch resists me. I turn over and from its depths rise sounds of snapping springs—*Why hast thou disquieted me, to bring me up?*—the water in the pipes shudders and hiccups, suddenly bubbling in the plug hole of the sink, the whitewash on the wall cracks, bare feet run past with a dry rustle—I switch on the light—a gigantic tick is advancing towards me!—

If I screamed, nobody heard. I'm leaving. Now. Right away.

But where to?

What is alive and lit up and full of people and movement twenty-four hours a day? I get dressed, keeping an eye on the tick waving its feelers next to the clawed foot of the Biedermeier. Don't you dare move from there, I say and order a cab to the airport.

At the airport it's neither day nor night, the air is filtered, processed, humming to itself and glittering with neon and stainless steel. People stray, stare, ask, what? What did you say? In the creaking whisper of the wheels of the trolleys, you may as well stop looking, sir, you won't find one that rides smoothly to where you want it to go, the flight attendant's half-complaining, half-demanding drawl over the loudspeaker fills everything, but in what language? Hebrew sounds like Turkish, English like ancient Scottish, who understands what, what did she say, what passengers on what flight, what plane growls now before takeoff on the invisible runway outside, from here you see what, black windows and walking reflections, passengers parting from their luggage after questions and answers and security checks, parting from the people seeing them off, should I take the umbrella? Where's my passport? And money, money, have you got enough? Did you buy me a newspaper? They hand them out in the plane! But there are never enough, buy one, don't be so mean, it'll cost you another two shekel, Ya'akov! Ya'akov! buy me a carton, okay, okay—and here the awkward embraces of *they haven't seen each other for forty years*, a few tears mixed up with laughter and how are you and fine, thank God, we've prepared a room for you, a bed, no, there's no need, what do you mean there's no need, I've booked in at a hotel, a hotel? They'll quarrel in the taxi to Holon, I smile at the security guard who remembers me and is sure that I have a flight and go up to the duty-free hall, into the smell of leather and Irish Cream and Courvoisier, and running shoes and sapphires—an international smell of yearning and money. Soon the people collecting at the head of the stairs will get onto the plane and flight attendants in dark suits and trained smiles will supply them with food wrapped in cellophane and reasons to complain. I go downstairs. You didn't fly? The security guard wonders, no, I only said good-bye to a friend—

When I get back to the house the darkness has already thinned and the birds are in full voice. I remain outside, trying to attach a voice to a bird, but it isn't easy: who, for example, is voicing that jagged lament that starts high and draws a descending arc, who is gargling raspberry cordial in her throat, the only one to be seen today is a big black-gray crow, hopping with folded wings, important and suspicious as a kashrut inspector from the rabbinate—

The air clears, warms, fills with crushed grayish light. The orange grove etches a pale silhouette. There's a tall weed growing next to the faucet. Only with the help of a stone do I succeed in loosening the bronze bowtie spigot of the faucet to a splutter—a sneeze—another splutter—the water hurries down the black hose, bursting out from somewhere or other in a seething hiss accompanied by brief coughs. I follow the direction of the sound and discover between the palms and the jacaranda tree a little iron pipe—it's the sprinkler: from its head a trembling glass sunflower opens, and the wind suddenly pouncing from the orange grove tears a wet shred off it, but the shred bounces back and again it is torn away and again it returns and remains whole—

What's fire made of, the memory suddenly assails me; you and Daddy squatting on your heels, busy with the camp fire. Nahum is already in the lake, and I, just woken up, pick my way carefully over huge stone eggs to the place where the edge of the Kinneret folds over in a thin, transparent, shining line. Na-hum! I call, but my voice drowns in the thick light which has swallowed the lake. Nahum's drowned, I announce so that you'll pay attention to me, but you're busy with the fire; the fire is almost transparent, only its edges are zigzag gold and keep changing shape. You carefully free a twig with a flaming head and insert it beneath a coffee can sitting on three stones, making a daughter-fire. Soon we'll have coffee, you say to Daddy or to yourself. Daddy's fire hasn't been diminished, I suddenly discover.

What's fire made of? Daddy removes his glasses; when you see very clearly it's hard to think, he once said to me—fire is made of everything that burns in it, he says after thinking briefly and puts his glasses back on, and then you rise from the daughter-fire—lace-up boots and khaki socks pulled up to rocky knees—and your voice passes right over my head: Of everything that burns! You say in that voice, a voice trembling inside itself, of every-thing that burns, you repeat in a louder, more trembling voice, almost sing-ing a black psalm. Wood burns, you seem to choke on malicious laughter, flesh burns, fat—fat burns very well—Daddy gets up and encloses you in a semi-embrace and leads you to the water. And here's Na-hum, he says in a sweet, soothing voice, a voice unfamiliar to me, and indeed Nahum surfaces and emerges dripping from the water. Loya, bring a towel! Since when does Nahum need help? I throw him a towel, and he wraps himself in it and goes up to you. How's tricks, Davidi? He doesn't call you Daddy. You've already calmed down. This time it was short. The three of us go up to your fire. A purplish-brown grown-up smell rises from the can. You, too? Nahum initiates me for the first time into the adult order. Yes! Daddy hands me a white, blue-rimmed enamel mug, careful, it's hot, I hold it gin-gerly and blow into the smell to cool it. Then I try. After that I cry; I can't understand why something that smells so good tastes so bad.

"Loya?"

"What?"

"Did I wake you?"

"What's the time?"

"Here or there?"

We both laugh.

"What's happening? How are you getting organized?" Hedva on the other side of the sea and ocean has controlled herself up to now, she swore not to nag, but she can't keep it up. She has to know—"Have you met any-one?"

"Only Missus-Morgenstern-the-grocer's, if you must know—"

"And?"

"She didn't recognize me—"

"And apart from that?"

"It's hot."

"So what else is new? How are you getting organized?"

"I'm not. Yesterday I took a taxi and ran away to the airport because of a bug—"

"What's happening to you?"

"I don't know. In the meantime I'm sleeping in the living room—"

"Did you find the . . ."

"Yes."

"What are you going to do with it?"

"I haven't decided yet."

"Do you feel all right?"

"I'm not sleeping—I haven't slept through the whole night once since I got here—"

Hedva laughs.

"What's so funny?"

"Two weeks in the country and you've already turned into a proper yenta. How are you? Don't ask, I didn't sleep a wink all night—"

"Very funny—"

"Loya," her voice changes, "Should I get on a plane?"

"*Nienada*. No need. It's okay. Another day or two—"

"Have you seen Ora?"

"No. Who knows where she's living now—"

"Will you look for her?"

"One thing at a time, Hedva. Maybe, when I've finished everything here, when I 'get organized'—"

We both laugh.

Gilgamesh and Enkidu, Achilles and Patroclus, Alexander and Hephaestion, Achates and Aeneas, Horace and Virgil—what were you to each other in your lives and mine, will I ever know? All the witnesses are dead.

"Take that one, take round challah special for holiday," the-grocer's grumbles, "no health's bread today. Holiday now." I buy the round challah, rummaging for change in my purse, "You got house of *meshuggener*," she takes me by surprise, "you not sell?" I don't reply. "Is buyer," she promises and fixes me with a hard look, "You's young girl, you musts go Tel Aviv, place for young peoples, not live where not one boy—" She insists, "Is first-class buyer—" maybe she's been promised a commission. "I'm in no hurry, nothing's burning—" I take the challah. "Why you say nothing burning?" Her eyes flash at me from behind the counter, "You buy newsespaper today?" She's forgotten. "I subscribe to *Haaretz*," I lie. "And there it doesn't say burning?" Her three chins quiver, "Burning! All country burning!" "*Sha-na To-va*, Mis-sus Morgenstern," I warble in honeyed tones and turn to go. "What kind of a good year is this," she mutters in Yiddish, sure I didn't hear her.

And if—if—if I go on walking straight ahead, straight and then left and then right to Ussishkin corner KaKaL streets, to the house surrounded exclusively by fruit trees—each in its own neat basin—if I knock at the door and wait on the mat until Ora's mother peeks through the spy hole and pretends to be surprised when she opens the door with a cry of "Loyinka! It's ages since we saw you! Come in, come in! Ba-ruch!" she'll call over her shoulder as I enter the living room—the same sofa covered with a sheet against bum dust, the same two armchairs—"You probably want Orinka"—she'll point me to the kitchen, I'm not worthy of the living room, sit me down next to the yellow Formica table, pour me a glass of water without raspberry cordial for reasons of economy and dental health, and seat herself opposite me with a creak. Orinka, she'll speak slowly, relishing every word, examining my face as she does so, Orinka is the head of the school of social work, or perhaps, Orinka is a doctor in charge of the maternity ward in a hospital in Tel Aviv, or Orinka is a senior lecturer at the university and you, what do you do? All these years in the air? Of course your father, may he rest in peace, was a professor in Jerusalem, and we all predicted great things for you, she'll accompany her words with that tsk-tsk-tsk shake of her head, wasting her sympathy on me, running around the streets, not eating a hot meal at midday, ruining my eyes at the cinema, and she repeats her standing invitation, but how many times can she ask me, you don't like the nourishing food we eat, as if food is a question of liking or not liking, you don't want to take a nap in the afternoon, I hear you running around barefoot when normal people are sleeping—and Ora standing next to me, tall, beautiful: Mother—leave her alone—

A new silence outside. Cool strips of wind pass through the hot air. A holiday eve. What is a holiday eve made of? Cars—far fewer—and perhaps this is the reason for the silence—pull up quietly outside houses, unload running children, parents carrying covered pots or flower arrangements—the sound of muffled singing rises—fills the air—dies down—I am apparently walking towards it and like me others, on the left, on the right, alone, in small family groups, most of them dressed in white, filling the street with the sound of hurrying feet, if I stop suddenly I'll be an island in the stream, they'll pass me by, move on like then, but then it was cooler and later, the air was already black and a moist halo was shining around the street lamp, we were coming back from the movie screened on the co-op wall and I said to Nahum that I was sorriest for the horses. You're sorry for the horses! I didn't know you'd heard. Yes, I turned to you, making an island among the tall people hurrying home to sleep, to get up in the morning for school, work, wash-day, concealing-revealing the light from the single lamp—and for the people you're not sorry? You raised your voice and Nahum pinched my arm to make me shut up but I couldn't, the horses were so beautiful, galloping-gliding past in colors of coffee and cinnamon and milk spotted with cocoa, and the people shot them, and they fell, turned onto their backs, lay bleeding on their sides— No, I'm not sorry for them because they're guilty, they're always guilty! I said defiantly. Guilty? You raised your voice and people moved away, I was close to Nahum, arm touching arm, he was trembling. Take her, take her home, my father said to Nahum, and Nahum hesitated, knowing I wouldn't come with him. I'll go by myself! I say angrily, insulted, what did I say already, hurrying to be swept along in the tide of people hurrying home to bed, *meshuggener, meshuggener*, they say above my head, but they say it about every third person in the neighborhood, *meshuggener arop von kop*, or *meshuggener arop von dach*, lunatic off his head, lunatic off his roof—"Loya, Loya!" Nahum is behind me but he hasn't got a chance, I run, run, run, run, run to the end of the people and the beginning of the absolute darkness—

From the orange groves the wolves' eyes shine like fireflies, babies wail as they are devoured, I'll go there and they'll eat me alive and you'll all be sorry when all you find of me is the scalp with my bangs, I cry and turn back, but not right away, first you have to worry, first you have to be sorry for my death in the bloom of my youth, first you have to know what you did, softly I knock on the Horovitzes' door so they won't hear and won't let me in and I'll have an excuse to sit there on the step, under the light, but Hasia opens the door. Daddy asked—the lie dries up in my mouth and she lets me in. Shlomi sleeping. And also his father sleeping. But I never sleeping—never—she ignores the tears wetting my cheeks, maybe she doesn't notice in the reddish glow of the boiler light—she puts a warm hand on my head and leads me into the living room. You sitting here, she whispers, and I to bring you nice hot glass milk—without the skin, I begin to ask and start—oh dear—to cry again. Hasia returns—heavy, soft, steaming, in a minute she'll ask me why I'm crying and what will I tell her; because they killed horses in a cowboy movie? But she doesn't ask, she removes the embroidered cloth from the strange mound in the middle of the dining table, revealing two loaves of bread, takes one, wraps it up to its waist in the cloth, and puts it in my lap. You holding this tight-tight till I brings you milk—it like your dolly, yes? And I hug the loaf of bread—it had a thrilling smell—almost fresh—and beyond the covering of its crust it was soft, springy to hold, more like a baby than a doll, its head—that my father cuts off and keeps to give to Haim Markowieczi's chickens, because I don't want to eat the hard end—its head presses against my wet cheek, its crust softens, one more minute and I'll find myself nibbling the top of this baby's head, what will Shlomi's mother say, my mother changes the bread every day, he told me the next day, after waking up and getting out of bed to see what was happening and saw me sleeping with my cheek on the bread, and what does she do with the old loaves of bread? If you come to our house I'll show you, he tried to squeeze another visit out of me, but three years passed before I dared to go back there, one ordinary weekday on my own, hoping that Hasia, like all grown-ups, had already forgotten, and Shlomi took me to his parents' bedroom and went up to a chestnut wardrobe with rounded corners and at its center a big mirror and in it me—skinny, blonde, severely freckled, and Shlomi already half a head taller than me, and the mirror creaks as it opens to reveal five or six shelves and on them loaves of bread lying one next to the other like in the co-op, this is the graveyard of the bread, Shlomi announces solemnly, trying to impress me, perhaps to frighten me with that word, but at the age of ten I'm not afraid any more of graveyards or dead people or ghosts either . . . Where the co-op used to be they've built a synagogue and that's where the singing is coming from, and that's where all the people are going this evening, the singing rises and subsides according to a secret law, and in front of me and behind me murmurs of *Shana Tova*, Happy New Year, how's Edna, is the boy done with the army? The light from the high windows hollows faces, deepens shadows, how can you recognize anyone, I elbow my way through them, excuse me, excuse me, swallowed up by so many people, all of them strangers, as if everyone who ever lived here had sold or rented their apartments or left and faded out—

"Loya?"

I turn around, almost bumping into a stout, half-bald man—

"Loya Kaplan?"

The voice is familiar—

"Don't tell me you don't recognize me—she doesn't recognize me!"— he appeals to the people around us for sympathy, and the gesture rings a bell—

"Bilu!"

I hold out my hand for him to shake it, but he bends down and plants a moist kiss on my cheek. A new fashion has come to the country; and now, the other cheek—

"It's been years, years!"—it's his voice, the slightly whistling s, the titter like grains of sand at the bottom of his voice—but all the rest of him is different: the paunch, the bald pate gleaming in the slanting light from the synagogue windows—"Anat! Where is she?" he stretches his neck, scans the crowd—"go and find someone here—the whole neighborhood's here; I want to introduce you to my wife—so are you back for good? No? Just home leave? How long are you going to be here? We're going on vacation tomorrow—we'll be back after Yom Kippur—as soon as the holidays arrive we pack up and take off like the rest of the people of Israel—will you still be here after Yom Kippur?"

"Maybe—"

"Where are you staying? With Ora?"

"Ora lives here?"

"They built on top of her parents' house—don't tell me you didn't know!"

"Her parents are still alive?"

"Her father's half-dead half-alive, but her mother, Mechora—"

"*Mechora*—motherland—"

"Some mother, some motherland . . . Polish yentas never die—"

"Are they still at the same address?"

"Sure they are, but wait a minute, it's the same place, but they changed all the street names here about ten years ago—"

"So it's not Ussishkin corner KaKaL any more—"

"No . . . Yankele," he turned to a man standing with his back to us, "what do they call Ussishkin now?"

"Ussishkin? It's been Etrog for years already—"

"He's from the council. Let me introduce you: this is Loya Kaplan—is it still Kaplan?—one of the old-timers in the neighborhood—we used to call it the block then, remember?—and this is Yankele Hadar, who's responsible for all the changes of recent years—"

"And KaKaL Street?" I ask.

"KaKaL's Marva Street now—"

"When we were kids we used to call it Kaka Street," Bilu says to Yankele, putting a patronizing arm around my shoulder, what's happened to him, "Loya and I have known each other from the era of Rasco Housing C—"

"A lot of water under the bridge since then," this Yankele looks completely uninterested, all he wants is to get away from Bilu, "you'll excuse me—" he turns back and is swallowed up in the crowd. Bilu's arm is hot and heavy on my shoulder. He turns me slowly around, as in a dance, obviously looking for someone to show me to—

"Shula, Shula, I want you to meet someone," a tall, bespectacled woman looks at me with a faint smile, "Shula works with Ora," Bilu says to my hair, "this is Ora's best friend," he announces to Shula who isn't impressed and inquires half-heartedly: "Ora Bronstein? Ora Gadot? Ora Azulai?"

"Ora Gadot—"

And now I know your name.

A quarter of a century. Without a letter, a phone call, a postcard. I'm in the air, and you're here, on the ground, above your parents in Ussishkin-KaKaL—all I have to do now is walk for ten minutes. And knock on your door—or not walk. Just stand here and wait; sooner or later the service will be over, and then, like always, you'll spill out of the synagogue with all the congregation: tall, slender, two braids, no—perhaps a soft wavy mane, eyes like the half-risen sun, dimples—somewhere in the crowd someone calls Bilu, and he presses my shoulder in parting— "Remember, after Kippur—don't disappear again—" the service comes to an end, and a slow stream of people pours out of the doors and mingles with those gathered outside, *Shana Tova*, Happy New Year, the crush is unbearable, and I decide not to wait; if I'm going to meet you then not here, not like this—

The silence continues the next morning too, except for the birds. I try to find out which of them is a *bona avis*, a good omen. Here's a pretty one, completely new: the face of a crow, the colors of a pigeon, and at the front of its wings a patch of gleaming azure blue with a tracery of black lines. It looks at me with a suspicious eye and opens its beak: is it going to sing? It croaks, squawks, in a minute it will begin to talk. What bird is it? I hurry to the guide—wait, wait, wait, wait—it's still here and there—there—that's it: in Hebrew *Orvani*—but scientifically—you hear? They've given you the name of a Roman emperor: *Garrulus glandarius*—who decides what to call who—I, for example, had to correct almost every new teacher at least once. Loya. With an o. Not Levia—a natural mistake after the Reuvena, Benyamina, Shimona, and Yosefa before me on the roll call. It's in the Bible. About Solomon's Temple. The class behind me giggled. And Bilu, who was very short until the tenth grade and always sat behind me, would pass me a Bible open at I Kings 7, and I would pass it to the teacher to read with her own eyes: verse 29, "Beneath the lions and the oxen were *loyot ma'aseh morad*" . . . We had a Rahamim Rahamim in our class too, and a Samuel Samuel ("First name I Samuel, last name II Samuel") and from the eleventh grade also Bilu Bilu. When he was issued an identity card he changed his first name to Bilu too; nobody ever calls me Moshe anyway, he said—strange, the fuss we made about names—no one was satisfied, everyone envied the other kids' names—in the class parallel to ours were two pretty twins called Yodfat and Masada, and a year above us were Gilad and Efrat—it's a shame they didn't call me Efrat, Ora once let slip a small envy.

Only Ora's mother needed no explanations about the meaning of Loya. A kind of *shvantz*—from Solomon's Temple! I was determined to defend my name, even though I didn't like it either; it was peculiar—it required explanations—what's a *shvantz*? Ora was standing next to me. A kind of garland, half a loop, in short—*patchkerai*—Mechora's Hebrew was flawless, but when she wanted to be insulting she always had recourse to Yiddish—Ora was convinced that my name was the result of combining two grandmothers; Leah and Zoya, for example, or Leonora and Sonya. We knew kids like that; Marganit after Marina and Nita; Tzafrira after Tzippora and Mira; Reudor after Reuven and Theodore—but the one that beat them all was Minaleh; Mina after Miriam, Yentel, Niota, and Hinda, *Mem, Yod, Nun, Heh*—

Nobody had living grandmothers. Maybe an uncle in Netanya, a few cousins on a kibbutz or half an old aunt in America who sent big parcels of secondhand clothes. Only Tikva had fourteen uncles and aunts and over fifty cousins. We didn't believe her until she brought New Year's greeting cards to class from France and Canada, from Petah-Tikva and Ashdod. One Passover eve we walked past her house: lights and voices and unfamiliar songs and little children running in and out. Nu, that's what it's like with those Sephardic *Frenkim*, said Ora's mother, no wonder they end up criminals. I didn't understand the connection. Every few days I would go over to Tikva's house. In summer salt diamonds would sparkle on the balustrade of their porch and on them black watermelon seeds laid out to dry. Let me water the mint, I would always ask. The water produced a fresh, green smell from the mint. Why don't we grow mint in the garden too, I once proposed to my father. He raised his eyes to me from a distance. It wasn't a good time to ask. I didn't ask again. I'm going over to Tikva's, I announced, and he agreed, from far away. I never dared to check how much he actually listened to me—I'm popping over to the South Pole—Fine, just be back in time for supper—there were days when I even preferred Ora's mother—she always had something to say about whoever Orinka was going over to see; about Tikva and Tikva's mother she had sour reservations—Tikva's mother in her headscarf whose ends crossed over on her nape and were tied in a little bow on top of her head, in her gold-threaded slippers, in her always-black dresses, serving us salads chopped so fine they could only be eaten with a spoon. Short and fat—like Hasia Horovitz, but more compressed, more solid—and when she passed her hand over my bangs narrow silver bracelets clattered on her arm. She never takes them off, said Tikva, it's a present from The

Father. Every year he gave her a bracelet. I counted eight bracelets. Every week Tikva's mother would go to talk to The Father in the cemetery, and when she came back she would lay a thick hand on Tikva's head: May-He-Rest-in-Peace sends you health and for you to have a good heart and succeed in your studies. In second grade I was sure that there was a connection between the blessings showered from the grave and the long luxuriant braids coming down to Tikva's waist. They were blue-black, like Elizabeth Taylor's hair in the movie *Ivanhoe*, and they ended in two quivering snow-white taffeta bows. Do you go to Tikva Toledano's house? Ora's mother asked with evil eyes. She's teaching me French! I knew this was an unimpeachable excuse. Languages were important. Tikva had piles of photo-romances in which narrow-waisted women with little round collars and pale gloves looked at men with narrow moustaches and gleaming combed-back hair with sharp-pointed triangles coming out of their mouths expanding into ovals containing the words *Je ne veux pas* or *Je suis occupé* and sometimes *La chose est impossible* while from the women's heads musing little bubbles rose into clouds of thought—*Pourquoi?* Or *Que peut-on faire?*

Your French! Jean-Jacques was part amused, part scandalized.

Alors, it isn't my mother tongue, monsieur—

And what is your mother tongue?—

Hebrew!

Hebrew—he tapped his pen on his lower teeth; this was his way, I learned later, of expressing doubt and at the same time being ready to write down your version; he was always ready to write. He tilted his head, slanted his eyes. He had big, gray eyes, pink-rimmed, as if he had just stopped crying.

But you weren't born in Israel—he said in the end.

I was born in Italy, so what? I only learned Italian from Adriana's mother—

Jean-Jacques smiled. He already knew the story.

So what language did they talk to you in when you were a baby?

Who can remember a thing like that?

Bon. What language did you say *mommy, Daddy, food, wee-wee* in?—He accelerated the tapping on his teeth. He had wonderful even white teeth, and a big mouth with wide, flat lips and shadowy, drooping corners.

Daddy—food—wee-wee. I tried to remember. I couldn't remember.

Maybe in German?

Are you crazy!

In Czech? Czech was dense and black like Minaleh's sweaters; her mother knitted them with thick wool on thin needles in moss stitch, so she wouldn't be cold. She always went on class hikes and trips with two sweaters in her rucksack—in case one got wet—on the trip to Jerusalem she lent me a sweater; heavy, stiff, surly, and scratchy—a *shkorifinsczech* sweater—

In Yiddish?—Jean-Jacques never let go until he found out the truth. What do you want, he's a journalist, Hedva defended him in the first months of our relationship.

Not on your life! My father said that Yiddish was jargon—

What language then? They must have talked to you—

Maybe in Latin—I joked, but Jean-Jacques raised his eyebrows and wrote something down in the notebook he took out of his shirt pocket.

What did you write there?

Father tongue: Latin—

You remind me of the story about Frederick the Second, I said. Jean-Jacques raised his eyebrows. They never taught you about him in the monastery—you never heard of Frederick the Second, Holy Roman Emperor, King of Sicily, Germany, and Jerusalem, *Stupor mundi*, Wonder of the world, he wanted to repeat the experiment of Psammetichus the First, King of Egypt—you never heard of him? I celebrated a little victory, Frederick decided to repeat his experiment in order to find out for once and for all what language babies would speak if nobody ever spoke to them or in their presence from the day they were born. Psammetichus ordered the mothers' tongues to be cut off—he didn't believe that they would be able to restrain themselves—but Frederick the Second who was a humanist and also an orphan from the age of four, gave the babies to nuns and swore them to silence.

In Psammetichus's experiment it turned out that the only word the babies said at the age of two was "*bekos*," which means "bread" in Phrygian: ergo— regrettably, the Phrygians, and not the Egyptians, were the first people on earth. But Frederick the Second, who spoke six languages and founded the University of Naples, rejected this pagan conclusion; his scholars guessed that the babies would talk Hebrew; he betted on Greek. What language did the babies speak? They didn't speak, they died, but wait, that's not the end— James the Fourth of Scotland who didn't believe the whole story, performed an experiment of his own. He wanted to find out what language they spoke in the Garden of Eden—and in his experiment—believe it or not, but it's written in the chronicles—the babies spoke Hebrew—

Morgenstern-the-grocer's nags everyone. "You son already officer?" she asks a woman of my age, and another, younger one: "You sell auto for peoples I sending you?" And from one thing to another small talk too: "Heats-wave now. And they saying on radio same thing tomorrow." She counts the coins I placed on the counter with her lips moving and raises her eyes to the woman waiting behind me: "You see catastropha what happen?" I linger, pretending to examine the loaves of bread. "Big big catastropha," she lays her swollen hand heavily on the pile of newspapers on the corner of the counter, "That man think there no God in world." With this sentiment I, standing with my back to her, definitely agree. There is no God. There's nobody here but us—

And the birds, of course. On the pomegranate tree peach-colored pome-granates ripen, and from the foliage a sudden bird shoots, tiny, blueblack— who is it? What does it want? What does it eat? Leaves? Pomegranates? It's autumn. Without rain, without clouds, without falling leaves. Only the haze is momentarily torn by a gust of wind carrying a bitter scent of pines and a hint of warm, distant figs. At the edge of the plot four squills pale to the point of transparency stand like sentries. I try to pick a pomegranate. It resists. You had your own word for lamp: "*rimonor*"—a "light pomegranate." *Panas*, you said, was a Greek word, whereas *rimon* was a Hebrew word derived from Accadian which was derived from Cappadocian, which was derived from who knows what, you have to decide on a *terminus post quem* at some point, you said, or else we really will end up at the Garden of Eden—

The mornings are still unstitched by the jagged call of a bird I haven't yet seen, but the light tarries. Four in the morning—dark—half past four—still dark—at five, only at ten past five, the air turns pale blue—and then—the punctual bird. I go out barefoot in spite of all the catastrophic possibilities—snakes, scorpions, poisonous centipedes, broken glass, rusty nails—feeling the film of dust that renews itself every morning on the doorstep, the flaky dryness of the leaves shed by the ficus tree flooding the path afresh, stumbling on a root sticking out like a brown vein, feeling the scratchiness of the conch grass, the floury soil between my toes—twenty-seven years on high heels have made me almost deaf in the feet, and now, as I place them stunned and groping on the ground they send up memories in great pulses: the damp chill of rounded white rocks, boiling asphalt, the rough tickle of sand rushing away underfoot with a wave returning to the sea, coiling around my ankles in thick, transparent ropes—it's the sea! You came to rescue me. And my father, where was he? He had gone with Nahum to look for the hoarse *lemon-popsicles-eskimo-pies* who had disappeared among the deck chairs, the mothers, the babies—

The sea, the sea. At high noon a slightly wrinkled golden skin, a dull brocade with glints and gleams and sudden shivers of brilliance. Ever since the night in Eilat I had not been at its edges nor on its waves, nor under them. Thirty, forty thousand feet above it, I would sometimes succeed in stealing a glance—an old, cracked, golden skin, every island rising like a bas-relief surrounded by a pale rim, opaque against the background of the scaly skin rippling in green-gold, blue-gold, gray-gold, at night dense black framed in golden pearls—one day, I promised myself. One day—

we were going to sail to Gibraltar in a Phoenician ship—you and Daddy and Nahum and me—its horse-head prow like a chess knight, its stern a fish's tail—I had read about the voyage of the Kon-Tiki. I knew it was possible. On a ship like this the Phoenicians—the ancient Hebrews—had sailed from Tyre to Cyprus, from there to Rhodes, from Rhodes to Malta, from Malta to Sardinia, from there to Spain, which is Tarshish. In the year 1100 B.C. the sailor-god Melqart had crossed the straits guarding the opening to the Mediterranean Sea, and the sailors who followed him had discovered America long before Columbus—they had filled their ships with gold and silver and gemstones; when there was no more room in the hold and on the deck for all the treasure, they had exchanged their bronze anchors for silver ones, is this why you changed the direction of our Saturday expeditions; instead of making for the hills baking in the light we drove to the sea. Quivering, flickering, sending out a salty tongue—where did we go to? To Caesarea, to the environs of Caesarea—in the gluing room you built models. Where are you going to get twenty oarsmen from, Daddy wondered, and you mentioned the latter-day "Canaanites" and the society that called itself the "Rulers-of-the-Waves"—the Odyssey, you claimed, was nothing but the story of the voyage of a Phoenician ship—a certain professor argued that—but your professor made no impression on my father; he had professors of his own—in the arguments suddenly flaring up against the background of a sea burning in the light the names of Virolleaud, Schaeffer, Conteneau crackled, who was on whose side, who was for who was against, neither Nahum nor I had a clue, all we knew was that the moment was fast approaching when you would snap "Nahum— come on!" and stride purposefully to the cabin, and Nahum would hurry to get in next to you, and Daddy and I in the back, among the ropes and the black rubber baskets and the sieves and the broom heads and the grating of the sand in everything and Daddy purse-lipped, withdrawn into himself, and the pickup jolting, you're racing it furiously, I lose my grip, fall onto my father, and he helps me to sit up again and hands me the warm canteen. What do you argue about all the time? The wave of his hand dismisses the question, the answer, any attempt to understand what there is between you: love, hate, envy, friendship.

You should have seen me, Jean-Jacques, eating canned food standing up next to the kitchen counter—feeling almost as if it was the annual class excursion: the trip to Tiberias—an adventure, the trip to the Baron de Rothschild's grave—an experience, the trip to Eilat—the end of the world with a bright-yellow taste of corn from a can or green peas mixed with carrot cubes. Or grapefruit segments in a sweet syrup hiding the hint of something bitter, grown-up, secret, and almost as forbidden as smoking—

Every day I realize that I have spread out a little more; yesterday I found a towel on the porch balustrade, today my sunglasses in the bathroom—in the meantime my kingdom is limited: living room, kitchen, bathroom, toilet, entrance hall with four padded parkas—I already know which floor tile wobbles, am adjusting to the sounds at night—rustle, sigh, breath, scuttling feet, something alive stirring under the floor, an unexplained gurgle, electric hum—the fridge, the fan—and when the air turns blue—the birds; that one first. In the new center, in a store selling backpacks, pocket knives, boots, and travel books, I found a hammock, and now it's here, between the two jacaranda trees, with me in it, like once upon a time. What are you doing? I hear Hedva inside my head; for years we haven't needed phones. Have you gone to see Ora yet? No. Not even the house from outside? No. Aren't you curious? No. You're afraid. What of? Why haven't you opened the rooms yet? Why don't you walk around the block more—you walked all over Paris, Brussels, Amsterdam, Rome, New York—and here you're afraid to go five hundred meters? I'm not afraid. Oh come on. I'm not afraid. Tell that to somebody else. I'm not afraid. I haven't got anything to be afraid of—okay, let's see you then: get up, go out—

Hansel and Gretel succeeded in finding their way home from the forest, because Hansel marked the path with little stones. But the second time they were abandoned in the forest, he marked the way with bread crumbs; birds came and ate the bread crumbs and the way home disappeared—who called us Hansel and Gretel—Eliot, when I showed him an old photograph: you and Daddy—both of you in knee-length khaki shorts and round cloth hats hiding the main difference: Daddy's bronzed bald head as opposed to your silver-gray mane—and in front of you Nahum and me hand in hand; fair, scrawny chicks—not resembling you or Daddy, but each other, if anyone, Hansel and Gretel, Eliot snickered—with that Hansel I would never have gotten lost, I protested, insulted. Right? Wrong?

It's cooler today. The windows are open and the radio follows me from street to street, so what have you got to say about the Yom Kippur War, a reserves colonel is asked and clears his throat before answering, but I am already in the next street, *love is a vow*, someone croons in a velvety voice, *a broken vow*.

Etrog corner of Rimon street, Etrog corner of Marva—this is it: the shutter—repainted dark green, but still double-winged with those wooden slats that can be turned to prevent the western sun from drawing stripes of fire on the floor and disturb the afternoon nap. The trees have grown taller—a faint smell of guavas—is it the season already?—no, not yet—the smell will still grow stronger, denser—take them away!—Ora's mother sends me to pick guavas and take them home, but Daddy stops me at the door—take them away!—on this side they've built a coarsely plastered white wall, above it a fringe of creeper, and next to the high wooden gate a mailbox made of matte stainless steel: "Mechora and Baruch Berger" printed in one window, "Ora and Mordechai Gadot" in the other, and underneath, written on a copybook label, "And Vered, Gilad, Udi and Yinon too." Married. Four children. A school principal or senior physician, her husband a chief engineer or bank manager—what happened to "and if you tell me not to then I won't—even if you like him a lot"? We were fifteen. I move away, cross the street, and stand on the opposite pavement and look. From here you can see the join between the new apartment and the old one—a crude concrete seam between the end of the roof of the original one-storied house, with its burgundy-gray tiles stained with verdigris, and the spotless white wall climbing a story higher and ending in wavy roof tiles of a bright orange color. The shutters in both houses are closed. Under the windows— planters full of geraniums. What else will you ask of us *Mechora*—

A snake! A snake! Upon my life—a snake! Flowing half a meter from me, disappearing under the bougainvillea separating your house from another house where nobody is living now. Once the police came with a flashing sapphire-blue light, and I, who saw it from a distance, ran here barefoot; I was sure it was for you—

A snake. This is the season. End of summer. Height of the heat. Once a snake emerged from your toolbox which was—look, here it is, it's still here, under the hibiscus staring at me with red eyes—Nahum jumped onto the balustrade of the porch, he didn't make it all the way, he hung there, his head inside, his legs kicking outside, Loya get up! in a choking voice because his stomach is squashed against the balustrade, the snake between him and me, and I grab hold of a rake and beat its teeth behind me, in front of me, at my sides, the snake vanishes and you appear, its corpse at the end of your hoe—it was only a blacksnake—Nahum jumps down, goes to see, but I go on hitting and hitting, hey, hey, hey, Anat! You freeze me, snatch me and Nahum up, each under a different arm, bring us in here, scold us for the sandals. Daddy and you never wear sandals. Always in laced-up boots, and when you go to excavate with buckled khaki puttees too, in khaki socks pulled up to bare knees and above them long, baggy workers' and immigrants' shorts, not like, not in the least like the handsome pith-helmeted archaeologists in the cinemascope-in-Technicolor with Hebrew-and-French-translation-in-the-body-of-the-movie, discovering to the hissing of a rising cobra a treasure chest slightly ajar, and in it—hundreds of dazzling gold coins—not like, not in the least like the ones you discovered—once in a blue moon!—blackened, eroded, they're here, in the Biedermeier, apparently worth a fortune—but this knowledge is powerless to sweeten in hindsight that disappointment, Daddy and you arguing in the sun, like a poodle and a dachshund fighting over a bone, Nahum said once, we were sitting under a solitary tree with our hands sticky from lukewarm oranges, bored, cross, oof, come on already, it's hot, and then Nahum lay back on the pique blanket and raised his eyes and called me to see: beyond the meager foliage the sky was like an upside-down sea, high and blue, and in it, on an enormous transparent spiral, scores of storks silently gliding—

"I went to see her—"
  "You went to see Ora!" Hedva knows at once.
  "Yes."
  "And . . . ?"
  "They weren't at home—"
  "Did you ring?"
  "Ring?"
  "Knock at the door—knock knock, anybody home?"
  "The gate was locked—it was impossible to reach the door—"
  "You're something else. Have you decided what you're going to do with the—what do you call that thing?"
  "Pyxis. No, I haven't. In the meantime it's here, two meters from me. Watching and waiting—"
  And now I go up and look at it. Even through the glass I can see that I was wrong: it's not a centaur's torso rising there, but a phoenix stretching its neck to free the tips of its wings welded to the lid—if it succeeds in rising it will raise the lid with it—

On the grocery counter is a flat cardboard box containing an entire phalange of memorial candles. "You not buys this on Yom Kippur? Mother not die? Father not die? Nothing die?" I buy three. I light them as soon as I get home. Does God have a calendar? I pass my finger through the flames. If you do it quickly it doesn't hurt. That's why the real test was to hold your open palm over the candle and leave it there. Bilu counted the seconds. I gritted my teeth, if Sarah Aaronsohn and Hannah Szenes could take it—so can I. The burn had a coin shape. You're crazy, Ora pronounced when I showed her. So how do you know you'll be able to withstand torture, I challenged her. I don't know, she stood up. Shimon the janitor walked down the corridor and rang the heavy bronze bell. And neither do you, whispered Ora before going to sit in her place—at the back. She always sat at the back; up to the sixth grade she was the tallest in the class; there was no need to keep an eye on her to make sure she wasn't daydreaming or cheating—and neither do you, she said to Yosefa on her way, and neither do you, she said to Bilu and Elhanan, who had no idea what she was talking about. Ora wasn't with us in the underground and she didn't help us to collect matches, nails, bottles, rags, and steal anything that could serve as food and weaponry, if the *fedayeen* came, if the Nazis returned to make children into soap, Minaleh buried bars of soap but she wasn't in the underground, she was too fat and too white and she was afraid of climbing trees and being outside in the dark, but Ora knew Morse code and knots and how to put up a pup tent and make a camp fire just like the boys and walked all the way to the end of the block to the "Hashomer Hatzair" den in her blue shirt with the white shoelace threaded through the holes in the neck, and went with them on Saturdays to work on kibbutzim—How-how-how, just explain to me how you can go to synagogue on holidays and fast on Yom Kippur and then drive to work on the Sabbath? Elhanan mocked her, perhaps because like all the boys, he was in love with her, but Ora wasn't put out: It isn't work, it's helping out—even though after those Saturdays it was impossible to get her to go with us to the movies at the meeting hall, her mother would open the door with a shhhhhh . . . Ora's sleeping, recovering her strength for the school week—and because of that she missed *The Bicycle Thief* and *Witness for the Prosecution* and *La Dolce Vita*.

Mrs.-Morgenstern-the-grocer's offers me a round challah, asks if I've ordered fish at Yosef-the-butcher's. The pomegranates are already ripe.

People—suddenly there are more people in this street, I haven't been here yet, the little one-family houses have turned a bitter gray, some of them have sprouted new white-walled, orange-tiled additions, in the gardens a swollen Persian cat or professional dog barking at the world, after the holidays, the lawyer said, after the holidays we can close the deal. Now there's nobody to talk to. The country's closed down. I wander, every day a little further, checking what's changed. Aren't you homesick, Hedva asked once; we were standing at the front of the plane and saying good-bye to the passengers and the sun was already roasting us at half past six in the morning. What for, I asked her in a gap between passengers—the old gang, the hummus, the heat—Hedva looked at me with eyes narrowed in the sun. Every time we land here I remember that verse from Genesis 28—Remind me?—"*How dreadful is this place,*" I begin, and then we're separated by a family clump; father, mother, two grandmothers, four walking grandchildren, one baby—Your memory kills me, Hedva on more than one occasion complains—Me too, I assure her, but neither of us believes me.

I'm thirsty. I only have to think of Yom Kippur and I'm already thirsty. Where does the water begin? From the movement of two fingers on the brass bow tie of the faucet. A water snake bursts out with a hiss—first fury and needles in all directions—and only afterwards a transparent braid trembling in my mouth from corner to corner, wetting my chin, sliding down my neck to the opening of my shirt. I turn it off. In the mouth of the faucet a round drop forms. And then another one. A bird comes to drink. Black head, white cheeks, a black bib around its neck and a black stripe descending from it to divide the yellow stomach precisely in the middle. It utters a prim, pinny chirp. It looks like a distant cousin to the wagtail, which for some reason has failed to put in an appearance here, even though it's almost autumn.

Not a car, not a radio, not a sprinkler, not a vacuum cleaner, not a washing machine, not a television program—absolute silence, high and deep, except for the birds, of course, and the sound of distant singing in the synagogue—should I go? And what should I wear? What do you wear on Yom Kippur? I don't have white. Where's my blue dress? You should have seen me, Jean-Jacques; opposite the suitcase with all my lightweight un-creasable clothes that wash in two seconds and dry in a jiffy spread out around me—searching for a dress—I, who opened your luggage, sorting, refolding, leaving one out of three, and tell me if you lacked for anything, *mon cheri*, saying good-bye at the railway station for Marseilles, for example, seven hundred kilometers you would travel and you wouldn't fly, if you were a bird you wouldn't be able to get off the ground, I can barely lift your suitcase into which you insisted at the last minute on cramming two volumes of Proust, one Julien Gracq, one Camus, afraid of being alone without a book, but I'm not a bird—you peck me on the cheek, a short, civilized kiss, and neither, *ma cherie*, are you—

The paved space in front of the synagogue is more crowded than it was on Rosh Hashanah. From the long windows a familiar melody swells and subsides, the people standing outside—because there's no room? From choice?—chat in undertones, move aside, because—incredibly—weaving between the people, two meters from the synagogue, are children on bicycles, one of them nearly runs over my foot, Hey! Be careful! I recoil, "You be careful!" he retorts and zigzags on, how old is he, nine, ten, what is it about this day that brings out all the contrariness in children—

On this plaza, when it was still red soil, we played the potters are coming and red light green light and from the old synagogue the melody rose like a great wave, swelling, pulling, we ran there, to carry on with our five sticks and catch and hide-and-seek, anyone behind me and in front of me and at my sides is it! I announce out loud and from the synagogue a white ghost emerges and waves his finger: Sha! Sha! Go away! Behind me in front of me at my sides are strangers, and I make my way between them to the synagogue door, lady lady where do you think you're going, stretching my neck to see past the women clustering at the entrance, all dressed up, some with scarves on their heads, some with hats like Princess Diana, lucky there's Yom Kippur otherwise when would they wear those hats, inside they stand facing an arabesque screen separating them from men wrapped in prayer shawls, I've never come so far, I've never gone inside, come inside, sit next to me, I'll show you the place in the prayer book, Ora urged me every year, but I refused. My father went to Hasia Horovitz instead of to the synagogue. That's my Yom Kippur he said, without explaining, and he didn't ask me to come with him. What do they do there, I asked Shlomi, and he shrugged his shoulders: They talk. My mother cries. And you shut yourself in the gluing room—it was a day of pure freedom; without grownups, without meals, without cars, without danger, in our games of hare and hounds we reached the main road, we played catch in the schoolyard, we ran around the water fountain—almost every Yom Kippur there was a terrible heatwave—Bilu whose mother was from a kibbutz, Elhanan whose parents voted for the Communists and read their newspaper, Adriana who Ora's mother called a "goyshka" because she was too blonde, too pretty, Yosefa, Arlozora, Moshiko, Hanna, Dina, Yossi, and Shlomi, of course, who wasn't allowed to fast, even though he wanted to and tried—All the boys fast, not because of God, but to prove—Hezi goes with his father to the Sephardic synagogue—All year long he steals sharpeners and erasers from satchels and cheats in tests, and on Yom Kippur he's in the synagogue like a saint—Because his father makes him—His father's a thief too—Can you prove it?—Me? Even the police can't prove it! And the laughter bursts out around the water fountain, and I open a faucet and drink with all my mouth and throat and all the buttons on my blouse down to my belt. Water! I cup it, splash it. They all recoil as if I've sprayed them with fire. What's the matter? It's only water! Go on, have a little drink! I laugh. Nobody laughs with me. Do you believe in God? I turn to Elhanan; tall, straight auburn hair, green eyes, handsome as a movie star. If he says no, they'll believe him that it's a lot of nonsense. Elhanan is silent. You? I turn to Bilu. He shuffles in embarrassment, stares at his sandals; I fast because we took a bet—That's not an answer! I know that I'm talking in my truculent

What-would-we-do-without-you-Goddess-Anat tone, but I don't care. Idiots! Retards! Cowards! You're just chicken! I stand in the middle of the day, in the middle of the sun, in the middle of Yom Kippur, next to the water fountain in the schoolyard and open the faucet to flashing water. There isn't any God! I sing out in a rhythmic chant and stand up straight to prove that nothing happens to me. There is too! Shlomi surprises me in a whisper. Then let him punish me! I demand in the middle of Yom Kippur, in the middle of the heatwave, and throw back my head and put out my tongue to the gray smudge of the sky. But you've already been punished, whispers Shlomi, and Elhanan suddenly turns on him: Why don't you shut up! Shlomi shrinks as if he's received a blow. And I add for good measure: Idiot. Coward. Why don't you run to the synagogue to your God, why are you standing here like a dummy watching me drink, don't you know that He punishes for that too? Go on, run and ask him to forgive you—

Shlomi, twenty years later, in the plane—a tall, good-looking man, with a John F. Kennedy haircut, he looks American, he is American, a professor of Yiddish in a New Jersey college—married, father to a son, another one on the way, and you, Loya, what about you? What did you mean then—suddenly that scene next to the water fountain comes back to me, I even feel hot, even though the windows of the cafe we went into are steamed over inside, streaming outside. Classic melancholy; thin, quiet, endless rain, gray light, glistening streets creating reflections, licked by car tires, their headlamps shattering into stars. Shlomi opens the door for me, moves the chair for me, hands me his visiting card over the table—Professor Shlomami Horovitz—looks at me with his father's blue eyes, reminds me of his mother. Something in the expression—Your curses—he smiles, absentminded—that's all he remembers—Curses?—Demagogue, conformist, reactionary—

I learned them from you, of course. Anyone who didn't think like you was a fool, a narrow-minded, ignorant peasant, mean-spirited, a benighted idiot, a hypocrite, a coward, a demagogue, a fanatic, an obscurantist, ignoramus with a ghetto mentality, conformist, reactionary, feeble-minded, weak-hearted, a conceited ass, mischief-maker, fence-sitter, willfully blind and deaf, a silly donkey, an Einstein, no less (said in the appropriate tone), insane, demented, dangerous, a traitor, a quisling, a Kapo, a Judenratnik, a spy, foreign agent, destroyer, Flavius Josephus—

I go to visit you, look for ways of making you angry, of arousing the furious words from their slumbers—listening to them with a joy bubbling up and firmly suppressed—gleeful as in a hard winter at the sound of the hail pelting down, spoiling the oranges, damaging the crops, and in spite of that—let it pelt, and because of that—let it pelt—

The service is apparently over. The women all stand up and turn to each other with saccharine-sweet expressions, nodding, dabbing at their noses with little handkerchiefs—the smell of lavender—one of them smells of lavender—the smell of the little handkerchief that Ora would tuck under the strap of her watch, because it always stinks in the synagogue, Yosefa explained, but I knew that it was in order not to faint from hunger and thirst. I didn't understand how anyone could fast, precisely on Yom Kippur I was always assailed by a passionate hunger; Ora, who would pop over for half an hour during the prayers for the dead, would look at me as if I was about to be struck down by lighting or as if the floor was about to open under me, and I—with my chair and slice of bread—would fall into the pit like Korah, Dathan, and Abiram in the illustration by Doré. God can't see—I take another bite of the fresh black bread covered with a mountain of processed cheese and a few olive butterflies—He's in the synagogue. You want a glass of water? Orange juice? Grape juice? Her fast drives me crazy. Drink already. Just a sip. She shakes her head left and right in a wonderful movement No-o tha-ank you, and accompanies the vanishing slice of bread with the look of a prophetess. I ate last year too—I drink grape juice, spread another slice of bread with cream cheese, decorate it with omegas of pimento—and I got almost-very-good in arithmetic. Which in my opinion was irrefutable proof. How much do you want to bet that nothing will happen to you if you eat? I can't stand seeing her not eating and I can't stop eating. I don't make bets like that—Ora glances at her watch. The prayer for the dead is short, too short. Stay—just a little longer—I plead, and regret it immediately. Ora gets up. She's pale. Her lips are dry. If there is a God, I hate him. Next to the door she looks at me. My second slice of bread is almost finished. I pray for you too, she says. Maybe that's why I got almost-very-good for arithmetic, I panic for a minute, but I recover immediately: stuff and nonsense.

Taste—Jean-Jacques carefully lifts the pot, stops the coffee from boiling over. It smells terrific, I admit. If I had cloves and black pepper and cinnamon, I would make coffee like that now and drink it bitter and boiling. Precisely now. Precisely today. Then a sip was enough for me. You don't know what's good, protested Jean-Jacques. He decided to teach me immediately after getting off the plane alive. The whole flight he was very pale, following me with big, Kafkaesque eyes. The plane was half empty. Most of the passengers slept with their heads falling to the side or sagging on their chests. You call that coffee? I thought he was joking, but he was serious. He stood up and followed me. I noticed that his hands were shaking. You'd better sit down, monsieur—this was all I needed in the middle of the night. I removed the cup from his hand, and he sat down in an empty seat from where he could see Hedva and me in the galley—Loya—you have a suitor, Hedva smiled. Nonsense—just another poor wretch who's frightened to death—after the flight it turned out that we were both right.

The plane's about to split apart—and you open-and-close, switch-on-switch-off, heat-up-take-out-serve, Jean-Jacques summed up his impressions. During that first meal he confessed that he was half a chef, wrote about restaurants, and that I reminded him somewhat of Michele Morgan. I stream with the returning worshippers, and suddenly I see Elhanan, no, it's not him, but who's that, not Yosefa? No, she's too young, perhaps it's her daughter, a frizzy ginger pile on her nape, should I tell her that—no, what can I say, where's your mother? And what if she's not her daughter at all, and the tall blonde's not Adriana? How is it possible that in a crowd of hundreds nobody stops, nobody calls out Look-who's-here! Where's Bilu, he promised to return, here, here he is, and next to him an attractive stranger, she must be his Anat, and behind them Ora. At long last Ora—

No.

My mistake.

"Well? Have you decided where? He told me you would take your time—okay, I'm not in a hurry—I'm just reminding you that until you do—okay, you know—you said you wanted to get it over quickly, the ball's in your court. What are you doing over the holidays—staying in the country?" The lawyer called to check before taking off for Majorca. "You know how many years I haven't been here over the holidays?" "Okay, whatever," I can hear his snicker speeding towards me from Tel Aviv, "stay, why not. It'll be an experience!"

In a house with crooked floor tiles, cracks like rivers course from the heights of a plane branching over the walls, the earth is indeed at work. One winter it swallowed a donkey. I remember how we stood on the edge of the steaming pit on a sparkling sunny morning and peered anxiously into the darkness. The donkey stood there and brayed. I told you, astounded, and you hurried to inspect and announce: It's nothing. A hundred years ago a farmer plowing his field south of Sidon discovered that the little mound in the middle of the field had suddenly collapsed: from the landslide rose a black stone sarcophagus with twenty-two lines of Phoenician writing on it: it was the coffin of Eshmun-Azar King of Sidon! In 1709 an Italian peasant dug a well and discovered Herculaneum! In 1879 the Spanish aristocrat the Marquis de Sautuola set out to excavate the cave of Altamira which had recently been discovered by hunters. His little daughter, Maria, wandering about with a candle, entered a low-ceilinged alcove and discovered Stone-Age paintings of bisons! And here in Israel? Nine years ago a Bedouin shepherd was searching for a lost goat around Qumran. He walked and walked and walked and arrived at a cave. He threw a stone inside, thinking that if the goat was inside it would run out in a fright. But the stone hit something that was not a goat and made a ping! He ran away and came back with a friend. Together they gathered their courage and entered the cave and discovered jars—jars—jars—and inside them no, not gold coins but the scrolls of the book of Isaiah!—From the Bible?—From the Bible!—And the goat?—What goat?—The one that got lost—That goat has not been found to this very day—you conclude in the tone that I can never guess whether it's serious or mocking—Ah, if only you had the time, if only you had the money like that Evans who bought a hill of anemones in Crete and within a few weeks—did you tell me—uncovered the palace of Minos and the lair of the Minotaur—

That was one of the scary stories. At night, before I fell asleep, my room was wide and high and full of enemies; the darkness sulked under the bed. In the closet door a cave gaped and out of it stared the Minotaur with one gigantic eye—there was no point in asking my father to come back, to switch on the light, to open the closet door: when it was open every shirt turned into a ghost dipped to the waist in a river of darkness, while the old boatman Charon rowed his raft to Hades—Is he dead too, that Charon, I asked. I didn't understand what he could do with the silver coin awaiting him under the tongue of the dead on the rivers of the underworld—my father was at a loss, smiled in embarrassment, reminded me that it was only a story passed down from generation to generation, closed the big mythology on his finger and switched off the light; immediately Charon was carved into the wood of the door, strong and dark, holding his oar and balancing on a little rubber dinghy on a stormy sea, looking at me—want a ride to Hell?

Everything begins from light. Especially the birds. Even when I seem to be asleep I'm awake, hearing dense chirpings, and above them all—a clear, jagged sickle of lament—I get up. Perhaps I'll see it. The air outside is thick and gray and presages a heatwave. I go outside. A bunch of basic birds, probably sparrows, shoots out of the cypress tree, and framed in one of the diamond-shaped holes in the fence a tiny one, gleaming like black obsidian—and suddenly—a flame of turquoise and azure-blue with a flicker of white, brown—is it him? What's it like to be a bird? What's it like to feel the air tickling under your armpits and the effort coming from your shoulder blades? What's it like to glide without twitching a feather on a spiral of hot air—and here's the hoopoe. Do you know, *proszę pani*, what they say about you, that your beak was a sword, the pick on your head—a helmet plume, that you're the reincarnation of Tereus the Thracian, pervert and murderer, a horror story, wait a minute, I sit down, try to come closer, but so far and no further, she opens striped wings—and she's gone. I lie with my chin on the back of my hand, my stomach on the ground, in the Yom Kippur silence I hear it growl, I hear it turning over, I feel down to my bones the mighty creaking of its effort as it revolves around its axis.

Time doesn't always erode. Sometimes it thickens and glazes into a patina of violet blue and pale green like on that alabaster scent bottle you found near Caesarea. Red limestone hills eaten away by salt. A narrow strip of sand. In it, once in a while, half a marble arm, a dull blue marble of glass, potsherds smoothed by the hand of sea and time, without a name, without an inscription—and the sea, very black at midday, a blackboard boiling with letters of fire—

Shall I begin today? First I'll eat a pomegranate from your tree; a royal fruit, its stain lasts forever. At this time of year I would clean my father's library: Polybius and Livy and Thucydides and Plutarch and Xenophon and Flavius Josephus and Theodor Mommsen and Ranke and Burckhardt and Gibbon—now, if I want to clean, I'll open and slam shut books about plants and birds and seas and rivers, a thousand and one ways of making a kite, deserts, volcanoes—Nahum's books; everything you wanted to know about life on earth—not a single novel. I'll work here, on the porch. In this silence they'll hear the bang-bang-bang all the way to the synagogue, and then maybe Ora—I'm out of my mind; what am I cleaning for, why am I tidying, I'm not staying here more than a week, and if the mountain doesn't come to Mohammed, who needs it.

Three keys: to your room, to Nahum's room, to the always-closed gluing room, powdered with dust and smelling of sweating iron. For hours you would sit there, sticking together jars, bowls, clay lamps, ossuaries, little figurines—I would knock at the door, knowing there would be no reply, wait anyway and then open it. You would be busy gluing potsherds, eyes close to the crack—and I would shuffle my feet, cough, clear my throat, until you raise your eyes and look at me as if caught in a web. Is Champollion in a big hurry? That's what you called me when you chose not to annoy me with what-would-we-do-without-you-Goddess-Anat. Jean-François Champollion learned half a dozen languages—including Coptic!—by the age of sixteen and he was the one who deciphered Egyptian hieroglyphics, no, I wasn't in a hurry, you offered me red soda pop in this kitchen, you told me about the labyrinth in Knossos or the exploits of Hannibal or Atlantis who was swallowed up by the sea and only her hair floats on its surface to this very day, and this is where the eels spawn, and are borne, slender and transparent, in the Gulf Stream to the rivers of Europe, swim against the current, live a dozen years in the cold European water—grow big and fat and silver—but in order to reproduce they return to the drowned continent of which all that remains is a great raft of golden seaweed—

Why do they want to go back?

Why and why and why. Because of nostophilia. Memory of the womb, *zeher-rehem*—you translated everything that moved or grew into Hebrew.

But that's impossible!—I interrupted you; no, I wasn't buying your tall tales—She's arguing again!—you spread hard hands and shook your head.

I don't remember anything before I was five! An eel remembers better than me?

Let's see; you remember the apartment in Haifa?

The porch. And the ships in the harbor—

But the apartment?

A sliding door with glass in a frost-flower pattern. And dense, black, whispered Czech, stifled tears—

No—

Nothing? You examine me with narrowed aquamarine eyes, but to all your questions I answer—No. No. No. No. No.

I try a shortcut through a pedestrian lane between oleanders and honey-suckle, cross a hard red dirt lot, walk to the end of the street and reach a field plowed with rough furrows to distant cypresses—from close up they're gray with dust—and beyond them they haven't pulled down the orphanage yet, it's still abandoned, its doors torn out—when Ora's mother lamented my fate, she would ask herself, only herself of course, if it wasn't a shame for a little girl to be roaming around the streets, it was a well known fact that it was precisely the gifted that became criminals if their education was neglected at an early age, the professor didn't want to remarry—that was up to him, but why didn't he send the child to a suitable institution—for years I was sure that she meant this orphanage, this ruin—the smell, the same smell. The smell of dry shit and thorns and the ash of old bonfires, for some reason the beautification campaign had not reached here, they hadn't taken over the building or even scrubbed the graffiti off the walls. What if I— what if I sold the house and bought this place and moved in—a large house, arched windows—after renovating it would look like a palace—yes, why not, I would live in the orphanage, now it was actually the right place for me because I was an orphan from all sides, everyone who was before me and behind me and at my sides is already underneath me, turning into bones—

I go back. The air is no longer sour milk—it's already early evening—in spite of the heat—it's all blue movement—in this silence you can hear the season turning and time passing and changing; what was will not be again.

A blue evening. Blue people are returning from the synagogue, the street lamps are still off but a few cars are already warming up their engines, and here comes the first, gliding slowly, without lights, as if stealing past, and suddenly it gathers speed and flees—but there's nothing to flee from; all at once the spell is lifted—everything starts to move—people hurrying home to eat, drink, make it in time for the movie, and here comes Ora. Ora? The tall girl with the braids turns around only in the corridors of my memory, comes out of the synagogue, sees me, I give up! I'm not playing! I yell at the others in the game, one look from her is enough for me to understand that—I have to go to the bathroom, she whispers to me, should I come with you? I offer immediately and she nods, we hurry off to Ussishkin-KaKaL—the door's not locked, who would steal on Yom Kippur, she goes into the toilet and I wait in the living room, in the dark, there's a faint light coming from the kitchen, a strange, flickering light, almost white, a spooky light—I go to look; the kitchen is trembling with eerie light, rays coming from inside the sink—I go closer—standing on the bottom of the sink ten, twenty, thirty-six memorial candles are burning—

Loya, are you coming?—Ora is standing in the kitchen door.

But what is this?—the almonds of fire hypnotize me.

It's my father's family—Ora turns to go, with me behind her, both of us groping in the dark.

But why in the sink?—I have to ask.

She strides ahead of me, taking big steps so as not to miss too much of the service, I run behind her, only at the threshold of the synagogue she turns to face me:

So they won't burn the house down—are you coming in?

But I refuse.

"You wants I saves you newsespaper on holiday," Morgenstern-the-grocer's grumbles. Another holiday? Already? But I've been cured of the addiction to newspapers. People pack their best clothes, buy tickets to fly as far as possible from the local stew—and the minute after takeoff they stretch their necks, follow the flight attendant with anxious eyes, worried there won't be a paper left for them—In English? Isn't there anything left in Hebrew? What is this?—An airplane, not a newspaper stand, I once answered and was reprimanded for my impertinence. But you heard the news this morning, I tried to persuade someone else on another flight—with half an ear, the passenger refuses to be appeased, I was in a hurry to get to the airport—and what can already happen between breakfast and lunch time? Oho! Other passengers join in: "A terrorist bomb" "War" "The religious zealots could bring down the government" "Jerusalem Betar could fall from the national soccer league"—after handing out the newspapers half an hour of quiet; they read, turn the pages, poke their neighbors in the ribs, hey, hey, d'ja see this? Total strangers exchange the sports page for the gossip column—and outside, through the windows, alabaster and amethyst—the first thing, a passenger left, alas, without a newspaper waves his finger at me—you know the first thing I'll do when I get to Paris? I'll buy a Hebrew paper. But why, I try to dissuade him. I dunno, I can't do without it. It's in my blood—Look at those lunatics, I would whisper to Hedva, but Hedva was on their side: Little green men from Mars will land on Earth and you'll be the only one not to know—during the first months of my affair with Jean-Jacques she really gloated: Now you'll read the paper from the headlines to the sports! And indeed for a few months I read all the French newspapers I could lay my hands on, I looked for his articles and for ones by the colleagues he admired and those he couldn't stand, I arrived at our dates ready to agree with him, to disagree and give my reasons, but I soon discovered that everything— the scandals and the demonstrations and the economic programs and the political statements—were rapidly blown up and collapsed immediately into nothing—It's only once in fifty or a hundred years that something really important happens, I heard myself quoting my father, agreeing with him about something years after his death, but Jean-Jacques was sure that this too was connected to airplanes: You live in the air, eat plastic—he had a theory; man is what he eats—eighty percent of the time that you're awake you wear a uniform—he raised finger after finger to count all the plastic in my life—most nights you sleep in hotels, not at home, not in your own bed, you drink Coca-Cola that destroys your taste buds—and friends—do you have friends? No! You have colleagues! Every year they change—What do you want, they get married—And you?—I'm happy the way I am—How can you be!—How can I explain it to you? You think that everyone who flies is crazy!—Not everyone who flies. Just everyone who flies when he doesn't have to—But it's my work!—Your work? Jean-Jacques stood in the middle of the street and spread out his arms—And what about your life? Where's your life?—There—I raised a finger. Above it was the foliage of a tree. Above that was a low gray woolly cloud. But above that, I knew, I got off a plane this morning, was a great, arching sky of crystal and sapphire—

On one of the branches of the jacaranda tree I saw it this morning: too-big head squeezed between shoulder wings, long, strong beak, slightly open, and issuing from it the jagged bray that starts my mornings. I stood still hardly breathing until the colors began and I saw that it was mostly cocoa brown with a triangular white bib on its neck. It reminded me of someone. Especially in profile. I took a step forward to make sure—but it took fright, spread bright blue wings and disappeared into the light—

Children going to school; carrying big colorful schoolbags, wearing big clumsy running shoes with the laces undone, once we would bring sneakers in cloth bags, only for gym, hide them, lie that we'd forgotten them, that there was no money at home to buy them, that somebody had stolen them, do gym barefoot so we wouldn't have to put our feet into that sweltering punishment, and now—are the shoes different? Are the children different? For a quarter of a century I'd moved from place to place, leaving others looking after me receding into the distance, married to the same woman, working at the same job, living in the same neighborhood, still meeting the old gang from the army on Independence Day, and now—life is passing me by—and I'm stuck on the bank, in a minute I'll grow roots—

"You didn't feel grounds moving?" the-grocer's asks me or perhaps the girl who came in after me, a little transistor radio perched on her shoulder like a tame parrot. "Listen, listen," she says, there really was an earthquake in the center of the country. What steps can people take, the morning news-anchor asks the expert. "First of all—build differently—" the expert embarks on a long sermon, listing catastrophic earthquakes in San Francisco, Japan, Agadir, Mexico, in 1837 an earthquake had destroyed Safed, we were sitting on the edge of a geological rift and completely ignoring the facts—"I don't believe it! I don't believe it!" a blonde woman holds out her arms to me, a basket in each hand, enclosing me in an embrace that slaps my back with a brick of ice cream and a container of milk—"And you haven't even changed, damn you!" She takes two steps back and looks at me, only her eyes and voice are familiar, yes, her voice—"Neither have you—" I try to gain time, who is she, who is she, "We thought—that's it. We're not good enough for you any more. You caught a millionaire—you conquered America"—it's Tikva! Tikva Toledano! She's lost weight, she's bobbed her nose, she's turned into a blonde Cleopatra—"She doesn't remember me!" Tikva complains to the-grocer's, but I do remember, now I'm sure of it, "You had a plaster cast in the fourth grade, Tikva Toledano." "Tikva Ben-David," she holds up her right hand and displays the ring on her finger—"Do you live here?" we both ask, only Tikva answers. "Of course I live here, what do you think, we built on top of my mother. Come, you must come, holiday eve or not."—"Today's the eve of a holiday?" "Tomorrow, tomorrow, haven't you landed yet?" She opens the boot of a silvery Renault. "The super-market's a madhouse—a million people—I didn't want to go there just for ice cream and milk." A beautiful, elegant woman. Dressed for the-grocer's as if for a business meeting in Wall Street. "I came straight from the bank," she gets into the car, opens the door for me, "I'm assistant manager now, come on, get in, the ice cream's going to turn to water in a minute," "Listen, Tikva, it was great to see you, but I'm in a bit of a hurry now," she gives in with a rather insulting ease, starts the car, but pokes an elbow and chin out of the window before driving off: "Just tell me; did you marry that character in the end? No? Then who? The Canadian? No? You're impossible!" She switches off the engine: "Listen. I've got a cousin—a wonderful guy. Well-off, with a great apartment in Neve Avivim. Don't say no now. Wait till you see him. You'll be in the country for another week won't you? Then you'll be able to meet all the gang and him too in our *sukkah*—it's already a tradition—*Sukkoth*—at Tikva's, Independence Day—at Ora's—where are you staying? With Ora? No? At the *meshuggener's* house? He left it to you in his will? Lucky you! I'll be in touch to tell you exactly when—don't get on a plane before you meet him— maybe he's your fate, who knows?"

And here it is—metallic blue on the back and tail, in the front chestnut with a bib, turning a brown eye and a strong beak in my direction, in pro- file it looks like Dubček. *Dobrý den*, I approach, good day, *jak se máte?* How do you do? It lets loose a loud, tremulous chirp: *Nemám náladu.* I'm not in the best of spirits. What's the wonder.

On the right, the wall of books gives off heat and dust, opposite the glass glint of the Biedermeier enclosing the iron Anat, beakers, coins, and the pyxis that I haven't yet decided, you hear, not yet, I know that we all return to dust in the end, but why like this, on the armchair a pile of clothes turns into a Rottweiler of darkness, someone is rustling papers, nibbling corners with small teeth, dragging feet under the floor, sighing, I lie supine, care- ful not to turn my back on the room, breathe in deeply and let out long whistling breaths the way Eliot taught me to do in order to fall asleep, perhaps to dream, floating over dark seas of sleep with no soft-fingered sea anemones or starched fans of red-hot coral, no black sea-urchins with mercury eyes, no eels, nothing but a black continuum like the luggage car- ousel at the airport, going on and on even when there are no suitcases or passengers left, only lonely nights and empty roads—

QUILLS

When exactly did you begin to fade, to blur into the background, to merge—every year a little more—into the complex tapestry of memory in

which I myself am no longer quite sure of the identity of the unicorn looking at the mounted knight dressed for the Crusades, or the knight reaching out his hand for the carved amphora held by the nymph with Brenda's
eyes, and you are apparently that figure, part boy, part girl, half-hidden in
a forest of foliage, always in trousers, in wide Robin-Hood sleeves, every
year more leaves, less face—

I didn't know you lived here, if you come out to me I'll say, even though
it's not absolutely true, but the lie is shorter and also not so far from the
truth, I was sure that you lived on a kibbutz, if you come out to me I'll tell
you, and not in some villa—will you react to the spite in this remark, or
blind to every kind of malice, pure and innocent as you once were, will you
smile: We built here—Mordechai's work—the children—my parents—and
I'll say, so neither of them have died on you yet, and you'll say, I'll probably die first—no, no you won't, for so many years you lived in my head,
I spoke to you, you answered me, when exactly did you begin to fade, to
answer me what I would have answered myself, to become more leaves,
less face—

I've spread out a pique blanket and I'm lying on my stomach; my eyes on
a level with the grass, not moving, scarcely breathing, a meter away from
me a mafioso glittering in the sun, next to him his faded replica, his wife,
according to Nahum's book, that's the way it is with them, he's a prince
and she's a housemaid, maybe they'll come closer to see what happened to
Gulliver, but they keep their distance. Okay, I can wait. Under my stomach I hear the earth belch, trying to get rid of two-thousand-year-old air
imprisoned in tunnels, in caves, threatening to close its rocky jaws on us
and flatten us into a flimsy sandwich or stamp us into the ground as the
fossil of a family, father mother son and daughter, in another twenty thousand years they'll discover us precisely etched in the rock down to the last
hair on our heads, if we're lucky, we'll die in the middle of a meal—you
once brought me, is it still here, a drop of amber with a five-thousand-
year-old insect in it, but I said, yuk, what I wanted then was a plastic ball

with a snowstorm whirling in the water-air above a log cabin and three fir trees—

In the meantime I'm still on the crust of the earth. The ground beneath me continues to gargle; it has cold iron pipes in its stomach and inside them lies a transparent and endless snake of water; it has tendons of electricity, voices run inside it in the dark, between the roots, echoing in the caves, making their way through the sand dunes, sinking into the sea, emerging on the other side, I love you, when are you coming, I don't know yet but me too, you what, I miss you, really, I can't sleep, and the dead in the shipwrecks complain, even here there's no peace, and Caribbean sharks bite the cable in a rage—trrr-trrrr—

"Tikva?"

"Yes, write this down quickly, it's a madhouse here today—I'm at work—yes, at the bank—so are you writing? Thursday at nine in the evening everybody's coming to me to the sukkah—who's everybody? Ora and Yosefa and Arlozora and Bilu and Hezi and Dina and Ruthie and Uri and Yohanan and maybe Adriana will come from abroad—did you write it down? You're coming. You remember where I live, right?"

I return to lie on the ground. The cypress tree—peach and cream; like dead butterflies the bougainvillea flowers collect around its trunk. From here I can see its summit—veins of pure silver to the heart of the sky—and a car coming closer, with a clear, carrying voice on the radio: "How do you explain the fact that in seventy-three they knew—and nevertheless . . ." and the interviewee with a scratchy voice and a kibbutznik lisp: "We trusted the . . ." and the car drives past, what did we trust, who insists on driving up Y.Y. Rosenberg Lane, today it's called Rosemary, an herbal bush with blue flowers, now they've discovered there's no exit and they're coming back, *Let it be, let it be,* the radio sings in a woman's voice, *May all we wish for come to be—*

Today the summer split apart; at noon the heat cracked, the haze evaporated, leaving a silken sky like the sky above the clouds with here and there a tickle of wind—the mafioso and his gang hop in the grass like wooden birds on springs, a couple of Polish yentas peck energetically and between one burst of pecking and the next they advance left-right on quick, stilt legs, their heads bobbing—now the birds have grown used to me, sooner than Mrs.-Morgenstern-the-grocer's who is still trying to sell me the newspaper, this morning she raised her head from the death notices, "That Dr. Finkelstein dead. You knowed him?" and I shake my head, no I didn't know him—"Him young man!" the-grocer's protests at my indifference, reminding me of you; of all the people I have ever known only you and Shlomi's mother studied the mourning notices, but Shlomi's mother was seeking townspeople and you were seeking justice. Look: mourned by his parents, his brothers, Grandmother Matilda, I don't understand why God kills people when they're so young!—How do you know how old he was when he died?—What do you mean, how? Look: no wife, no children, no grandchildren—Maybe he was a ninety-years-old bachelor!—With parents and a grandmother? You were right again. So what do you want to read in the death notices? Mourned by his great-grandchildren and his great-great-grandchildren—and I, looking for a way to annoy you, would like to read for once: "Hallelujah, I'm an orphan"—I wanted you to be an orphan, or at least half an orphan, like me, I even fasted half a Yom Kippur in the fifth grade—I was trying to make a deal with the God of the synagogue: I'll fast, and you'll kill Ora's mother—but I couldn't keep it up, and she's alive and kicking to this day—

And if you were half an orphan, would everything have been different, or then too would you have been obliged to volunteer for work days on border kibbutzim and for the first aid and to go to the synagogue on holidays and to be a counselor in the youth movement and to speak to the headmaster on behalf of the class committee and to organize a readers' strike because of the librarian and to deliver the valedictory speech at the graduation ceremony and to be the top student in the class in science and mathematics and physical education and the prettiest girl of the year—there's no such thing, Loya, there's no such thing, Hedva would respond to my stories about you, there is, I promised her, in your dreams, warned Hedva, when you wake up let me know—

The day before Yom Kippur in the tenth grade you came to me with your schoolbag. There's nobody here? You glanced around the living room, the passage, no, I assured you, and then you took a big brown envelope out of your bag and slid a short stream of old photographs onto the kitchen table, part of them matte brown and part glossy gray with white, serrated edges—You pinched them? I couldn't believe it. Ora!—I just wanted you to see. I'll put them back right away—there were about thirty, some of them of castles, no, the same castle from different angles, a bit of forest and a few figures in riding breeches, girls standing in a pyramid, babies in heavy baby carriages with little wheels, little boys with damp side-parted hair and little girls with ringlets—the important photos were left for last; they were in a separate, smaller envelope; you cleared a space on the table for them and laid them carefully in the middle: in all five was a beautiful blonde who looked like Rita Hayworth—she should have been my mother, you picked one of them up: Rita Hayworth sitting at a piano, tilting her head, laughing, yes, if there was any justice in the world, because it was almost impossible to believe that you had emerged from the squat, thin-lipped Mechora, with her plucked eyebrows and sparse mousy hair and "Golda Meir" legs—she was my father's first wife—you said—her name was Vera. There was no point in asking what had happened to her. You thought that you should mourn for her. Your mother thought not. You thought you should. Your mother said that only orphans stayed in the synagogue for the prayers for the dead. I almost forgot—you rummaged in the schoolbag, took out a memorial candle: You light it for her; I won't have time to get here and back before Kol Nidrei, but you light it before the holiday begins, at four o'clock, okay?

Immediately after my father left for Hasia Horovitz, at a quarter past five—God doesn't have a watch, believe me—I lit the memorial candle for the beautiful mother you didn't have and placed it carefully in the middle of the kitchen sink. Then I went to the synagogue plaza. The boys were still fasting to prove themselves, the girls were already fasting to lose weight—and I was uneasy. When all was said and done I had left a fire burning in the house against all instructions—Are you fasting? Adriana had noticed something—I'm just going home for a minute—Should I come with you?—NO, no—I hurried home and found my father drinking tea standing up, looking at the sink: Loya—what is this? His tone was almost scolding. We don't light memorial candles or pray or perform any pagan rites. We're modern people—Ora asked me to—Ora? He was surprised and I was surprised at his relief. What had he expected? It's in memory of her father's first wife—I offered in explanation. My father nodded as if he was familiar with the story. Were we the only ones who hadn't known all these years?

The candle went out after twenty-six hours. I hurried over to your house. Your father opened the door in silence. Tall, dark, you resembled him, I saw for the first time, you came out to me, we stood under the guava tree, among the shadows of the leaves, branches and fruit, in a heavy yellow smell—when it was time for the prayer for the dead, you told me in a rapid, almost trembling whisper, my mother said to me: Now you're leaving, and I said no, and she said, leave at once, and I said on-no-account, and Mrs. Mendelkern and Mrs. Kosovitzki who always sit behind us began saying shhhhh . . . what's going on here, and I got up and went to sit on another chair, at the end of the row—And your mother thought you'd left?—No, but she didn't want to make a scene in the synagogue—And what did she say when you went home?—Nothing. She isn't talking to me—and it went on almost until Hanukkah; you, deliberately cheerful, hiding your distress, but I rejoiced: you came to me every day after school, sharing the falafel I bought with the money my father left me in the table drawer or spooning food from cans standing up, and afterwards we would roam around the citrus groves or smoke a cigarette made from grass in the ruins of the orphanage, or come here, to your house, you were a welcoming host, volunteering over-long explanations in reply to every little question, telling Ora about an amazing Hebrew world—hurrying to unroll a map of the Mediterranean basin—a mighty Hebrew empire stretching from Jerusalem to Tyre to Carthage, who founded the colonies of the sea if not the tribes of Asher, Issachar, and Zebulun, and "Naphtali a hind let loose," let loose to where, in your opinion, to here, to here, your finger travels to Cyprus, to Crete which is Caphtor, to Carthage, to Spain—the finger returns, your hand fans out, sweeps from Ezion-gaber to Tadmor, the Hebrew empire protected its Phoenician relations from the east—you pronounce it "Phoinikian" after the Greek name Phoinike, meaning "the land of purple," we are all Canaanites, girls—who are you studying now? Amos who-was-among-the-herdsmen-of-Tekoa? Isaiah the-ox-knoweth-his-owner? All our prophets were small farmers and big reactionaries! They wanted us to remain a small nation surrounded by enemies and never to mix with the goyim, because the goyim are *tfu-yasna-cholera* and we are the chosen people. Pour out thy wrath on the gentiles—you turn to Ora, speaking only to her, I am already familiar with the material, and Ora, aged sixteen, holds her breath—you know when this is said?—You test her, Ora doesn't reply, it's beneath her dignity to answer such a childish question—and who has the door opened for him at the Passover Seder? You ask and answer yourself—Elijah, that ruffian who took four hundred and fifty people down to the Kishon river and khhhhttt—you draw your finger gleefully across your throat—what did he care that his king had made an alliance with Sidon and married Jezebel, so people worshipped Baal and Astarte here a bit, assimilated into the Semitic region—

And another time we take you out of the gluing room and you don't mind, not at all, but we can't go into the room with its enormous table, potsherds, bookshelves—What are you studying in the Bible now, girls, you ask, Jeremiah, I reply, hoping you won't start again, "For death has come up into our windows and is entered into our palaces" you quote from Jeremiah 9, our prophets, you turn to Ora, only to Ora, were minor poets and major plagiarists, you raise pale eyes to the astonished Ora, tell her where it comes from, Loya, and I know that the virgin goddess Anat will immediately appear, threatening to send her old father to a bloody death if he refuses to erect a temple to her brother Aliyn-Baal after death came up into his windows, "Thou brakest the heads of leviathan in pieces," this isn't enough for you—Loya, you send me away in order to remain for a minute alone with Ora, go and find a Bible in Nahum's room, but I am on my guard, I know the passage off by heart, "Thou didst divide the sea by thy strength; thou brakest the heads of the dragons in the waters. Thou brakest the head of leviathan in pieces," Psalm 74, and who did all this? The goddess Anat! I preempt you in the competition to astonish Ora, quickly throwing in the half-remembered "I shall smite leviathan that crooked serpent, I shall punish the dragon in the sea"—Ora's very pretty, you remark casually two days later, and again, in the course of the following months, from time to time, as if by the way, how's that pretty friend of yours, or, aren't you friends with that pretty girl any more, why don't you bring her around sometime, you even dare to ask, aren't you ashamed, behaving like the boys in our class even though you're old old old, how old were you then, more or less my age now—she seems like an intelligent young woman, you said, and I shrugged my shoulders and thought "You can go to hell!" I was angered by the "young woman" which made her about five years older, I was angered by the "intelligent" because how could you know, you hardly let her get a word in edgewise—but Ora didn't want to come back here anyway: you frightened her, you upset her, you insulted her Bible, she even stopped coming to our house so often, maybe she was afraid of meeting you there, come to my place, I kept on inviting her, no, you come to me, come to me, you haven't come to me for ages, no, you come to me, it's more comfortable at my house, in a kind of tug-of-war—it really is more comfortable at her house, padded, brightly lit, there's always yeast cake and cocoa, in the course of the years carpets on the floor, curtains, a big electric fan in every room, a full fridge, and her mother keeps opening the door to bring cold drinks and fruit or cookies, what are you studying, overflowing with advice and information, choking me with fury because she hates me—a sugarcoated, clucking, hypocritical hatred—and I hate her plain and simple—and I can't say a word—

The heatwave breaks. I go out to water the garden. Does the ficus tree need to be watered? Its roots are thick and muscular—its crest is huge—it probably lives on ground water—"*mei-tehom*," the Hebrew word still gives me gooseflesh. What does this sound like, I once asked Jean-Jacques. It was a kind of game. Listen—*mei-tehom*, I made the *h* imprisoned in the word sound like an echo in a cave. "*Meit-hom*" Jean-Jacques divided the word, tasting it in two little sips as if it was wine. He had a theory that you could guess the meaning of words in an unfamiliar language with a surprising degree of accuracy simply by means of the sound. I was sure that he was wrong. How many languages do you know? This was on one of our first dates. We were both trying to impress. All the civilized languages, he smiled. Latin? English? Spanish? Italian? Russian? I started to compile a basic list, but he accompanied it with shake of his head, no-no-no-no. Then which? French, French, French—at our next meetings I devoted not a little time to proving that his theory lacked all basis in reality. I would ask him to guess the meaning of a word in Italian, Spanish, Latin, English; to tell the truth he guessed quite well until we came to Hebrew. Hebrew to him was the language in which the mummies whispered in the tombs of the Pharoahs. And *mei-tehom*? A dangerous dog? Or perhaps, a stepmother? Or a small house?

I water the garden. The splashing of the water wetting the ground does something to relieve the dryness all around—the papery bougainvillea, the fallen ficus leaves, the islands of earth cracked by dark fissures of thirst— the water trembles, unravels under the pressure of my thumb into palm fronds, soft horse manes, all according to the changing thickness of the jet and the tightness of my thumb—I create collapsing chandeliers in the air—and the birds come to see; here come the black ones, the mafiosi, flying straight, low, with surly, plummy gurgles—*Buon giorno!* I try to placate them, *Benvenuto! Sono io! Loya!* They respond quite well. One gliding blackbird settles on the pomegranate tree and looks at me attentively. *Piacere di conoscerla!* Perhaps I'll be able to tame her, Lo-ya, I repeat, Loya,

Lo-ya, I hear from the top of the ficus tree, am I hallucinating? I go closer. The water draws supple figure eights in the air, and the Imperial bird, *Garrulus glandarius*, is revealed on a sturdy bough, obviously interested. *Aspetta qualcuno?* I wonder; if he's a Roman emperor he'll speak Latin, if she's a songbird she'll break into song in Italian, Hebrew is out of the question, a language full of harsh gutturals, only Dutch is harsher. The Caesar on the tree averts his head, apparently preferring Latin—*Ave Caesar, morituri te salutant*—but he looks disapproving, *Va bene, va bene*, I return to Italian, drawing a spectacular treble clef of water in the air, *Ti amo*, I say to him what I have never had the chance to say to any man up to now, not in Italian—"Are you talking to the birds or to yourself?" a familiar voice, full of sea sand and salt, asks behind my back, I turn around—Hey! Someone recoils from the water, I go to the faucet, turn it off, stand up to see who— "Tikva told me you were here!"

A first swallow.

Yosefa. Who else.

Still slim, she can afford to wear tailored slacks, a flimsy silk shirt, I hold out my hand, she looks at it, afraid of getting wet? Apparently not— "You're not married" is what she has to say to me after a quarter of a century, she hasn't changed, despite the lines at the corners of her mouth, the corners of her eyes, the faded carrot hair. She encloses my hand in a painful grip with three silver rings, "And you, are you married?"—What did you tell me, Davidi? With the mean be mean—her eyes are a murky blue, she's not as tall as Ora, but still tall, the school champion one hundred meter sprinter, a member of the underground but not really a friend, always knowing everything before everyone else, cross-examining: So what did you say to him? Are you wearing a bra yet? What number? Summing people up in one cutting word—idiot—moron—blockhead—"Not any more," she replies, devouring the house with her eyes, "So he left you the house, the *meshuggener*?" striding up the path, stumbling on a paving stone displaced by the ficus tree, "Fuck that tree—" cursing like before, she hasn't changed, "I'm going inside—" she announces, the front door's open, how can I say "No"—Yosefa? But she's already inside, "It's dark in here, switch something on, open a window," I push the shutters open, the living room fills with a faint light, my clothes lie in heaps, shoes, books, "What's going on here? How long have you been here?" Yosefa measures the room, counting the floor tiles, "they built big once, eh?" She glances over the bookshelves, "Whose are all these books?" "Nahum's, apparently," I say "apparently" in order to blur the information, leave something in the shadows—"Nemecsek," says Yosefa with a giggle, recalling the nickname she gave him after reading Ferenc Molnár's book *Who is a Hero?* with its tragic little hero. "He fell at the canal, didn't he?" "No, he fell in the Kinneret—" "In the Kinneret?" "There's an entire squadron in there—" I repeat the black joke of the air control unit, Yosefa leaves the living room, tries the doors of the bedrooms, "What did you lock them for?" "They were locked, I haven't had a chance to open them yet—" "How many rooms have you got here, three?" "The same as you." "No, not the same as us, we lived in the row houses, don't you remember?" I try, but no picture comes to mind. "Me and my boyfriend are looking for a house in the neighborhood," she returns to the living room, hands in her pockets, her shoulders a little raised, "While you were away our slummy old block became really smart, and you—you've got more luck than sense, now you can make a pile." She's on the porch, leaning on the balustrade, smoking a Marlboro Light, "How much do you want?" "For what?" "For the house." "I'm not selling," I sound firm, to my surprise—"Are you staying?" Yosefa looks at her hands lying on the balustrade. The light explodes on her massive silver rings. "Yes!" I am far more unequivocal than I meant to be, "Okay, okay," Yosefa raises her head, half turns her face to me and shoots "Have you had a face-lift?" "Yes, twice," I lie gleefully. "In America?" "Once. And once in France," I'm beginning to enjoy myself. "They did a good job on you," Yosefa brings her face closer before throwing out "I'm thinking of having one too, but first the house. One thing at a time," she abandons the balustrade, "I'll still persuade you to sell it to me—" She's on her way out, with me on her heels, to sweep her out as quickly as I can, what did I come back for, why am I still here—Yosefa slides into a dark green BMW, sticks a thin, freckled arm out of the window and looks at me. "So you're coming to Tikva's, right?" I nod. The hose is back in my hands again. In a minute I'll turn it on her—"Remember the underground?" I can't decide if she's reminiscing or mocking. I say nothing. "Don't you remember? Don't you remember how we had to practice being tortured? Hold our palms over a burning candle for ten minutes?" "Three—" I can't help correcting, "did it leave a scar?" She misses the irony, shows me the palm of her hand. Dry, yellowish, crisscrossed with many thin lines. "No—" I pronounce, "nothing at all!" I step back, but she bends down to the glove compartment, takes out a card proclaiming Yosefa Hertz-Rubin, Hertz-Rubin-Abramov Attorneys at Law, so that's what became of her, she turns on the engine, one hand on the wheel the second waving, "Good luck!" I call through the water fanning out under my thumb, "With what?" she calls out of the window as she reverses, "The face-lift!" I shout from behind the fan of spray.

I wonder who else Tikva has told that I'm back on the block, talk of the devil, here she is, with a basket "to take a few pomegranates," she smiles, both of us next to the tree, I pick the low ones—Are they for the sukkah? "We've already hung some in the sukkah—I'm making goose liver with Cointreau and pomegranates," it sounds to me like one of Jean-Jacques' recipes, "Broche de corail," he would call such a concoction, "coral brooch," or "Bronze clouds flaming over Polynesia" or simply "Gauguin. Etude." I don't understand, I would shrug my shoulders, it's just chicken with a bit of broccoli and red pepper, why do you call it "The Little Prince among the baobab trees"? Jean-Jacques would point the tip of his fork at the broccoli on my plate and say, that's the baobab. And where's the Little Prince? I want to know—he had a strong tendency to talk in metaphors and for a year or two it infected me too—This is his cloak, Jean-Jacques spears a red pepper. And the Prince himself? I ask with my mouth full of chicken. You've already eaten him, *mon amie*, didn't you notice?

"I'll see you at my place the day after tomorrow," Tikva concludes, picking up the basket, "Bilu's coming too, and Adriana—she bought a boutique in the new center—I organized a loan for her, and Arlozorova and Dina

and Shmuel and Minaleh if she feels okay and Uri—you remember Uri?"
I accompany her, this time she came by foot, listening to the names, being
brought up to date, who's a grandmother already, whose son was killed in
Lebanon or badly wounded in the Intifada, how many are divorced and
how many married-divorced-married to be continued, who got rich or
famous, she invited Shlomi too but he can't come, not now, when, when,
when will she get to Elhanan, to Ora—"My cousin's coming too—" Tikva
gives me an almost black look strangely at odds with its Cleopatra-blonde
framework—"And Elhanan, did you invite Elhanan?" I can't ask about Ora
but Elhanan is close—"No one will invite Elhanan any more," she averts
her eyes—"What happened?" These petty score-settling squabbles. Nothing's changed with the years. A small, crowded place, stewing in its own
juice—"He's in Kiryat-Shaul." "So? Hasn't he got a phone?" I say sharply,
annoyed, and Tikva says: "In the military cemetery—" "Since when?" I
ask, my mouth dry. "The war of attrition," I can sense her looking at me
now, but I look at the eucalyptus. How tall it is. And they're still peeling
its bark off in strips, exposing its skin, the skin of plump women in Renoir
paintings, "Minaleh called her son after him." Minaleh soft and white like
salt-free cheese, always in white socks, was hopelessly in love with him, but
he, according to all the signs, like all the boys, was in love with Ora—we go
on walking, Carob Street, Chrysanthemum Street, Cyclamen Street—here,
here it is—the Persian Lilac trees have grown so tall, they've changed the
street—once Brigade Street, today Cypress Street—a high wooden fence
painted green, a gate—Tikva opens the gate and reveals a big lawn with
a garden gnome in its center and at its end an almost new house, with a
steeply sloping tiled roof, on the heavy front door a brass lion's head with
a knocker in its mouth, above it a reindeer's head with branching antlers.
"And Ora?" If I don't ask, I won't know that she isn't here. Two months
ago she went abroad with her husband and two children on a sabbatical.
How ironic, I say to Hedva in my head, when I'm here at last she's there,
somewhere or other, in New York, or Oxford or San Diego, and I went to
her house, I stood before the locked gate, I almost rang, lucky I didn't ring,
who would have let me in—"Who do you think helped me to organize

everything if not Ora?" Tikva closes the gate—"Does she know that—" I start to ask. Bit the tip of my tongue. "What did you say?" Tikva turns around, already next to the front door. Nothing, I wave my hand weakly. If Tikva knows. If Bilu knows. If Yosefa knows. If the mountain won't come to Mohammed, who the hell needs it?

At night I toss and turn in a comfortable sarcophagus lined with white satin like the casket of a mafioso in the movies, thinking, if this is what it means to be dead it's not so bad, it's even comfortable, lying like the yoke in the white of the egg in its shell in a cardboard box in a coffin in the ground, with nothing to do, not even breathe, you can sleep and sleep, it's so quiet in the ground and warm and safe, there's nowhere to fall to from here, this is the last terminal, the absolutely final end, nothing more to expect, nothing to fear, the worst has already happened, I fill with happiness, feel it spreading through my body, but there's something sticking into my back under my shoulder, someone left a drawing pin or a nail here, I turn a little to the right, grope and fish up the thing that is depriving me of the pleasure of death, something full of sharp corners is enclosed in my hand, I open it to discover a star—

The hammock between the jacaranda trees sways slightly and I see the sky from its belly; flooded at noon with a strong dull light and towards evening becoming transparent, almost greenish, until lying in the hammock is almost like lying at the bottom of the sea. Did you see? asked Nahum when we came out of the water, the fish have backs the color of water and stomachs the color of light—we saw them gliding above us without moving their fins. So why do planes—I was thinking of the planes in the air force—I sometimes asked silly questions—Nahum looked at me incredulously, and then he giggled: Because we don't always fly belly down, he demonstrated by turning over his hands. When a fish floats belly up it's either a dolphin or dead—I extricated myself, Nahum laughed, and I remembered Bilu's aquarium. Once he invited me to come and see it and discovered an upside-down goldfish. He fished it out of the aquarium with a soup ladle. Your mother will kill you, I assured him, even though I wasn't really sure; Bilu's mother, with her sandals, her braid, her pampered kibbutznik lisp—Bilu stared at me with wide, Huckleberry Finn eyes: Because of the fish?—Because of the ladle, idiot!—I'll wash it, promised Bilu. We went to the kitchen together. I waited while he rinsed and soaped and scrubbed and rinsed again. But germs don't die in water, I informed him. What germs? What do you think it died of? A heart attack?—I think it died of old age, it was my oldest fish—

The hammock sways slightly. Above the delicate foliage the night sky from the bottom up, so many stars, dead stars too, Nahum told me on that same night, I glanced at him, but he was serious, it takes them a few billion years—but they die too in the end, a dry black wind blew without stopping, the water of the bay ran up to the sand with a continuous swishing whisper, I never told anyone about that night, not even Ora; was it from then that the rift began, will she come this evening, will she come up to me and hold out her hand for a formal shake or—will she smile, her eyes sparkling, press me to her in a short, warm embrace, and push me away to look at me, as she did when I finished basic training in the army, let's have a look at you, she'll say, and then we'll both say at once, what will we say, we won't say "I missed you," maybe "I thought of you, all these years I thought of you," no, not "all these years," just "I thought of you," we'll say at once, like then, sending each other exactly the same New Year's greeting cards, buying each other the same paper angels, saying together, "I was sure you'd like it," you won't believe it, I told Hedva who didn't believe it, when we finally got a telephone I always knew if the ring was Ora's, I was never wrong, we studied together for all our exams, we got the same grades—except in arithmetic; she was better than me in arithmetic—what will she wear this evening, I could always guess if she would consider the event festive enough to undo her braids into a dark mane and now I don't even know if she's cut her hair short or if she hasn't touched it, as she promised me once, and wears it in an aristocratic bun, like Martha Graham, beautiful, she's still very beautiful, I'm sure, beauty like hers only improves with the years, becomes radiant and regal, what will I wear this evening in her honor, you won't believe it, I say to Hedva in my head, I've changed three times already, put on make-up and taken it off again, changed my hair, as if for a date with someone I've fallen head over heels in love with, I know she's angry, I can feel her anger reaching me like a low sea wave, hissing, snapping at my toes, if all the time I've been here and she knew, she hasn't dropped in to see, hasn't picked up the phone, even if she came as far as the gate—stopped next to the solitary cypress tree, didn't come any further, thinking to herself what, I haven't known for years what she thinks to herself, but this evening I'll know, I choose black pants and a white shirt, tie a blue and yellow silk scarf around my neck, take it off again, try a necklace of turquoise stones, take it off, choose pearls, sporty but elegant, this is how I want her to see me for the first time after two thousand years, she'll wait for me at the entrance to Tikva's sukkah or even at the gate, she'll say "You're late," yes, those will be her first words to me, "You're late, as usual," and I'll tell her that I knew that's what she would say and that I came late on purpose just to hear her say "you're late," in the past quarter of a century I've never been late for a flight, and she'll smile and say that coming late is evidently a kind of sickness that only afflicts me on the ground, no, she won't say that, what will she say, the conversation dies down, fades out, if I don't go there I won't know—

A distant plane passes between the leaves; up there, in the aisles, flight attendants cruise, dispersing faint smiles, seeing in the illuminated windows the same plane, the same passengers, a flight attendant resembling the one looking—a ghost plane suspended in the air, materializing without a sound—when I was in a crew with Hedva I sometimes permitted myself to retire, sit on the jump seat and press against the window, darken it with my face and hands, erase the reflections and see what was outside; what was really outside; on a moonlit night the clouds are silver sheep and filmy blue and the sea is suddenly enamel and silk—

To go or not to go?

When I was still reading *The Secret Gang and the Iron Fist* Ora was in the middle of *Les Misérables*, by the time I got to *Les Misérables*—she was already after *Jean-Christophe* and *Zorba the Greek*, always two or three ahead of me, she regarded the underground as childish, and Adriana's mother as shallow and superfluous, even though she was the only person in the neighborhood to own a dressing table with three mirrors so that she could see what she looked like from the front and from the sides, she would brush her hair opposite the mirrors, while we—Adriana and Yosefa and Gila and Arlozora and Minaleh and Dina and Tikva—clustered around, hypnotized by the strokes of the brush sweeping through her soft, abundant hair, a hundred times from the top and a hundred times from the bottom—listening to her mellifluous Hebrew—soft, rapid, lilting—she talked without stopping of hairdos and face creams and what to eat for a skin clear of pimples and what to wear when and what color, before parties she agreed to make us up just a teeny bit, so it wouldn't be obvious but it would make all the difference, that was the whole secret, just a hint on your eyelashes, Loya, and what a difference, now you can see the green, a little rouge on your cheeks, Minaleh, she was the youngest of all the mothers, she had given birth to Adriana at the age of sixteen and a half and when Adriana was fifteen they looked like sisters, they wore the same blouses, they exchanged bangles and sandals, a good friend is better than silver, better than a husband, said Adriana's mother, she had a childhood friend in Milan who sent her so many letters that Adriana had a magnificent collection of Italian stamps—a good friend is kindhearted and wise—her eyes left her reflection and scanned our faces to guess who would have a good friend and who wouldn't, I smiled, I knew I had one, that nothing and nobody would ever come between Ora and me, no mother, no father, no secret, when you get your period tell me, she got hers three years before me, she told me how and what to do, bought the sanitary towels for me, when you buy a bra show me, she wore one two years before me, forging a road into the unknown for me, and I, in the wake of the orange-peel-path of her life, to go or not to go, the jacaranda leaves like black velvet feathers above my head, the hammock underneath me sways from side to side, and the belly of the sky is revealed and concealed—I simply like seeing the sky from the back, I explained to Jean-Jacques on one of the times when he started with his "why do you have to fly" again—nobody sees the sky from the back, pronounced Jean-Jacques, except for God—

I'm going to Tikva's. To Tikva's sukkah. Tikva, who we called "Nits" after the school nurse found lice in her hair: she would come into the Bible or arithmetic or calligraphy class, whisper to the teacher, set a tray with a glass, a bottle, cotton wool, and an antiseptic smell on the teacher's table, pick up a glass knitting needle and in a slow, pedagogic voice ask a-all the gi-irls to undo their braids and pony-tails, the teacher would call out the names, and one after the other we would go up and stand under the glass knitting needles that made mesmerizing paths on our heads—I could have stood for hours under that spell-binding movement, feeling as if I was about to fall asleep standing up, but with me—straight, thin hair—it was all over in five or six sweeps, like with the boys; how I envied the girls with thick hair and curls, like Ora, Tikva, Yosefa, whose heads the nurse investigated at length, separating strands, blinking, usually not finding anything, but once she found lice on Yosefa and Tikva and sent them home immediately with a note. The next day Yosefa came to school with her hair cropped, looking shrewder, more dangerous, Wow, it suits you, the girls said warily, while the boys whistled, and Tikva came back two days later with her braids giving off a nasty smell and nobody wanted to sit next to her—was it then that she began bringing French journals to school and reading them on her lap in class and also in recess, until she fell and broke her arm and came back from the hospital with a plaster cast and everyone wanted to write something on the cast or at least sign their names, and Tikva didn't favor everybody, she didn't let Yosefa sign, or Shmuel either, first they insult me and then they suck up to me, she pursed her lips, but she let me, apparently in orphan-solidarity, and then I asked her if I could borrow one of her journals to take home and read, but she said: You won't understand a single word because it's in French. And anyway they belong to my aunt in Paris and my mother won't let me, but you can come and read them at my house if you like—

Once, twice a week I would walk this way—always invited to eat too, different, pungent food, even the rice, even the rissoles, even the tea—very sweet, very dark with floating boats of mint, let's go and water the mint, I would ask after we were tired of the French, and we would go out into the garden, and I would water the mint which covered the whole area between the porch and the fence in order to awaken its smells against coughing and colds and tiredness—the smells of a felt beret on a shampooed head on an autumn day in Paris—your French really does have a Moroccan aroma, chuckled Jean-Jacques—

Every third house had a sukkah, shining in the night like a Chinese lantern, with its paper decorations rustling in the hot wind blowing in intermittent gusts, bearing a smell of dust and rotting mandarins from the citrus groves—from the corner of Cypress and Cyclamen the sound of laughter and loud voices is already audible—Cypress Street is full of cars, parked on the pavements too on both sides of the open gate, its Welcome sign waving and Ora isn't there, the lawn is lit, empty, on the door under the lion's jaw is a note saying "We're in the back" with a red arrow pointing the way, I follow the arrow, circle the house, it's hot, hot, very hot, sweltering, here's the sukkah, a big cube of light full of shadows and blaring voices and "Welcome" at the entrance and Ora isn't there, it's hot, very hot, sweltering, boiling—thirty, no, forty people crowded around tables laden with pita bread, hummus, pickles, falafel balls, finely chopped salads, mountains of pickled cabbage and heaps of green olives and every couple of meters—a cluster of bottles; Cola, Diet Cola, Kinley, Sprite, Diet Orangeade—and arms stretching, crossing, cramming something into half a pita—Pour me a drink, will you? and a bottle balances in the air over the plastic glass at the end of the outstretched arm—people a little past the middle of their lives eating and drinking because in another thirty years there'll be only half of them left, in another forty—only a sample, in a minute someone will ask—Yes? Are you looking for somebody? I made a mistake, I mistook the date and the place, I don't know anyone here, and Ora isn't here— "Loya!" Tikva's voice behind me proclaiming "People! Look who's here," she tries to overcome the voices of the chewing, laughing, talking, drinking crowd, *"If we die bury us in the wine cellars of Rishon LeZion"*—silence falls gradually, heads are raised, eyes turned in my direction—here's Yosefa and next to her Bilu waving a piece of pita at me, two strangers away from him Arlozora with streaked, bobbed hair, dramatic make-up, and next to her—Minaleh? Is that Minaleh? Bloated, pale, almost bald, sick, opposite her Hezi with a broad grin, with a heavy gold chain glittering from the V of his shirt, and Hi! Hi! From the corner signaling gaily Adriana, like her mother but not as pretty, and Dina and Leah and Yossi and Amnon who have doubled their size and Shmuel Shmuel, him I would have recognized—"You know everybody here," Tikva skirts me with a loaded tray. "Not really," I say to myself, "because of the husbands and wives," a small, well groomed woman sitting next to the entrance helps me—Ruthie? "Yes, Ruthie—and this is Misha," she indicates the stranger next to her—"Loya, Loya, come here!" Adriana calls from the corner, and I squeeze past, smiling to the right, smiling to the left, some of them grab my arm with a "Hi-how-are-you" without a question mark, they don't really want to know, the others just look, nobody is too excited, so we once had some Loya in our class, skinny and blonde and jittery, last seen throwing, screaming, breaking, they brought a nurse, police, and nobody's seen her since, anyone with information regarding her whereabouts—*anyone with information regarding her whereabouts*—Nahum listens, I listen every afternoon, some of the names keep stubbornly coming back until an imploring note seems to creep into the broadcaster's voice, *anyone with information regarding her whereabouts*, what does the person being searched for feel—knitting needles in her hair? breathing down her neck?—how can it be that they're searching so hard here, there, somewhere, and the search fails to touch even the tip of the fingernail of the person whose traces have been lost—

"Hi Loya!" in a voice full of hummus, eggplant, and pickles, on my right, on my left, I push on, climb onto a bench between two strangers, step onto the table, balance between the tahini and the pickled cabbage—faint applause, brief laughter—step down with the help of two arms raised to me—one has a cold hand, one has a warm hand—thank you—I'm past the bench, on the way to Adriana, but the warm hand doesn't let go—I turn to see—a middle-aged woman looks at me from her seat—heavy, loosely dressed to hide how heavy, short, limp hair, dyed aubergine-black, her face sweaty, her eyes—a half-risen sun surrounded by a halo of gray—

Ora?

It's impossible, not to such an extent. But she looks at me with clenched lips and nods her head with that majestic movement—

"I—" I wave my hand in the direction of Adriana who has made room for me next to her—"We'll talk later—" the stranger with Ora's eyes lets go of me abruptly and turns a thick back to me, and Adriana—she, at least, has only turned into her mother—hugs me, plants a big kiss on my cheek. "So many years!" she exults, as if the quarter of a century that has passed only adds charm and spice to the meeting. "You look wonderful!" someone I don't recognize exclaims on my left. "You too," I assure her. "Tell us, tell us what you're doing—" Adriana holds my hand, hers is cool, smooth. "Now I'm here." "Yes, I heard, in Davidi's house—" the rumor spread like wild-fire—Adriana laughs—"And what about you?" "I got married-divorced-married-divorced and now I'm here with three daughters—" "Better three daughters on the street than two sons in the Suez canal," chorus Shmuel Shmuel and—Nissim? Yes, Nissim—"I have two sons," Shmuel Shmuel smiles, "And I have three!" Nissim raises a plastic glass, "L'chaim, Loya!" and the unidentified woman hands me a glass of red wine so sweet it stings and Tikva comes up, leans over me. "You see that guy there? That's my cousin. A wonderful guy—" A dark, good-looking man, like ten thousand others, the ones you see in the middle of New York and know immediately: an Israeli—and in the meantime an argument flares up—That Rabin—What about him, what do you want of Rabin—If there's another bomb—

"That's enough, we said no politics!" Tikva hurries to the arguers, "How can we not talk about politics?" Shmuel Shmuel protests—The settlers won't leave—it won't be as easy as it was in Sinai—In Sinai it was easy?—It was nothing compared to what will happen now—"He was evacuated from Yamit," Adriana fills me in, "you were already gone then."—Right, and all the news reached me muffled, veiled by distance, translated into foreign languages, squeezed between a terrible earthquake in Chile and a devastating typhoon in Japan. "There'll be murder," promises Shmuel I Shmuel II, "What murder are you talking about?" Nissim hands him a pita, "lay off and eat, the hummus is terrific." But I don't touch a thing, I keep looking at where I came from: Ora is talking in a low voice to someone next to her, there's a hump at the back of her neck already, her hair is thin, dyed, dead, there are three lines at the corner of her eye, her dimple has turned into a sad crease—"Are you looking at Ora?" Adriana whispers, I nod, "you remember how she used to be?" Adriana sighs, I nod, Ora, characteristically, is preceding us into old age too, she is the evidence and the knowledge of what awaits Adriana, Yosefa, Tikva, Arlozora, and me, we're still okay, but it's a temporary state, a combination of genetics and cosmetics and dieting and exercise—in another two or three years—"A Prime Minister is going to be murdered here!" Shmuel I bangs on the table, making the hummus jump, overturning a plastic glass of diet orangeade. "That's enough, look what you've done now!" Tikva hurries up with a bunch of paper napkins, she looks fine, plastics and cosmetics, dieting and dyeing—"Ever since she got married she—" Adriana starts and stops, examines me carefully, I want to ask ever since she got married what, why, but I can't, I look at her old nape, her rounded shoulders, I can see her pale scalp through her sparse hair, Adriana goes on talking and I can't listen, can't react, I turn my face away and stare at nothing so as not to cry—

I wake up with Dubček. Go outside barefoot, disheveled, feeling the clean morning light finally waking me from my sleep in order to discover that all the fields have been covered with polyethylene—when do these people work, I wonder—from the plane flying low overhead a tourist with violet-silver hair is sure that there's a little lake here, why do you say there's no water in Israel, someone like her once asked me indignantly as I poured her coffee, pointing her teaspoon at the window, it's plastic, ma'am, just plastic, I assured her, and she put on her glasses to get a better look: Ah—so it is—

A new gang is perched on the electricity wires: pale stomachs, black frock coats—in a minute I'll find out who you are, but first the-grocer's. All this week she's only open until eleven in the morning, "This holiday for me too" she says defiantly, "I human being too" as if I said she wasn't. "Come by—" said Ora before we parted, older than me by twenty years, a stranger landing up between us would have said—but there are no strangers here, they're all the same age, passing between us as they make their way out, each to his own past, pardon me, pardon me, her weight transforms her height into a presence that takes up space, blocks, a thousand times I've imagined this meeting without guessing how. "Drop in to see me," she continues, unbelievably, from the place where we left off thirty-three years ago, come to me, no, you come to me, but it's more comfortable at my house, but I've come to you three times already, "But when are you at home?" I insist on a more explicit invitation. "Every afternoon." "Tomorrow?" my heart jumps into my mouth; tomorrow! "Tomorrow—not tomorrow, we have a staff meeting." "The day after tomorrow?" The sentence is postponed for a day—"Only after six—I have to take Yinon to Judo—" "Then the day after tomorrow after six," I make it final. "But Tirza, my trainee teacher's coming at quarter to seven, never mind, you'll meet her, she's a very nice girl—" "What about Wednesday?" I try to get her all to myself, to ask, to tell, to know at last what has mounted up between us over the years. "Give me a ring—have you got a pen? I'll write the number down for you—" "No need, just tell me what it is—" "Do you still remember everything?" "Let's see." "Nine five zero one one nine zero" she says rapidly, almost in a whisper, as if she's trying to trip me up. "It's easy," I smile, it really is easy. "We'll see—" she's still testing, something very bad apparently happens to anyone who goes on teaching for too many years, "950; the building of the temple. 1190; the destruction of Troy. Together 9501190, that's your number, right?" "I wish I had your memory—" she sighs, lets go of my arm, people are unraveling, parting, the cars behind the fence are starting, in the light filtering out from the sukkah she looks better or maybe I've already grown accustomed. "Tikva told me you were here—" she volunteers an apology, "but I didn't have the time, with the holidays—" "Yes, the holidays," I mumble (two women in orthopedic shoes selecting a victim for their gefilte fish from the fishmonger's tank, talking to each other in the meantime, how did we turn into them)—

When I had to confide a secret or an insult, when I needed to ask for answers or advice, or even when I suddenly had nothing to do, ninety times out of a hundred her mother would open the door a crack, let me wait on the mat, ask me what I wanted to tell Orinka, promise me she'd pass the message on word for word, and shut the door in my face. What did I have to tell Orinka?

Only once did she pull me inside. There's something I have to ask you, Loyinka, she spoke in a whisper, rapidly, like a conspirator, do you have a moment to spare? I didn't, but she wasn't asking to get an answer—you have to swear to me that whatever I tell you will never reach Ora's ears. I didn't answer. Promise me—her hand tightened on my wrist until the watch left a print on my skin—you promise? She was really hurting me. I nodded, but in my heart I said, "Go to hell!" She let go. Sit down, she pulled out a chair for me in the kitchen. She sat down opposite me. You and Ora are bosom friends—tell me, what's the matter with her recently? I shrugged my shoulders. That's not an answer! Her voice was full of anger. And if I may say so, that's not a becoming gesture for a young girl either—I shrugged my shoulders again. She wasn't going to educate me. But she didn't see. Her eyes were lowered to her hands lying clasped on the table—thick, dry, tired hands—Ora isn't eating, she isn't sleeping, she isn't doing her homework, she isn't going to the youth movement—as soon as she comes home from school she gets into bed and reads—do you know what kind of books she's taking out of the library? I knew: *The House of Dolls* and *His Name was Piepel* and *My Hundred Children*. Have they been talking to you at school about the Holocaust? Ora's mother demanded to know. Of course not! What an idea—really! Or perhaps some boy—Why don't you ask Ora? I interrupted her—Ever since her uncle came to see us—she shook her head, stood up, picked up the kettle, filled it with water—I'm putting the kettle on—she said with her back to me. What uncle? I demanded. I wanted to hear what she would say. Baruch's brother from America—liar! I bowed my head so she wouldn't see my glee. She was lying! Ora's mother was lying! And who to? Me!—He isn't Baruch's brother, why do you say he's Baruch's brother, I said cheekily. She turned to face me, flushed, stunned, the full kettle shaking in her hand, then she turned to the gas stove, put the kettle down, and lit the flame under it. So . . . you know too . . . she said with her back to me, I begged Orinka not to tell anyone—it's a family affair—a terrible tragedy—I begged her, I really begged her . . . She sat down opposite me again, defeated. I'm the only one she told, suddenly I felt sorry for her and regretted it immediately, because she raised her head and demanded: You? What did she tell you? About Vera and . . . I hated her for forcing me to repeat the story; there were many like it circulating on the block, whispered from mouth to ear, horrifying, like the stories about the Kapo living in the shipping crate who hanged himself in the citrus grove, or the giant on the way to school whose house we make a big detour to avoid, the Giant-and-his-garden we called him, his garden was frightening too, surrounded by a high wall, he was from the Sonderkommando and he would make any child who fell into his hands into jam or laundry soap and a lampshade from his skin—they sent Ora to bed because she had school the next day, but she shut herself in the bathroom and even though they spoke a mixture of English and German she heard and understood almost everything.

When I get an ID card I'll add her name to mine! she announced, and on that Yom Kippur she stayed in the synagogue for the prayers for the dead, and her mother, who hardly spoke to her till Hanukkah, brought her face close to mine, hissing, she didn't have to run away! At such close quarters she has a bristly, bleached little moustache, which moves as she speaks; I can't take my eyes off it—And you know why she didn't have to run away? She was a German, and the children were half-German—she divorced him—did she tell you that?—and he went back to Vilna, Ora's mother coughed. I hoped that she would choke on tears or rage, but she stood up, poured herself a cup of tea, forgot about me, sat down opposite me again and talked and talked, but I wasn't listening; if Vera was a German, I could think of nothing else, then the uncle, in other words her brother, was a German too, and Ora was in love with a German—something had to be done—she had to be told—so she would know and stop immediately—

Before I left—I was there for almost an hour, and when I left it was already dark and a fine rain had started to fall and I didn't have an umbrella—before I left Ora's mother asked again for this conversation to remain between the two of us, on my word of honor, and I didn't even nod, who did she think she was, I left angry, tense, almost on the verge of tears, I couldn't go home like this, or to you either, you would sense something immediately, ask me what happened, get it out of me and set out—girded with rage—to avenge me, to make a scene, I ran from there to the empty lot and from there to the cypresses and from there to the abandoned orphanage, sheltering in the ruins from the rain that was coming down harder, sorry that I didn't have red paint and a paintbrush—*Mother Russia!* I would have written in big letters *Father Stalin! If only we were orphans!*

On the ficus is a Roman Emperor and another Emperor, or maybe an Empress, in *Garrulus Glandarius* there is no difference in the plumage, thus the bird book, he remains married to his empress to the day he dies, he does not migrate, he is happy here, he can imitate the voice of a cat, of boughs in the breeze, in conditions of captivity he can even be taught to say a few words—Garrulus! I appeal to him, say Davidi, say Davidi! Davidi!

I couldn't tell Ora about that conversation, and the secret stuck in my throat, not to be swallowed or vomited up, I tried to behave as if it wasn't there, and she didn't sense anything, if you hide anything from me I'll sense it at once, what happened to that, she was busy with school, with the youth movement—Have you written to your uncle? I once ventured to put out feelers, hoping to start a conversation that would lead to the revelation— Yes, she replied, and immediately changed the subject, concealing, not telling, if I fall in love I'll tell you, what happened to that, and I, as if poking the tip of my tongue into a dull pain in a wisdom tooth in order to sharpen it to a clear point, said to myself, she's turning away, keeping things to herself, what happened to that love in the end I don't know to this day, nor if it was indeed love, but two years later there was Giora and I went to her with that love like Elhanan's cat with the wagtail's body, she came and deposited it in the doorway, she thought she was giving me a gift, that she deserved a prize, said Elhanan—only six days—we once did the sum—132 hours gross, 21 hours net—and the rest—the love—for a year and another year and almost another year there was nothing but words in letters, in long conversations lasting all night long, over the phone, walking from my house to hers and back again, with me accompanying her, she accompanying me, while I returned to those 21 net hours, dissecting them into minutes, half-minutes, what he said exactly, when he laughed, what he meant, what he promised when he said, "We'll keep in touch—" and Ora asking, sympathizing, interpreting, cultivating hopes, preaching patience, giving examples from life, I would have sent him to hell already, stopped looking for his photograph in articles about the retaliation raids, in articles about archeological digs— perhaps he was part of the expedition to Masada, perhaps he was digging in Megiddo—in the death notices—perhaps he had been killed in the army, perhaps he had been killed in a road accident—but the earth had swallowed him up. Adriana's mother arranged for her gynecologist to perform the abortion, she paid for it, and I paid her back in minute installments until I rose into the air and received my first salary and paid off the rest of the debt, but about this I said nothing to Ora, not one word—

It's time to decide. To open one room at least. The gluing room, for instance. Is that where you crammed all those books—Loya no, Loya no—Herodotus and Plutarch, Tacitus, Julius Caesar, Polybius, Cassius Dio, Ranke, Carr, Mommsen, Flavius Josephus the traitor—So why do you read his books?—In order to know—But if he was a traitor he must have been a liar too!—That has to be investigated—and so we drove to Yodfat during the Sukkot holidays and spent hours in the sun on a bare, round hill, almost as hollow as a skull, careful Loya, careful Nahum, eroded by caves, riddled with water cisterns, sprouting squills, from a distance bald as Ben-Gurion, at close quarters covered with potsherds, big stones, echoing pits, a rather low hill surrounded by mountains, no "ravines of extraordinary depths," no dizzying precipice, both a traitor and a liar and a cheat who remained alive to tell the tale to future generations—Without him, my father said, we wouldn't have known, he was there when everything happened, like Xenophon on the march of the ten thousand from the Armenian mountains to Asia minor and back home to Greece—He was a traitor too, you seethed, an Athenian who fought for Sparta and even took refuge there—But without him, my father insisted in a low voice, we wouldn't have known, because he was there like Polybius at the side of Scipio the younger weeping at the sight of Carthage burning, quoting Homer's lines on the destruction of holy Ilium, which is Rome—He was a traitor too! you thundered, a Greek exiled to Rome, and what does he devote his life to?—propagating the power of the Roman Empire, joining Scipio the younger to see with his own eyes the destruction of Karthadshat at the hands of Rome—In 146 B.C., I intervened, to remind them that I was there too, ready to take part in the argument—Carthage and Corinth were wiped out, you ignored me, and who remained? Rome, Rome, terrrrible Rome, what did it give the world, bread and circuses, gladiators, Popes—Horace, Virgil, Daddy interrupted you quietly, but you waved your hands, you were standing here in the middle of the living room—Horrrace! Virrrgil! Did you tell her what they did to Archimedes? "*Noli istum disturbare*," I quoted at once, offended, *do not disturb that*—what did you think, that I didn't know? They not only spoiled his circle, they killed him, killed him, killed him, murrderred him—and who remained to tell the story? The traitors, *sauve qui peut*, correct, Professor Kaplan—starting with that dark laughter, and Daddy got up, saying quietly, Loya, we're leaving, not trying to soothe you this time, offended himself, you had insulted the apple of his eye, the historians who were there and who wrote and without whom we wouldn't know, at home we return to Gaul divided into three parts, "*Gallia est omnis divisa in partes tres*" Julius Caesar, author and general, 1300 words at his command and what Latin! Lucid, trenchant, *Veni, vidi, vici* he wrote to a friend after his stunning victory at Zela, *I came, I saw, I conquered*, and went to visit the ruins of Troy not far from there, not even a trace of them remains today, he said after a long silence, everything ends in blood and fire and scorched earth, Athens and Sparta and Corinth, Carthage and Carthagena, Tyre and Sidon and Jerusalem, Yodefat, Gamla, Beitar, Masada, what remains standing, strong and invulnerable except for Switzerland—

On the train to Haifa I preferred to sit with my back to the engine, facing backwards. Because you're sick with nostalgia, Eliot sniggered when I told him—he had a psychologist in every town—I, he smiled down at me from his heights, am very fond of people who turn to look back—Like Lot's wife, I couldn't resist the jab—But Lot's wife wasn't turned into a pillar of salt because she looked back, but because of what she saw there! "The overthrow of Sodom and Gomorrah," I said in Hebrew, Whatever, Eliot agreed and immediately demurred, but you and I don't have a past like that, praise the Lord—he would slip "praise the Lord" into every second sentence, it was only after three years that I realized it had been there all the time and I hadn't noticed: I thought it was just another way of ensuring that nothing bad would happen, like insuring one's apartment and holiday home, one's life, property, health, and earning capacity—We live forwards but understand backwards, you said to me, holding both my hands tightly, trying to persuade me that no, no, no, Loya no . . . I returned to that sentence, you're right I thought, already far away from you, safe from you, just like on the train to Haifa bringing me back from the base along the coastal road, rushing backwards, gathering into a single point as if someone beyond the landscape was sucking it into a cone of disappearance, a black hole, even the light, Nahum told me on that night, can't escape from there—

And now I'm going to Ora without phoning first, without arranging in advance, when it suits my convenience, why not, what can already happen, Hedva said yesterday from across the ocean, "You know what she looks like," I lamented, "old, shabby, not in the least like the Ora I had in my head—" "Which of us looks like we looked thirty years ago, Loya," said Hedva. "But she looks like Auntie Mania from Romania!" I protested, "You're the same age, aren't you?" Hedva tried to balance the picture, but in my case the exterior is stainless steel—all the rust is on the inside—

Going there with my heart pounding in my throat, in my ears—Tamar Street, Semadar Street, Yasmin Street, Etrog corner of Marva, not too early and not too late, after the siesta, before the evening meal, is the time suitable, and if it's not so suitable so what; I ring the bell next to the gate. One mail box says Ora and Mordechai Gadot, and also Vered Gilad Ehud Yinon, the one next to it says Mechora and Baruch Berger, which of them will let me in. A hoarse croak announces that the gate has been opened by remote control—I push it and go in—of the big garden all that remains is a small lawn bordered with a few flowers, a big parking space for two cars, both of them are here, everyone's home, which of them will open the door—

"Baruch! Baruch! Look who's come to visit us! Ora's friend Loya! Loya Kaplan!" Ora's mother has hardly aged; as if all the changes had taken place in her up to the age of forty and from then on nothing had changed but for a wrinkle here and there; hair dyed copper, teeth white and even, even the moustache plucked, she looks almost the same age as Ora—and her father sits bowed—his fine mane of hair has gone—staring at me with empty Ora's eyes, obviously he doesn't recognize me, doesn't remember—"Morgenstern-the-grocer's didn't recognize me either," I try to improve matters, but Ora's mother waves her hand as if to wipe the offered explanation off the air; she grips my hand and brings me closer to her husband—"Orinka told me she met you in Tikva's sukkah and that you look very well . . . Baruch, Baruch, here's Loya—" She stands me in front of the rocking chair. "Baruch, look here. It's Loya. You remember Loya." "Granny, leave him alone," a boy's voice intervenes, brown skinned, dark haired, eyes like the half-risen sun— "Hi!" he throws at me with a white, dimple-producing smile, "I'm Yinon"— but Mechora tightens her grip around my wrist—"How many times she ate meals with us! She went to school with Orinka until the end of high school—" "Hel-lo!" she is interrupted by a voice proclaiming the arrival of its owner, "This is Motik, Ora's husband"—Motik glances at me briefly, nods, and concentrates his attention on his son. "What are you doing here, haven't you got training today?" A little fat, a little bald, a little blond, a little tanned, a little smiling-all-the-time, what did Ora see in him, only his voice is heraldic, Ora's mother continues gripping my hand, crushing it, talking more to me and Motik now than to her husband. "I remember there was a time when Loya wanted us to call her Ilil!" she smiles triumphantly at the surprise on my face, "I remember everything!" "What kind of a name is that?" asks Yinon, slender, tall, volatile, smiling, conscious of his good looks—"Don't you learn Saul Tchernichowsky's poetry at school any more?" I ask. "They don't learn anything there—" it's Ora entering the room, intending a joke but sounding bitter. "We learn computers!" protests Yinon in what is apparently a continuation of an argument that has been going on here for who knows how long, "Computers are the future," Motik supports his son, "Quite true," Mechora joins in, Motik approaches me with his hand outstretched, "we've heard a lot about you—" and at that moment a soldier comes in, "Hi everybody!" and right behind him Ora, God almighty, Ora—"And this is Vered," says Ora, but her younger edition doesn't even say "Hi!" taller even than Ora by half a head—a meter eighty and how much? She speaks to Ora over my head, "Have you fixed my skirt yet?" "Say, Vered, have you ever heard the name Ilil?" Yinon circles her bouncing a ball, "Yinon! Not in the living room!" scolds Ora but he ignores her, "Stop spinning around me like a top," says Vered, "Yinon, that's enough!" Motik's booming voice fills the room and Mechora bends over

Baruch. "Here's Yinon, and Ehud's arrived as well, and Vered's here too—" and the door opens again and a young second lieutenant enters, "This is Gili, our firstborn grandson," Mechora straightens up and the officer corrects her, "Gilad," and holds out his hand to me, "Loya," I say and look straight at him, his eyes, Motik's eyes, already searching the room, find his younger brother—"How's it going, bro," he asks, "Don't ask," replies the soldier glumly, and Yinon bounces his ball and Mechora and Motik and Ora—I feel that I have landed up in an Italian movie at last—except that here everything is in Technicolor and there everything was black and white, and the conditions too, of course, broken steps, moldy walls, a little square, a well, two donkeys, and one Sophia Loren, narrow-waisted, wide-hipped, leaning a tubful of laundry on her hip, striding energetically, shouting, waving, and from the windows people wave back, call out questions, greetings, all at the top of their voices, and then inside the house, the baby and the child and the boy and the girl and her mother and his mother, everyone has something to say and so does she, she serves up a bowl of steaming spaghetti, calls them to the table, in spite of the obvious poverty there's a bottle of wine, a tablecloth, they all sit down to eat, smack their lips, stretch across the table for the salt, argue, a neighbor comes in, his wife, their daughter, always crowded, always seething, a child overturns a glass, gets a slap, begins to cry, I can't stand it any more, says the beautiful Sophia, wipes her forehead with the back of her hand, I'm going crazy, Come to us, I offer, turning the translation-on-the-side, in our house it's only me and Daddy chewing with our mouths shut and no talking at mealtimes, what wouldn't I have given once to step into an Italian movie, but now I'm not so sure. "Ilil, Ilil—" Yinon bounces his ball around me, Motik bends down and grabs the ball and Ora explains, "It's a poem by Tchernichowsky"—Tchernichowsky died on Sukkot, 1943, but we didn't know. We admired him more than Bialik and Shimoni and Rachel—we knew that he was a doctor—we saw that he was handsome—terrifically handsome—next to him Bialik looked like a shopkeeper—we hoped that he would come to our school—Ora carefully detached his photograph from page 3 in the book and kept it in an envelope in her diary. I couldn't. It was your book. Thick, heavy, full, not a selection for schools. I read it all and learned "Facing the statue of Apollo," "Poems for Ilil" and "Baruch of Mayence" off by heart. We tore up five drafts until we perfected the final version of the invitation on behalf of Grade Six B in the Alumot school and we went to the Post Office together and asked Nehama where to send it to and she said, the Education Ministry in Jerusalem, that's your safest bet, they'll locate him for you, and we sent it and waited. We knew that such things took time. In the meantime I learned more of his poems off by heart: *My sword, where are you, When the shadows spread, Facing the sea, Happy are they that fall in war.* I knew that if he came to us, Ora would be asked to welcome him on behalf of the class. My only chance was that our teacher Devora would turn to us and ask, which of you, children, remembers a few lines of Tchernichowsky's poems? And then—then I asked everybody to call me Ilil. We went through a stage like that; Adriana shortened her name to Diana, and then to Donna, but she couldn't get used to the changes or accustom us to them either, her own name was tailor-made for her, she was tall, blonde, long limbed, a little ungainly, a perfect Adriana, Yosefa decided to become Josephine after reading "*Desirée*," Ora asked us to call her Efrat, but that was out of the question, Tikva tried to return to Allegra, and I asked everyone to call me Ilil. If they called me "Loya" I didn't turn my head and I didn't respond, until Ora arrived at school one day in a tempest a minute before the bell rang and managed to whisper only—Don't ask what's happened! I waited impatiently for the break—Ora didn't pass notes during class—and then I ran behind her to the girls' toilets—this was the place for bad news, gossip, insults, tears—Ora took a deep breath, stood up straight and said in a solemn, disaster-announcing voice: He's dead. Who's dead? I asked in alarm. Tchernichowsky! Saul Tchernichowsky! whispered Ora. Who told you? I didn't believe it. My mother! Girls ran in and out, washed their faces, drank water, washed their hands and shook the drops onto the floor. How does she know? I demanded furiously. I was angry with Ora for telling her, for including her. She was at the funeral.

Tchernichowsky's funeral? When? When was she? Don't you believe it? Let's go and ask a teacher—Ora pulled me outside, into the passage. In the distance we saw the teacher on duty patrolling with half a sandwich in her hand, but Ora changed direction because the headmistress suddenly came out of her office—Headmistress! Headmistress! Ora hurried up to her without me, I didn't ask teachers questions at recess or go anywhere near the office. The headmistress stopped and smiled, she liked Ora. Everybody liked Ora. May I ask you something? Go ahead! Saul Tchernichowsky's dead, isn't he? The headmistress swallowed a smile, narrowed her eyes as if she was trying to see into the distance: Of course . . . he passed away on Sukkot 1943 or '44 . . . Any other urgent questions?—She didn't believe me! Ora turned her head to indicate me. I made off. I felt cheated, betrayed. If they teach him at school it's a sign that he died long ago—Ora hurried after me—But you were sure he was alive too! I retorted—No, I wasn't sure, I just thought he might be—"Mrs. Berger, were you at Tchernichowsky's funeral?" It was now or never. Mechora raises her eyes to me in surprise, "Yes, of course I was, and at the funerals of Weizmann and Ben-Gurion and Ussishkin and Berl Katznelson too—" she sits down next to me, ready and willing to elaborate, "Wallah!"—Yinon pushes himself between us—"Gran the man! Are you a funeral fan or what?" he smiles at her, smiles at me, if only I was thirty-five years younger—"Only of historical figures," Ora giggles over her Sprite, "Avi says that Mechora is a walking history book." Motik's voice fills the living room—"Avi is his brother, Ora's brother-in-law, a professor of the history of the People of Israel," Mechora explains, "Only a doctor—" Motik corrects her, "he'll be a professor, give him a few more years, Mechora." "That's my son-in-law, always joking," chuckles Mechora, "When are you going back to the base?" Gilad asks his brother. "Mother!" Vered returns—when did she leave? I can't take my eyes off her—"How's my sister? Isn't she an eyeful?" Yinon notices, elbows me without embarrassment, "She looks exactly like Ora," I can't help saying, "Wallah, Vered, did you hear that?" Vered drops a skirt into Ora's lap, "Fix it for me, I need it urgently, did I hear what?" she looks at Yinon, "That you look exactly like ma." "Says who?" Vered protests indignantly as if it was some sort of insult. "Loya, ma's friend from the Palmach," giggles Yinon. "Loya? You're Loya?" Vered sits on the arm of Ora's chair, piercing me with dark looks, "You're the best friend who didn't come to the wedding and didn't pick up the phone for twenty-five years?" Her voice is like Motik's; too loud, overbearing, leaving no room for anyone else. "You see, we haven't got any secrets here," Yinon elbows me. "Apart from the secrets we have got," Udi puts in from his corner. "We have no secrets! We have no secrets!" Mechora protests, "Mother, are you going to fix it or not?" Vered demands, "Let your mother finish her drink first," Motik comes to her defense from behind Udi's chair, "First I'll do Udi's washing, Udi, where's your kitbag," Ora gets up and so do I. I accompany her to the laundry room, stand next to her as she pulls the crumpled uniform and the stinking gray socks out of the kitbag, sorts the items out and crams them into the washing machine, I want to say something to her, console her, perhaps, for her life, and I can't find anything. "It was nice at Tikva's," I say to her bowed back. She straightens up. "Don't be cross with Vered," she starts the machine. "Why should I be cross with her?" I shrug my shoulders, "she told the truth, no?" Ora bows her head, pressing her chin down in a movement which emphasizes her wrinkles, her double chin, she raises her eyebrows the way she used to when she didn't want to cry, and then she looks at me. "Yes, but she wasn't absolutely accurate; it wasn't twenty-five years, it was twenty-seven." "Time flies," I whisper, like two mothers meeting at the grocer's, how did I turn into them.

Your radio. Sometimes it works, sometimes it doesn't. A hard smack on the head brings it back to report that a huge migration is now passing over our heads: from Eastern and Middle Europe the birds are gathering on the ancient high road, songbirds and storks, cranes and pelicans, raptors of all varieties—the airports too are full of travellers—the fares are already cheaper, the flights less crowded, tickets are available, there are no longer Israelis everywhere—I'm popping over to London for ten days, It's Paris for me, pal, only Paris, there's nothing to beat it, believe me, Why, have you already been to Vienna? Those anti-Semites? The language is enough to give me the creeps! And Turkey? Take it from me—Turkey's the place, half the price of a hotel in Eilat and that includes the plane ticket! Maybe next year. Last year we went to Bali and came back on the eve of Yom Kippur. Are you nuts? What's Yom Kippur to you? We visit my sister's son's grave. He got it on the canal in the Yom Kippur War. We don't show our faces here till the end of Sukkot—who needs all those holidays and shopping and cooking? Enough! Only this year we put it off—our son graduated from an officers' course, there was a ceremony, the Chief of Staff, the chief of G branch—GHQ, believe me I was in the army for three years without parents and visits, the army's turning into a kindergarten, grade one, parents' day, meetings with the teacher, I haven't got the strength for this country any more, believe me, so we're off for a bit of a break, I only hope there's room for my legs in this half-assed plane, if it wasn't for the security I'd fly Air France, forget about those frogs, Swissair's better, no, they're not what they used to be, have we got time for the duty-free? Yes we have, they gave me a list from here to London, bring me bring me, kids today aren't what they used to be, nothing's what it used to be, pal, I'm not either, excuse me, excuse me, let me out please, just let me out of here, did you forget something? Yes, I forgot something, you poor thing, should we keep your place in the line? No thank you, there's no need, okay, let her out, she forgot something, what did you forget dearie, my passport, oh dear oh dear oh dear, let her out, let her out, and so I extricate myself from the baggage-check line at the airport, how did I get here again, flight number 343 is departing in another—I leave the nasal drawls of the attendants behind me, the glass doors close, all the people waiting in the line will take off in fifty minutes, see combed fields framed by cypresses, roads deeply etched between the bas-reliefs of buildings, diamonds flaming on the solar-heater reflectors, soft sand dunes and the sea sending foam-embroidered waves to the receding shore, and I, in fifty minutes' time, will raise my eyes and see them passing over my head in a plane migrating from the lands of the blazing sun to countries easier on the eye and the skin—

Tonight I was in Tikva's sukkah again. The smell of guavas rose from a covered pottery bowl, under the napkin, I knew, they lay one on top of the other, pale yellow, lumpy, white-fleshed, and Tikva's mother keeps coming in with more and more fruit—pears and grapes and peaches and plums, and everybody reaches out, tears off a grape, takes an apple or an apricot, they all talk at once, *come stai*, Adriana hugs my shoulders, and Shmuel Shmuel sitting next to her turns, hello, talk Hebrew, what is this, she forgot Hebrew because she was a flight attendant, says Ora, do you all live here? I ask, ye-es, they chorus, maybe I'll come to live here too, I suggest hesitantly, but you haven't got anywhere to stay, says Tikva, but she has friends here, Minaleh comes to my defense in a pampered voice, lucky her, she's married to Elhanan, what friends, where friends, says Yosefa, at our age we don't have friends any more. Girlfriends are good up to the sixth grade, maximum the eighth grade, but we haven't reached the eighth grade yet! I protest and wake up.

My life? Proceeds slowly. At a snail's pace, I'd say. At ground level. I go everywhere on foot. Once in a while I raise my head, see treetops above me, above them the sky, in it a plane, I feel stifled—I could have finished everything by now, but I still haven't decided how—where—

The people I love? Let's start with you. Or maybe my father. Or not: if love is a heatwave and crazy birds, then Giora. And after a few lemonades—Jean-Jacques. And then Eliot. For a very short time, disturbing and confused, Brenda. And Nahum—for one bad mistake—

The people I love are all far away. Some of them are under the ground, some above it, longings come in fits almost like Hedva's migraines, she could hear them coming in the distance, swallow aspirins—you have to kill migraines when they're small—is it the same with longings? What do I think about the people I love. They're alike, they have to be alike, according to Hedva on a snowy night in New York, reading women's magazines, always managing to sound far wiser than anything written there, here, read this, she would sometimes hand me one. Tell me what it says. We always end up falling in love with the same type, she sums up the wisdom of the month. Nonsense, I protest, I actually try a different salad every time—

You, for instance; you loved objects—potsherds, seals, figurines, bones, once you sent Nahum to see how far it was from where we were to the sea, count double steps, you instructed him, telling me in the meantime that three times more people had been killed in battles here than in the final battle for Carthage, and that's not counting the ones who died of starvation, fire, plague, the ones sold into slavery, utter devastation, and in the meantime, in Usha and Zippori, they engaged in Talmudic hairsplitting, those clowns stayed alive, and Daddy was cautious, he didn't believe the Romans, or the sages, he looked for inscriptions on potsherds, buildings, something scratched on the wall of a cave, he calls your stories *"bunkes,"* you soon switch to dense, unintelligible, unguessable Czech, not like English, or Italian, or Latin, or French, or Yiddish, and I already know more than a few words in all of them, but Czech is like a fortified wall—

Or, for example, Nahum: Nahum built kites. Model airplanes. An hourglass. A telephone from little plastic containers and sewing thread. He knew *Wonders of the World Volume One* off by heart. He had good field glasses. A compass. A canteen. It was from him that I heard about the power of the moon to draw the sea to it like a glittering, viscous blue sheet, about the poles shining in the wake of magnetic storms, about the Fata Morgana in the desert—he wanted to be Nansen; Captain Cook; Marco Polo or, at least, Thor Heyerdahl—what will you do if everything's been discovered by the time you grow up, I worried. Then I'll fly to the moon, he promised. He always meant what he said. He never told tall tales. In the course of the years I learned to believe him more and you less—all those stories about the Semitic lands, about Gval and Arvad and Tyre and Sidon, about enemies within and without, about spies and traitors who—wonder of wonders!—always knew what side of their bread was buttered and always stayed alive—were repeated over and over until they grew threadbare, and one day at the end of high school I discovered that of all the stories swarming around me I believed only in the weather. And in love, of course. Then, still, in love; larger-than-life, in black-and-white like in the movies—one and only from the cradle to the grave—now all I had left was the weather: autumn mornings, for example. The gray silk of the air decorated with little flat-bellied clouds—soon this frisson too will fade: to extricate myself from whatever coils or climbs on whatever stands still for too long in one place—bougainvillea, honeysuckle, gossip, habits—to rise into the air and land in Paris. Paris net, without Jean-Jacques. Houses like palaces surrounding squares from which streets radiate like the rays of the sun—attractive cafes, small round marble tables on one arabesque wrought-iron leg, flowerpots cascading greenery, waiters in black suits even in thirty-five degrees in the shade, it isn't hot in Paris, only in the Levant, in all weathers they officiate with their table napkins and menus and French which is the deputy beauty queen of languages—

He wanted the good for you, but you don't believe him, *mon Dieu*, you believe nobody, only you—Tikva's turbaned aunt read the coffee patterns on the sides of my cup. After the hummus etc. and before the cakes Tikva beckoned me to extricate myself from my corner between Adriana and Shlomit and come and help her, see something, meet her cousin, no, to come into the kitchen, where the aunt who used to send the journals from Paris was waiting for me—what, she's real? After the sukkah, the lights, the white sheets, the glittering decorations, the interior of the house is crinkly-brown, like a baked apple. I pass through the living room—the tapestry with the swans on the river bank still commands a whole wall, but more than the swans I see the shadow of myself on it, gliding past, reaching the rectangle of light escaping from the kitchen. I waited you, says the aunt in the satin gown, the blue satin turban, the one and only mother of the cousin, she's heard about the match, she wants to check me out. This your coffee—she pours it from a little jug into a miniature gold decorated china cup—think very well on your life when you drinks—Think what about my life? I insist on not understanding—Love, she says, "*A-ha-va*," separating the syllables, pronouncing the Hebrew word with difficulty, and I close my eyes and hope that this coffee whose marvelous smell is tickling my nose won't taste like coffee for once. When I return to the sukkah I ignore Tikva's looks, the cousin who's talking to Bilu, maybe about me, who knows, and fit into the conversation branching out from Adriana to everyone around her; what did we think we would be, what did we become. Take Shlomi, the Professor of Yiddish in New Jersey, who used to get so cross when we called him an old Yiddish-speaking "Vus-vus," and Minaleh—we thought she would be a writer—remember the stories she used to tell in recess . . . ? And what did she become, a pharmacist! And about Tikva we thought she would be tops a hairdresser, and look, she's the deputy manager of a bank, arranging loans for whoever needs them, and Ora, we thought she would be Golda Meir, and what did she become—a primary school teacher, and Yosefa—maybe she'd take part in the Olympics, but she's a lawyer, and Loya—we thought you'd be a professor of languages—and I turned into a flying waitress, I put in, and everybody laughs, and Elhanan—here people sigh, glance at their watches, some of them begin to stand up, say good-bye, leave, but the holes of grief are covered up again, Hezi—weren't we sure he'd end up in jail like his brother? And just look at him today, a company that imports automobile accessories and spare parts, and what a villa, he could buy up all of us and still have money left over, and his wife, did you see her? A real Swedish Viking, no, she isn't here now, they left already, we should be going now too—"Didn't my aunt say anything to you about Maurice?" Tikva whispers to me on my way out. Maurice? I decide to lie, yes, she said there was no point in trying, he isn't my fortune and I'm not his, what a shame, Tikva glances at the little group with Maurice on its fringes, and then Ora leaves the sukkah at last and Tikva gives up.

"Shalom Loya," says Ora in a "Greetings to Grade One" tone. The light filtering out of the sukkah illuminates half a cheek, half a forehead, a bit of nose. Her eyes are wells of darkness.

"Greetings your Majesty the King," I recite, my mouth suddenly dry.

"Greetings my dear daughter," she replies after a slight hesitation, "where have you been and what have you done for the past quarter of a century—"

"Should I tell you here, now, everything?" I too try to sound amused—

"No, come to us, you remember where the house is, right?"

"When?"

"Whenever you like—"

"Tomorrow?"

"Not tomorrow, tomorrow we have a staff meeting—"

I see there is the wound here and here and here—the aunt pointed the tip of a scarlet fingernail at the tears in the dregs of the coffee settled on the sides of the cup, and I, instead of getting up at this nonsense went on sitting there, thinking of Jean-Jacques; perhaps because of the French present like a subterranean river in everything about this aunt, in her gestures, her fingernails, her language. Did he find the courage to fly to Algeria? He worshipped Camus, but he was afraid of flying and apprehensive about sailing, when a flight to London once ended in a forced landing in Brussels he shut himself up in the apartment and cooked enough for five families. One more forced landing—and you can come and visit me in the lunatic asylum, he grumbled in the aromas that greeted me, rich, seductive, foxes with golden tails—are you telling me that you'll go back to flying after that? I raised the lid from a chicken cooking in white wine and wild mushrooms—But nothing happened!—Are you hungry?—the table was laid—Not particularly, but the smell is to die for! Jean-Jacques pulled out a chair for me. Why don't you want to be a chef—I ventured. *Mais non*, he would be a writer, he would win the Prix Goncourt. I couldn't understand; when he cooked he was so happy, he even hummed to himself, almost danced between the saucepans, and the writing, *bon*, the writing! Jean-Jacques scowled, served the soup—when you write you're insufferable, I informed him. The rest of the soup we ate in silence. Then Jean-Jacques took the souffle out of the oven, removed a perfect triangle and put it on my plate: That's what you get! He said. It's wonderful! I announced with my mouth full. He cut himself a slice too, but he didn't touch it. Eat, it will get cold, I pointed my fork at his plate. Loya-Loya-Loya—he smiled, with the accent on the last syllable, resting his chin with its Kirk Douglas dimple on his fists—talking with your mouth full, waving your fork, dropping your table napkin—Not this time! I protested, picking the napkin up from my lap to show him, nobody had ever tried to educate me like he did, "polishing the diamond" he called it, I'm not a diamond, I warned him from the beginning, maximum an Eilat stone. He didn't know what an Eilat stone was, and I, at the first opportunity, bought myself earrings studded with the bright green stone, it's a simple stone, he was shocked, I'm a simple girl, I assured him, but he was not convinced. I have three things to say to you—he said at the end of that meal—I will be a writer. You will be my wife. I love you. He looked at me over the napkin hiding his mouth and waited. And waited. And laid his napkin on the table to the right of his plate. And looked at it. Do you love me? he asked the napkin. I tightened my lips. I couldn't say yes. I couldn't say no.

Or Eliot. After that last supper. Phoning half the world and finding me in the end in a London hotel, packing for a flight. Let's keep in touch at least, he pleaded. But I refused to be another name in his address book. I'm calling Janet, he would announce in all his honesty, talk at length, laugh, she used to be his girlfriend fifteen years ago, now she was happily married with twins, but they kept in touch, or—You have regards from Evelyn, his girlfriend from high school, gorgeous, a divorced architect, you must meet her, he phoned her too from all over, chatting, laughing, speaking in a code exclusive to the pair of them, he had an Israeli girl on his list too, "Israela" with a full American "l"—don't you know her? He was sure that in such a small country everybody knew everybody else—almost, I had to admit, and nevertheless this Israela I hadn't had the honor—so we'll keep in touch, he implored me from the other side of the Atlantic, and then I told him about Alexander of Macedon and the Gordian knot. What am I supposed to understand from this story, sighed Eliot. Whatever you like, I said quietly and replaced the receiver.

Jean-Jacques in a monastery? Nonsense. But the turbaned aunt was positive. In a closed place. Perhaps a hospital? She turned the cup around slowly, contemplating its sides through blue-framed glasses which had slid halfway down her nose, here, look this—what you see? I saw three wineglasses standing on three wineglasses lying down. The letter "d" in Ugaritic, I said, but she had a different interpretation: house you live in no good—here—show me—something bad—big danger for you—you see here like knife? I didn't see. All I saw was her nail, large, slightly curved, painted dark crimson. What you don't know do you no harm—she continues, her eyes on the cup turning slowly around in her hands, here, look this—you know some man Gira? Gora? My hands are sweating, but I immediately work it out: Ora told Elhanan, Elhanan told Bilu, Bilu told Adriana, Adriana told Yosefa, Yosefa told Tikva, who told her aunt, and so my first wonderful, terrible love passed from one to the other like the ball in the sports commentary on the radio—I see the house can to fall on your head, the aunt warns me in parting, and now I look at the veins of darkness branching out over the walls and I think, can to fall, can to fall—

At dawn the birds were particularly agitated; Dubček shook the air with sickles of lament; the hangmen barked at each other excitedly; the mafiosi exchanged ringing commands, and in the Biedermeier the figure of Astarte you once stuck together so laboriously fell and broke into abstract pieces again—another earthquake? Impossible! This isn't San Francisco or Japan, but still, two earthquakes since I arrived, is it a dress rehearsal for the end of the millenium, the end of history, the overthrow of Sodom and Gomorrah and a reversion to chaos, impossible to buy a plane ticket at such short notice, but I have to go, I'm already in a taxi to the airport, running away from the prophecy, maybe this house will fall but not on me, I'm travelling, I'm in motion, soon I'll be in the air, how they've built here, a whole town on the fields that used to be to the right of the road, on the left is still the seminary, a kind of hotel, cypresses, the sun in the west dazzles the eyes, we're driving right into it—

And here's the airport, so drab and utilitarian, an airport in a remote township in a third-world country, I buy a ticket on a plane the size of a bus, we'll be in the air for thirty-five minutes, so little, so short, but essential to open a distance between myself and this earth about to gape and bury, fly, metal, the sound of the engines fills the plane vibrating to its last screw and beginning to accelerate over the runway studded with blue diamonds, fly metal, the acceleration increases, and suddenly, most wonderful of all, the takeoff which only exists when you look back, at what is being left behind, fly metal, I see a smiling reflection in the window, the dangerous moment in every flight is for me a celebration, as in love, love to the nth degree, and here's the sea, all slanting and not spilling, embroidered with light and salt, the west is as transparent as gas, and in the east, after the turn to the north, Tel Aviv for a moment at an altitude of a hundred: an azure beauty in the pale flicker of electricity starting up—and further north, northeast, and it's already evening, dark earth curving, a bonfire of ashes shooting sparks, live coals covering the land, necklaces of cinder lamps, orange traffic lights, cars sending out pale feelers of light and already we're coming down, already, already people are collecting bags, flight attendants are smiling, and already we're landing, a black desert, what am I doing here—

There are no more planes, not tonight, so how do I get out of here, you can take a taxi, where to? Haifa, I decide on the spot—"Where in Haifa?" demands the taxi driver, "The Dan Carmel," I blurt out the name of the only hotel I remember from the days of my army service, and here I am, I asked for, got, a room high up, opposite a steep slope spotted with lights ending in ships ending in sea—

The same view, almost. Nahum and I on the balcony, looking at the night ships, trying to ignore the voices escaping from behind the flower-frosted glass. What are they arguing about there all the time, I ask Nahum, and he points to one of the ships: You want to sail on a ship like that? To a completely different place, for example the block where we separated into two houses, next to the Sick Fund clinic—Daddy and me, next to the citrus grove Nahum and you, I hardly returned to Haifa before I joined the army. From the air control base there was a view almost like this one: a dark slope spotted with lights to a sea full of a gold Morse code of harbor lamps and ship lights and reflections—dot-dot-dot dash-dash-dash the lights pulsate, SOS, SOS, save our souls, and what about the bodies. The base is surrounded by a fence, the fence by dogs, the dogs can't be seen—only the squares of dense darkness of the kennels and the short, hoarse, vicious barks, I wanted a dog so badly, but Daddy said "No," dogs die after ten years, they break your heart, so what doesn't break, what doesn't die, even stones wear down, even metals, Nahum told me on that night, even stars— you know person name Gira, the fortune teller repeated for the third time because I kept denying it, no, I don't know him, but it's not so far from here, perhaps I should stop running away. I'm here. Isn't it time to find out at last what we had there: love—affection—lust—a mistake?

Outside, very close, runs the blue strip of sea, disappearing from time to time behind a limestone hill and on it—one-two-three-four—thin and trembling—squills. Autumn. And not far from his kibbutz now. To ring the bell, get off the bus—thumb a lift—why not. Explain to me why not. Who's waiting for you except for a cracked living room in a house full of books and plundered antiquities and three locked rooms? Ring the bell. The driver will stop. You'll get off. Hitch a ride. Everything's so close. So small. You can walk across the country from sea to sea—ring the bell. There. Was that so hard? You're on the road. Raise your arm. Someone will stop soon. They'll ask you what you do and where you're going and where you served in the army and if you know Zvika's brother and what you think of the Maccabi Tel Aviv football team—

A small Peugeot stops for you. The elderly woman at the wheel scolds— why hitchhike? She's ready to give you money—"I don't want to see your picture in tomorrow's paper." She has a daughter your age. (She apparently thinks you're ten years younger than you are.) In fifteen minutes she manages to summarize five stories of rape-murder that took place in the area in recent years—"It wasn't like that once, you're right, but it's like that now, and I always tell my daughter—" and I just-a-minute-just-a-minute-what-is-this; we drive past a dark orange sign with black letters saying THERESIENSTADT. "Is it here?" The driver slows down, "No, a few kilometers further on—"

The sloping lawn is smoothly mown just like the one in my bad memory of this place, but behind it is a different dining hall—gray concrete alternating with pale bricks and huge, screened, closed windows, they must have air-conditioning inside—what did they do with the hut which housed the old dining hall? Burn it on Lag Ba'Omer? The lawn is lined with rose beds instead of the luxuriant oleanders—pointed leaves—rich pink flowers— a poisonous plant—how miserable these roses are in comparison, dusty, sparse, not made for the heat, the dirt path to the members' rooms has been covered with asphalt, instead of the children's house is a members' club in the same depressing combination of concrete and bricks, and here are the members' rooms in the old row-house building, looking crowded and lost in a mishmash of dead potted plants and torn mats and rusty bicycles and sneakers with the laces undone—and everything around them too—the rusting vine, the morning glory, the jasmine—has grown wild as if no one here has the strength left to fight what goes on growing or to part from what has accumulated—children's toys, agricultural journals, macrame for which no suitable flower pot had been found, a balding besom, a deck chair made of wood and canvas, the canvas faded, the wood gray and cracked, from one of the windows, hidden behind a cluster of plastic water canteens and rubber flippers, a woman is singing on the radio about partly clear weather and a girl peeps out—can I help you?

Nobody—I discover after two hours wandering—can help. If there was ever a Giora Bar-Netzer on this kibbutz thirty years ago, not a trace of him remains, no parents, brother, sister, uncle, perhaps he came to the kibbutz as a child from outside, as a boarder, the only one who might be able to confirm this is someone who might have served in the army with him, he works in the factory. "Can you wait? You can have something to eat in the dining hall in the meantime," on the stainless steel counter is a pile of trays, thick china plates, light cutlery—there are no more serving trolleys, everyone serves himself from rectangular containers arranged in two groups—cold—tomatoes, cucumbers, and so on—and hot—plastic schnitzels, dry white rice, squash in tomato sauce—and the smell, the smell—a repellent, sour smell of food cooked in large quantities—

I peck at something. If you lived here, Giora, this is what you ate, this is what you saw. The man from the factory arrives, is led to my table—someone was looking for you—me? He smiles at me from a brown, furrowed face, his thinning hair is gray, no, no, he can't be from Giora's age group, "How can I help," pours me watery juice from a jug, "Perhaps you know—I'm looking for—actually I've been looking for years for—" I address his head bowed over his food, his bald pate, and if he tells me that he knows him from then, so what, and even if he gives me an address, will I get up and go there to find out what became of that beautiful youth, all of him variations on gold—the hair—curls of baked gold, the skin—brown gold, the eyes—shining, transparent gold—"I've been looking for years for—on the way here I saw a sign," I change gears, the man opposite me doesn't notice, he is very hungry—"it said Theresienstadt," he lifts his head in surprise. "Yes, there's a museum in Kibbutz Givat Haim Ihud, not far from here," he bows his head over his food again, eating almost voraciously, bowing his balding head before me—"Thank you," I stand up to make my getaway, "Did you find what you were looking for?" the woman in charge of the soup asks me—no, I shrug my shoulders—"That's the way it goes," she sighs, "once everybody knew everybody else—and now?" She fills a ladle for an old woman waiting with demonstrative impatience for her soup. "Now everyone's stuck inside his own navel—right, Sonya?"

After the conversation with Hedva ("You went to Giora's kibbutz? And what did you find out? Disappeared without a trace? Well, what did you expect. I hope you don't intend taking it up with the police—can you bury that episode already? Thank goodness. One less—") I go out for a walk. I haven't got the strength for another Italian scene at Ora's, not today, and this evening they're showing a movie at the community center. There is no advertisement behind a glass case closed with a cute little lock; no seductive series of stills from the movie, before which we would gather to confer, looking at the beauty pointing her profile at the moustachioed Latin, the air between the two profiles stretched tight and full of possibilities; the boys with hair falling onto their foreheads, loose sandals, short pants turned up until the lining of their pockets peeped out, wanting to know if it was an action movie, and the girls in wide elastic belts on full gathered skirts, in flat court shoes, asking someone who had already seen the movie—me: do you cry at the end?

This evening the movie shown will be *Cinema Paradiso*. The transparent black air is full of major smells of guavas and jasmine—will there be big women with watermelon buttocks under too-thin dresses, carrying baskets, sweating, wiping away the sweat with the back of a shapely hand, swearing, calling someone to come *subito, subito*, cooking, shouting with hands flying, pinching, slapping, saying sorry, hugging, crying, *mama mia, mama mia*, what wouldn't I give for the chance to step into an Italian movie and introduce some order there at last, I suddenly realize, but the mouse-kennel hatch of the ticket booth is firmly shut—all the tickets are sold out—

Dubček wakes me with a cry of fearful, clamorous lament. I go out barefoot to see what it is this time. Sparrows here and there, a raven, a pigeon. Nothing out of the ordinary apart from one high-pitched shriek. And the plot: from the polyethylene whales a lump of earth detaches itself and straightens up to become someone coming towards me—I need glasses!—and turning into a short man in khaki holding out a hand rough with mud—Amitai!—Loya! And afterwards the inevitable clarification—

"You're staying here?"

"Yes."

"Since when? I've been growing strawberries here for five years—there was some other character staying here before—"

"When are they ready?"

"The strawberries? At the end of February. I'll bring you a box—"

"Thank you very much . . ."

"Do you want to make a garden here? I noticed you watering a few times. I'm a gardener—"

"I just watch the birds—"

"Did you see that one?" A phosphorescent green parrot parts from the fronds of the palm with a shriek.

"A parrot!"

"A rose-ringed parakeet," Amitai corrects me, skin the color of clay, hair the color of red loam, "a colonizing cultural refugee—"

"The Emperor Augustus had a parrot who hailed him whenever he returned from war: 'Ave Caesar Victor Imperator!'"

"Are you a history teacher?"

"Me? I'm retired . . ."

"Retired from what?"

"From what? From life, I think—"

"Aren't you a bit too young?"

"'It's not the age, pal, it's the mileage' . . ."

"What's the mileage?" he laughs. He has nice teeth.

I try to work it out: "A million—no two million kilometers—maybe more, actually—"

"That's not the mileage of a human being! It's the mileage of an old stork!"

"How many years does a stork live?"

"Forty years, more or less . . ."

"Are you interested in birds?"

"Know your enemy—"

"Who's that enemy?" I had just discovered a new one, walking up the palm trunk in a black-red-white-gray Norwegian sweater—

"A woodpecker. Listen, he's knocking on the tree—"

"Against the evil eye?"

"He's claiming the territory—do they bother you?"

"The birds? Not at all. I even have some friends—"

"Who?" he smiles. He has nice teeth.

"One who wakes me every morning as if it's the end of the world—"

"White-throated kingfisher—"

"And that one—" I raise my eyes to the branches of the ficus. The emperor stands on a thick bough, peering at us and bristling his crest—"Hello Garrulus! Say Davidi! Say Davidi!"

And the sky-blue and pearl and smoke-colored bird opens a strong black beak and announces: "Sayvididi! Sayvididi!"

POTSHERDS AND DREAMS

I have time. Calm, continuous time, time that flows hour after hour past things that happen slowly; the pomegranate, for example; only two or three pomegranates are left on the top branches—the leaves are more faded, thinner, here and there some have already turned yellow, if I'm here I'll be able to see them fall and the tree turning into a bunch or twigs in the rain—the sky too—in spite of the heat—is different; a pleasant blue with floating clouds, sometimes open triangles of birds changing climates. Morning comes late. Yesterday I discovered a slim, elegant wagtail hurrying somewhere with its tail quivering. The Persian lilacs are blooming in the orange-pink of "Pesia's Corsets, Guaranteed." I forgot they bore flowers. I remembered the pointed leaves, the fruit like miniature apples, the naked arms in winter, purple-brown with pendants of rain like a sad chandelier—

I have time. I've discovered that I have time. I put it off because I have time. Like Shlomi's mother stroking, feeling, sliding through her fingers the new fabric she has been given to sew a dress for a wedding or a bar mitzvah, calling me, whispering, look at this cloth, touch it, touch it with your hand, I let the days slip through my fingers as though they were some unimaginable fabric in a translated book—tussore silk—plush—damask—

Advocate Betzer returned from Palma de Majorca, picked up the phone to ask: "Well?" He has a buyer and I have an opportunity—but I have time, I say to him, what's the rush . . . I could decide to stay here all winter too, till spring, till next summer, till the holidays—"You drives me crazy," groans the-grocer's as she bends down to get me precisely that yogurt over there, I've never tasted it before. "Believe me," she slaps it down on the counter, "everything the same." Everything the same? No, I think not, aren't you going crazy, asks Tikva, who sometimes stops at the greengrocer's, or drops into the-grocer's for something she forgot, what do you do all day, she demands to know, and I reply, think, I think, and Tikva warns me, "It's not enough to think. Do something, Loya. Life is passing." Right, I agree, but not so fast. "I once saw a television program about an old age home," I tell her over a mound of ice cream in a cafe in the new center, "an old age home in Canada. They interviewed some old man there. Are there any love stories here? they asked. Yes, he said, like everywhere else. And what's love like at this age? Much better, he replied, everything happens, but more slowly; it warms, it doesn't burn. I recommend this age, he said. How old are you? they asked him. Eighty-eight, he replied, so I still have another forty years to wander in the wilderness—" "Maybe it's like that for men," Tikva attacks the ice cream, "but for women—" Has the fashion of "Men Are from Mars, Women Are from Venus" reached here too? Hedva knew the book almost by heart, quoted it in almost every conversation about "the situation," in other words the situation of my loveless life, "Really, Loya, look where they are and look where we are!" Where they are I don't know. Where are we? Sitting here and eating ice cream—

After the ice cream I go home with two tomatoes, a cucumber, and a rad-ish in a plastic bag. Old age home? In the fifth grade we had an argument about the best age to die; Yosefa and Arlozora wanted to live to a hundred. Adriana quoted her mother: up to the age of forty, a woman could still be beautiful; and she announced that as far as she was concerned, forty was enough. And I declared the age of twenty-five to be the point at which the body began to wrinkle and decay, and wished that I would die before then—in the first years in the air I still wished that on one of the flights, all of a sudden, without knowing or fearing anything, we would explode like a gigantic firecracker, the flesh and blood would turn into stars and the spirit would evaporate into absolutely nothing: no bodies would float on the Aegean Sea.

When I go to visit Ora in the evening I catch her in the middle of a terri-ble, furious "Yyy-e-ssss!" on the point of tears. I remember myself in that kind of rage after we moved here. Crying and screaming and kicking and dirtying the floor with lines of brown shoe polish from the heels of the boots I hated so violently and Daddy forced me to wear because they're good for your flat feet. And I so badly wanted patent leather pumps with bows, like Adriana's—"Yes!" yells Ora. "Yes! Yes! Yes! Yes! I'm coming! I heard you! In a minute!" And then she discovers me and breathes a sigh—"Oh, Loya . . . come in, sit down for a minute . . . sorry for the . . . sit, sit. I'm so glad you came. I'll make coffee in a minute . . ." And again, to the depths of the house, in response to the unclear voice of one of the boys, in a yell—"so look! Look under the bed! In the drawers! It must be there! If you've lost it, you're buying a new one yourself!"

Heavy running steps, after which Yinon enters the kitchen sweating, opens the fridge, takes out a big bottle of cola, unscrews the top, and in response to a yell of "Not from the bottle! How many times do I have to tell you!" opens a cabinet, takes out a tall glass, fills it, drinks, leaves the bottle on the counter and the glass in the sink and runs out again. "Yinnnon!!" Ora roars after him. I have never heard her yell like this—not even in debates about the military government and capital punishment for and against. The boy comes back. "In the fridge!" Ora points to the bottle left standing on the counter. The lad gives her an amused look, sees me, says "Hi," and puts the bottle in the fridge. And turns to go. "What about the glass!" Ora stops him at the door. "It's in the sink," he pretends not to understand. "What's all the fuss about," Ora's mother opens the door joining the kitchens. "Wash up behind you!" Ora demands of her son, ignoring her mother. "What's the dishwasher for?" the boy smiles with the eyes of the woman who was once my best friend and is now about to burst into tears. "Orinka, why are you so angry?" Mechora's saccharine voice is the same as it was; the voice of a nasty woman trying with all her might to sound like a nice woman. The boy dances from foot to foot, shadow boxes, demands: "You see? Even Grandma thinks I'm right!" and he turns back to the door. "Yinon!" Ora stops him. He returns walking backwards, clownish, humorous. Her anger amuses him. "You didn't say hello to Loya." Now I should have said, "Yes, he did," but I say nothing. Yinon doesn't take it amiss. He bows and doffs an imaginary musketeer's hat with a flourish— "Hello to Loya!" he announces, winks at me over her anger, if I smile back at him, I'll betray her.

"Clever as a devil," Mechora breathes admiringly after he's gone. His head pops up again in the doorway. "I heard you! It's not nice to gossip!" Smiling, radiant, charismatic, if only I was twenty-five years younger. "Shalom to Loya," Mechora Berger now turns her attention to me. I hold out my hand. She holds it in hers, a hand as hot and dry as fire. "I'll make us coffee," mutters Ora and turns a broad back to us. She faces the stove. I suspect she's crying. "What beautiful hands Loya has," says Ora's mother and strokes my captive hand with a touch like sandpaper. Her hands are roped with veins, freckled with brown liver spots. I hope I die before I have hands like that, I say to myself in dismay. "Real coffee or Nescafé?" Ora asks in a choked voice from the stove. She still has her back to us. "Loya does not drink coffee," Mechora pronounces. "You remember!"—the exclamation escapes me. "How should I not?" Her Hebrew—high, pure, with its old-fashioned Ashkenazi pronunciation. "My memory has not yet failed me," she grins at me with snowy dentures, "I remember everything!" She pulls up a chair and sits down next to me. "Orinka, tea for me please." Ora still has her back to us. "For you, too, Loya?" she asks from there; judging by her tone I too am already cooking in her anger. "No, no, something cold if you have it." Ora sets the kettle down. "Something cold, something co-o-old," she sings to herself in a flat, nervous tune and I think to myself, why did I come? What did I think I would find? A hint of the fast friendship that had existed between us thirty years ago? I've changed, she's changed, life has changed, even the garden is different; of all that big garden, an orchard full of blossoms and smells and fruit and shadows, only a pocket-handkerchief lawn and a row of stiff, joyless flowers are left. "What flowers have you got next to the fence?" I try to make small talk while Ora serves me Sprite, her mother pale tea with lemon, and herself coffee. "Birds-of-paradise," Mechora answers in her place, "look how beautiful Loya's hands are—" she says to her daughter. Ora glances briefly at me, at her mother, at her coffee. And suddenly I realize: Mechora Berger doesn't mean to flatter me. She means to hurt Ora. I peep at Ora. Her face is preoccupied, she doesn't have the patience to sit here, soon she'll get up and announce that she has to go, now she's getting up, what did I come for. At this age, Hedva quotes her latest bible, being naive isn't a luxury, it's simply stupid. "Loya and I want to have a little chat," says Ora. "Chat away, how am I disturbing you?" Mechora draws the tea towards her, slurps loudly and goes on, "have you seen my four grandchildren?" "At Sukkot," I remind her. She takes another slurp. "Mother! I think Daddy's calling you!" "Orinka wants to chase me away," Mrs. Berger smiles with gleaming teeth, "and you? Are you married?" she asks. "Mother! Daddy's calling you! Can't you hear?" Ora raises her voice. In the distance, from one of the rooms beyond the two adjoining kitchens Mechora's Polish name is called: "Mara! Mara!" is heard. "Coming—" answers Ora's mother in a voice that has no chance of reaching the person calling her from the depths of the house, "just let me finish my tea—" she grumbles to herself. Afterwards she raises her eyes to me looking refreshed. "Did you know Frieda Gurevitch? The dressmaker who lived here, in the neighborhood! You must have known her!" "Mother!" Ora interrupts her with demonstrative impatience. "She passed away!" Ora's mother continues slurping and talking, "three months ago! A young woman!" "Seventy-three years old!" Ora's voice is venomous. She is no longer saintly; something has happened to her; the level of malice apparently rises with age. Like blood pressure. Like cholesterol. "And Mr. Zinger passed away," Mechora Berger takes a bought cookie and crunches, "the Kalmanovitches too, the same night, you probably heard of the tragedy, and Hasia Horovitz—" Hasia Horovitz, Shlomi's mother, who put bread in the middle of the table in the living room instead of gladiolas. "You didn't come for the funeral," Mechora dunks the rest of the cookie in her tea. "Mother marked you absent on the attendance register—" Ora circles her mother's shoulders with a heavy arm, almost lifts her from the chair and leads her toward the door. "The memorial service is on the eleventh of Adar," Mechora continues from the threshold. "Daddy's calling you!" Ora opens the door wide and now the call is clearly audible, "Mara! Mara!" "She wants to shut me up with the old man," Mechora grumbles and leaves the room, leaves the room at last.

Ora takes a deep breath and lets the air out in a long exhalation.

"I thought your mother loved your father," I can't resist saying.

"She got over it." Ora rummages in a drawer, fishes a crumpled packet of cigarettes from between the paper napkins. "Now she only loves herself." She carefully extracts a cigarette. "Let's go outside, I'm dying to smoke—"

We stand next to the fence and she smokes. She scatters the ash over the birds-of-paradise. I want to rebuke her, but remember what you once said to me, ash, you said, is a fertilizer, damn it, ash is a very good fertilizer.

This morning winter began: all night the wind blustered in the ficus leaves, shook the palm fronds, tapped on all the shutters, checking; closed? closed? All night I walked on the Great Wall of China which was actually a part of the abandoned orphanage and reached the tomb of Qin Shi Huang. I passed between the life-sized terra cotta soldiers, touching them, feeling the roughness of the clay on the tips of my fingers. Next to the last soldier I saw you. What are you doing here, I asked you. A bit of digging, you replied, even though you too, like all the infantry and cavalry, were made of hard, fired clay, and I knew that if you bent down to dig you would break. I looked around for something to dig with. I saw a little pick. I bent down to pick it up, and when I straightened up I no longer knew which of the Emperor's soldiers was you. I felt the ground flowing, running away beneath my feet, like the sea sand when the wave returns—I woke with a short scream to the wind streaming around the house strong and invisible testing the shutters and the door—closed? closed?

Outside took on the colors of abroad; the light blue-gray, the sky cloudy, the bougainvillea, the cypress, the honeysuckle, the grass, the polyethylene whales putting on a murky patina—happily Adriana burst into this mood smelling of Estée Lauder and croissants. "Still warm from the bakery!" she announced. I make Jean-Jacques' "*chocolat apres-amour.*" Adriana takes a sip, blinks with pleasure. Big mouth, big nose, big, green eyes—she was more beautiful once—her complexion creamy matte, no longer tanned, she too is apparently wary of the hole in the ozone layer—her hair dyed dull blonde—once our hair was almost the same color—a little green scarf echoing the color of her eyes—yellower than the ones painted in my memory—

"Is this from your French boyfriend's cookbook?" she asks when she's finished drinking. "How do you know?" "Have you forgotten what it's like on the block?" she laughs. Married, divorced, married, divorced, and she hasn't lost her gaiety, her good humor, her cheerful generosity; she comes, gives, she doesn't keep count. "Let's see the house," she gets up, goes to the living room, with me behind her—"once they built on a grand scale, eh?" She looks up at the ceiling—"I adore these ceilings!" Is she also going to ask me how much I want for your house? "Have you seen those cracks?" she points to the western wall. "It's not a good idea to live in a house with cracks in it," she seems genuinely worried, is she going to predict that in the next earthquake the house will bury me beneath it, advise me to call in the local council engineer? "It invites all kinds of negative energies," she says to herself more than to me, goes up to the Biedermeier. "Antiquities, eh?" "Yes," I say. She opens the glass door. "Real antiquities? Authentic?" "Mmhm," I reply. She takes out an alabaster figurine, examines it, puts it back, a few turquoise beads, puts them back, touches the pyxis—"That's not so ancient," I say in a tone that makes her snatch back her hand as if burned and move further up, where she carefully extricates the goddess Anat from behind the broken Astarte. "She's exquisite! Listen, if you don't know what to do with all this stuff, I'm prepared to buy a few things from you to put in the window of my boutique," she holds the iron goddess in her big, cupped hands, creating a cradle for her, as if she were a baby bird. "She's an Ugaritic goddess . . ." "Hey!" she remembers, "you tried to teach us to write Ugaritic . . . it was so complicated . . . do you remember any of all that?" I nod. "You're staying, right?" She returns Anat to her place and closes the glass door on her. "In the meantime," I say. Adriana examines me with her head on one side. "The *meshuggener* left you the house instead of leaving it to the local council. Ask Yosefa. He left you the house so that you would come back. It's your karma." "My what?" "Karma. Don't you know what karma is? Everyone corrects in his present incarnation what he did wrong in his last one—" "What nonsense are you talking, Adriana!" Adriana takes my hand and leads me to the sofa with the steps of the prince in *Swan Lake*. "Sit down for a minute," she says. She bends over the armchair, bundles the clothes strewn over it into her arms and carries them into the kitchen. "That's better," she says on her return, and sits down on the seat she had cleared, facing me. "Karma," she says, her beautiful, manicured hands drawing an arabesque in the air at about the level of her diaphragm, "you sold your house twenty-seven years ago . . ." I nod. "You said you would never come back, remember? After that whole scandal . . ." I nod. "You were really in a terrible state . . ." She rouses herself from a melancholy reflection, "and all of a sudden you get another house and you have to come back—" "To tie things up, just to tie things up." I don't want anyone to get the wrong idea. "Excuses, excuses." Adriana smiles. "You can't run away from it, Loya, there's unfinished business you have to attend to here, you have to make a *tikkun*, to put things right . . ." No doubt about it, the New Age has reached the old country too. "Why don't you tell me precisely what it is I have to put right?" I inquire. Precision is a good pin to deflate spiritual balloons. "I don't know, that's for you to know," Adriana rises to her feet. A tall woman. Full, but still good looking. "A striking woman," Eliot would have called her. She walks around the living room. "I have the feeling there's somebody else here," she sniffs the air with her eyes closed, suddenly freezing in her place. "What was that?" "A mouse, maybe." I am already used to the sounds of the house. Adriana rummages in her bag—a big blue-green bag. "I brought you some crystals to purify the air"— she fishes out a lump wrapped in tissue paper and reveals a jagged, milkily transparent crystal shaped like a miniature dinosaur. "Where should I put it, where should I put it—" she roams around the room, holding her hand with the dinosaur out in front of her, waiting for the crystal to give her a sign. "Adriana, you've gone off the rails!" I haven't got the patience for pagan rituals. "Shhhhh . . ." Adriana stands in front of me, carefully sets the crystal on top of my head. "You had a bad dream last night," she whispers. "Not bad, strange," I admit. "What did you dream about?" "China . . ." "Have you ever been to China?" "No, but after I sell the house and the orange grove I'm going to fly to China and Alaska and New Zealand." "If that was your karma you would have been given money, not a house," pronounces Adriana and at the last minute catches the dinosaur slipping from my head. "Tell me, do you sleep in the living room? What about the rest of the rooms? Closed? Let's open them, it's not good for rooms to be closed, negative energy collects inside them—only the toilet should be closed. It's just like our house." We're in the passage. "What happened to your house?" I try to postpone the moment. My mouth is dry. "Mother sold the house after my father died in seventy-six . . ." "How is your lovely mother?" "My mother? She returned to Milan . . . she married a fashion designer eight years younger than she is—" "Is she still so beautiful?" "She's even more beautiful, now that she's had a makeover . . . Come on, fetch the key for this room. We'll open it first.

Whose was it? The *meshuggener*'s? Nemecsek's?" "It's the gluing room." "The gluing room?" "Yes, Davidi's work room, where he stuck the sherds together, reconstructed the pottery and so on." "So let's open it." "It's full of potsherds and papers and it stinks of glue." "Open it Loya." The keyhole stares at me in the form of the moon goddess Tanit, cut out of darkness, armless. "You see, it doesn't open," I am happy to say. "Patience, patience . . . there, it's turning. No, you open it. You have to. It's your karma."

A wave of stale, sour-smelling air almost thrusts us back, nails us to the threshold: the room is smaller than I remembered; on the right shelves crammed with books, pushed up against the left wall the huge table, at the far end two tall stacks of cardboard files full of papers, next to them the enormous books that no shelf could hold, sticking out tongues of impro-vised bookmarks—brown packing paper, envelopes—on the side of the table closest to the door shallow open boxes, inside them, like the petals of a dismantled rose, potsherds waiting to be stuck together, this is a water jug and this is an oil lamp, I hear your voice, this is the handle, I can see the broad tips of your fingers, here's the mouth and this is where the wick goes, the eye of the lamp, you see?—"Bye, Loya," Adriana whispers—is she still here?—"I'm late for the boutique already—I'll leave the crystal here." She puts it on the edge of your table. "Ciao!" "Ciao!" I reply, going first to the huge books, not Livy, not Tacitus, not Suetonius, but big biblical letters making a long rectangle and around them broad frames of Rashi script and on the margins tiny Rashi script—volumes of the Talmud—did you become religious? Impossible! I go to the end of the room, pull the win-dows towards me, push the shutters out, letting the autumn into the time that has congealed here in smells of clay and glue and pressed paper. What were you working on? What were you trying to prove? What wasn't I able to detach you from in all those years when it was still possible—

Rome! Wouldn't you like to fly to Rome? I phoned, I wrote, I wanted to appease you: What do you do in Rome? In Rome you do as the Romans do, drive like a lunatic, eat pizza and cold watermelon in a trattoria sitting right on the street, breathe in a passing bus, or motorbike, see beautiful Italian women, fill a spoon with Parmesan served in a glass bowl with a lid like a sugar bowl—or London! Fly with me to London! In London there are houses the color of bitter chocolate, solid gray light, eternally green lawns and dim pubs with beer a shade between brown and yellow— and the British Museum—and the theater—you still hate the English? So maybe Scandinavia? The water of the fjords as black as ink, the air crisp with cold—you can chew it like crushed ice—the white houses have slate roofs colored a metallic gray, and when it rains there you can die of melancholy—I don't understand. You don't want a change of air? Of climate? Scenery? Mood? *Animum debes mutare, non caelum.* It's the soul that needs changing, not the climate, you reply sullenly. What's keeping you stuck there in Rasco C; come, come to Spain, the boycott's over, Franco's dead, Madrid's fantastic. On every square marble horses draw marble chariots through sparkling arcs of water, the palaces have gates like black jewels, once there was a prince living in every palace, today there's a bank—but Europe does not attract you. Europe is rotten. Moldy. If you ever move from Rasco C it will only be on a northbound train, to Tyre, to Sidon—

Of course: Tyre. Sidon. Phoenicia. Here's Slouschz's *Thesaurus of Phoenician Inscriptions* and Charles Virolleaud's book about the Royal Palace in Ugarit, *Carthage, the Maritime Power* by Zvi Herman who told you that even Ben-Gurion regarded Hannibal as a Hebrew general, and here's the green book by Cassuto about the goddess Anat from which I copied the Ugaritic alphabet, and the brown book by Contenau and here's the book about Hannibal you gave me when I had measles *One Against Rome* which I read over and over again and whenever I reached the bit about the sick elephant who waved a branch with his trunk in the way he had seen humans doing when they begged for mercy, I had to stop reading to blink away my tears, and here's Kathleen Kenyon's *Amorites and Canaanites* and books about Bar Kokhba—Abramski, Dvir, the book about daily life in Karthadshat by Charles Picard, the book by Juster—

And where are Daddy's books that you wouldn't let me sell—Loya no, no, no—chasing the rag-and-bone man away almost with blows, creating a commotion, people came running, Shlomi's father, Bilu's mother, Ora's mother, the nurse, someone phoned the police—where are the blue Flavius Josephus, Livy, Plutarch, the four volumes of Roman history with the men in stone robes, the armless women, the mosaics of wine drinking and kindly, smiling wild animals, and where is Tacitus, the prince of darkness—

New sounds wake me in the throes of the night: sounds of the disintegration of matter exposed to a fresh light—a page creaking in one of the Talmuds, a mended piece of pottery coming apart, a fibre snapping—I lie and listen: I left the door to the gluing room open—and the murmurs are coming from there, the rustling of time like the whisper of fire—I leap to my feet—the whole house is surrounded by sounds of trickling and lapping; the sound of water on leaves and the sound of water on the roof tiles and the sound of water on the asbestos and on the door step and in the throat of the gutter—all the garden is plashing and splashing, and the smell of the earth in the rain fills the air—lightning floods the garden with pure electricity—after it an explosion and the noise of complex temples collapsing, and again the slanting lines of rain glitter in the dark—the sound of the water on the fallen leaves, on the islands of bare ground, the grass, in the thickets of the ficus, the crests of the shaken palms—everything is one gurgling, drinking, glittering black—how many years since I was in the rain like this, as in the heart of a giant chandelier, barefoot, bareheaded, who can forbid me, and precisely now the rain subsides and the wind blows cold and the ficus shakes off raindrops like a huge black poodle and the water clatters in the tin throat of the gutter and the earth gurgles in satisfaction—

I close the gate opened by the wind. Everything is washed and ringing. Tomorrow will be a clear winter day full of wagtails.

Is somebody knocking? Is somebody knocking at the door? Who can it be—not the milkman and not the laundry man with clean pressed sheets, not the head of the council and the nurse to say they are very sorry but, I'm a spinster orphaned on every side, there's nobody who can suddenly die on me, but someone is knocking on the door, knocking, and there is something desperate about this knocking, a stubborn buyer? Betzer would have informed me—maybe the character cultivating the plot? Let him knock, I'm not here. The light between the slats of the shutter is faint and dull, what's the time, half past eight in the morning, I slept like a bear! And they're still knocking at the door, damn them, they won't stop until I answer, I shuffle my feet in open sandals, wrap myself in a robe, just a minute! The peephole is clouded over, until I open up I won't know who is so determined to see me—"Ora?" wearing a tasteless tracksuit like a refugee from Eastern Europe, "Aren't you working?" "It's Saturday—" her smile is worn, dull, almost painful at the corners. She is hugging a big swollen envelope to her chest, "Don't you have a calendar?" she follows me into the living room, sees the corpses of the clothes strewn over the armchairs, the sofa in disarray, turns back, "Come into the kitchen. Make me some coffee. Did I wake you? I'm sorry, but otherwise I wouldn't have been able to come, and at my place—you saw for yourself—" she lets out a sigh. "Now, everyone's still sleeping," she glances quickly at her watch. "We've got till ten—" I make myself tea, her coffee, sit down opposite her. We both look terrible, but who's there to see: the balding pomegranate tree behind the screen spotted with oil fumes and dust? The peeling whitewash on the ceiling?

"Look what I brought you—" Ora lays the hugged envelope on the table and on top of it a hand with fingernails cut to the quick, and I am sure that in a minute the photographs of the castle, the human pyramid, the beautiful Vera at the piano with her mouth open in song or scream will come sliding out, but from the tilted envelope pour postcards, postcards, postcards, from every capital, a museum, a picturesque village, a snowy mountain, a lake with wooded banks—"You kept everything," I say in astonishment. My handwriting on the other side of those landscapes. Ora smiles sourly. "Somebody had to—" understanding without needing to be told that I threw hers away. Until Eliot I dragged the flat box around with me at the bottom of my suitcase, and then, when I sorted out what to keep and what not, I came to Ora's letters, too. She wrote long letters. The last one—after a few months of silence—was an invitation to her wedding—I spread the postcards out, turn them over, my young handwriting looks at me, Switzerland is like the postcards, I wrote to her, to see Rome and die, I wrote, her letters I didn't even take the trouble to burn; a decade and a half after they were written they seemed childish to me, boring, superfluous. I tore them up and threw them into a trash can in Toronto. Who was going to read them. "I had this fantasy—for years; I thought that one day you would get on a plane and—" Ora bows her head, shakes it from side to side. "What? Don't tell me you never went abroad?" "We were on the way three times, and something always happened at the last minute," she raised eyes the color of muddy black coffee to me, "my father was hospitalized, Motik's mother died, I discovered I was pregnant with Yinon . . . the last time we packed our bags, the Gulf War broke out—" "Where were you going to go?" "Germany." "Germany!" "Are you still boycotting them?" Ora giggles. "And what did you do when El Al landed there?" "I usually managed to change places with someone, and when I had no alternative I flew, but I didn't get off the plane. Once I stayed to sleep on the plane with a security guard posted to watch over me and we argued half the night . . ." Ora laughs. No, not laughs, lets out a small, dry laugh. "And apart from Germany—you've been all over the world?" "No need to exaggerate, there're a few places left where I haven't set foot yet—" "Have you been to Eilat?" I can't decide if she is teasing or asking in all innocence. "No, I never went back there—" after that night. But what does Ora know about it? She glances quickly at her watch. Stands up. That ghastly tracksuit, the sparse, dyed hair. She goes into the living room, with me behind her. That restlessness, like a caged lioness, like an old caged lioness—"So, Adriana's already been here," she discovers the crystal in the Biedermeier. I can't decide if there's a hint of jealousy in her voice, I've lost that old ability to guess what she'll say, to sense what she'll feel—"You haven't opened any of the rooms yet," her eyes wander over the clothes. "Actually I have—the gluing room." I'm glad, why, to upset her assertions. She gives me a surprised look, follows in my foot-steps and I open the door to the room she, too, remembers. She peeps in, peeps at me and then into the room again, as if asking permission, and then she steps inside, barely able to insert herself between the table and chair. "The Talmud?" she is as surprised as I was, bends over the notes in the file I opened yesterday, trying to find her way in the tangle of scribbles, question marks, exclamation marks, gives up. "Did you read it?" "No, I haven't managed to yet—" She looks at me from inside the room. She sits on your chair, squeezed against your table, speaking like a prosecutor. "At least don't throw it all away like—" and I, from the doorway, defiantly: "Why? Why keep things? Can you tell me why you kept all those idiotic postcards? The Loya who wrote them doesn't exist any more! All the cells in her body have been changed, all the particles in her soul—" Ora con-templates me from the depths of the room, her head resting on her fist, her eyes twinkling. "But the temperament is the same—" she smiles and averts her eyes from me. "You always knew how to part," she adds quietly to the wall opposite her. Is she going to cry? I try to examine her assertion, like probing an aching tooth with the tip of my tongue. Did I know how to part? Maybe. I like the idea. "And I'm married to my first boyfriend," whispers Ora, her eyes on the wooden box holding the open potsherds still waiting for the touch of your hand: to fit, to glue, to close up an open mouth of darkness. "You didn't write a word about him—you didn't tell me anything about him—and suddenly—boom—there's a wedding invitation waiting for me at the Avia hotel—"—unbelievable what hurt my feelings twenty-six years ago—"And if you don't like him, say so," we promised when we realized how complicated and dangerous it might be. "And if you say no, then it'll be no," we promised, we were determined to look out for each other, we didn't take jealousy into account—

Ora gets up, extricates herself from the clutch of the chair-table with a clumsy inclination of her body, leaves your room. "Davidi was a little in love with you," I don't know why I say this, betraying your secret. Perhaps as a kind of offering to a goddess in decline. "I know," says Ora impassively, glances again at her watch, walks into the living room. "I got married because I was pregnant," she says with the same passivity of defeat. She has her back to me. I can't see the expression on her face. I go ahead of her, open the doors to the porch. It seems to me that she can't breathe. We stand next to each other, our elbows on the broad balustrade. I want to ask her, did you consider an abortion, and immediately understand that there's no point; she didn't consider an abortion. "Vered isn't twenty-three," she says and then she turns her face to me, "and that's the first and last lie—" I smile. "Ora—you're allowed to lie—the sky won't fall!" We both look at the rusting whitewashed ceiling of the porch which lets a bit of damp plaster fall onto the balustrade and burst out laughing. "Oh-where-have-you-been-all-these-years?" Ora puts her hand on my shoulder. "Where haven't I been?" I giggle and leave the porch. Ora follows, glancing at her watch again. We're in the kitchen. "Should I leave the parcel with you?" "No, you keep it, I—you know me—would destroy all the evidence—"

What do the birds do in the rain? What can they do? Hide, apparently. Before evening two cranes flew over the house with a bitter honking. Lightning dazzled coldly for a moment, dragging a collapsing train of noise behind it. They must have lost their way; something went wrong with the sense connecting them to the magnetic fields of the earth, with the brain cells judging the length of the day, the temperature, perhaps love confused their calculations of the nesting season and the migrating season and the angle of the rays of the sun and the distance from the one flying in front of them; there are so many things, it says in the book, that they have to remember: the face of the earth changing with their flight, mountain peaks sharp among wisps of cloud, their slopes powdered with snow, forests of triangular fir trees, the twists and turns of rivers, the sparkle of the sea changing with the light, the smell of the salt, the algae, the fish—how many of them die on the way of exhaustion, of cold, of old age. Airplane pilots hate them; they crash against the cabin windows or are sucked into the engine—sometimes causing near accidents—accidents—Oh that I were a fowl of the air, sang Yona, the singing teacher, vigorously opening her accordion, but as far as we were concerned a fowl was what appeared on your Friday night dinner plate next to the mashed potatoes—

I polished the stove with a scouring pad and steel wool. I bought kerosene and a new wick. There—the mesh cap reddens, and heat rises from the stove with a quiet hissing sound. What else is missing. The smell. I peel a long ribbon from a bought orange and lay it carefully on the blazing bars. Everything's here. The transparent red of the heat, the aroma of the roasting orange peel, the sound of the rain around the house, the checked slippers with the zipper, yes, they still exist, people like them so the manufacturers make them. We sat around this stove and you lit candles in the Hanukkah lamp Nahum made of a plank and upside-down bottle caps. Daddy served cold doughnuts he'd bought in a cake shop in Jerusalem. I licked the powdered sugar carefully, refraining from the sticky lump of fried dough, while Nahum opposite me, eating his with methodical thoroughness, grew a moustache of white icing sugar. We were both sitting on a small striped rug. Nahum gave up his turn with the top and I played for both of us, spinning it once for me and once for him, but it kept falling on *Po*.

I sit in the gluing room, opposite the open flower of the potsherds. I try something. Give up. "The pots are broken and the game's over!" We used to chant. Why pots? Maybe the word pots, *kelim*, was a corruption of the word rules, *klalim*? Maybe the game was over because the rules were broken? But we didn't ask then, not even ourselves, why they broke the pots or what was so terrible about potters coming in that children's game that it put all the players to hysterical flight, or why potters and not cobblers or tanners or smiths, or why the barn of Mizra was burning—"The barn of Mizra is burning!" we sang and shouted as we danced, where exactly is Mizra anyway and what's there to sing and shout about if its barn is burning? The pots are broken. In the pots they always kept something—a rare, precious commodity—fine olive oil—choice flour—myrrh and cinnamon and aromatic roots—and when the pot broke, and its priceless heart spilled out like water, what was the point of playing games? But you never gave up—digging, exposing, collecting, contemplating, fitting, and piecing together, restoring the outer shell, creating a hollow black heart staring at us from the mouth of the jar—

The pomegranate tree is balding. Now, as in an X-ray its skeleton is revealed: a bunch of thin sticks turning every which way, without a central trunk, without a crest. With every day that passes it grows clearer that it's more of a bush than a tree. The cypress, on the other hand, has renewed its vigor; from below it's like a gigantic ancient dagger fished from the bowels of the sea—a short handle and a huge blade, encrusted with shells, stone and time, thrusting its point into the sky. And the sky—high and transparent, full of light, slowly streaming clouds, seems to flow. But after lengthy contemplation, everything changes; the sky with the clouds sculpted in it is still as the sky in a painting. And the cypress—it and the earth at its roots and the earth connected to the earth at its roots, the cypress and all its surroundings—is moving. The earth is sailing. I lose my balance and sit on the damp grass. Underneath it, with the palms of my hands open to the earth, I feel a movement like the slow flexing of muscles, a heartbeat muffled by great depths and the sound of distant splashing and bubbling, as if down there, at the center of the earth, the drum of a giant washing machine is turning, washing molten iron in burning water.

I squeeze in between the table and the bookshelves, push the chair out of the room and reach for the books on the shelves; for a moment the smell stops me—a smell of vanilla and old time and darkness; a sweet, stale smell of things that return in dreams. I pull them out one by one with hands suddenly recognizing the covers, the weight, the serrated edges of the coarse, brownish-yellow pages, here's *The Hebrew Underground in the Period of the Talmud* by Mandil and Vahalman with the front page picture of Roman storm troopers with their enviable pleated skirts and round shields and on the other side of three cypresses at the entrance to a cave, six sages dressed in galabias guarded by Bar Kokhba's boys in short togas and sandals. And here's another one—"This book was published in Warsaw in the year 1924 without any connection to the situation in Eretz Israel," the Jerusalem publisher B. Ben-Aharon declared. I read it once. I remember one story about a Roman princess and the ivory-sounding name Tur-Malka, Queen's tower—and this book, red, with the gold coin at the center of the cover, which I quite often dipped into as well, opens at page 48, against a pitch-black background facing each other the Emperor Trajan and the Emperor Hadrian, Hadrian has a nice little smile and close marble curls, he was an enlightened emperor, my father told me, and I was very sorry that we revolted against him rather than one of the lunatics like Caligula or Nero—the book ends with an appendix, "From the lips of the parchment." When I was a child I thought that parchment was a kind of corpse. Today I know that I wasn't completely wrong. And here's a relatively new one, *Bar Kokhba* by Shmuel Abramsky. The war is mapped on the first page, the area of the fighting grows darker and shrinks from year to year, until it blackens into a single dot: Bethar. In the middle of the book are pages of photographs, Hadrian again, this time closer up, less friendly, and an aerial photo of the ruins of Bethar like the rings of an ancient tree stump. And fragments of letters from Bar Koseva to the men of Ein Gedi—was his name Simeon? Simeon Bar Koseva? I loved Bar Kokhba because of the smell of the bonfires and the magic of the sparks and the statue in the museum in Safed (tensed to leap with straining stone muscles, stone locks on a stone forehead beneath which stone eyes look at us wherever we go—a special technique, the guide explained) but mainly because of the name, *Kochav*, star—and here is a black book whose title is engraved in curlicued handwriting and filled in with gold faded to khaki, *When a Nation Fights for Its Freedom*—opposite the picture of the author, haughty and cropped, a circle, a black eagle spreading its wings over the words "Political Publication" traversing the circle, beneath it the country from a bird's eye view; wrinkles of mountains, the three lakes—the small, the medium, and the large—connected by the thread of the Jordan river. Historical essays, the subtitle promises, by Dr. Joseph Klausner Professor of History at the He-brew University in Jerusalem. At the head of each page, for the reader's benefit, a condensation of the matter discussed below; "Bar Kokhba or Bar Koziva?" "Petronius arouses the wrath of Caesar," "Prophetic Socialismus," and here's something new: *In search of Bar Kokhba*, an album-like volume, heavy pages, clear print, photographs in color, in black and white, woven baskets out of which skulls stare with eyes of darkness, scraps of fabric, mo-saics, a view of desert creeks, avalanches of pale gold, brown gold, ending in the blue strip of the Dead Sea, and the diggers—silhouettes with a mine detector at the entrance to a cave; and here's Yigael Yadin in a balaclava—you and Daddy were part of that expedition, you came back tanned, ex-cited, I was supposed to accompany you there on the Passover vacation, but everything was thrown into confusion by the trial in Jerusalem, and so, instead of spending the holidays in the light-eroded landscape of the Dead Sea, I spent it in front of the Cyclops-eye of the radio blinking nervously, as if to echo, in its own way, the intonation of the prosecutor with his strange "r," "As I stand before you, Judges of Israel, to lead the prosecution of Adolf Eichmann, I do not stand alone. With me, in this place and at this hour, stand six million accusers. But they cannot rise to their feet . . . for their ashes were piled up in the hills of Auschwitz . . . their blood cries out but their voice is not heard. Therefore it falls to me to be their spokesman . . ." And afterwards the witnesses with hoarse, faded voices, sometimes sup-pressing a sob, apologizing, answering his thundering questions—days, weeks, months, you and Daddy travelling to Jerusalem to see with your own eyes, Daddy coming home with full notebooks and you shutting yourself up in this room, my knocking elicits nothing but groans of go away, Daddy summons Nahum from the technical college, I fetch the nurse from the Sick Fund, she the doctor who succeeds in reaching you, recommends rest, going to the beach, breathing "gut air mit iodine," I am placed in charge of the picnic hamper, do you want something to eat, something to drink, but Daddy is silent as a stone and you have no appetite, you get up and begin to prowl, to probe with a finger burrowing in the sand—

The days grow shorter, the light changes, the birds change too. Dubček no longer wakes me at daybreak. The Polish yentas no longer peck at the ground in a sewing-machine staccato; left behind are the sparrows, the executioners, the mafiosi and the wagtails, who arrived not long ago; nervous and elegant they step with nodding heads like a bank clerk on his way to the safe, draw waves of flight in the air, as if swimming in the element others breathe. And yesterday, after a night of rain—slow, straight, whispering rain—a pale black flock flew past with hoarse, brief cries. None of them bothered to land in order to see if this place too was an option.

The earth at ten o'clock in the morning after the rain is damp and brown with a fine mist rising from it. I carve cones in it with a big butcher's knife, in every cone I lay a plant removed from a plastic cup, its pale roots trembling as if shivering with cold: I can hardly believe it myself—I drove with Tikva to the plant nursery and came back with a cardboard box full of baby flowers. The nursery at the entrance to the neighborhood is open every day of the week, including Saturdays and holidays, blooming in the shade of dark net veils. Every group of plants boasts a Latin name, rare and important as the name of a malignant disease. "Who gives them their names?" I ask the mustachioed man at the counter with casual interest. "The guys at the Volcani Agricultural Research Institute?" he asks in reply, glancing at my cardboard box. "But you chose common flowers?" Yes, petunias, snapdragons, pansies, everything familiar from then, Tikva standing next to me with three pots of overgrown crimson cyclamens that look like living plastic. I, without knowing exactly why, break the ground and plant and pat down. "Very good," Tikva encouraged me, "if the house looks less neglected, you'll get a better price for it—should I send you a painter?" Not for the time being—for the time being I'm trying out the new road, to see where it leads, giving myself courage for another hundred yards, what can already happen, the road bends, nearly leaves the neighborhood and returns to it, no, it ends at the edge of my drying-up citrus grove, on its south side. The ground is patched with light, the trees are meager, small fruits of a dull orange shade replacing the old, lustrous ones. Some of the trees have been attacked by asparagus ferns—this grove has been abandoned to die, and I—what is that smell, a bad smell, the smell of a carcass, where is it coming from, the ground is covered with branching furrows full of toffee and cocoa-colored silt, spotted with chips of gravel, the smell of the carcass is close, almost suffocating, is the body buried under this mound of gray building debris, broken cinder blocks, Arab floor tiles with green and ocher patterns, a broken toilet bowl, the door of a fridge, even a torn army blanket, the things people throw away, I remember you bending down to retrieve old books from the bowels of a trash can, once you brought me a parcel of Russian books translated into old-fashioned Hebrew, *Panfilov's Men, Quiet Flows The Don*, these citrus trees won't live long, most of them have skinny, sooty arms, I walk further, here's the dirt track and here are the crates—in a crate like this you once tried to make me a house smelling of wood and oranges, like Alice in Wonderland after the "Drink Me" syrup I filled it up to the walls and the roof—and crates are lying on their sides, dry and cracked on the sunny side, rotten on the side of the ground, a long, long line—the smell of the carcass fades, I leave the track, go back into the trees, how did the skeleton of a Volkswagen get here, without wheels, without doors—I touch—the metal, leprous with rust, breaks on contact—metals too get tired, Nahum said to me on that night—what doesn't get tired. What isn't eaten by the teeth of the wind and the water and time and habit, the smell of the air full of sun between one rain and the next at the edge of the plot, at the end of the grove, from here your house is a child's building block between the jaws of the ficus tree—

I said, let's take a taxi to Sde Dov, get on a plane to Eilat, how much can it already cost, we'll stay for one night and come back, but Ora smiled bitterly and it was clear that no, it was simply out of the question, then come to Tel Aviv, I suggested, I haven't been in Tel Aviv for twenty years, they tell me it's changed beyond recognition, come on, show me around, and Ora said, but—and I didn't wait for the explanation or the excuse, then the new center, I decided to rest content with what was possible under present circumstances, the new center for an hour or two, and she said, all right, and now she's sitting opposite me in the cafe, between us the slice of cheese cake and the slice of chocolate cake which we share like the things we shared forty years ago, a ring with a heart, a hair band, gold stars, paper angels, fluff from an angora sweater, dried flowers, but Ora is with me and not with me; her eyes wander around the mall on the other side of the glass as if a knight on a white horse will suddenly reveal himself there, Mica was like that, Liora, Shula—none of them became a close friend of mine, and now Ora too.

"But it wasn't only that—" I attack at once. Going for the soft underbelly.

"It wasn't only what?" Ora tenses. Now she's with me. Leaning towards me, listening hard, in a minute she'll guess the tail of my sentence before I end it—

"The reason for this estrangement. It wasn't only because you got pregnant and got married and didn't want me to know—why didn't you want me to know, in fact—"

"Because you would have told me to have an abortion—not to get married like that—" Ora looks into my eyes. Her eyes are narrowed.

"Right—I admit it—but why didn't you tell me afterwards, you didn't write a word—"

"Did you write?" she turns her face from me.

"I wrote you postcards . . . but you were angry with me. You were angry because I sold everything, because I became a flight attendant—you were angry even before your marriage, before your pregnancy—"

"No—" Ora begins, but she has to stop because the waitress comes up to us at last: slender, young, blonde, a round tray in her hand—

"One small Nescafé and one black coffee with sugar?"

"One English tea and one latte—" Ora corrects her in a voice containing a hint of rebuke together with a hint of stern pedagogic astonishment at her failure to master the assignment. The chastised waitress mutters "Sorry, sorry," and retreats to the depths of the cafe—

"You weren't angry with me?" I try to bring Ora back to the conversation. Her eyes are on the empty seat next to her. Somebody left a newspaper there and she's reading it.

"No, I wasn't angry—" her attention is no longer fixed on me, "I was a little jealous, I think—" she lowers her eyes to the newspaper again as if she hasn't just dropped a small, quiet, and dangerous bombshell between us.

"You were jealous of me?" I have no intention of letting it pass. But her eyes are on the paper.

"Ever since Udi and Gili were drafted I can't see a newspaper without . . ." Her voice fades. She reads. I sit opposite her and see her reading. A chirping sound rises from her bag. She detaches herself from the newspaper, rummages in her bag in a panicky way, fishes out a cell phone, opens it, answers. "Vered might come to the mall, she wants to buy a blouse, she wants me to come with her—"

"A twenty-five-year-old girl needs her mother to choose a blouse?" I meant to tease, but Ora is still immune. She smiles sweetly.

"Yes, why not. We go to the movies together, shopping . . ."—her eyes return to the newspaper not before scanning the mall through the cafe window again. She has forgotten me. I can get up and go. I've already left love in the middle of a meal—"Listen to what it says here." Ora doesn't look up from the paper, but she retells it to me, reads to me from it—"A fertilized egg was implanted in the womb of a sixty-two-year-old woman and she gave birth to a healthy baby—"

Is she hinting that it's not too late for me either? I feel the blood rushing to my face—"And you think—"

"That it's a good thing?" There, it's happened. Meeting me halfway, completing my thought or returning my ball. "No, I think it's terrible." She raises her eyes from the paper. "Old people have stopped dying." She surprises me, she sounds bitter. "Soon the whole world will look like one big old-age home; every senior citizen will have a face-lift, liposuction, organ transplants, hormones, and at the age of eighty he'll marry for the fifth time some chick who's managed to survive the trip to India and the acid parties and AIDS—do you take hormones?" Without waiting for an answer she digs into her bag again, a vast, brown leather bag, fishes out calcium, zinc, vitamin D, vitamin E, vitamin A, vitamin B12, sets them on the table in a row. "Yesterday I left eight hundred shekels at the pharmacist—where is that waitress?"

Here she comes—golden haired and pale in her black uniform, asks coyly:

"Which of you is the English tea and which of you is the latte?"

Ora answers with a jerk of her chin, waits for her to go, contemplates the parade of bottles, tries to open one of them, gives up, sweeps them all back into her bag.

"Sometimes I feel like doing what you did—" she waves her hand in the air, almost hitting the glass wall.

"You've done a lot—" I say carefully. She sounds furious. Will she spit poison like her mother?

"Sending the whole world to hell—getting on a plane and—" Her lips tremble.

"What's stopping you—" I bend down to sip my tea. Her undisguised agitation embarrasses me. "Seriously," her silence forces me to raise my eyes, "what's stopping you—"

Her lips tighten in a grimace new to me. She covers her face. A spasm under the skin makes the cheek turned to me twitch.

"Two sons in the army and a son in high school—" She breathes a sigh of what-do-you-know, what-do-you-understand, "and my parents—"

The waitress, a tender narcissus in a black sheath, approaches, clears the empty cake plates onto the round tray, simpers—"Was everything all right?"

What are all these Jewish books doing here? *Lamentations Rabbah*, published by S. Buber in 1899. *The Book of Josiphon*, Warsaw 1874, in Rashi script. *The Produce of the Land* by Yehoseph Schwarz, first published in Jerusalem in 1845—and maps—in this cardboard file are ancient maps—of what, of Terra Santa or of Palestine, what were you looking for in maps dating from 1600 and something, a new country? Because these maps don't even come close to the coastline on the Jewish National Fund collection box that hung in our class, the Dead Sea looks like a nibbled banana, and all the land to the West of it hills and towers and baffling foreign names and the Mediterranean wavy to very wavy with ships with billowing sails or a shining scroll surrounded by clouds, and there's a map in Hebrew too—Bravo!—with a character looking like Maimonides hovering over the sea on which is written "Philistines" and, a little to the north, "The Great Sea" and here you've drawn an arrow, underlined a name, I have to open a few drawers to find your precious magnifying glass—neatly wrapped in flannel—here, I see, it's "Bethar"—Bethar? Isn't Bethar somewhere in the vicinity of Jerusalem? In the Judean desert? Apparently I'm wrong, but here's another Hebrew map, which calls itself a "True Map," but its truth is very strange, to the south of Beersheba is an enclave called "Abode of Ama-lekites" and between Jaffa and Caesarea, almost on the coast Beth-Tor—according to Graetz!! And also Yabetz!!! Your exclamation marks exult on the pages next to the maps, scribbles, quotations, several layers of notes, in blue ink, in black ink, in changing script, and question marks, exclama-tion marks, advice to yourself, check in Tacitus, in Dio Cassius, in Rashi (sic!), Bar Kokhba was a king of the Herodian dynasty? A struggle between the Herodian and Hasmonean dynasties? How should I know—one thou-sand ships, you write, whose thousand ships, it's a huge number, how many ships took part in the battle of Salamis, sixty-seven if I'm not mistaken, who had a thousand ships?—Eleazar ben Harsom, you send an arrow to a character I've never heard of; Eleazar the high priest? you ask, as in the Bar Kokhba coin bearing his name we found near Caesarea, one of the ten sages martyred by the Romans? you ask, Eleazar of Modi'in? You shoot three arrows from the name to three possibilities—spy and informer, with the name "Ha-Moda'i" referring to his role, "the informer," rather than his place of origin? Double agent? From the Hasmonean family in Modi'in? A triumvirate of Eleazar–Bar-Kokhba–Akiva? Rabbi Akiva, according to your notes, is a kind of James Bond, sailing the seas, meeting Hadrian for secret talks, conducting a passionate affair (sic!) with the wife of Tinneius Rufus the Roman governor of Judea in order to milk her for information, a male Mata Hari, no less, are we talking here about the same Rabbi Akiva, that legendary scholar and sage, martyred by the Romans for teaching the Torah? According to you the whole story of the four sages who entered the *pardes*, the sacred grove of esoteric speculation, and only Akiva emerged unscathed, is nothing but a disguise for the description of an espionage mission, four were sent and only Rabbi Akiva returned, he came ashore in the vicinity of Caesarea and went by foot to Bethar—and perhaps that's when he was arrested—tortured to death with iron combs—his students = Bar Kokhba fighters attacked the town to rescue him, but were killed by *askara*—not diptheria!!! I can hear you thundering through the three exclamation marks, but *askarei* = a title for officials (soldiers?) in Turkish/ Arabic, you note in green ink, they didn't succeed in rescuing him but nevertheless they accomplished something: the Tenth Roman Legion was destroyed! The Twenty-second Roman Legion was destroyed! The Emperor Hadrian did not open his report to the Senate with the standard formula of "I and my soldiers are well"—

Anger begins to rise in my throat: What the hell is all this doing here when you are gray powder and splinters of bone—

The ancients, you said, equipped the dead with everything necessary for a good life: biscuits, dried fruits, wine, weapons, jewels, money for the journey—in your story death turned into a long excursion which sometimes included dogs and horses, servants and wives as well—and they agreed? asked Nahum from the mouth of the cave. He hated burial caves. I don't think they were asked, you answered with a sour smile.

The pomegranate tree is sick, but the garden is flourishing. The ficus gleams like volcanic glass, the cypress bleeds bright purple, the jacaranda leaves are studded with diamonds of water, the palm trunks are washed clean, they look like three silver masts sailing in the sky—a wagtail here. A wagtail there. And a phone call from Adriana—

"Have you heard about Minaleh's son?"

The body loses control over the production lines, Eliot explained to me, as a health freak he knew a lot about all kinds of diseases, he ran to keep them at bay, he swam, he ate fresh fruit and vegetables, he didn't touch white sugar, he didn't touch red meat, I'll live like a Balkan peasant, he promised me and himself, to a hundred and twenty at least. He worshipped yogurt; he explored the possibility of having his body frozen until scientists in the future could thaw people for chapter two—but every few months he would get fed up with it all, abandon himself to a rich meal in a French restaurant, polish off three desserts, recover with a searing cup of coffee, raise a toast, "Life is short!" to celebrate the holiday he had taken from the rules and restrictions obliging anyone determined to cheat life and death—"They diagnosed it after he came back from a class trip to Poland," Adriana continues, sure that it isn't a coincidence, in Minaleh's case too, just a minute, she has a customer—

> My dear Hedva,
>
> Soon it will be Hanukkah here. The grocer's already has trays of doughnuts saturated with oil disguised by icing sugar and thin candles for the Hanukkah lamps. But I miss the December cheer of abroad: the snow—the shop windows with Christmas trees and ribbons and silver balls, the crisp combination of fiery red and dark green—the shoppers, the excitement—here the year ends without sparkling, without snow, almost without cold—the last days have been all gold and blue—I haven't worn a sweater yet—would you believe it?

Saturday. Breakfast for six. At your place. "This house—he never changed anything, right?" Minaleh hugs her elbows, her eyes wander over the walls, the tops of the door frames, don't treat her as if she's dying, don't feel sorry for her, Adriana ordered, "I adore houses like this," says Yosefa, if you could have seen us you would have pulled a face, what did you bring those Hadassah ladies here for, you didn't like middle-aged women, but look, I'm a Hadassah lady too now, and so is beautiful Ora, Arlozora lays out on your dining table cosmetics produced by a friend of hers who lives in the vegetarian village of Amirim from all kinds of plants that survive in harsh climatic conditions, "Loya, did you put the water on?" When I come back they're all ready: Arlozora has bound all their heads in wide elastic bands—with their hair pulled back they all look frightened. "And now, girls," she says archly, "all of you moisten a piece of cotton wool in face lotion" the bottle passes from hand to hand, we all clean our faces—Yosefa and Ora with brisk movements, Tikva slowly with her eyes closed, Adriana with a smile, Minaleh delicately, gently, with great care, Arlozora with businesslike efficiency. "You too, Loya," and I obey. "This is much better than your Hungarian cosmetics, in Hungary the sun doesn't fry your skin, the water's soft, it's a well known fact that the best cosmetics are local, here, rub this in, you'll see." Arlozora passes around a flat pot of day cream. "It's made from olive oil, aloe vera, sage, and minerals from the Dead Sea—" "I was at a conference at the Dead Sea last week," says Yosefa, "the place was full of archaeologists, they're apparently excavating somewhere around there." "Where?" I jump in. "Wadi Murabba'at? The Hever river?" "Look what an expert she is! You used to go out on Saturdays to dig—" "Girls! Girls!" Arlozora claps her hands to silence us—she's a teacher too—"Now apply this mask—" A white tube which produces a white snake with a sulphurous smell passes between us. "Careful, not next to your eyes." "They took us on a tour of the surroundings," Yosefa goes on talking while she smears the stuff on her face; she can't keep quiet for a minute. "They showed us that Lot's wife is on her way out; if it rains again like it did last winter she'll simply collapse—" "So we'll have Sodom without Lot's wife?" asks Minaleh with her eyes closed. "Don't worry, they'll find some other rock to take her place," Arlozora promises and commands, "Shhhh . . . that's enough. The masks have to harden. You mustn't talk now. Close your eyes and relax—here, I'm putting it on too—keep quiet for twenty minutes and you'll feel the difference—"

We keep quiet. We keep absolutely quiet. Outside a tit saws glass plates with a silver saw and a honey-sucker chirps as if it's swallowed a cricket—I open my eyes and feel a moment of alarm: around me are six eyeless plaster masks, like the busts of six Roman emperors.

I have to decide. Soon it will be New Year's. The civilian new year. Who but the religious and elementary school teachers still thinks in terms of the Hebrew months, of Heshvan-Kislev-Tevet? I have to open the rooms and choose which ghost I want to sleep with—you?—Nahum?—but first to shake out the handbag that accompanies me wherever I go—unzip all the zippers and simply let it vomit out everything it's holding in its guts—Passport. Identity Card. Theater ticket from four years ago. Narrow gold bracelet I forgot to take in to be mended and forgot altogether. A few cents. Two French telephone tokens. A pale pink lipstick that doesn't belong to me. A sunglasses case. An entrance ticket to a museum. An earring. A key! So I didn't return the key to Jean-Jacques in the end! A pen that doesn't write. A pair of tweezers. A squashed rectangular cardboard box and in it—a watch with green phosphorescent hands and numbers—my bat mitzvah watch!—I remember myself looking for darkness in the middle of the day so as to see the glowworm light of time—no—it doesn't shine any more—I wonder if it can be fixed—I wonder if it still closes around my wrist—yes, I only have to move one hole—I can throw out the box—crumple it up and throw it out—no, there's something in there, pushed between the paper lining and the back of the box—a small, stiff rectangle, good wishes from you and Nahum that have been waiting for thirty-six years—I tear the lining and discover a white card inscribed Ziegel et Ziegel fully guaranteed.

HANUKKAH

Tonight they came to me again with covered pots, full of food smelling of family and crowded togetherness, talked to me without stopping, plied me with glass after glass of orange juice, offered Valerian drops, spoke about Daddy who had donated his body to science, look, Elhanan's father showed me his eyes, one dark and narrow, his, and the other round and slightly protruding, just like Daddy's, he donated his hand to me too, turning it over to show me, but it was big and white, with blurred lines, more like Jean-Jacques' hand, no, I said, don't you believe it? Don't you believe it? They stood up, came closer, crowded around me in concern, and some annoyance, but you'll believe it in the end, you'll believe it in the end—

I woke up crossly. I'm not mourning or sitting shivah, I said, but they came anyway, with covered pots, offered tea, coffee, Valerian, your father, what a gentleman he was, he gave everyone the time of day, they never forgot that he was a professor at the university and took the bus to Jerusalem five times a week, colleagues of his arrived in a little group and spoke in turn, as if they had agreed beforehand, one of them recounted how proud he had been that at the age of six I could write ancient Hebrew script and at the age of ten I copied the story "Three Gifts" by Y.L. Peretz into hieroglyphics, did I want to study ancient history, perhaps languages, a scholarship could be arranged, my father had told them about how I used to do the translations-on-the-side for the movies they showed in the neighborhood, that I caught languages like other people caught influenza, it was enough for someone near me to sneeze in Russian—and I knew it, I even got the accent right, it was a gift some people were born with, had I heard of simultaneous translation, I could travel to all kinds of congresses in the most beautiful cities in the world, this wasn't the right moment, but it was something to think about—

Shlomi's mother dished out peanuts and salt sticks and too-sweet tea and asked me every few minutes if I was hungry, if I was thirsty, if I was tired, she insisted on staying to sleep in the living room all week, and Shlomi, who had been exempted from army service because of a heart murmur, came and was sent to shop, to bring, to notify, and came back and looked at me from a distance and didn't dare approach me, and Nahum came a few times from the base, sat in the corner and didn't say a word, and you came every afternoon; when you came in there was a slight stir in the room, neighbors suddenly found reasons to hurry, and only Shlomi's mother wasn't afraid, she made strong coffee for you both and sat down next to you for a hushed conversation in Czech, be careful, I understand every word, I lied, I was twenty and a half, and Shlomi's mother wrung her hands over me, you're so young, you're so young, but I felt a hundred years old—

The boys dropped in for fifteen minutes, in uniform, Elhanan an officer, Bilu in the navy, Hezi in a red paratrooper's beret, Adriana came with her mother, Tikva, Yosefa, Arlozora, and Ora, a platoon commander, came for one night:

Loya, you're not crying?

He's dead—what's the point of crying. That milk's already been spilt—all that's left is to mop up the puddle to keep the ants away—

You're angry—

Me? *Adversus solem ne loquitor*—

Translation on the side, please—

You don't argue with the sun. Being angry about facts is like banging your head against the wall—but I was angry, I was boiling mad at the whole world, especially at my father for dying before I was ready, out of the blue, without any warning signs, without weakness or illness, dying suddenly of cardiac arrest in the middle of the university library, where he was only found two days later. And exactly in the interim after the army and before life, when I was far away, entangled in a difficult love affair, I didn't want advice and I couldn't see a way out, I learned French and Russian and Italian but I didn't know why, I already knew that I wasn't going to be a second Champollion, I didn't want to be, and for that too I blamed him; if he and Davidi hadn't urged me I wouldn't have gone with them to the excavations, and I wouldn't have met Giora there, under the ground, popping out of the tunnel, first a storm of bronze and copper curls, then a broad forehead shining with sweat, then the eyes, in the deceptive light of the candle golden eyes, with stands of fire in the lashes, and one sturdy shoulder, powdered with tunnel crawling, its muscles rounding with the effort of pulling up and out into the columbarium where I was waiting for Daddy and you, holding a potsherd in my hand, perhaps an ostracon. The golden eyes smiled, and I, facing a statue of Apollo, that's what I thought in spite of the tractorist's moustache, in spite of the grin below it, in spite of the slightly protruding canines. "With the mole I struggled from darkness, stubborn and under a spell," he said jokingly, sitting with a half-jump on the edge of the tunnel, his torso already here, his legs in the dark—what?—Nathan Alterman! He rose from the pit, all gold, casting a giant shadow on the rock wall. Pleased to meet you, Nathan. I'm Loya, Loya Kaplan—he laughed out loud, throwing his head back, filling the columbarium with echoes. I didn't know what to say, he explained the next day over morning coffee, you gave me a fright. It was hard to tell if he was serious, teasing or conceited, there was an ironic note deep down in his voice, he argued with you too, and you were furious; he knew far less than you did, that was clear even to him, but he spoke with absolute confidence, it was only after a few minutes that I realized he was playing a game, that he enjoyed challenging you, making you lose your temper. "Nathan Alterman," I called him, to make him stop, to make him come, and he did come and stood behind me warm and tall and put two big hands on my shoulders: The mole at your command—closed his arms around me and rested his chin on my head, behind us, around the camp fire sat the excavators—Daddy, you, another seven—four students and three volunteers, a small, semipiratical expedition. Do you know any stars? I tried to stop the giddiness. Giora released one arm, waved it at the sky: there, he pointed, is the North Arrow—is it really pointing north?—more or less—and there? I pointed to a nearby, shining star. That's Sirius—And is it always in the same place?—What's the matter with you? It moves!—It moves, or we move? In the darkness above me I sensed him chuckle, lift the weight of his chin from my hair, and then a warm breath on my nape and a tongue sliding dizzily from the lobe of my ear to the base of my neck; for a second I lost my balance—We move, Giora steadied me, don't worry, it's impossible to see anything from light to

darkness—he meant the people sitting around the camp fire, Daddy, you—
Let's go back there, I freed myself, with a sweet, stunned, melting body
enclosed in a shrivelled shell of what-will-you-think-of-us, in a distress of
yes-but, not now, not here, striding ahead of him to the camp fire: Giora
was showing me the stars—explaining before being asked, but you were
deep in argument—bunker or not bunker from the time of Bar Kokhba,
the lessons of Gamla and Yodefat and Masada, a guerilla war was fought
here, you insist, that's Sirius, I point to the brightest star as proof, and only
then you raise your head to protest: The Hebrew name is Avrek—others
raise their heads too. And that's Orion, says one of the diggers, pointing to
the North Arrow. That's Ksil, you correct. "Hebrew is the sky above us—
Hebrew the air—Hebrew the wind!" Giora declaims in a theatrical tone,
and you perceive the mockery, fall silent, look at me as if to say that I will
have to choose between you and Giora, but why on earth should I, I shake
off this ridiculous idea with a shrug of my shoulders, go back to looking at
Giora who is now teasing the dying fire, stabbing its heart, turning coals
into kernels of fire, the argument dies down, one by one the excavators get
up to climb into their sleeping bags, Daddy almost last, giving me an in-
quiring look. Everything's fine, I say, I'll go to sleep soon—and when only
Giora and I are left, Giora gets up, shakes the dirt from his trousers and
whispers: Tonight there'll be an eclipse of the moon—that night we saw
the full moon veiled by a semitransparent shadow. And the stars bigger
and brighter in the dark. Next to the North Arrow a single star blazed red,
and Giora put his arms around my waist from behind and kissed me on the
side of my neck. Not here, I whispered. The sleepers were very close. Then
come—Giora pulled me. We went down through the water cistern. Giora
had an army flashlight, and its round light danced on the chalk rock—
a concentrated little circle, and around it a halo of thin, almost watery
light. The tunnel gave off a damp cold and a smell of limestone and clay.
I can't even see my own hands as I follow the light shining on either side
of Giora's silhouette walking in front of me and warning—bend down—
there's a step here—careful, from here we have to crawl—feeling almost

as if I'm inside the chest of winter clothes, blind and giddy from danger-ous smells—naphthalene, consumptive dankness, Jane Eyre-ish sadness—come on, whispers Giora, his shadow straightening, I straighten up too, at long last the columbarium. Giora drops down with his back to the wall, his knees folded, tucks me under his arm, lets the circle of light waver on the walls. The darkness gathers in the hollowed-out alcoves, deepens them unbearably, turning them into forty-eight eyes staring at us. They bred carrier pigeons here, I say to stop this staring, and Giora chuckles and pats my arm in time to his reply: Here-they-buried-dead-people-burned-and-ground-to-dust-in-little-boxes—Oh please! I protest, and the echo bounces off the walls and Giora switches off the flashlight and sentences us to darkness.

And in the darkness he laughs a quick nervous laugh, and then he em-braces me, encompassing me with a dry, almost electric heat, searing me with kisses, groping over my skin with burning hands, you're freezing, he notes, soon you'll be warm, he promises, what exists in the dense darkness is not his hands, not his face, not his chest, only his skin, his voice, his touch, the columbarium fills with echoes of the whispers of fabric pushed aside, hair stirring in the dirt, breathing, heartbeats, we are one tangled, heavy, almost suffocating, blazing darkness, and when I feel the cold again it is no longer dark, I can see Giora's eyes flashing as his moustache makes my skin bristle: Let's go—Not yet, I shouldn't have said it, I did say it, I upset the very fine balance between what-he-wants and what-I-ask-for, but then I knew no better, there was a sour, bitter feeling between my legs, and he rolled onto his back, his face to the rock ceiling, ran a rough hand over my face, declaim-ing ironically from that same poem as before, "My every thought besieged you—the hairs of my head upright." He has nothing to say and therefore he quotes perhaps even from the same poem, two months later I bought *Stars Outside* and *Joy of the Poor* and searched and found "The Mole" in one of them and learned it off by heart in his honor, but I never met him again—

What a story! Jean-Jacques exclaims, he had never known anyone who made love in the secret tunnels of guerilla fighters from the second century

AD before, and I can't convince him that it was much less exotic than it sounded, *Alors non!* he protests, and the poem, he reminds me, I still have the book, I confess, and a week later, sailing down the Seine on a long tourist boat, I read it aloud to him, You can tell at once that it's poetry, he pronounces, but he fails to guess a single word, he removes the book gently from my hands, studies the vowel-pointed letters at length, looks up at me, and before I can understand the reason for his distress he stretches his hand over the railing and drops Alterman into the streaming Seine—

Do you really know so many languages, Giora asked me as we got up to go. I know how to say I love you in twelve languages, I said playfully, instinctively understanding that this was the right tone, this was what was required now on the way out and up, to the morning—Go on, let's hear, demands Giora, ahead of me again, and I walk, crouch, crawl, straighten up and as I do so I list the neighborhood selection, Yiddish, Hebrew, Russian, Rumanian, Bulgarian, Greek, Polish, English, French, Italian, Ladino, Hungarian—and in which language do you really mean it, Giora's hand is on the first rung of the last ladder, his eyes looking down at me from the heights of his six foot something: It only commits you in Hebrew— he says, begins to climb, I go up behind him rung after rung, he's already outside, looking at me, a dark silhouette—only his eyes glitter, and I take a deep breath before I commit myself in the language of the Bible, but Giora bends down and gives me his hand: If you said it in Hebrew—we would both be lost—

We would both be lost, how many times I returned to those five words— was he trying to warn me? Was he mocking me?—I couldn't make up my mind and neither could Ora, I chose to remain silent, but Ora urged, Write, what can already happen, you can't leave it like this, and I wrote, hinting that the night of the eclipse of the moon would not be soon forgotten, deliberately choosing high-flown words, trusting him to dilute them with irony, but he didn't answer, and in the meantime the fear of pregnancy, then the certainty, I write again, not about that, not a word about that, choosing a different tone, a kind of hoarse humor, wait for an answer, and in the meantime the abortion, write again, this time briefly, almost defiantly, and on the envelope "In the absence of the addressee—return to sender" but the letter does not return to me, perhaps it followed him to Easter Island, to the graves of the Aztecs, and there he disappeared, South America is not America, Ora and I agreed, and I restrained myself until the end of my army service and then I wrote again, I'm at home in the meantime, I told him, learning a couple of languages, I still haven't decided exactly what I want to do, I didn't remind him by so much as a hint of the night in the underground tunnels, the bloodstain I glimpsed from the corner of my eye, already brown-black, soaked into the ground, my thought that somebody would still claim it as evidence of the heroism of the rebels fighting in the dark to their last drop of blood—Giora did not reply. One day I gathered my courage and went to his kibbutz. Should I come with you? asked Ora. No, I preferred to face him alone, I could imagine his grin: You brought reinforcements? His measured look, comparing us. I got onto the northbound bus, I got off at the wrong station, I walked for nearly an hour, I reached his kibbutz thirsty, hungry, sweltering, angry, I crossed a lawn to reach an open sprinkler and catch water to drink and cool myself down. Can't you read? Someone roared behind me, standing on the concrete path, waving his arms, I approached him with my face wet and he pointed an accusing finger at a small sign: KEEP OFF THE GRASS! I didn't see it, I apologized, I was very thirsty, I'm looking for, I started to say, but he turned his back on me: Thirsty! She was thirsty! he repeated scornfully to himself, a nasty old man—I went up to the woman standing on the path but she had no idea and neither did the youth for some reason riding a child's scooter, who turned his head to stare at me, during the entire visit inquisitive, malevolent eyes followed me, to my questions they replied with a shrug or with demonstrative reluctance. You're not the only one, muttered the comrade distributing tin bowls to hold the leftovers to all the tables in the dining-room hut which would also disappear without leaving a trace. For one, two, three years later I went on wondering how the flesh and blood had evaporated without a trace while the memories took on volume, turned into a place to which I returned, feeling the dense darkness again, breathing a mixture of damp limestone, clay, and also salt, and the bitter sourness of rust, hearing the hiss of breath, sensing the pulsing of the blood filling my ears, the heat rising from him like an aura, his smell, the smell of earth and ashes from the campfire, the passion, the sweet, painful melting, how could all this have vanished into thin air, I protest and Ora listens, nods, clarifies: But are you sure? Are you sure that's what happened? That's what he said? And I return to the night of the eclipse of the moon in almost the same words, clinging to them because with the years what was between them grew tenuous, my safety net, I discovered, was made of diamond shapes of nothingness, but ever since I came here— perhaps because of the colors of the sounds, the colors of the light, the smells, many things have come back to life, returned from words to sights: the darkness that turned transparent gray, diluted by a distant light, come, says Giora, not yet, I try to draw the moment out, losing everything, we'll both be lost, he said. Behind him widens a clear silver sky with strips of gray cloud. The people in the sleeping bags look like lumps of basalt. In a minute there'll be coffee to wake the dead, says Giora, he's already started the fire, the smell is already rising, purple-brown, pungent, I skip from foot to foot, hugging myself, *if I am not for myself who will be for me*, I feel cold, miserable, in a minute, in a minute, his voice is tense, as if I pressed him to hurry up. He raises his eyes to me, two little fires dance in them; here you are, he pours the coffee into a wide-lipped little cup without a handle, drink and you won't be cold, he pours himself a cup too, I take a sip with pouting lips—the sugar does nothing to alleviate the bitterness. Ah! Giora relishes his handiwork, peeps at me from behind his cup. It's bitter, I say. Shrew, he smiles, showing his canines, and before I can protest: I adore shrews—

"What are you doing?" Ora's on the phone. A teacher on vacation over Hanukkah, but she's busy, things to do, arrangements to make, she hardly has time to breathe. And what am I doing. Very little, to tell the truth.

Yesterday, for example, I decided that I could no longer stand the pyxis on the shelf in the Biedermeier next to the alabaster figures, the seals, the coins, Gulliver among the Lilliputians, I carefully opened the glass door and moved it to the gluing room. I put it down in a flat, open wooden box, among the potsherds which no one would ever put back together as a lamp or a chalice or a jar. But there too it is too big, blunt, demanding attention, in other words, a final solution. You can be as angry as you like, but who bequeathed me this last task if not you, and what is it if not a punishment. Afterwards I went to lie down in the hammock; you don't need wings in order to move from place to place. You can just lie on your back and let the clouds, the wind, the birds, be, pass by, and suddenly discover that for long moments you weren't there, you were wandering through unexpected mazes of memory, careful of the Minotaur—

"So come to me for the third night tomorrow at six—"

Why not? In for a penny, in for a pound—including the Hanukkah lamp, the candles, the potato pancakes, the songs—I arrive at six on the dot, but everything is still in the process of coming into being: Motik has gone to fetch his grandmother, Yinon isn't back from soccer yet, Gili is still on his way home from his base, and Ora sits me down in the kitchen, red and white in a jolly Italian style, and fries potato pancakes. I page through a book of drawings to the homeroom teacher Ora from grade 3A. It's a long time since I saw children's drawings and I can't decide whether to admire them or not; I look at the names of the artists under the pictures of Hanukkah lamps, oil jars, and burning brands. Children have different names today: not a single Danny. Not a single Yoram. Not a single Zvika or Dalya. Dotan—Omri—Ahaz—the names of those who did-evil-in-the-sight-of-the-Lord, I wonder if there is an Ahab or Jezebel too, no—but there is a Hiram, the King of Tyre's name is writ bold above a red-and-yellow top, a girl named Kinneret has drawn Judah Maccabee with an oil jar in one hand and a pistol in the other while Sahar's picture blazes with burning torches like the ones it always rained on in our Hanukkah processions, marching through the wind and the mud to the classroom shining in the distance with its stained-glass windows made of black Bristol paper and colored cellophane. "I'm going to change." Ora leaves a moment before the door between the two kitchens opens and Mechora enters, smiling with gleaming dentures. "Shalom Loya—what are you looking at? That was a present to Orinka from her pupils." She approaches the table, sits down opposite me. "Orinka is very well liked both by the pupils and teaching staff, soon she will be appointed to the post of headmistress—but she must have told you that herself—no? Nu, she's modest. Perhaps too modest. We did not bring her up to boast of her talents—and perhaps we were wrong—what do you think? Did we do right or wrong?" leaning over the table towards me. "Actually Ora—" "Yes, yes, I know. Exceptionally gifted. The best student in the school. In the army too she was outstanding—" "I remember that—" "Yes, yes, I'm sure that you remember. The headmistress, Dr. Hermona Shealtieli, constantly sang her praises. And now Orinka herself will be a headmistress—it isn't easy, two sons in the army and Yinon so mischievous—have you met my grandchildren?" "Mo-ther!" Ora rescues me from her, and the front door opens to Motik's thundering "Hel-lo-o!" He's here and so is his grandmother. "Ninety-three years old," Ora whispers in my ear. "And who's this?" the grandmother approaches me, thin like me, inquisitive to the point of sniffing. "This is Loya, my good friend—" "And I'm Gertrude," she offers me a shriveled hand in a grip from which only Motik extricates me, shepherding her into the living room, into an armchair. "A German Jew, *yekketa*!" Ora's mother whispers to me. "From Berlin," whispers Ora. "That makes a difference?" "It explains—" says Ora, indicating the trim, upright old lady looking alertly around her. "Is Avi coming?" she asks. "Motik's brother," whispers Ora, and the door opens again and Yinon bursts in—

The days are shorter, but toasted, almost crumbling in the light. "Israeli winter," says Amitai who now comes every day to the strawberry field to bring workers and supervise them. Between the beds new birds hop on long thin legs; their breasts are black and white and their folded wings a smoky cinnamon, their fastidious steps remind me of Monsieur Hulot in the film *Mon Oncle*, but Amitai throws stones at them and adds a string of energetic curses for good measure. "They look for worms and ruin my strawberries," he grumbles in reply to my "What do you think you're doing?"

In the evening I go to visit Adriana in her rented penthouse in a new eight-story building that went up after they demolished the old, low buildings typical of Rasco Housing C. Adriana. Bilu and Anat too. She's cute—plump with white skin, curly hair, and wide blue eyes, she reminds me of Hedva, and he's different-different-different, paunchy, balding, intolerably sweet. "How long do you think you can go on sitting in that old ruin of Davidi's and counting birds?" Adriana shakes her splendid head from side to side. "I'm starting a course in Numerology soon. Every Monday from nine to midnight—want to come?" Adriana has also studied palmistry and astrology and Tarot cards, Bilu explains to Anat without a trace of irony, remarking that it all began after the Six-Day War, when she held a seance and Dudu from the parallel class who was killed on the Canal and Kobi from the class above us who fell in Jerusalem answered all the questions, Adriana nods, what am I doing here, they've all turned into complete pagans—the wall is festooned with bronze, silver, ceramic Hamsa hands against the Evil Eye. "Aren't you afraid to sleep alone in that house?" Anat turns to me, "What's there to be afraid of—" I shrug my shoulders. "Don't you read the papers?" Here it comes, fortunately at that moment Tikva comes in with her husband, Kobi, pleased to meet you, a good-looking version of Enrico Macias. "Tikva says you didn't want to meet her cousin, a real shame, a wonderful guy, you want to know my rule?—pay attention now—Kobi's rule: never say no. A single woman—at your age?—don't say you don't need anyone, I don't buy it, I simply don't buy it—you don't know what you need—listen to what Kobi says: don't turn up your nose at anyone—so you were a flight attendant, so what, what's a flight attendant today, a flying waitress, no? Yes sir, no ma'am, once they only took beauty queens, now they're not so fussy, and what I say is—anyone who serves the public should look presentable at least—no?" Bilu looks at him disapprovingly, Adriana with a faint smile, but Anat nods, and Tikva fishes a little phone out of her Gucci bag, taps a number and murmurs, "I'm just phoning home to see if my mother's back from the cemetery—" which gives Kobi a new impetus: "She's incredible, that woman, incredible. Forty-five years—and every week at the cemetery; brings him flowers, tells him her troubles—I'm telling you—love like that doesn't exist in our generation, it just doesn't exist, even Tikva and me—if I died Tikva would visit me in the grave for forty years? Where from! There aren't any women left in the world like our mothers—" he looks around for agreement, Adriana smiles, Bilu smiles, Anat smiles too, they all had wonderful mothers. "Mother isn't back yet," Tikva announces in a tense voice. "I'm going to drive in the direction of the cemetery, she must have missed the bus—" "I'll come with you!" I decide on the spot and a corridor, elevator and five minutes later we're in Tikva's turquoise car, on the way to the cemetery.

Tikva drives slowly, close to the pavement, she asks me to scan the pavement on the other side of the street. A fine rain is falling, glittering in the lamplight. "Your father is buried there too," Tikva gives me a reproachful look, "have you been to visit his grave?" "No—" "You really are screwed up—" She looks away from me, at the pavement. "Tikva. Do you believe that your father is lying there under the tombstone, listening to everything your mother has to tell him?" I attack. "You know how many times I've told her to take a taxi, but she says no, it's a waste of money—" "Do you believe that?" I insist. In the deceptive yellow light of the street lamps, pavements, low stone walls, hibiscus hedges flit past. A few people with their collars turned up. A little girl with braids on skates, taking no notice of the drizzle, smiling to herself, suddenly reminds me of the Ora who no longer exists except in my memories. And maybe hers. "Why shouldn't I believe it?" Tikva mumbles, "the person dies—but the soul—" She stops with screeching brakes, "here's Mother!" and turns around to open the back door. "What happened to you?" she scolds her mother who squeezes in, wet, lumpy. "Never mind, my eyes, never mind," Tikva's mother settles herself on the back seat, "I had a long talk with your father, may-he-rest-in-peace. He said you mustn't despair. Everything will come right in the end. And I say so too. You must never despair. In the end everything will come right—right, Loya?" I want to say, "Come off it." But I compromise with "Maybe."

First they stretched transparent pale blue polyethylene over the beds; afterwards, like patches of color, Arab women bent over in the furrows between the beds and tore the sheets in order to let the leaves of the strawberries breathe. Then Amitai came with a few workers and stuck slender iron hoops into the ground over each bed and covered them again with fresh sheets of polyethylene, arched by the hoops, easy to open, all this was explained to me by Amitai, the strawberries grew between plastic and plastic, almost without contact with the soil, clean, ready to eat—

I walk between the beds that have been exposed today to the mild sun, see the leaves, always in groups of three—here and there a flower with a lemon heart or a half-red strawberry, big and firm as if made of wax, springs out, and between one plant and the next the earth chokes on big damp clods—at the end of the rows the citrus grove awaits me. The last rain has refreshed it. The ground between the trees is covered with a green down—when I returned to Adriana—Kobi came down, took my place in the car, shook his finger at me "Remember what I said"—Bilu and Anat had already left and Adriana showed me her apartment—this is her room and this is Sharon's and this is Natalie's, she likes to read, I fixed this up for her like you used to have, she opens the door to a little room, mauve-pink-white, a bed whose cover matches the curtain, a small desk and above it—a blue felt board on which epigrams and aphorisms are pinned with colored tacks, Adriana smiles, "Nice, no?" and I am alarmed; how could it have been wiped out of my memory to this very minute, the green felt board over my desk on which Daddy would change every few months the epigrams pinned to it, *Dum spiro, spero*, where there's life there's hope, and next to it *Sic itur ad astra*, thus one ascends to the stars, and in the middle an exhortation that stayed there for a particularly long time, *Festina lente*, make haste slowly, and beneath it *Timeo Danaos et dona ferentes*, which you used to hum in a synagogue chant whenever Shlomi's mother arrived with compotes and preserves, and on top of them all, in fancy print letters *Historia magistra vitae*, history is the teacher of life—What do you think? asked Adriana, what could I answer her, you can't step into the same river twice, in spite of your will, which sent me, as in a game of Monopoly, back to square one, to advance again step by step, to sell houses, plots, to fall into the hands of the police, to go to jail for speeding for two turns, to see all the other players passing me on the way to victory—the end was the victory, if you hadn't brought me back I would be in Boston now, perhaps sailing on Hedva and Leibo's yacht, certainly not here, on the edge of the grove, on the border of the plot, which is deserted but for the Monsieur Hulot birds, stepping delicately on their long legs, leaving a fine trace of footprints—but what's this—on some of the strawberry beds the print of rough steps, someone human was in a big hurry here, fleeing, chasing, trampling, perhaps you know what happened here, I ask the birds, but they are indifferent, your thoughts, complains Hedva, stray, you're running away, said Brenda, simply running away, whenever something important or painful turns up you switch channels, once in my life, I told Jean-Jacques, who also had complaints of the same nature, once in my life I got on a train and rode to the last station—and that was enough—but Jean-Jacques didn't want to hear anything about trains travelling to the last station and Eliot was actually in favor: Why suffer? Suffering shortens life, and he had decided to live like a Balkan peasant to a hundred and twenty and then to place himself in the hands of a company that froze bodies, should I register you for the program too, Loya? Loya? Loya! On the far side of the plot, next to the palms, someone small is waving energetically, calling me, Amitai? Amitai? I need glasses! "Loya! Come at once!" he shouts from there, I stay where I am on the edge of the grove, asking with hand gestures what it was all about, and he shouts and comes closer with big strides, suddenly stops, illustrates his intention with a brisk arm movement like a tank commander signalling to his forces in a movie "Move your ass already!" he yells at the top of his voice, ah, Mister Hummus, Israeli to the marrow of his bones, crude, boorish, rough, growling good intentions, knowing best about everything, I advance towards him at a leisurely pace, balancing in the furrow between the beds, what's happening, what can happen already, there's nowhere to fall from, nowhere to crash onto, no fire or flood in sight, "Faster! Run! Run!" he waves his arms. "You want me to trample your strawberries?" I yell back at him. "Never mind, run already, run!" and now he's next to me, grabbing my hand, pulling me, almost dragging me to the end of the plot, to the palms, over the petunia bed, under the ficus, to the house. "Did you lock the door?" "No I didn't, I only went out for ten minutes—" He flings open the door, shoots a quick look into the kitchen, pulls me there, commands, "You stay here now. Don't move," organizes his belt, feels his waist behind his back, straightens his shoulders and enters the living room like Daniel going into the lions' den. "Will you please tell me what's happening here?" I have no intention of standing still and keeping quiet, I follow him, watch him walking around the living room, checking the shutters, the windows, he peeks under the sofa, suddenly opens the porch door, closes it, locks it and locks it again, pushes a chair to the door, tips it and shoves the top of the backrest under the handle. "What are you doing?" I demand, but he's already in the passage, flinging open the door to the toilet, the bathroom, struggling with your door, Nahum's door, "Those rooms are locked!" "When did you lock them?" He's gone mad, he's preparing a massive shoulder to break the door down. "I haven't opened them at all yet—" I cry, he flings open the door to the gluing room, almost falls headlong into it. "Be careful!" He shoos me away from the door, shifts papers, books, looks under the table, touches the pyxis, opens it, "What is this pot?" I rush in to stop him. "Okay, okay—" he gives up, grips my wrist roughly, pulls me out, glances briefly at Bar Kokhba, Bethar, and company again and closes and locks the door. "Why don't you tell me what you're looking for—I'd be happy to help," I go back to being a flight attendant taking care of a disturbed passenger. "A telephone—" his eyes dart around. "In the living room—didn't you see it?" I precede him, reach the telephone, pick up the receiver. "And now will you please tell me what's going on here, who's dead—" "You, stupid, you—" he snatches the receiver from my hand, dials 100, asks for the duty officer, phones the Civil Guard, the Local Council—his worker has disappeared, he may be connected to the murder, the householder (me?) is here next to me, she's all right, no, he isn't in the house, the house has been checked, he has a pistol, only now I notice it, under the shabby sweater, he's staying here, but they should send reinforcements immediately—a commando in the reserves, I bet myself, I've become an expert in the genre, I recognize them the minute they step onto the plane, pantherish, like coiled springs, looking around them, always suspicious of a few passengers, whispering to the male flight attendant, pushing their way to the cockpit—one of them once overcame a character who went beserk before the security man had time to move from his seat—"Amitai," I try to sound patient and amused, a tried and tested panic-killer, "perhaps you will be so kind as to explain to me who murdered who, when, and why precisely here?" But Amitai walks past me on his way to the front door which he locks twice after which he stands in front of the padded jackets and examines them. "How many parkas were here? Three?" "Four," I know, I counted them, but Amitai folds his arms opposite the evidence: "Three!" "Then perhaps I was wrong—" I shudder. Someone was here, entered the house and stole—out of all the antiques worth a fortune—an old parka? "You have cupboards here—" Amitai walks around the kitchen, opening the cupboards, the pantry. "Are you looking for a mouse?" I try to sound indifferent, almost mocking, but he ignores the act, sits down at the table, takes out his pistol, puts it down on the table in front of him and announces, "Coffee. Now you'll make us coffee and I'll sit here with you and wait for the security forces—" I put the kettle on to boil. The world will collapse—and there'll always be someone who'll ask me for coffee. "Perhaps you'll take me into your confidence in spite of everything and tell me what happened?" "Don't you read the papers?" Good morning. No, no I don't read the papers. "Did you listen to the radio this morning?" "The radio here is half-dead, it works when it feels like it." "You live without a radio? Haven't you got a transistor?" It was as if he was asking if I lived without air. "What's so funny? There are all kinds of bad people wandering around here. The Islamic Jihad. The Hamas. Izza el Din el Qassam." "*Fedayoun*—" I contribute, but Amitai doesn't even smile. "Where have you been living? They murdered someone two days ago here at the junction. Yesterday the security service came and arrested two of my workers. The third one ran away. I was instructed not to move around the area unarmed—" He doesn't touch his coffee. He stands up, peers through the kitchen window, sees a naked pomegranate tree, behind it bougainvillea, glances at his watch with an expression of how-long-does-it-take-those-bastards, "What exactly is the 'area,'" I try to clarify, "your strawberry beds? My citrus grove?" But Amitai does not consider my question worthy of a reply. He picks up his pistol, looks at me. "Do you know how to use this?" "No, certainly not, take it away—" He cocks his head and now I too hear sirens in the distance, hysterical, piling up on top of each other, getting closer and louder, "When I was walking in the citrus grove a couple of weeks ago there was the smell of a carcass—" I suddenly remember, "Why didn't you say something?" Amitai jumps up, the sound of the sirens outside is joined by the sound of screeching brakes, running feet, dogs barking, "They're here!" Amitai turns the key and commands, "Lock it behind me. And lean a chair under the handle. And find yourself somewhere to hide, for God's sake, you shouldn't be here at all, I was sure you'd been told—" and leaves. And I lock the door behind him once hard and once soft and one more half-turn and I still can't grasp how suddenly, in the middle of everything, in the middle of a little walk, in the middle of a partly cloudy winter day, and where, right here, in your house, on our own block, in the middle of the state—from outside heavy footsteps. Shouts. The chirping of radio transmitters. Barking voices. Running. Panting. "Moishe-Moishe" repeated at high frequencies, "Do you copy? Do you copy?" Security forces surround the house, trample the flower beds, I go to the living room, excited hiding-away butterflies are going wild in my throat, my chest, but your house is too big to be a hidey-hole, a nutshell, and I raise the slats of the shutter, peep into the garden. "Lady! Get inside! This isn't a movie!" a border policeman barks at me and slams the slats down with his hand from outside. Unbelievable—all about the storm rages, and I stand in the living room and look around me—the walls are far away, Niles and Danubes branch out in the white-wash, behind the glass in the Biedermeier little Canaanite gods look back at me—hide somewhere, but where? Under the sofa there's no room for anything but a cockroach, under the table in the gluing room—no, there's no room there because of the drawers and it's too exposed as well, I seem to have lost the talent for folding up like a Swiss pocketknife—I go to the kitchen, take the bread knife out of the cutlery drawer, wrap it up, for some reason, in a kitchen towel, what exactly I plan to do with it isn't clear to me, outside it's a little calmer, but more tense, like an ambush tightening around your house, but who are they hunting, me. I open the pantry—no room for anything to hide here but canned goods—but here!—I open the broom cupboard—how come I didn't think of it before—lucky I hung the floor rug outside this morning—I pull the door towards me—it has a handle on the inside too—your doing—you were thinking of Malina, I'm sure, be-hind a double door, in a room opening from the depths of the wardrobe, families hid, strangled crying babies so they wouldn't betray them, some-thing like that happened in Nahariya too, when we handed out the paper in the plane a few of the passengers burst out crying—but it won't shut like this and if I take out the broom and the mop anyone searching will realize right away that someone has taken their place, I collapse onto the brush of the broom, feel the handle sticking into my back, hug my knees to my chin—the joy of concealment in small places sends a few peppermint but-terflies to my diaphragm, but my mouth is dry, my hands are frozen, my blood is roaring in my ears like the sea in a conch shell, the wrapped-up knife is squeezed between my knees, if anyone widens the slit of light into the kitchen I'll draw it immediately and aim it at him, but how exactly, one of my hands is pressing my knees to my chest, the other is stretched up, holding the handle, if anyone suddenly opens the door—I'll fall on top of him together with the broom and the mop and perhaps I'll be able to run a few steps to the living room, the passage, maybe the gluing room, climb onto the table, open the window and jump outside—the broomstick is pressing against my back, my hand holding the door handle has gone to sleep, I have to change position—one of my knees slips out of my grasp and touches the door which suddenly opens onto a dazzling kitchen— terrifyingly big—and I'm thirsty—thirsty as on Yom Kippur, what, in God's name, will happen if I emerge from this idiotic cupboard and fill a glass with water from the tap, get up, Loya, one-two-three-and, but I can't move—so at least shut the door again, disappear into the cupboard, be swallowed up by the wall like the stork in that Chinese legend—I can't move and outside there's someone desperate at the door, shaking the handle, pounding fists, maybe hitting with a hard shoulder, calling the others—now they're shouting back, "Moishe-Moishe it's okay" and again running around, the house is being attacked, right under my feet a continuous creaking, shaking—the sound of stones tumbling, soft stuffed objects falling and thudding—cut-off groans—the place I thought was ground full of tangled roots is nothing but a trembling black void, beating its fists to get out—I am no longer thirsty, no longer cramped, I no longer see, I am totally concentrated on what's happening under the wooden floor of the cupboard, you were sure it would happen to me in the air, especially after Nahum, don't listen to me, you hurled at me on the phone, what would you have said if you had known that here, here of all places, on the ground, in your house, in the broom cupboard they killed me because I couldn't cope with the knife. "Here! Over here! Did you catch him? Moishe-Moishe—" Right under my frozen backside—a scream, blows, thuds, dragging—"Get the demolition squad! Get the demolition squad!" the crackle of a transmitter, "Abutbul do you copy? Do you copy?" and running feet, "Everyone get the hell out of here!" and a very long silence and suddenly a loud banging on the door: "Loya! Loya open up, open the door at once! It's Amitai! It's over—they caught him! They caught him! You hear me, open the door and come outside immediately! They're checking to see if there's a bomb in your basement!" I try to say, I hear you, I'm not deaf, why are you shouting, but instead of words all that comes out is a croak. I stretch one leg. The door opens, the wrapped knife drops, could I have stuck it into someone, not even into a cat, not even into a rat. I stretch the other leg—my legs are full of prickly soda—I hobble stiff-kneed to the front door, move the chair, turn the key, open the door—Amitai, who was leaning on the door from outside, almost falls on top of me—he pulls me behind him and runs towards the plot, where about thirty policemen and soldiers and a few men in civvies are clustered—someone says something metallic on a megaphone—next to the cypress a small group of men in civvies surrounding someone—small and thin like me, maybe a boy, maybe just built that way, they're the most dangerous, Eliot opined from the heights of his meter ninety-one, the Napoleon complex, he explained, check out generals, war heroes, actors—all of them short people who have to prove that they're a combination of Tarzan and de Gaulle, would I have been capable of sticking a knife into him if he had attacked me? They're hitting him there, I can see from here, a few hard slaps, a kick, "He's been living in your cellar for a few weeks," a police officer standing nearby informs me. "That's impossible," I protest, and remember the missing parka. "They found a whole stockpile down there—canned goods—candles—matches." "But have you checked when they're from? All that stuff may have been there from before he showed up at all—" "In a minute you'll be able to tell us whatever you know," the officer looks at his watch, from the other side of the house the demolition squad appear one after the other, wearing flak jackets and carrying little cases, "that's it, they're done, it's clean, we can go down—"

Surrounded by policemen and plainclothes detectives, I go down to your basement. I was here only once before, immediately after it was built in 1957, after the retreat from Sinai. As far as I remember it was a big, dark concrete room, with a small air shaft which could also be closed and sealed, a toilet corner and a sink. The rags on the mattress are not familiar to me, but here's the parka, and the mattress—an antique—one of the policemen lifts it with the toe of his shoe. "Yes, I remember the mattress, it was here before," but not the gray metal shelves or the cans lined up on them—corn, peas, olives, carrot cubes, tuna, Spam, pickled cucumbers, sauerkraut, pineapple chunks in syrup—and also matches, candles, batteries, rolls of toilet paper, mineral water, a dusty suitcase which the policemen take for a forensic examination. "I'm sure that's his," I try to get my hands on your suitcase. "Whose? The former owner?" asked the police officer. "Yes, I'm sure." "Just to be on the safe side we'll take it nevertheless, and you'll get it back safe and sound after it's been examined—" the policeman gives the suitcase to one of the men in plainclothes, apparently from the secret service, who disappears with it, my eyes fall on a first-aid kit, did you know about our hideout at the edge of the block, is that why you were so generous, without asking too many questions, with matches, rags, nails, empty bottles, because you too had organized a survival bunker here—the door is wide open, but the police officer trains his flashlight on the walls, the ceiling—rough concrete, still preserving the lines of the beams supporting it, and in the corner—what's that?—almost hidden from the eye, painted gray for camouflage, an escape hatch opening upwards straight into the broom cupboard; how did you think you were going to climb up there? There's a little ladder under the sink—"And you didn't hear anything?" the policeman asks for the third time. "Judging by what he left behind he must have been here for about three weeks—" He pokes the pile of rubbish in the middle of the floor with his shoe—empty cans, squashed, empty mineral water bottles—"No, I didn't hear anything," what can I say: sometimes there was a sound of gurgling, bubbling, rustling, the snapping of old furniture. "You're one lucky lady," the sergeant accompanying him says to me, but their superior officer waiting for us outside isn't so sure—"Ma'am. Take a change of clothes and a toothbrush, you're coming with us—we have a few questions to ask you—"

It's happening, I pinch myself to make sure that it's happening, even though it can't be, it can't be happening, it isn't me sitting here in this little room, if aliens had abducted me for a visit to Mars, if I had been sucked into another universe in the Bermuda Triangle it would have been more or less like what's happening now as I, in this little room, am asked, do you smoke? No. Do you want coffee? No, just water, thank you, opposite me a policeman, then an officer, then a plainclothes detective, ask me over and over again, how long have you been here, when did you leave, why did you return, do you have family, names please, and ID numbers and dates of birth if you remember, and the water? In a minute, just answer a couple of questions first—what is this? Am I under investigation? Are they depriving me of water? "I want to speak to my lawyer," I quote a thousand and one movies, who is your lawyer, Shmaryahu Betzer, all right, he'll be contacted and in the meantime before he gets here you can answer a couple of simple questions, like, for example, where were you born? In Venice. In Venice? As if people aren't born there, they only go there to sail in gondolas and feed pigeons. And when did you come to Israel, in January 1950, and where did you live before, in Haifa, until what year, until . . . '51, and where did you move to from Haifa, Rasco Housing C. Who moved, my father and me and Davidi, the one who left me the house, and Nahum, his son, can I have glass of water? Someone's gone to fetch it, I don't believe you, you know what, I won't answer any more questions before I get some cold water to drink, okay then, we'll wait, he sits opposite me in silence until a policewoman arrives with a thin plastic glass containing the kind of mineral water airline passengers are given to drink, what is this miserliness, isn't there any water left in the country? "Bring me a whole bottle," I order her from my chair, if everyone's gone crazy then why not me, the officer nods, gets up, leaves me alone in the room, I wait, remember that once, before the air-control course in the army, I was interrogated by— what was his name—Mishka from field security, we sat in a room on the base—the paper Daddy subscribed to for a few years bothered him, he asked a lot of questions about communism, but I laughed, the right one, and he was quite quickly convinced, he almost apologized, shook my hand, wished me success, warned me of course that not a word to anyone, even Daddy didn't know that the secret base was on the Carmel in Haifa, the entrance was from a side street, next to a monastery, a few antennas covered with camouflage nets were visible from below to anyone driving on the road who knew where to look and what to look for, but even so it was more logical than—a short man dressed like a civilian enters the room, he has a straight hairline from which springs rusty iron wool and eyes so sunken that it is difficult to make out their color or expression, perhaps this was the reason they had chosen him to interrogate citizens in shock, he holds out his hand for a short, dry handshake from the other side of the table separating us, Mike, he says, a false name, of course, I say mockingly, I know these types a little from the airline security, he doesn't react, what about the water, I demand, and where's my lawyer, one thing at a time, he smiles sourly, so you say you moved to Rasco in '51, yes, why are you asking me stupid questions about things that happened over forty years ago, we have our reasons, believe me, he tries to sound friendly, but I don't believe him, in the house in question, as I understand it, lived Barak Davidi and Nahum Davidi, and you lived on what street? Olei Hagardom, but they changed the name. Yes, yes, we know—he opens a little notebook— Gefen Street, who lived on Gefen Street? My father and I. And your mother?—What about her?—That's precisely what we'd like to know, he fixes me with a penetrating look, and waits, and I shrug my shoulders, if they intend to confuse me or break me or make me cry they don't know who they're dealing with, where's my lawyer, I fold my arms, Mike picks up the receiver of an internal phone, talks, puts it down, says, he's on his way, are you in touch with her? He suddenly shoots, oh sure, every day! I snap angrily, he's surprised, raises his eyebrows, at last I can see the color of his eyes, brown, you don't know how ugly that is, ginger hair with rusty eyes, I say to him silently, I wouldn't joke if I were you, he says in a stern voice, why joke, I mean it—I have a friend, Adriana Ferrera, she holds seances, after the Six-Day War she succeeded in conjuring up Kobi and Dudu, ask anyone you like, ask Bilu—he takes a pen out of his pocket—What Bilu?— Bilu Bilu—now he's sure that I'm lying, making fun of him, he purses his lips, in a minute he'll try another tack, he picks up the phone, asks for water for the lady, the same policewoman brings a half-empty bottle, "Saving money?" I say to her, drink straight from the bottle in big gulps, I'm thirsty, parched, Does the name Slansky mean anything to you? the secret service man suddenly shoots at me, the name sounds familiar but I don't remember, Dr. Vasco? Who? Mordechai Oren? Something to do with a trial? Yes. But what have all these questions got to do with me? You don't need to get upset, we're just exploring a few possibilities, you served in the army—he opens his notebook, flips a few pages, in an air-control unit, he lets me know that they know, and when you were in the army you kept in touch with all kinds of people? What exactly do you mean? Did you write letters? Of course I wrote letters. Who to, do you remember? Home, to Ora Berger, to Yosefa Minikovsky, to Adriana Ferrera, I could go on but he has apparently had enough, he takes a packet of cigarettes out of his pocket, is it all right with you if I smoke? Absolutely not! I am determined to make things difficult for him, not to ingratiate myself, he puts the packet back in his pocket, it's unopened, he had no intention of smoking, he just wanted to confuse me, you wouldn't believe it, I am already conducting a conversation in my head with Hedva beyond the ocean, an insane state, a police state, you've spent a lot of time abroad, he states, I nod, I was a flight attendant, did you visit many countries? I nodded. Did you go to Libya? Libya? Of course not! Algeria? No. Hungary? Once. Czechoslovakia? Not yet. Do you know Giora Bar-Netzer? I feel as if my face is on fire, I keep quiet, what is this interrogation all about, until Betzer arrives I'm not saying a word. You were in his kibbutz a month and a half ago, Mike gives me a penetrating look. I keep quiet. Let me give you a piece of advice, he leans towards me, his elbows on the table—I'm all ears—you're getting into deeper waters than you can imagine here simply because you refuse to answer elementary questions, I answered all your questions, sir. Have you visited Gaza? Hebron? Ramalla? I have never set foot in the territories, I assure him, and you know what? Not in Tel Aviv or Jerusalem either, for twenty-seven years I've only visited the airport and the Avia Hotel, and you know what? I was right! Where's my lawyer, I want to know, until he arrives I'm not saying another word—and I fold my arms and clamp my lips and he folds his arms and clamps his lips opposite me, and thus we sit for a minute, two minutes, until I see myself and can't believe that this is happening to me and bust into laughter that stops only when he says in a stern voice: "May I see your passport?" I take my passport out of my bag and he studies it chewing his lips. And then the telephone startles us both. He picks up the receiver. Says hmm. Hmm. Yes. Okay. Good. Then he looks at me. Memorizes me. Turns me into Mata Hari. "Good. We'll check out your version," he says in the end, and gives me back my passport. Can I go now? Yes, on condition that you sign here— he takes a form out of the briefcase standing on the floor—I undertake not to leave the country, to come in for questioning when summoned, to remain, of course, at the same address—I'm not signing! I say in the tone that would have elicited your "What-would-we-do-without-you-Goddess-Anat," it's a pity you're not here to see me now, looking the rusty-haired interrogator straight in the eye. "I demand to speak to my lawyer," I coolly repeat the text glibly recited by every gangster in the movies. "He's on the way," the detective leans back in his chair as if the interrogation is over and the making-friends is about to begin. Be careful, I warn myself, they've lost their minds here, and again the old black dialing phone rings, yes, bring him in, and a moment later Advocate Betzer is in the doorway, a mountain and not a man, flushed, sweating, a human samovar—

"What do you think you're doing!" he scolds the interrogator, extending his censure to the policewoman trying to squeeze past him; he blocks the way into the corridor. "We'll lodge a complaint, you won't get away with this—Miss Kaplan, come along!" And I get up and go into the corridor, where's the toilet, and Advocate Betzer is beckoned into the room, beckons me to wait for him, and three minutes later we're both on our way out—

"So am I at liberty? Can I buy a plane ticket and get out of here tomorrow?" I interrogate him in the car. "What's the rush?" Advocate Betzer drives carefully. "What did that detective say to you?" "They're conducting a complicated investigation—all kinds of old issues have surfaced—they've got that suitcase that they found—don't you want to get it back?" "Yes, but what has that got to do with the scrawny little creature they found in Davidi's basement?" "I'm surprised at you," Betzer turns a glinting lens in my direction, "an intelligent woman like you—apparently they suspect you of sheltering a terror suspect—he was hiding there for quite a few days, no? Maybe you invited him, maybe you supplied him with food—" "Me?" "I told them you were pure as the driven snow—that I can guarantee it—I told them about Davidi, about his will—by the way, have you thought about what to do with the—" "When did you have the time?" "They held me for questioning too—remind me—is it here? To the right?" And in front of the gate he asks, "Are you sure that you don't want to sleep at some friend's place or in a hotel?" "No, why should I? I'm going to take a big flashlight and go back to the bunker and maybe even sleep there—" but the police have locked the horizontal door hidden under a wave of honeysuckle with an enormous lock, glittering among the leaves. "Are they allowed to do that?" I ask Betzer. "Until the investigation's over," he follows me to the house. "That ficus." Yes, I know, I open the door, he follows me in, "I want to see with my own eyes that everything's all right," outside it's already twilight, I switch on the light in the kitchen, the living room, the gluing room. "You see—everything's all right," the phone rings, but Betzer grips me by the elbow. "You're not to say a word about what they asked you," I shrug my shoulders, Ora's on the phone. "Loya! How are you!" "Everything's okay, I'll get back to you in a few minutes." "So what are they looking for here?" I ask Betzer in parting without much hope of hearing anything new. "I assume," he says in an important voice, a courthouse voice, "that they're looking for collaborators." Collaborators. Traitors, Judenratniks. Kapos. Quislings. I thought that we had already left that station far behind us, but maybe we've been going around in circles. "Left-wing extremists," volunteers Betzer. "Jews?" I ask stupidly. "Does the name Udi Adiv ring a bell?" "But—" I begin to protest, give up, everything is so stupid, I don't care about that small, radical, left-wing group from '72. "Are you in favor of a Palestinian state?" the interrogator suddenly asked me. "I'm in favor of a Canaanite Empire from the Euphrates to the port of Carthage—" I wisecracked. "Where's Carthage?" surely he must have known, but it's a fact that he asked. "Do you know where Libya is?" "Have you been to Libya?" was the next question. And now Advocate Betzer glances around the living room again and sighs. "It will take a good few months before we'll be able to find a buyer—"

I beat off the press, shut myself away from the television, but against old friends I can do nothing but assure them that yes, everything's fine, and no, it wasn't as bad as it sounded, they were exaggerating, the newspapers always exaggerated, no, I didn't want to be interviewed, yes, it was over very quickly, the whole thing only lasted a few minutes, no, I didn't hear anything, thank you, I'm staying here, they locked the basement with seven locks, what can already happen, no, Amitai didn't save me, the paper made him out to be a hero? Good luck to him, no I didn't read it, why should I read it, I was right here, in the center of events, no?

Only to Ora who arrives with Motik "to be with you a bit after the shock" I show the broom cupboard where I hid without knowing, of course, that if the suspect had wanted to take advantage of the escape hatch you installed he would have come out through my bum, Ora doesn't even smile. "Were you frightened?" she examines the little cupboard, she thinks, I wouldn't have fit in, perhaps she even thinks, I wouldn't have hidden, she thinks, who knows what she's thinking now, "No," I lie, and she believes me, she doesn't sense anything, she drinks the tea I make her and tells Motik about the underground I organized for a few kids in the fifth grade, the initiation test, Motik listens with his arms crossed on his little paunch. "And is that what helped you now?" he asks in a too-loud voice, almost like the prosecutor in a court case. "No," I confess, "No—the strange thing is that," I begin, give up, but Ora won't let me, the old Ora comes back to us for a short visit, lays a gentle hand on my arm, "The strange thing is that—" she repeats the beginning of my sentence, urges me, without words, to go on, to get it out "to put it on the table," but I don't know how. "It's as if the whole thing never happened, not really." I try and fail and try again. "As if it was a kind of practical joke—" I fail and try again. "As if it was all happening but not to me, as if I was seeing myself acting in a movie that would soon end and then everything would go back to being—normal." I'm getting closer, Ora is leaning towards me, looking at me intently. "I couldn't even feel really frightened—it simply didn't seem real to me—it seemed like some stupid parody or something that couldn't happen. That simply couldn't be happening. Unreal—" Ora straightens up, turns her head to Motik who is still sitting with his arms crossed. "You know who Loya should talk to?" he addresses Ora but looks at me as if forming a diagnosis. "To Avi," they both say as one and smile as one. "Avi is Motik's brother," Ora finishes her tea, "he's a historian." Motik raises his tea to his lips, did my face betray something—"A historian of the Holocaust," he enlarges, and I breathe a sigh of relief—not the roots of Western civilization and not Bar Kokhba and his friends and foes, of those I have had quite enough. "When he did his doctorate, he went around here with a tape recorder—almost from house to house—" Ora gets up, glances restlessly at her watch. "How many years ago was that?" I ignore the signals, relying on the fact that Motik is still sitting in his place, he looks up at Ora. "Nine years? Ten?" Ora nods. "Did he talk to Hasia Horovitz?" I tense. "No, she died a few months before that, but it all began after her funeral, actually, when I told him about the shivah at Shlomi's— Shlomi's in New Jersey now, you know?" I know. "He left his father in an old-age home and went to Americhka to be a professor—there was an article about him a couple of years ago in *Haaretz*—" a trace of mockery in her voice and perhaps of envy. "You really must talk to him," concludes Motik and reluctantly joins Ora who is already standing at the door, obviously impatient, she's done her bit, and now home to bed—

Why must I talk to him? Will he record me on a little tape recorder, interrogate me like the prosecutor with the strange "r," why did you hide?

Did you think that hiding in the cupboard would save you? So what did you think during those minutes, describe to us what you were thinking, I wasn't thinking—in the middle of all the commotion I was a dead spot—Thank you. Your worship, the witness has concluded her testimony—

The keyhole of Nahum's room looks like the symbol of the goddess Tanit; armless, full of darkness, she waits for me to insert the key, easy to turn, and one more turn and I'll be inside the room which may not have changed since I remember it—

I didn't go to the funeral. Nahum was not supposed to be fished heavy and dripping from the blue grave of the Kinneret but to explode in the air into a rose of fire, like he said to me on that night after the flight that rescued me from the teeth of the neighbors, the policemen, the nurse, the rag-and-bone man, the boxes full of historians, Mommsen and Burckhardt and Gibbon and Niebuhr and Shirer and that Dutchman with the strange name, Huizinga, and the orange crates full of clothes papers pots and pans, come, I felt his hand on my shoulder, I'm taking her away from here, he announced and took me outside, I didn't ask where to, nor did the others, only Davidi shouted after us: Nahum! Nahum! And I'm already inside the army jeep and Nahum returns to the house for a minute and comes back and sits down in the driver's seat: Everything's all right, he says, satisfied, almost cocksure, and I lean against the windowpane, exhausted, finished, the jeep sways, rocks, I weep soundlessly onto the windowpane, but the movement of the vehicle and Nahum's blessed silence calm me. Where are we going? I ask half an hour later. Wait and see, Nahum sounds as if he's got a surprise up his sleeve and I can't imagine what until we park at the edge of a little airport and get out and approach a two-seater Piper—we're going to fly? I had never flown before, take me, I had often asked Nahum before, but I knew it was impossible, after the army, I promised myself, I'll work and earn money and I'll fly, at least once, at least to see what it's like, and now it's actually happening, Nahum helps me to climb up, and I'm excited, confused because suddenly I'm happy, almost jubilant, Nahum peeks over his shoulder at me before he begins talking into the radio, starts the engine, the little Piper shudders with excitement, strains, go, I address it silently, go! Go! Afraid it will die, give up, and we'll stay on the ground, but the runway rushes madly past under the wing, the plane shivers, roars, "Frightened?" shouts Nahum. "No!" I yell back, the plane runs amok in a frantic rush of metal and fuel to the limits of possibility—and then—it detaches itself from the curved surface of the globe, breaks the laws of gravity, confronts them with the other forces, of effort and will and in-spite-of-everything and to-hell-with-it, and Wow! I exult, I'm a kite, a bird, a cloud, and you stay here, I say out loud to the ground receding at a slant, from minute to minute growing smaller, more insignificant, like the shell of an egg I leave behind me the old house, the boxes of china and historians to the neighbors, to the rag-and-bone man, to Davidi, I want wings, maybe I won't be Amelia Earhart but I will be a flight attendant, why not, in a few months I'll leave Loya in cotton dresses and sturdy sandals behind me and turn into Catherine Deneuve in a tailored suit and high heels, every day I'll be able to look through the window and see everything from the perspective of a cloud—a shining brown string trimmed with green from which hangs a silver medallion shaped like a crinkled South America, and the string continues, but I turn to the West, the sea, all light, rises like a sheet of fire to our right, and then sand dunes, gray veins, here and there patches of pigmentation, the earth whitens, becomes mineral, all congealed peaks and mushrooms sculpted by the wind and the salt, glittering and breathing dense fumes smelling of sulfur and potassium, and here's the tip of another spectacular purple-turquoise medallion striped with white, salt! Nahum yells at me, from above the logic of the contours of the twists and turns of the silver road before they are ironed out into a gray strip is revealed, the gradual curving of surface of the ground, the topographical rhythms of the earth, fine, dazzled soil, rock-torn or salt-glazed, and here and there mangy trees, and a glittering lawn under the V of sprinklers, and again desert, but toasted, reddish, and here, already, one minute sapphire and the next sil-ver, the Red Sea, surrounded by sharply carved shaped mountains, pinkish, misty in the light, we've arrived! announces Nahum, and I protest, no, not yet, but we've come to the end of the country! Nahum shouts, busy with the landing—we're close to the ground; housing projects, wide empty streets, dust, scraps of paper, a few scrawny palms, no, no, no, no—and when we returned the house was empty and deserted, ready to be torn down.

A WINDOW IN WINTER

What if, we once had this game, what if Eve hadn't eaten from the tree of knowledge, if she had eaten from the tree of life—

We would have lived forever—

We would have met all the characters from the Bible in the street—Hi Moses, Hi Rachel—

What are you talking about. If all those characters from the Bible were alive they would be living in the President's house in Jerusalem—

Not in the President's house, silly, in the Temple!

And nobody would die any more—not Tikva's father not—

And not all my uncles from the Holocaust!

And not all of them from the flood! They would have swum and swum—

There wouldn't have been any need for Noah's Ark then—

And Cain wouldn't have killed Abel either—

It all gets more and more complicated—And all the stories where you cry in the end would have to be changed too, The Little Match Girl, The Happy Prince, Who is a Hero, The Call of the Wild, but if nobody ever dies where's the story, and anyway how would you win wars, the boys demanded, someone suggested that they could have fistfights, someone else suggested they could play something like "Sticking the Knife" but it was clear that it wouldn't work—

So let's say she didn't eat from the Tree of Knowledge but not from the Tree of Life either—Yosefa offers a magic formula.

Then they wouldn't have been banished from the Garden of Eden—

Then we would have been living to this day like Tarzan in the jungle—

And we wouldn't have to go to school—

And we wouldn't have any clothes!—cheers Bilu, whose mother as everyone knows showered with boys up to the age of sixteen because she was from a kibbutz and on the kibbutz they didn't make any difference between the sexes.

Would you agree to walk around without any clothes on?—Adriana whispers to me. The sentence seems to us too hard to bear, but the boys are jubilant—

We would see you! We would see you!

You wouldn't see anything!—Ora retorts—Because Eve did eat from the Tree of Knowledge—

And because of her we have to go to school—Bilu laments.

And on the second shift too—

The door to your room, Nahum, after so many years doesn't creak. A box of preserved air with a smell of dust and cold sheets and cracked wood—but I am already passing through this air like a knife through water and it closes behind me and presses at my sides and stands in front of me until I open the windows and the screens and the shutters and hasten to draw the curtains over the two squares of too-bright spring light outside, but it's winter now, it's winter.

The room is blue and trembling with airplanes: Dakota, Vautour, Black Spitfire, Super-Mister and Mirage, Sky Hawk, Phantom—I remember myself sitting with my chin resting on my fists, watching your blond fingers opening a box, sliding everything inside it onto the kitchen table—separating the parts with a light click—and almost without looking at the page of instructions fitting together fuselage, canopy, wings, how come you don't get mixed up, I ask or think, and you lift puzzled eyes to me, what's there to get mixed up about—in the wind swelling the curtains the old fighter planes move, among them a Messerschmitt and a Mig 19, and here's a Norad—the plane with a balcony, it's a paradrop aircraft, you already knew as a child, which made the balcony logical—I was sure that the parachutists had to step out and walk along it balancing themselves until they reached the middle and only then spread their arms and jump—this balancing act on a narrow strip in the middle of the sky was in my eyes an act of supreme Hannah-Szenes-like heroism. So how did you become a flight attendant, Jean-Jacques argued with the fact. In the air I don't have to jump from anywhere or walk on air, I explained, over and over, patiently, what should have been obvious. But the whole plane is suspended in the air! protested Jean-Jacques. It isn't suspended in the air—it's flying! But Jean-Jacques obstinately cut out from the newspaper items about plane crashes in the Philippines, Honduras, over the Indian Ocean, in Portugal, Japan—circling in red the words *no survivors*—there was no point in trying to tell him about the lift power you speak of, picking up a feather, ruffling it and combing it again, explaining how cleverly it is constructed to be part of the wing keeping the bird airborne, and once, one excavation Saturday, we raised our eyes from the sieve and the dust, and—Loya, you whispered to me, as if your voice might alarm them up there, and I sat up and then lay down next to you and saw how they drew receding transparent circles almost without moving their wings, until Davidi suddenly blocked out half the sky: You want an orange?

From the bed the airplanes look like fishes from the observation point of a drowned person—and the shelves—what have you got there—I get up—*The Little Prince* with a dedication in my youthful handwriting, "Antoine de Saint-Exupery is the first sentence you need to know in French," and here's *Cuore: The Heart of a Boy*, third edition—"This book is intended mainly for children from the ages of nine to thirteen," but Daddy gave it to me when I was six; how I loved those silky-gray illustrations—and the teacher's monthly stories—especially "Blood of Rome" with Giulio Ferruccio and his paralyzed grandmother and "From the Apennines to the Andes." In the nights I tried to gather courage, once I even stuffed some clothes into my schoolbag and emptied my piggy bank, but I didn't wake up from the alarm clock's ringing which was supposed to wake me at dawn in order to steal out of the house and hitchhike to Haifa, and there to smuggle myself onto a ship sailing to Italy, for example, and in reply to the question of an angry sailor or surprised captain as to what I was doing there etc. to answer with eyes full of tears (I had already practiced crying at will by remembering the puppy run over next to the meeting hall) I'm going to look for my mother—and how I regretted not having Shirley Temple curls which would have guaranteed the success of my ploy—who would dare to disbelieve Shirley Temple, who would dare to refuse her—and what is this in a cocoa brown cover? Nordau's *Legends* falls open of its own accord at story number 16, "My child, replied the Children's Minister, the strings of the heart can never be cut, not by me nor by death itself," and this book too is mine, like *Pretty Butterfly Pray Fly To Me* with the vowel-pointed dedication in Daddy's copper-plate European handwriting, "To sweet Loya who can already read"—twenty-seven years after his death he is still talking to me in the third person, Loya, Loya, open the door, it's not terrorists, it's me, behind her the ficus is green-black and the morning light dappled with voices—three executioners holding an election meeting, mafiosi cutting across the air on urgent missions, sparrows coming and going, and on the telephone wire a humming bird turns into black jet—

"They're tearing down the house next door to you," Yosefa points to the empty house behind the ficus—when did anyone ever live there—she comes in, uninvited, her hands hugging her elbows, her eyes darting around, examining the walls, "It's full of cracks here too—haven't they come to you from the council yet? I think this house will have to be torn down too—look, look what it looks like—" she points the toe of her boot at a row of rising floor tiles, "It's cold as the grave in here. Aren't you cold? Let's go outside—bring chairs—" she goes out, looking around her, "Have you seen what's going on here?" "The ingathering of the exiles," I think she is referring to the birds, but she is referring to the ground, the plot, Amitai in the distance, the bright patches of the Arab women picking the strawberries—"Who would buy this house from you?" Yosefa abandons herself to the mild winter sun with her eyes closed, "but the land—do you know that you're sitting on one thousand two hundred meters?" "Here's Amitai," I change the subject, Yosefa opens murky blue eyes, claps her hands. "Amitai the hero—we read about you in the papers!" Amitai comes closer, he is holding a white Styrofoam box full of fire-colored fruit. "Amitai—this is Yosefa—" I stand up. "Good," he isn't impressed, pushes the box into my hands. "Go and wash them and bring plates and sugar. And cream, if you have any. And spoons." He sits down in my place, stretches out his legs. "And bring yourself a chair!" Mister Hummus in every fiber of his crude, patronizing, self-satisfied being—I return with the washed strawberries in two saucers, sugar, two teaspoons, two paper napkins, a container of cream, all on a tray. (I have to get rid of a few flight-attendant habits as soon as possible!) "I'm just giving her something to do," says Amitai from the depths of his round cloth hat, he doesn't know that I'm standing behind him, listening—there were two or three like him on every flight—giving us something to do as if they were doing us a favor—Yosefa sprinkles sugar on her strawberries, takes each strawberry between two silver-nailed fingers, sucks it between dry lips and then licks the pink sugar off each fingertip and nail, "Ah, that's good—why don't you bring yourself a chair?" "Never mind, let her stand—" Amitai finishes the strawberries and cream he has organized for himself, plants the saucer in the grass and wipes his mouth on the back of his hand—

"I'm off," he stands up, his face to the strawberry beds shining in the sun, "Goddamn birds," he bends down to look for a stone, fails to find one. "Your strawberries are delicious"—Yosefa says flatteringly to his back, "You have to know how to grow them," he is already on his way, talking as he walks, he doesn't even take the trouble to cast a backward glance over his shoulder. "What a hunk," says Yosefa aloud, apparently intending him to hear, I shrug my shoulders, "So you waited for the terrorists with a knife in your hand?" she peeks at me over the tops of her Jackie O sunglasses that have come back into fashion, I keep quiet, what can I say, that I hid in a cupboard with my back to a broom like someone from the camps, we used to say that about Minaleh, "How's Minaleh?" I move to sit in the vacated chair. "Oof—I haven't got the strength for her troubles now," Yosefa sighs, "but Adriana and Ora are sure to know—" she stands up, stretches. Long, lean, dried up. "They'll build a four-story building here—" she points to the area beyond the mane of the ficus. "Are you sure you don't want to sell the land?"

I go back to the blue room. In your not-large wardrobe there's enough room—with a squeeze—for my not-many clothes—how many months have you been here and you don't even leave your toothbrush in the glass when you leave, complained Jean-Jacques after three months, four months, eight months, a year—do you miss my toothbrush? I tried not to understand what he meant to say. Eliot actually liked it, he would leave me the keys to the apartment in Toronto, the apartment in New York, impossible to tell you were here, he would say—and now I revert to my old ways: go barefoot, eat with my hands, heap clothes on armchairs that sometimes turn into a pair of Cerberuses at night—

So should I move your checked shirts aside and hang my clothes up next to them? What do you say? Okay. I'll decide. For over a quarter of a century I've been deciding on my own what to do and what not to do, and my decisions oblige nobody but myself. "Free as a bird," Hedva's mother called this state of affairs on the one and only occasion when Hedva succeeded in dragging me to see the famous attic and the wedding gown that visited the dry cleaners every year before Passover. Doesn't it make you want to get married? Hedva stroked her wedding dress and smiled at me, it even makes me want to get married again—why should she get married? Hedva's mother intervened, and Hedva exclaimed: did you hear her? Lately she's turned into a wild woman, what's happened to you, Mommy—and Hedva's mother—Rica—glanced at her watch and invited us to join her and her friends for coffee and toast and talking about life; Talma was widowed two years ago and Pesia a year ago and Mira was born a widow and there's only one really fresh one, Hayuta—Did you see them? Hedva couldn't get over the meeting even when we were already back in the air—I've known them all from before I was born, and believe me—their husbands kicked the bucket and it took twenty years off their age—it must be because of the restoration of their energetic aura, Hedvaleh—I referred to the latest best seller from which she had been quoting pearls of idiocy at every opportunity for the last few months—I mean it seriously! Hedva was almost offended— Every twenty, twenty-five years, we change; for the first twenty-five we're— lettuce salad with lemon? I stole a culinary metaphor from Jean-Jacques' stock; and for the next twenty-five years, continued Hedva—meatballs and mashed potatoes? I suggested, and Hedva cocked her head, considering: Could be, could be—so what are your mother and her friends? *Kaffee-mit-Schlagsahne*—Hedva did a brilliant imitation of a German accent—and in the end?—After pondering this difficult question, I suggested finishing off with cheese: In the last twenty years we'll turn into Roquefort or white Bleu-de-Auvergne with blue veins, we'll stink to high heaven—No, Hedva laughed, in the last twenty years we'll turn into meat aspic—having once eaten this horror at Ora's I said, without garlic, I hope—

So should I hang my clothes up next to the clothes that have remained empty of you, perhaps suffering from phantom pains, who was it who told me about them, Brenda—I was once a nurse, so you'd better believe me—it was hard to imagine a nurse's uniform closing around her—the part amputated, she related, hurts more than the stump left—So Trumpeldor was even more of a hero than they told us, I couldn't resist saying, and Brenda asked "Trumpel-who?" and I told her about the one-armed hero and his famous last words about how good it is to die for your country, and also what my father said: He didn't invent it—see the Iliad, book 16—

So. Now my clothes hung next to yours, black silk blouses next to your Marlboro-Man checked shirts, did you want to be like him?—Perhaps—in any case you deserved to look like him, you, who were a *Corvus albus*, a white crow, odd man out—how easy to say to a closet full of empty shirts—

Both for Jean-Jacques and Eliot I bought checked shirts. There's no one like the Marlboro Man, the saleslady smiled at me. He's got cancer, you know—said Eliot as he buttoned the shirt which was too small for him even though I bought extra-extra-large—the cigarettes—Eliot never touched cigarettes, he was no less afraid of dying than Jean-Jacques, who was actually afraid of living—you were in another league, but you didn't have a choice: Davidi brought you up not to be afraid of anything—to survive in every situation—what was he, your father, apart from everything we know: an avenging partisan and a Canaanite and a robber-archaeologist and an inventor of Hebrew words and a writer of angry letters to the newspapers and an assaulter of dog owners and Public Works Department workers, what was he under all that? You said to me more than once "We should have switched fathers—" it's true that he never shouted at me, except for that one time and then you yourself came to rescue me and the neighbors held him back—when we returned from Eilat he didn't speak to me, he hardly spoke to you, he told you to tell me that there were a few boxes waiting for me here, and I took some clothes and a photograph of people on a dig with Giora's face the size of a pea, and to this day I'm still living out of suitcases—

It didn't take long; my clothes next to yours like Mili Bilu's clothes next to Bilu Bilu's, brother and sister in the same room, what's there to be ashamed of, said Bilu's mother who grew up on a kibbutz and showered with the boys to the age of sixteen, she buttonholed me once for an educational talk, I was waiting for Bilu to return from the Sick Fund clinic in their puritanical living room on a high bed instead of a bourgeois sofa that left my feet dangling in the air. Shame is a bourgeois emotion, lectured Bilu's mother who had beautiful blue eyes and a long, unmotherly braid. When we were in the underground I suspected her of being a phony mother, maybe a spy; she didn't look like mothers and she didn't behave like mothers, she wore short gathered pants in the summer, and from behind, because of the braid, she looked like a schoolgirl, and she had fervent, half-baked opinions, as if she were still in the youth movement, the way she talked reminded me of Ora, what was her name—it didn't sound like a mother's name either, it was Michmoret, but Bilu's father called her Miki, which was definitely a boy's name, or a dog's, and her sister from the kibbutz was called Ze'eva, a she-wolf—

My clothes next to your clothes almost like Bilu and Mili, we said, brother and sister and father and father, a family for outings on holidays and Saturdays—here's *A Thousand and One Ways to Make a Kite*—Hold it, you would ask me, hold the string—putting a thick ball in my hands, taking the kite and running uphill or downhill—Let the string out, let the string out! you would yell at me in the distance, and sometimes you would come back running yellow and pink, take the ball away from me, scold, you nearly let it get away, you nearly let it fall, and demonstrate, with vigorous movements, how to persuade the paper diamond with the tail to fly higher, higher, and I was too hot or too cold, usually too hot, and my eyes hurt from the light and I wanted Daddy or Davidi to finish investigating the bunker tunnel or the burial cave and call us to come and see, the tunnel was a place to relax in after the heat and dust outside, it was always cool and dim and full of the smell of wet sheets, when they called us I would hurry first, you would stay behind to bring in the kite, to stand guard at the opening against inspectors, grave robbers, Bedouin, policemen, Arabs—I was sure that you, together with our fathers, had invented it in order to spice those Saturdays with fictitious dangers—I knew the three of you had secrets—I never imagined that we were really breaking the law; everything was so neglected at the places we went to, so uninteresting to anyone except for us—once they found a burial cave filled up with earth, they dug and cleared and cleaned and called us to see the wonderful paintings on the ceiling, the paintings were fragmented, faded, parts of jars, parts of animals—Nahum! I called you from a triangular burial alcove, but you stopped close to the opening and asked what in your eyes was darkness and in mine was us inside a kind of damp painted passage—How do we get out of here if it collapses?—It's been standing for over two thousand years, and suddenly in your honor it's going to collapse? Davidi was angry and Daddy proposed that we all get out, but then

Davidi's miner's flashlight lit up a Greek inscription, and I went out to you and the two of them stayed to decipher it and came out very excited, Daddy's notebook was full of beautiful Greek letters, and a few days later he handed them to me translated into scrupulously vowel-pointed Hebrew: "I can do nothing for you now, not even pleasure you, most dearly beloved. With another I now share my bed, although I loved only you. Your garment I still have with me as a token, oh Aphrodite, goddess of lovers, but I am absent. My soul has fled, and you are free to do whatever you wish. Do not beat the wall. Do not wake my death." I may have forgotten a line or two—so many years have passed since then; I can do nothing for you, that hasn't changed, most dearly beloved, neither has that.

I want to die like a meteor, you said when I told you about Arlozora's father—he died in the middle of a meal at a Romanian restaurant—fell face down into the okra—you wished yourself a death of light and cloud—you almost got your wish—and what's this—a picture—you meant to hang it up and you left it in the closet—a white astronaut standing on ground illuminated from the side, every little stone at his feet casting a sharp triangular shadow, Neil Armstrong is the distorted reflection in the visor of Aldrin's domed helmet photographed on the twentieth of June, 1969, on the moon, next to the date an exclamation mark in your hand—perhaps in self-reproach because someone got there before you—

How many stars are there in the sky, I asked Daddy on one of the Friday nights we spent outside, warming ourselves at a little campfire, sleeping in pup tents—me with my father, you with yours, and sometimes also the two of them in one tent and the two of us in the other—I waited for you to go to sleep first so you wouldn't find out that I snored—you would fall asleep immediately, wake up immediately, washed and dressed in a minute—and I always took my time—"Madam-wait-for-me" you and Daddy called me, and only Davidi related to my slowness in waking up with a kind of mocking indulgence, when I finally arrived he would turn to me with a smile—Glad you could make it, Goddess Anat! You want breakfast? We left you a little—how many stars there were in the sky Daddy didn't know. He sent me to ask your father. Davidi sent me to you, but the answer had to wait until Eilat—I heard you smile in the transparent whispers of that dry darkness—the little waves seethed on the sand—sand coarse with crushed stones—and the wind tossed ceaselessly among the palm fronds, and there was also a flag or a big shirt hung out to dry not far away, for sounds of wet flapping suddenly cracked and died down—How many stars are there, I asked you, and you clasped your hands under your head and blew your breath out, in which galaxy, you clarified, how many galaxies are there, and again a long exhalation into the whispering of the night, twenty million at least, and how many stars in each galaxy, ten to the power of ten, ten to the power of eleven, who can count them, whoever tries, and you raised yourself on your elbow and told me a strange story about a Tartar astronomer called Ulugh Beg who built an observatory in Samarkand and with its help composed a catalog of a thousand and sixteen stars but was murdered by his son before he succeeded in reporting everything he had seen—and I put my hands behind my neck and tried to count the ones you can see from here, not all of them are really blue, I suddenly discovered, good morning, there are all kinds of different types of stars, type A stars and type B stars, like blood types, I laughed, there are blue ones and red ones, like blood types, I laughed, what are you laughing at, what's so funny, you didn't know, and neither did I, there was nothing funny about that night, what exactly did happen then we can no longer clarify, not together—only Davidi was capable of producing a whole story from a fragment of an alabaster figure, a coin and a bead, *ex ungue leonem*, describing a lion from its claw, paleontologists construct an entire dinosaur from a single tail bone and a broken tooth, don't you believe me? Professor Kaplan, take the pest to the Natural History Museum so she can see with her own eyes, let her see with her own eyes, otherwise she won't be convinced—and he was right, of course. In the gluing room I saw him gluing together and filling in the missing parts of clay lamps, little figures, flasks—we were studying fractions at school then, and I found a name for the operation, the results—improper fractions, that only looked like the real thing. Although the fracture was real enough, it was only the repair that was virtual, only the filler was virtual—no, the filler was real too—but nevertheless—a piece from the present time was inserted to cover up a black hole from the past until it was impossible to tell the new from the old, I told Jean-Jacques who kept on quizzing me about my life up to him, with the curiosity of a vacuum cleaner he reached the corners that had always wanted to remain full of cobwebs, to be left alone, resurrecting and wondering, does it hurt? Does it still hurt? What are you doing, I would sometimes feel that it was enough, I'm studying you, he would reply, I'm much more interested in you than you are, he would sometimes scold me, you live very far from yourself, he once flung at me, what do you mean, I chose not to understand in order to avoid a quarrel, you live without rendering an account, who exactly am I supposed to render an account to, I, thank God, am an orphan from all sides, to yourself, Jean-Jacques whispered the word, almost shocked, I gave myself an exemption, I giggled, but Jean-Jacques had neither a sense of humor nor the ability to part from himself for even five minutes. As if you're afraid you won't find anyone there when you return, I once said to him, or you'll find someone else, you don't know how right you are, he was grateful for the diagnosis, it fueled the furnace of his thoughts for the ten days I was absent on a flight to London and New York, when I landed I saw him waiting for me at the airport, completely green. I suggested taking a vacation, hiring a car, getting lost among nameless villages, he agreed, and after completing all the arrangements he had three full suitcases—he took the whole house with him—he wasn't prepared to part from anything—he had suitable outfits for every place and every occasion—he wasn't a dandy, he simply lived according to the rules of what-to-eat-with-what, what-to-drink-with-what, what-to-talk-about-when-and-to-whom, what-not-to-do-where, you should really be religious, I sometimes mocked him without succeeding in annoying him—"religious" wasn't a word that called him to the barricades—but there really was something religious about him—perhaps the years in the monastery which he once referred to—in a single sentence, in brackets—

his mouth like a tense rectangle, his gray eyes blank—someone so ugly should sit in a corner with a beret on his head and take care not to let the light fall on him, from time to time this thought would cross my mind—not really a thought—more of a gleam—a knife in the light—but here he actually showed surprising courage—he always sat in the center, spoke with passionate excitement, loudly, quickly, accompanying himself with broad gestures, he stood out, walking upright, hands in his pockets, full of nervous energy, taking big strides, looking like an intellectual, hounded, hounding, mocking and critical—regarding himself as someone a lot of women—if he only wanted them—so why do you? Ora-inside-my-head argued with me, I don't know—he had the dark, tyrannical fascination of the persecuted; he was a jetty to butt up against, perhaps by way of my disagreements with him to draw my own borders—he agitated me and annoyed me and aroused me and distressed me, and I took it for love.

"And after him?" asks the Ora of now. She asks me to list my lovers like a new doctor who wants to know, first of all, what illnesses I have had: Measles? Mumps? Chicken pox? Ora only knows about Giora. "And after him?" "A French journalist—" I try to sound as if I don't even remember his name. "And what happened?" I shrug my shoulders. We are sitting in her red-and-white kitchen. On the stove—lentil soup for a winter evening. But it's not cold. I'm not cold. "You didn't love him," states Ora. "Depends what you mean by love—" Ora stands up to check on her soup. "The feeling that without this man your life isn't worth living," she says to the soup, stirring it with a slow spoon, "that if he leaves you—you'll die." "If Motik suddenly left you—would you die?" I can't resist asking. Ora laughs sadly, sits down heavily. "No, of course not—I'm talking about feelings—I wouldn't die, but I feel as if I'd die if it happened—" I am silent. If this is the yardstick—"What are you smiling about?" Ora examines me with narrowed eyes—two slits in her face—"No reason," I shrug my shoulders. Yinon entering at a run saves me from confessing. "Ma! Did you get them for me? I'm late already—" Ora gets up, opens the freezer. "Hi, Ilil, howzit" he smiles at me. "Is this all right?" Ora takes a package of frozen steaks out of the freezer, Yinon grabs it from her, includes both of us in his "Yallah, bye—" and Ora's "Do you want a bag?" loses track of him. He's no longer here, he's gone with a slam of the door—"They don't bake potatoes at their campfires any more," Ora dries her hands on a kitchen towel. "A kumzits without kartoshkes—would you believe it?" With their peel turned to crumbly coal, smelling of fire and charring, hissing hot steam with every lip-burning bite and all that was missing was salt, we always forgot to bring salt—"Could I have a piece of bread?" I feel suddenly hungry. "I thought you'd stay for supper—maybe Avi will come—" Is she trying to fix me up, no—she's already cutting me a slice of bread, giving up on me very quickly, too quickly, I want to say to her, you know, if there was ever anyone I couldn't imagine being parted from—it was you. Sometimes it seems to me that what we had together was more meaningful and special than anything I had with—"What with?" Ora intrudes on me. "With whatever you have," I reply, returning to the camp-fire, Bilu rolling a charred potato out of the embers, and Elhanan, always slightly hoarse, asking, who hasn't had, who hasn't had one yet?

"What are you dreaming about?" On a hexagonal plate lie two slices of bread—one with avocado and a slice of tomato, one with white cheese and pickled cucumber "Two?" Ora opens a drawer. "Too much or too little?" She takes out her forbidden cigarettes. "Too much," I remind her. "You'll die thin," a faint smile crosses her lips, she lights a cigarette and opens the window, "If my mother comes in—the cigarette passes to you—" she pours herself a cup of coffee, "I haven't got the strength to argue with her—" she sits down and looks at me with Ora eyes sunk in a worn face, "I wish I could lose weight," she takes a sip of coffee, her eyes widen, "where are my manners—what will you drink—Nescafé or Turkish?" "I don't drink coffee at all," I remind her. "Right-right-right," Ora presses a hand to her brows, hiding her eyes and nose, "you don't drink coffee, Yinon doesn't drink chocolate, Motik can't stand Israeli beer, Vered's allergic to diet drinks, my father gets heartburn from orange juice, my mother only drinks herb tea—" she sips her coffee and immediately remembers, "then what will you drink?" "Nothing. I'm not thirsty. Sit still for five minutes. Ever since I arrived you've been jumping up every minute, you've already put the dishes in the dishwasher and hung up the washing and ironed a uniform and sewn on a button and answered one phone call from a student and one from a teacher and stirred the lentil soup—"

"That's the way it goes," Ora gets up to stir the lentil soup again, "we'll rest in the grave," no, she isn't joking, Polish yenta-hood apparently passes like a torch from generation to generation. "Perhaps I dropped in at a bad time," I offer her a ladder, but she stays up in the tree. "No, it's like this every day in this house—" and I came to tell her that I had finally opened Nahum's room, that I had found my copies of *The Heart of a Boy* and *The Happy Prince*, to ask her how she remembered what had happened, she was there, on the sidelines, she saw everything or almost everything, but what came out suddenly instead was "Tell me—are you happy?" She rests her elbows on the table, her chin on the backs of her hands. "That question passed from the world a long time ago—now we ask: How are the children? How's your health? Have you finished renovating? How was the trip abroad?" I feel rebuked. "Do you still eat from cans standing up?" Ora takes me by surprise, no doubt intending to change the atmosphere for the better, her eyes on mine. The color of clear tea, the shape of the half-risen sun. Surrounded by gray ripples of tiredness. "How I envied you those meals!" She ate boiled chicken and mashed potatoes or white rice with lots of white bread after anemic chicken soup every day—but she had a healthy appetite, aren't you going to finish that, she would ask me and switch the plates so that her mother wouldn't kill me for leaving food on my plate when half the population of China was starving—

Dense dusk slowly fills the kitchen. The windows are open. "Look," Ora follows the smoke rising from her cigarette and floating out of the window with her eyes, "it isn't winter at all . . . last year we had a serious winter here and the year before that too—"

"There's no such thing as a serious winter here," I assure her. She doesn't like my tone, but says nothing. She smokes. I too say nothing.

"I moved into Nahum's room to sleep—" I say at last. Ora smokes in silence. Waiting for me to go on? "Nahum's room" doesn't prompt any "What, really?" from her. Well, about Eilat, about what happened in Eilat, she knows nothing. And she isn't going to know either. "It's a strange feeling," I try. Thirty, thirty-five years ago, she would have hurried to offer me fluent formulas for what I felt, for what exactly had happened, for why it upset me, right, I would have to agree, right, exactly, but now she asks from behind her cigarette "Why strange?" and glances very quickly at her watch. She's lost interest already. Lost patience already—

The kitchen fills with evening and mingled smells of coffee and smoke and sounds of a bouncing ball and a child calling to his little brother or his dog—"Perhaps—" It's beginning. Here it comes. It's coming back. Ora crushes her cigarette in a saucer, hurries to throw the stub in the trash can, washes the saucer clean and tries to wave the smoky air out of the window with shooing movements. "Perhaps what?" I prompt her. "Perhaps because you're living in that ruin of Davidi's after everything that happened—"

Oh.

"What exactly happened?"

The truth lies between the chairs, said Jean-Jacques on the evening we celebrated the first and last flight of his life and the meeting between us, when I'm writing an article I always ask more than one person what happened, otherwise there's no chance of coming close to anything resembling what happened, you remember that flight as an ordinary flight, without any mishaps, and I remember it as a nightmare, and how do you come up with an average between nightmare and routine, I put in a little of this and a little of that, mix well and add a tasty sauce—

"I don't understand the question," Ora says in a true teacher's voice; a voice trying to remain civil but actually impatient, not-really-interested, disagreeing-in-advance with the reply—

"You were there. You saw everything from outside, from the side—what are friends for?" Unbelievable—I quote her almost word for word and it doesn't remind her of anything—"*Then*? You mean then?" She means now, the terrorist hiding in the basement—"I was there and so was Shlomi and your neighbors, what was their name, Zukerman, and Arlozora's father and Elhanan's mother and Yosefa's mother and the nurse—"

Ask them, she's saying to me, not me. Why me—

"Shlomi—" I pick a name from the list "is living abroad—the Zukermans—are they still alive?"

No need to go on. She understands. She lights another cigarette. In a minute I'll hear another version of the truth—what are friends for—

"It was terrible—" Ora closes her eyes as if the picture of the memory is situated deep inside her head and her eyes are turning around to look inside, "you yelled—you screamed—I've never heard you scream like that—and you threw the cups from the Czech service—Shlomi's mother was scratched—and Davidi nearly killed you—"

"He yelled—"

The kitchen flickers, blinks, buzzes, and decides on a steady neon light the color of ice.

"Why are you sitting in the dark like a pair of conspirators?" Ora's mother asks with her hand on the switch. Ora passes me cigarette number two under the table as if she's passing a note during a test—"Loya has to leave," she says, and stands up. So do I. "Already? Why the rush? Who is waiting for you at home?" Mechora sniffs the air, "neither children nor parents," she smiles a sour-sweet smile, "Orinka is always complaining, and I always tell her that the time will come when she'll long for the days when we were all with her—do you smoke?" she stares at the cigarette in my hand, "ve-ry unhealthy—Orinka used to smoke too, and we would not let her be, her father and I, until she stopped—"

"Not Daddy," Ora corrects her dryly.

"Not Daddy, not Daddy, I am to blame for everything, it's all on my head—" Ora's mother takes big trembling plates, small trembling plates out of the cabinet, addresses herself only to me. "Daddy doesn't interfere. Daddy doesn't scold. Daddy is a saint. I too would like to be a saint, but then we would be left here without a Shabbes-goy to do what needs to be done—"

"Mother! Loya has to go—" Ora advances towards the door with me behind her. "Who is waiting for you at home apart from four walls?" Ora's mother grips my wrist, "you come so seldom . . . even though you're living here now, close by . . . sit, sit. Why don't you stay and have supper with us? Did you invite her, Orinka? Avi is coming too—have you met Avi? Ora's brother-in-law, Motik's brother. An important professor of Jewish history—only last week an article written by him was published in *Haaretz* . . . sit, sit. Why are you standing—just get rid of that cigarette of yours my dear—" Her tone is like cough syrup and the "my dear" is almost venomous. She offers me a little cup in which to put out the cigarette, "ever since Orinka stopped smoking—there are no ashtrays in this house—"

"Mother! Loya has plans!" Ora is waiting for me at the kitchen door. "Plans!" helps. Mechora lets go of my wrist.

"I still remember those days—run along and enjoy yourself. And when you have good news—we will be happy to hear it and also to invite your fiancé to our home . . . It's never too late; you must remember your English teacher in the tenth grade, Miss Kuperman, she—"

But we are already outside. Ora leading and me bringing up the rear. She opens the gate for me. Shuts it. Opens. Shuts. The gate creaks. "The hinges need to be oiled," we both say together, like we once did.

"People said that he chased you away—" Ora says suddenly, "that it was because of him—"

"Nonsense. It had nothing to do with him—it was my decision—"

"O-ra!" Behind Ora a rectangle of light opens at its center her mother's silhouette. "What about the broth?"

"Ten more minutes!" Ora shouts back.

"Does your mother cook for you?"

"Sometimes—" Ora is thinking of other things, she swings the hoarse gate between us. You won't believe it, I say to Hedva-inside-my-head, the queen of the class who argued with the history and Bible teachers and got tests postponed and organized a strike and was sent to the President's house as the best and brightest representative of our school, still hasn't left the shelter of her mother's wings. It's true that her mother is one of a kind, but still—

"Not because of him?" Ora returns to the subject.

"Ora!" Again the silhouette in the rectangle of light behind her. "The salad dressing with olive oil or corn oil?"

"What day is it today?" Ora whispers. "Wednesday—why?" I whisper. "Wednesday . . . so Udi's on duty today . . . with olive oil!" she shouts over her shoulder and turns back to me in a whisper. "And you never came to Nahum's funeral—" Does she too, like her mother, note absences from funerals? Has she forgotten that I don't believe in funerals, in tombstones, in cemeteries, in memorial candles, when you die you return to the earth and leave only bones to future generations—

"I couldn't make it—" I invent something, but I haven't got a chance—

"O-ra!"

"I'm coming!" Ora's voice is angry, impatient, almost on the verge of tears. "Keep in touch—" she whispers to me.

"I'll give you a ring," I reply into the darkness of the garden.

Yesterday it rained all night long; slow, straight, whispering rain—and this morning a raging sun again sending daggers of light in all directions, and a new voice—reedy, parched, the sound of a transparent squeak—

I went back to the nursery to buy new plants to replace the ones trampled underfoot by the security forces—I refused a jasminoid gardenia, a pink camellia, restricting myself to pansies and geraniums. "I understand where you're at," said the man with the moustache who recognized me, "you want an old-fashioned garden, something simple, without any fancy bullshit, I'm with you, believe me, I tell the customers, why don't you take vincas, petunias, what's the matter, nice little flowers, but no, today they want Gucci, sushi—where's your car? You came by foot? Tell me where you live. At the end of the day I'll load it on the pickup and deliver it to your door. How do you like that?"

Cold water. No, gazoz, the kind of soda pop once sold in sidewalk kiosks: colorful, refreshing, effervescent, cheap, restorative—

After his first visit here, Eliot, the good little boy from Canada, came back shocked to the core, and I found myself striding beside him—for every step of his three quick ones of mine—and vehemently—incredibly—defending the country in which I had not lived for twenty years, if I had to fall down half-dead in the street I would prefer to fall in Tel Aviv, not in Toronto or New York, that may be, Eliot smiled down at me, but most of your life you're not lying half-dead in the street—there was something about him, and Jean-Jacques too, damp and white, a little wormlike, as if they had been left too long to soak in water and aftershave, horribly clean, soft handed, without any angles—so different from the local product, made, perhaps, from war and harsh light, or perhaps from hummus, swagger, and sweat—how do like that? I try to lift the box. Easy. "Thank you, but no thanks. I can manage," I leave the nursery. "Some women are as stubborn as mules," I hear him say to his next customer, "and they say that women are smart—"

The knife flicks and sticks in the ground and the hand stretches to reach the knife, to extend the border within the circle, another wedge and another slice, "Knife in the Mud" we called this game, I don't understand where the knives disappear to, my father would complain at the end of every winter, Yosefa would draw the circle—she was the only one who could draw it like a compass—"What are you doing?" How could I have failed to hear him approaching me? "I'm trying to repair the damage your friends did to my garden—" I carefully overturn the black plastic container, extract the moist, almost black clod of earth netted with pale roots. "Now? They won't take—" pronounces Amitai. "Did you get the suitcase back from the police yet?" I set the young petunia inside the open cone. "That won't grow now. It's not the season—" insists Amitai over my head, but I take no notice. Tender plants and blades of grass have a guardian angel who hits them with his magic wand of light and half-blesses half-compels them, Grow! said our third grade reader. I almost saw this angel once on a winter's day in our garden, hovering for a moment over the strawberry beds, but Ora told me that if I didn't believe in God I couldn't believe in angels either. I didn't believe her. Angels were an entirely different thing; they were blond and almost transparent, they flew all over and made sure that the plants

would grow, that the grasshoppers would hop, that children who ate everything up would grow, there are angels in the world aren't there, I appealed
to my father, sure that he would confirm it, hadn't I seen one with my own
eyes, glittering in the sun like a big dragonfly, but Daddy smiled and sliced
black bread for our supper and said that there weren't, there weren't any
angels in the world. Not even one? I bargained. Not even one, he assured
me. So is that something people made up in their heads too? I clarified, and
Daddy said yes, and that night I hardly slept because the guardian angel of
sleep was offended and withdrew into the shadow of the curtains. There's
one in my room anyway, I said at breakfast the next morning, and Daddy
promised to check, not now, in the evening, when he came home from work.
Where is he? He asked when he came home, he hadn't forgotten, sometimes
next to the curtain and sometimes behind the bed and sometimes inside
the closet—May I come in and see him?—from the day we moved to the
block and I had a room of my own, he always took care to knock on the
door, to ask my permission to enter—No, no, no, I said to him, if he sees
you he'll run away, but Daddy came in anyway. Are you sleeping, he asked
in a whisper, and I didn't know if he was whispering because he wanted to
wake me gently so that I would see, or not to wake me so I wouldn't see. No!
I whispered back so as not to frighten the angel, and Daddy said, close your
eyes, and switched on the big light. Now open them, said Daddy, and I sat
up in bed, blinking. There are no angels here, you see, said Daddy. He stood
in the middle of the room and looked around. Perhaps he ran away and hid
under the bed, I whispered. Look, Daddy lifted the edge of the blanket and I
peeked; there was nothing there but for checked felt slippers and dust. Then
behind the curtain, I said, and Daddy drew the curtain and showed me the
windowpane, and behind it the screen, and behind it the shutter, and now
you can go to sleep in peace, he promised me, but that night I wept bitterly.
He had convinced me that there were no angels in the world and none in
my room and there was nobody to keep watch over me apart from him.

And most of the time he wasn't there.

Loya is an independent and responsible child, he would repel any attempt to adopt me on the part of neighbors and acquaintances, Loya can—

"Why are you planting flowers out of season?" Amitai perseveres, "What season is it now? Please tell me." I tighten the damp earth. "Winter—" "Winter?" I'm in short sleeves and the sun beats down, yesterday's raindrops turn to hedgehogs of light if you narrow your eyes, and a mist of light rises over the flower bed. "There is no winter here." I stand up. My hands are full of dark earth. "The boss forgot to make room for that season in our calendar—" Amitai sniggers, waves his hand dismissively, and returns to the plot. He didn't even notice that I said "our" without thinking.

I lie on your bed—hands under my head, ankles crossed, eyes staring at your fighter bomber squadron circling around its axis in the curtain light blue as the light of the ocean depths, it was my idea, you didn't refuse, you listened gravely to the instructions, asked questions—too many questions—reexamined me yourself—in the wetsuits we looked unreal, like black dolls. The instructor dived with us—a cautious beginners' dive—we glided over stone lettuces and petrified patterns of carrot leaves and underwater cauliflowers and swaying pink spaghetti and black needles sticking out of a black cushion looking at us with glassy eyes; and among all these, with the nonchalance of fashion models, impressionist fish displaying this side, that side, a sharp back, a tail like a scarf, a fin like a wing—schools of fish too changing from shiny to matte—Did you see the barracudas? asked the diving instructor after we had emerged from the water, and after we had peeled off the black rubber skins and started walking in the direction of the hotel you informed me: I was sure that I was choking—you wanted to die by fire, not by water. You always needed very wide spaces— you loved big birds—not the common or garden variety that come and go around here—albatrosses, condors—you loved kites—gliders—airplanes—astounding astronomical numbers—it takes the light light-years to get here, you told me on that night, we lay on the coarse sand, on the edge of the long scar of the Syrian-African rift, and looked up at the sky; everything you see there now isn't the stars, you took me by surprise, so what is it then, I said crossly. I wasn't in the mood for riddles. It's light that came from them hundreds of years ago, thousands of years ago, you began in the tone that announced an imminent lecture for the benefit of ignorant children, in this you were a little like Davidi, so the sky isn't fresh, I cut you short and suddenly I saw, look, there's the North Arrow, I pointed, Orion's Belt, you corrected me—Where do you see a belt? Those three stars—on a diagonal—you see? Alnitak, Mintaka, and Alnilam, and the fourth one there, Saif-al Jabbar—Are you trying to tell me that every star has a name? No, only the big, bright ones, the ones visible from the earth thousands of years ago, the ones discovered today aren't usually given names, just numbers—But where is Orion, I demanded and you showed me the shoulders, the right one studded with a big sapphire star—that's Bellatrix, the Amazon warrior, the left one wounded, with the big blood-star Betelgeuse shining over it, between the shoulders and above them Meissa, the luminous head—shoulders, head, arms? Yes, the right one a little bent the left one raised, and below the belt I see a kind of blurred luminous stain, that's the Orion nebula, M43, how big is it, twenty-three light-years, between it and us? No! that's its diameter! The distance between it and us is a thousand six hundred light-years—so that nebulous light that we see now set out when it was 367 AD here, more or less, and that's the leg over there—right? Yes, and that star is actually called Rigel, like the Hebrew "*regel*"—that blue one? Yes, it's a huge star—how huge? Its light is 14,000 times stronger than the light of the sun—so why doesn't it light up the sky? Because it's 620 light-years distant from here, the Black Plague, I said. What? The Black Plague, its light set out in our direction in 1348, dates are your field, three hundred years before the Chmielnicki pogroms in Russia in 1648–49, if you say so, five hundred years before the national revolutions of 1848, how can you remember, it's easy, I simply decide on a key date—the War of Independence, for example—and from there I add or subtract, the Black Plague is 600 years before the War of Independence, and so on—anyway, what about that red star on his shoulder—a giant star, but old—Nahum!—I'm absolutely serious; stars grow old too—in a minute you'll tell me that they die and are born too—quite right—so is it dying?—Who?—That red-red one!—Yes, and it will die too, not tomorrow or the next day, of course, in another billion years at least—what a relief; but theoretically—it may be dead already and it's only us down here that go on seeing it, that's to say, not it, but its light reaching us like a dog's leash without a dog at the end of it?—Theoretically? Yes.—So everything we see there now—I raised both hands to the black and very starry Eilat sky—is only the past?—Right. That sky is only the history of itself—I felt very disappointed, almost betrayed—theoretically there may not be a single star left up there!—Theoretically, you giggled, leaned towards me, pushed aside the hair that the incessant wind had blown over my eyes—Tell me, I had to find out once and for all—is there a group of stars in the sky that through a telescope looks like a question mark?—Sure, look, over there!—Where?—Take forty-five degrees from the end of Orion's right arm—Another red star!—Right, that's Aldebaran, take another thirty degrees to the right—there? Yes, those are the Pleiades—Atlas's seven daughters?—If you say so—Orion pursued them until Zeus took pity on them and placed them in the sky—If you say so—

I don't say anything. I look at the seven sapphire stars arranged in the shape of a question mark. In the Eilat night they were visible without a telescope too—When will we meet again, I asked Giora more than two years ago, and he put the binoculars to my eyes, turned my head to the sky and showed me a question mark. Look, you touched my shoulder to show me a blemished, pockmarked moon—in another year or two they'll land on it, you promised—who? The Americans—I'd die to walk on the moon!—So would I, you smiled. When I was small I was sure that there was a kind of induction center on it, I surprised you, I was sure that it was the first station of the dead. After they recovered a bit there from their deaths they were sent on to the appropriate stars—who sent them?—God.—You saw God as a traffic policeman?—More or less; Daddy and Davidi insisted that He was an invention of cowards, but—I know, they sold me that story too—you leaned on your elbow and pushed aside the hair that the wind which didn't stop tossing the palm fronds to and fro all night long had blown into my eyes—but ever since I started studying astrophysics I'm not at all sure—Nahum! Are you becoming religious?—I'm taking all kinds of possibilities into account—like what—like this, you bent down and I felt your breath on my face and afterwards, with very dry lips, the kiss.

Only you and I knew about that night, and since your death only I remained to guard it like the pile of rucksacks on the class hike when I sprained my ankle. Should I stay with you, asked our teacher Leah, and I thought, that's all I need. They left me two water canteens and sandwiches of black bread and mixed jam and three oranges with cuts in the peel to make them easier to peel, and promised me that they would be back in one to one-and-a-quarter hours. Was I comfortable, why didn't I rest my foot on one of the rucksacks, here's a crossword puzzle, by the time you finish it we'll be back—but they were four hours late and the sun set and it began to get cold and my sweater was stuck in my rucksack buried deep under most of the others, if not for my responsibility for all those rucksacks—Yosefa had a transistor in hers, Elhanan—fossils, Ora had pushed her new watch into hers—I would have tried to hobble to the main road and hitch a ride to the kibbutz—afterwards they apologized, fawned, even scolded; it's all because you refused to let anyone else stay with you on guard—I thought that the two of us were guarding this rucksack; and that one day we would open it and turn it over and empty everything out and find out what had happened then and what happened afterwards, how I became involved with you in the middle of the pain over Giora and perhaps precisely because of it, or because Daddy suddenly died, and I, boiling with rage over his untimely death, without any sign in advance, determined to destroy, lay waste, and liquidate, to sell, to sell, to go away, to forget, to leave scorched earth behind me—did what happened between us happen like a brush fire in summer—simply because of the heat and the dryness and the circumstances—with no chance of a future—not with me, not then, and how about you—or was it otherwise, utterly otherwise, and that night which began in a marvelous flight and continued in my idea of doing everything we had never done before, we were here, at the end of the world, who could say no to us, my father was under the ground and your father was up to his neck in difficult decisions about what to keep and what to sell and what to throw away, losing his temper, arguing with the rag-and-bone man, shouting at the policemen, frightening the fat nurse from the well-baby clinic who had also been roped in to calm, perhaps to offer pills until they located the doctor, we had left everything precious behind us and turned a new page, we dived in the Red Sea to discover that it was turquoise and azure blue like the wings of the amazing Dubček, there was no bird so beautiful when you lived here, you missed her, just like the chance to find out what exactly that night meant to me, to you, I tried once, years later, on a transatlantic call, and you, sleeping on this bed, woke up and asked first of all what's wrong, anticipating calamity, and then announced that it was the middle of the night and asked if it was urgent, and I said no, I just wanted to talk about what happened that night, if you remembered, and you were silent, and I insisted, in Eilat, after the flight, and you said in a very quiet voice, I know what night you mean. We'll talk about it one day. Not now. Not like this. What's wrong with now, why not like this, I argued with you, what can already happen, there's an entire ocean plus the Mediterranean Sea between us, so you can say whatever you like. Loya, Loya, Loya, I promise you, we'll talk about it, but not over the phone, okay? So when, how—Suddenly it's urgent?—Not suddenly, I've thought about it a lot since then—So have I, Loya—So why haven't you ever said anything to me?—Why didn't you say anything?—I had my reasons; one reason, actually—And what happened to that reason?—It doesn't exist, it hasn't existed for a long time—I had my reasons too, actually, one reason— And what happened to your reason? Does it still exist?—It still exists; I'll tell you one day . . . When are you landing in Lod airport?—I'm not coming back to the block. Never in my life. Why not Paris? It's so beautiful at this time of year—but you never came to Paris or to London either. In Rome I waited for you for two days, I hired a car, we'll go to Venice, that was the idea, do you still remember anything about the apartment we lived in, we'll find it, we'll go and see it, but you didn't come, you contacted me two weeks later in a hotel in New York. I imagined so—I spared you apologies—I saw our planes on the Italian news—So when will you be in Rome again, you asked, but suddenly I felt tired and I let you off abruptly, never mind Nahum, whatever happened happened, perhaps when we're in adjacent rooms in a retirement home you'll tell me what made that night different from all other nights, if you'll remember at all—I'll remember, you promised, and two years later the news reached me on the way to the plane—

What was your reason; in the sixth grade the nurse came into the classroom, sent all the boys out to play volleyball and explained the monthly cycle to the girls. She drew a teapot on the blackboard and said: And this is the womb. Then she spoke about tubes and eggs, deliberately avoiding the word "menstruation," and in gym lessons, she said, you can go to the gym teacher and say to her quietly, "I have a reason"—

Perhaps you left a letter for me among the papers in this drawer, To Loya— the real reason for everything—not to be opened after a meal—a kind of heavy-handed joke, or perhaps in earnest, To Loya—to be opened only after my death—but you weren't supposed to die—you survived a parachute accident, you once bailed out of your plane, you lived through two hard wars, raids, missions, who could have thought that you would drown in our national pond—you knew how to swim from the age of three—

No, there's nothing here, a few old documents, certificates, in your last years you didn't live here, and what's this, a pair of baby shoes congealed in copper, whose idea was that, maybe your mother wanted to preserve something of your babyhood for Davidi when he came back from the *partizanka*, where did I see shoes like this before, at Hedva's mother's on top of the piano. Would you believe it, Hedva stroked them with her fingertip; she always complained that she had feet like a kangeroo and she would never find Italian shoes to fit her, in China they would have put her in a freak show at the circus, would you believe that I once had such tiny feet, and her mother said, what did you think? That you were born like that? My mother keeps my birthday dresses from when I turned one in moth balls and she sends my wedding gown to the dry cleaner's every Passover, Mother, where is the gown—in the attic, said Rica, and we both burst out laughing; at some point in almost every black-and-white midnight movie an attic appears flickering in nervous candlelight or probing flashlight, and in it—festooned with theatrical cobwebs—a ruffled cradle, a musket, a doll with one eye in a Scarlett O'Hara dress and some musical box with a secret drawer holding the true will—Just like my mother's attic! Hedva would elbow me; when she and Leibo built themselves a house they would have an enormous attic—only you destroy evidence as if life is a crime—seriously, normal people keep things, you know that my mother has letters written to my grandfather's father by some Russian woman anarchist who was executed in the time of the Czar? Mother, where are those letters? You should see the handwriting! And she put her baby shoes in my lap, and for a moment it seemed to me that the embalmed leather shuddered and moved, living the horror of a mummy under the silver—

I return the shoes to the drawer—the shoes have been preserved, and the woman who went to the trouble of having them coated with copper—of her all that remains is her good intentions, not a single picture—why don't things taken out of a drawer ever fit back into it, I have to empty everything out—ai!—the shoes fell onto my foot—I would never have imagined that they were so heavy, I pick them up, on the right sole is an inscription engraved in round Hebrew letters: "Leah age one 23/7/47"—just a minute—that's my birthday—are the shoes mine? But it's written Leah, definitely Leah, not Loya—could I have had a twin sister who died—like Arlozora—Herzlina they called her, but she died when she was six months old—Leah and Loya—logical—even sounds good—and it also explains, I tell Hedva in my head, my obsession with having a best friend, a kind of soul mate like Ora and I were until halfway through high school—who can I ask: my mother's dead and my father's dead and Davidi's dead and Nahum's dead and

Hasia's dead and Shlomi's living on the other side of the ocean—but once he gave me an address—a visiting card—maybe it's still in the old holder for visiting cards under the zipper of the suitcase, just a minute, just a minute, here it is, visiting cards of dentists and a gynecologist and psychologist and naturopath, all from the Eliot era, you should always have insurance agent's and lawyer's cards on you too, and here it is, unbelievable. Shlomami Horovitz, Professor of Yiddish, telephone at the college, telephone at home—how many years has it been lying here—ten, at least—he's probably moved, changed his phone number, nothing stays still, but I can try—

"Shlomi?" So easy and simple. I recognize his voice as soon as he says "Hello"—

"Loya?" my hoarse voice gives me away. "To what do I owe the honor?" His Hebrew has an American flavor, spiced with Yiddish, but he looks—does he still—like JFK—

"I have a question for you—you're the only person who can answer it, I think—"

"So why over the phone? Where are you? In New Jersey? I can pop over—"

"I'm here, in Israel."

"Israel? What happened?"

"It's a long story—I'm living in Davidi's house—"

"Yes, I heard that he passed away—"

"And in one of the drawers I found a pair of copper-coated baby shoes—"

"There was a fashion like that once—"

"I thought that they were Nahum's, but on the right sole there's an inscription that says "Leah age one 23/7/47—"

"Yes—" Shlomi doesn't sound surprised or shocked. He's waiting for me to go on.

"On 23/7/47 I was exactly one year old—23/7 is my birthday—"

"So?"

"Maybe you know—did I have a twin sister?"

"As far as I know—" something between a laugh and a snort escapes him—"no, why should you think so?"

"What do you mean why? Because of the 'Leah'—"

"Leah is your name!"

"Leah? Is my name Leah?"

"Don't tell me you don't know the story—how you became Loya simply because of the unclear writing of some clerk at the harbor—"

"So why didn't they correct the mistake?" I hadn't heard the story. But it wasn't the only story I hadn't heard—

"Who knows? They had more urgent matters on their minds. In addition to which, they probably discovered that Loya is a much more original name—but my mother used to call you Leah—don't you remember?"

"Leah? No, she used to call me Leialeh—"

"Well?"

"I always thought it was a distortion of Loya—a kind of pet name—"

"My mother was very fond of you—how long are you staying there?"

"Where?"

"In Israel—"

"I don't know yet—I still have all kinds of things to arrange here—aren't you coming to visit?"

"Yes, maybe, around Independence Day—will you still be there?"

"Very likely—"

"So we'll talk—"

"Yes, we'll talk—"

Leah. Just plain Leah. A miserable, dreary name. And Leah was tender-eyed. The woman not chosen. And behold, it was Leah. Buying love with her son's mandrakes. What love? An obligatory quickie at most. Leah. A child bearer. Fat for sure. Heavy. With tits hanging down to her waist. Not my style at all. Maybe that's why you left it as Loya. What's your name? Leah. Brrrr. Only Yocheved would be worse.

Maybe Nahum is your true love, Hedva once suggested—Giora with all the ripples of heartbreak, sorrow, insult, longings, regrets, she brushed aside: it's all because you started too late, she was sure, who falls in love for the first time at the age of seventeen-and-a-half? It's almost like a childhood disease—if you get it at the right time it passes with no ill effects. When did you get chicken pox? When you were five? Good for you, I got it when I was sixteen and I had to be hospitalized—you simply caught the Giora bug! No, don't come to me with your French frog! Whenever you got onto the plane after Paris you looked as if you'd come straight out of the wringer, that's not love, it's punishment! Perhaps Nahum is your true love—she was almost sure after her marriage to Leibo, she was a great believer in lasting loves between two people who had sat on their potties together and consolidated firm, unembarrassed friendships, without secrets and dark corners—love is when you can fart next to him without wanting the earth to swallow you up, she repeated her creed with variations, Nahum should have happened to you years ago, she was sure, even though I never betrayed that night even to her—why get involved with some other frog who God knows what's eating him, you've known Nahum since you were a baby and you should hear yourself talking about him—one night I almost told her about Eilat, but at the last minute I refrained. I wanted to clear it up first of all with you. I called you on the phone—

Tonight I dreamed about rain. Light blue rain falling on the bay of Eilat. Continuous rain, not separated into drops, but falling soft and continuous like a thin waterfall in slow motion. The bay was filling up, look, I said to Nahum, we were both in a plane, sitting side by side, soon they'll have to evacuate all the people, but Nahum sniggered as if I was talking nonsense, and then I saw that the bay was surrounded by clouds, not mountains, do we still have far to go? I asked Nahum. I was worried. I couldn't see any airport below us. The curtains of rain went on falling and the water of the bay kept rising, you could hear it lapping the belly of the plane. We don't have far to go, said Nahum and glanced at the dials in front of him, look, he peered out of the window, here's Lake Kinneret—

I got up, showered, brushed my teeth, got dressed, ate a slice of bread and cheese and took a taxi to Tel Aviv. I hadn't been here for years. An ugly city—beautiful-ugly—beautiful—it hadn't made up its mind. It had changed in patches, not continuously. Some streets were almost as I remembered them—danker, darker, perhaps because of the trees that had grown to hide the sun—and others had been renewed, with sophisticated expanses of glass, glittering in the sun, shining brightly, more than seeing the articles on display behind them you saw the reflections of the people trying to see through the glazed light—clothes, shoes, household wares— here I am too—I've put on a bit of weight or else it's a hidden wave in the glass, short in comparison to the people standing by my sides, behind me, peering past my shoulders, they're changing the clothes on the mannequins in the window, stripping them to the nakedness of their plastic, no, they're wearing panties, around me people snigger, joke dryly, walk away, in front of the glass I remain with someone, who, looking at my reflection, he knows me—where from?—thinks to himself here I am and here's who? I turn my head to see the original. I know him, but where from. El Al? The army? The block? He recognizes me first. "Hello-hello-hello! Look who's here! The corporal in charge of the fourth shift! Wait, wait, don't tell me—you had an unusual name . . . Nofar? Timna?" "Leah—" I try my original name out on him. Still wondering who he is—tall, dark, smiling, he has dimples, beautiful brown eyes, of the black curls less are left—"No," he says—his voice is familiar too, "not Leah. I'm positive— almost one hundred percent positive." If he's who I think he is—"And I was almost a hundred percent positive that you'd been killed—that you fell on the other side of the canal." "There was a rumor to that effect," he's obviously enjoying himself. "Where are you, what are you doing?" Both of us reflections in the window where a man is buttoning up big mannequins. "Living in Nahum Davidi's house." "What do you say—so he finally died, the crazy old man—are you married? Children?" I shake my head in two no's and he grows serious, "then I lost a bet—" "What bet?" Our eyes meet in the glass. "About you—with Nahum." "About me?" For a minute I lose my balance, lean on the glass. "You had a bet with Nahum about me? When?" "After the flight to Eilat—" "Nahum told you about Eilat?" And I, all these years, keeping the secret with my lips pursed, as if if I opened my mouth a frog would jump out—"Who do you think got ahold of the Piper for you—"

It's a good thing we begin to walk. The sun warms, dazzles, how could I have come out without sunglasses? "What's up?" inquires Rogel, no, it can't be Rogel, over the head of a woman with baskets who passes between us. "He shouldn't have told you—" I give myself away, feeling betrayed, feeling foolish, just a minute—who knows what he told him—how much—"He was really freaked out about it," he makes a human island on the pavement full of people hurrying here, hurrying there. "I told him you don't die from one time or fall in love either—I bet him that in a few years we would see you married with children; I lost." I stand facing him. My eyes on a level with his shirt collar. "And how about you?" I ask. "Married—children?" "Three daughters and a daughter—" he confirms the myth with a brief laugh; pilots only have daughters. "Listen, it was great to see you—Leah. Leah? Are you sure? Well, my memory isn't what it used to be. I have to run—" and he is immediately swallowed up by the crowds and the shimmering sun. On the arm of the mirror of a parked car a wagtail quivers and can't believe its eyes; it cocks its head from side to side, and suddenly stretches its neck and gives the mirror one feeble peck.

The jacaranda trees are thinning out. On the almost bare branches castanets of shriveled bark shake, and the wind blows, rattling and tearing. Tomorrow, the next day, the clouds will return, what passes for winter here will return. I check to see if there's kerosene in the stove, even though it's not particularly cold—your house manages to be as cold as the grave. I buy grapefruit at the greengrocer's, drop in at the grocer's for milk and bread.

"It in your house police catch terrorist, big terrorist it say on radio"—
Mrs. Morgenstern grumbles at me. "it always hooligans there," the carpenter's pencil trembles in her hand, "from beginning hooligans there—"
"Mrs. Morgenstern—from the beginning is from nineteen hundred and
fifty-one—kapish?" "Nu, that what I say—" she gives me a suspicious
look, removes her glasses and looks at me through narrowed eyes, "you
Lealeh—what lived here once—" At last she remembers me. "My name
is Loya," I correct her with a dry throat. "Nu, that what I say," the-grocer's
says triumphantly and sends me on my way with a sour smile.

"Hedva—"
    "Do you know what the time is?"
    "I don't care what time it is. This is an S.O.S.—"
    "What happened?"
    "I found out that my original name was Leah—you hear—"
    "Leah?" Hedva greets my news with a peal of clear transatlantic laugh-
ter. "Welcome to the club."
    "But that's not the reason we gathered here tonight—listen. No, seri-
ously." She is still laughing there. "You remember the list we passed around
after the Yom Kippur War?"
    "The names of the fallen? What's come over you—"
    "Yes. Tell me—do you remember if the name Yohanan Rogel was on it?"
    "You're the only one with such a crazy memory—no, I don't remember
the names of dead people I never knew—"
    "Maybe Leibo remembers—"
    "Leibo doesn't remember our dog's name—but hang on a minute—his
cousin is on the committee for commemorating the fallen or some such
thing—I can give you his phone number at home—why is it suddenly so
important—"
    "I met him yesterday in Tel Aviv—I even spoke to him—"
    "You must have made a mistake—"
    "In plain daylight?"

"Okay, listen. I'll phone him now—I'll get back to you." She spares me explanations, embarrassment, agitation.

On your bed lie old Air Force magazines and photograph albums. I page through them to dull the taste of the betrayal, I never trusted anyone like I trusted you, you should have heard yourself talking about him, said Hedva, she was right, I trusted you more than I trusted Daddy, more than Davidi, and now—I feel like after a night flight, something's wrong but what, sleep, appetite, the absolute wakefulness at three o'clock in the morning, the heartburn, in these photographs your hair is orange-yellow and you're thinner than I remember, your nose is more hooked, I'd forgotten all about the birthmark next to your ear, each new photograph corrects you a little, proves to me how far I could have erred if they hadn't invented this business of look-at-the-birdie-and-click, Davidi's here too, at your side, different, no fireworks and flashes of lightning but gray, almost old, and Daddy—is that Daddy? Without glasses and almost unrecognizable, outside, in harsh sunlight, his face like a featureless egg, standing in a kind of excavation full of glaring light and at his feet, up to the knees, an unclear heap, who snapped him with this exposure—you? Davidi? Maybe me? They thrust the battered camera into my hands and said "Just press here"?

Possibly. Definitely possible. I lift the sticky cellophane page from the snapshot, try, with the tip of my fingernail, to separate it from the stiff cardboard, if I'm not careful I'll tear it—but here it comes—the paper on the back is a little torn but the writing is still legible—To Professor Kaplan and his daughter—a memento from the exca- here it's torn—5—maybe 1965—and in the corner smudged, almost illegible—Giora—

Giora photographed my father? I take the snapshot to the gluing room, clear a space on the table, switch the KGB lamp—that's what you called it—on over it, take your magnifying glass out of the flannel cloth; the photo itself, bathed in light and time, is almost black and white, *czernobili foto*, I hear Daddy's voice in a rare slip into Czech, almost a death mask; magnified too, his face shines featureless, expressionless, a stone egg, and the heap at his feet—wait a minute—there's something there—someone collapsing—someone hugging white knees with a white arm casting a strip of shadow—his head on his knees—and the sun white on his hair—good God—this heap is me.

"Loya?"

"Do you know what the time is?"

"Time for you to wake up and stop suffering from jet lag."

"*Yaefet*—"

"Ya-what?"

"They've invented a word for it in Hebrew—*yaefet*—"

"I'm so glad to hear it. Listen. Yohanan Rogel? The guy you asked about?"

"You found out already?" I sit up in bed, wide awake.

"So listen. You couldn't have met him in Tel Aviv. He was killed over the canal in seventy-three—"

"Are you sure?"

"A million percent. Leibo's cousin checked and he made inquiries in the Defense Ministry too—"

"So how do you explain it—" I don't know what to think.

"*Yaefet*—"

"I've been here for a good few months already—"

"And you still haven't calibrated your instruments—" Hedva tries to sound jocular, but I know her. She's worried. "So when are you selling up and coming back?"

"After they found a terrorist in the basement here—I haven't a hope of getting a decent price—"

"Keep your excuses for the police—"

"Don't remind me of them—they still haven't returned Davidi's poor old suitcase—"

On the windowpane behind my back a raindrop, and then another one, and a minute later rain, real rain drums with thin fingers on the windowpanes, tangles in the ficus leaves, clatters in the gutter, surrounds the house with big glass needles, stabs the earth, splashes off the long polyethylene arches under which red-green red-green red-green the strawberries hide.

GATHERING CLOUD

The weather's glorious. A transparent blue light refreshes everything—the eucalyptuses, the asphalt, the hibiscus bushes—and I walk aerobically and breathe in air smelling of Sabbath loaves that have just reached the grocer's and in the distance I see Tikva. "Where are you running?" she approaches, carrying a stiff plastic basket which contains parcels wrapped in brown paper. "You'll never guess what this is," she puts the basket down on the ground, "I went to the market in Lydda . . . they're selling fabrics at fifty percent . . . I'm making costumes for my brother's son's children too—" I'd forgotten all about her older brother—a brother from a different father, who lived in France. "They live here now, in Ramat Hasharon—" "What costumes are you making?" Both of us under the eucalyptus trees, for a moment like old times. "For the little girl 'Little House on the Prairie' and for the boy Ninja Turtles—the big girl wanted to be Madonna but my brother said no, apart from the fact that it always rains on Purim—" on the Hawaiian straw skirts, on all the frozen ballerinas and Queens of the Night, only the cats and cowboys kept warm, which is why I was a cat for three years and a cowboy for four, after which I refused to dress up—"Yallah bye" Tikva takes her leave and I go on marching energetically against osteoporosis and for the preservation of muscle mass, from the age of five to ten I longed to be Queen Esther but who could I borrow petticoats and tulle from—"Loya!" Tikva shouts at me from the end of the street. "Have you still got your flight attendant's uniform?" "Yes!" I too am obliged to shout, "So maybe I'll come around and get it—it's definitely better than Madonna—" dressing up as a flight attendant, something which has never occurred to me, but why not? A flight attendant: she's never tired and never irritated and never loses her temper and never eats and never even shits, and when everyone's dying of fear she's calm, she reassures, she smiles, in the course they plied us with real life examples of exemplary behaviour and cool-headedness of flight attendants in difficult situations, trained us to say in Hebrew and English, please fasten your seat belts, we've lost our back-up engine but there's no reason for alarm, place your pillow on your knees, and now bend over, hold your ankles, yes, in that fetal position we are all safer, breathe deeply, there's no reason for alarm, our pilot is very experienced, these are only precautions and thank you for flying El Al up to this moment—

In a book shop in New York I saw a book by someone called MacPherson entitled *The Black Box*. This sufferer from fear of flying had collected the last exchanges between the captains and the first and second officers and the control towers and here and there a flight attendant too—I bought the book after paging through it at length in order to send it to Jean-Jacques, I even wrote "Never believe flight attendants" on the flyleaf, but the next day I thought the better of it; you left? Leave him alone—

A flight attendant is almost like a nurse, said Brenda who was a nurse for fifteen years, what are you talking about, I protested, we were in a phase of constant tugs of war—She: You're just like me. Me: I'm not a bit like you—You don't care for? Serve? Clean up after? Display patience? Reassure? Sometimes tell lies to avert panic? To all these questions I answered yes, yes, yes, yes, but the passengers, I found a fundamental difference, are healthy, the passengers, smiled Brenda, are a group at risk—they are liable to die at any minute, just like patients in intensive care, even more so, but I'm in the same situation! Quite right, Brenda agreed gently, you're braver than I am, I'm not at all sure, for a healthy person to confront sickness, suffering, decay, old age, every single day you need so much courage, so much compassion, oh no, Brenda protested, if you feel compassion you won't be able to stick in the infusion, into Minaleh's room came one nurse and then another in silent shoes, in white uniforms, knowing and clean and almost faceless, were they lying when they said to her as she was about to leave, this time good-bye and not *au revoir*, did you notice, Jean-Jacques said once, taking off his reading glasses, that the murderer is very often a mailman or a doorman or an elevator operator or a monk—a monk? I couldn't conceal my surprise, he had been saved by monks—someone in uniform, he broadened the spectrum, a doctor, nurse, conductor, policeman—what's that got to do with murder? I didn't understand, when you put on a uniform you're no longer you, I still don't understand the connection, people commit murder in order to step out of line and declare *Je suis!*—he hit the table with his fist. And isn't there any other way? I was angry, I knew what he was getting at—there is, he opened his book again, spoke as if he was reading from it, to take off the uniform—

When I was a child the time train stopped on holidays. Perhaps because there was no school and perhaps because on most of the holidays Daddy was there and we—what: took trips to discover history under the ground, to float on Lake Kinneret in inner tubes or stayed home and ate different food on a white tablecloth ever since I'd complained we're the only people who don't celebrate the holidays, but it took time for Daddy to surrender; first of all he didn't think we had to, it was a waste of time, money, and effort, he hated rituals of any kind, when Shlomi's mother invited us he always sat on the edge of his chair and waited for the meal with the chopped liver and the chicken soup and the stewed fruit to be over already, he repeatedly suggested that we come when it was all over, just for the watermelon or the oranges, but Hasia would have none of it, the child's pale, she said, and Daddy, who didn't want to raise her blood pressure, sent me a look of silent resignation. Once he tried to recruit me; you don't like eating at Hasia's, he stated, yes I do, I surprised him, but you hardly eat a thing, you just sit and keep the food in your mouth, but they have a feast there, I explained, his thin eyebrows rose over the top of his glasses, we can have a feast too, he promised. With a white tablecloth and challah bread and malt beer! I demanded, and Daddy gave in, and after that, on every holiday and Friday night there was a white tablecloth, a challah loaf and malt beer and even chicken soup from cubes and soup-almonds from a bag, until the meetings of the underground and class parties ate into those hours, and I grabbed a thick slice of challah for the road and left Daddy reading some heavy history book on the snow-white cloth—the train stopped on holidays. On Purim, for example. In the haberdashery owned by Mr. Get-lost Hershkovitz, who chased children away and sold mothers buttons, thread and nylon stockings, and whose wife gave knitting instructions, in his haberdashery before Purim there were Red Indians made of sacking and Queen Esthers of white satin and black eye-masks and pirate/Moshe Dayan eye-patches and silver plastic swords and gold plastic king's scep-tres and red lining-fabric cloaks, and what's here now, in the new center, in Bridget's Ladies Lingerie rabbit overalls for toddlers and in the delicates-sen's printed on a piece of white cardboard "Fresh Haman's Ears Sold Here Daily" and in smaller letters—"Poppy-seed-walnuts-jam," in the air, Hedva and I agreed, you lose the sense of Goodness, it's Hanukkah again, or is it already Passover? After two years—no day and no night, no spring and no autumn, no weekdays and no holidays—and after three years above-ground—the only holiday left undimmed is Christmas: a whole month of stores in vivid green and bright red and trees producing fruits of light and reindeers and snow and red-capped grandfather doubles and gift-wrapped parcels festooned with octopuses of ribbon—

Tikva arrives to take the flight attendant uniform. "I don't know if it will fit her—" She measures me with different eyes, spreads the jacket out on the table. "She's very well-developed for her age—" Without any births or breast-feeding—the bosom of the thirteen-year-old, Eliot's mother spoke about me as if I weren't there, or as if I didn't understand English. "Don't you miss working?" Tikva folds the uniform. "Nnooo . . ." I admit, and she nods. "In the end everything gets boring—" she turns to the door. "What about that guy?" "What guy?" She's still bothered by my failure to get fixed up and my lack of effort in this regard. "The one who saved you from the terrorist—I saw a picture of him in the paper—" "What about him?" We're outside now. A marvelous day. The sky ringing with light—but suddenly baleful thunder comes rushing up and floods everything with deafening noise and recedes leaving behind it stunned air and trembling window-panes and a kind of continuous echo as if the silence is hard pressed to recover. And again clear skies, searingly transparent, and light filling the air like champagne. "Kobi wrote and complained to the Defense Ministry." Tikva walks with me behind her. She stops between the palms and looks at the bright patches of the women working in the strawberry beds. "He's only taking women now," she notes, waves, Amitai is approaching. "Yallah let's have a carton," she calls him. "A friend of yours?" he looks at me and I nod and he raises his hand in a gesture of assent and goes up to the make-shift little awning in the corner of the plot where for the past two weeks transparent plastic cartons have been filled with half a kilo of strawberries, half a kilo of strawberries. "He's cute," notes Tikva, and at that moment I look up and see them again; first bits of metal alternately glittering and disappearing over the plot, over the citrus grove, and only afterwards the sound, crashing down, making it almost impossible to breathe and impossible to think, and then they've gone, but the sound is still here, an angry grumble of metals forced to become a one-point-two Mach airplane, metals wear down, Nahum said on that night, like stones in water, like people in time, and the noise is still here, weaker but there, at the edges of the silence the echo of an echo of an echo—

I return to Nahum's room, to the mute squadron, discover that the winds that have invaded the room since I began to sleep here have changed something in the dancing array, a Sikorsky hovers over my hair like a giant grass-hopper, the Tupolev goes into a spin—on the radar screen they all looked like radiant chips, and the wonders of IFF—Identification Friend-or-Foe—which they promised us so that we would know which of all the shining blips on the radar screen were for us and which were against, this is the button, they explained, but it isn't working yet, when will it start working, soon, they said, and until then who could tell the difference between friend and foe; perhaps the birds—but they too belatedly, in other words, never—

In your bed-linen chest are dozens of posters rolled up like scrolls—what did your father call them?—*krazkirim*—wall-announcements—I spread out on the bed an almost life-size cockpit with all the dials, indicators, switches, the next one is an aerial photograph, the country from the air a patchwork quilt in yellow-brown or purple shadows between jagged basalt mountains like a dragon's spine or here a view of Sodom in the noon light, you can feel the heat pant, breathe the vapours of light and salt, see the chisels of wind and time at work, if there is a God—this is his angle of vision, who told me, Zvika, Zvika Saar who came with you to the base to scold me because of the storks, meet Corporal Loya Kaplan, in charge of shift four, you said, your sister, it wasn't even a question, we both smiled, to the black-haired, dark-skinned, all the pale "Soaps" looked the same, Zvika looked at me, at you, at me, and in the end he said, so you're the one who's making us scramble against storks, and I was offended and insisted on taking him up to show him on the screen how easy it was to make a mistake, those things, he said after staring for half an hour at the round screen behind the back of the radar operator, those things have brought down more of our planes than the Syrians, make a complaint, I said dryly, who to? He stood up, stretched his legs, walked out of the dark, buzzing cabin into the dazzling daylight, glanced up at the clumsy revolving antenna, as if it isn't enough that you can't take a spin in this country without encroaching on the neighbors, he grumbled, they had to stick Lake Kinneret in the middle too, what's wrong with the Kinneret, I didn't know yet, there's an entire squadron under water there, an entire squadron? And that's in addition to birds-of-the-whole-world-unite, every season the sky's full of new lunatics, we were on our way to the mess room, do you know the story of Icarus? I'll remember him when I get too close to the sun, Saar saved me from continuing—

One Purim we came back from the costume parade and saw death notices for Shmulik's grandfather nailed to the eucalyptus trees.

Dead means not breathing—said Arlozora.

And not feeling anything. Not even if you cut them—said Yosefa.

Dead people can't see—said Bilu.

Dead people can't hear—I said, because what else was there. Everyone looked as me as if I was wrong. But I was sure they couldn't, not even if you cried, or shouted at them at the top of your voice—dead people don't remember either, I went on confidently, and you can't ask them for anything—

They're buried in the ground—said Minaleh.

But their soul isn't buried, their soul doesn't die—said Adriana.

So where is it—asked Elhanan.

In the air—said Ora.

In the air?—Elhanan laughed—he was Captain Cook with an orange satin shirt, black waistcoat, eye patch, earring, and a hook at the end of his left hand—look!—he pointed with his hook at the air—there's Shmulik's grandfather! Phoo!—

Not that air!—Tikva—a black-haired Dutch girl—dared to contradict Ora. On this question she was more of an expert than the queen of the class. She was a certified orphan—the dead go to heaven—

Tikva was right; two days before Purim the weather stopped being glorious. She calls me up to ask if she can let the jacket out a little, at the chest, and I give my permission: "You can keep it," I say. "Don't you want it as a souvenir?" "What for?" After a minute during which she speaks to someone in the background she comes back. "You know who's here? Arlozora—she looks fantastic! Come around to see her—"

And I am already on my way.

Arlozora married first and she already has three grandchildren. Her sisters married young too, Minaleh filled me in at the hospital, they had funny names, right—Balfourit, who we all called Blufferit, and Ordit in honor of Orde Wingate, she gave her children more normal names, said Minaleh, only the eldest she called Moshit, after her father Moshe who died with his face in the okra, ever since they moved away from here nobody sees her, complained Ora, you'd think she was living at the other end of the country. I actually talk to her on the phone twice a week and believe me, she tells me everything that's happening here on the block, smiles Minaleh, we all three laugh, a white uniform with a nurse inside it comes into the room, says, I'm glad to see we're in a good mood today, what's the joke, tell me, I want to laugh too, and Ora explains, we're just reminiscing about an old friend, and the nurse checks the infusion and turns to Minaleh, it's great to have good friends, and Minaleh nods sadly, knowing as well as we do, that no good friend can or will offer to bear it in her place, not for an hour or even for five minutes, cancer isn't a heavy rucksack on a class hike—

Arlozora always knew who didn't come to school because he was really sick and whose uncle had come to visit from America and whose parents were getting divorced and that Shoshana's mother didn't come to the parent-teacher meeting because she was hospitalized, and she also knew that hospitalized meant shut up in the lunatic asylum, that Bilu's father was a functionary, that Nitza in the third grade was adopted, that Hezi's cousin was in jail in Ramla and that everybody in the government was corrupt; in their house the grown-ups didn't change to Yiddish when such subjects were discussed, or send the children to play on the porch, *A Baby is Born* stood in their bookcase in the entrance hall between *Do You Know Your Land?* and *The Book of the Palmach*—

"What's this I hear about you?" Arlozora without glasses and hair closely curled and dyed fiery red. "That you're having an affair with the guy who saved you from the terrorist?"

"Arlozora's coming back here. She's going to be the secretary of the local council," Tikva comes in with a tray of amber tea and a plate of date-stuffed cookies dusted with icing sugar.

"I'd be scared to death to live next to the citrus grove now—" Arlozora takes a cookie, changes her mind, puts it back—"Have they come to see you from the council yet?"

"Who was supposed to come?"

"The engineer and—I'll check it out. I'm still learning the job. You know that the house was supposed to go to the council," she decides to take a cookie, nibbles the end carefully. Her lips are covered with icing sugar. "I went over the papers. In '85 he undertook to leave it to the council on condition they renovated it and turned it into a museum in memory of the forest fighters—"

"Yosefa's husband has already presented a plan," adds Tikva.

"But they're getting divorced—" I say, confused.

Tikva and Arlozora talk about loans, parceling, building permits, demolition orders, interest, percentages, inspectors, and intrigues, and I think about you; what really made you change your mind, think that in order to force me to come back here—if only to sign a few papers and decide what to do with what's in the pyxis—Betzer passed it on to his intern, he'd had enough of dealing with this nutty will, most wills are predictable, he told me on the way from the airport, half to the son and half to the daughter or the lot to the widow, here and there some lunatic leaves everything to the state or the SPCA, some people settle accounts, one rich man left everything to the maid, left his three sons with their tongues hanging out, one lady left everything to her two Persian cats, but as a rule people did the reasonable thing, the question is what you call "reasonable," I wonder, well, even half to the lawful wife and half to the mistress seems reasonable to him—because if you think about it, both of them were married to the same woman—

"Who?"

"What do you mean who—" Arlozora takes out a cigarette and Tikva stops her: Not here; Kobi can't stand people smoking in the house—"What are you looking at me like that for—"

"Because it's exactly like Shoshana's mother's stories—"

"What Shoshana? Zilbershlag? The one who was hospitalized in Beer-Ya'akov?"

"She went to have dialysis." I was happy to put the record straight, if only after a quarter of a century—

"Maybe they took her to have dialysis from Beer-Ya'akov—" under the red perm Arlozora still twists things to make her come out right, if not completely then at least a little. "Don't tell me you don't know," she returns to me as if I came back here simply in order to lift the edge of a scab with the tip of a malicious finger to see what was underneath, blood or flesh—

In the mirror on your closet door, not to be believed: wild, unkempt, all blandishments suddenly abandoned, me just as I am, me making no attempt to please, not even myself. From the top shelf I pull down the down quilt; that's what I want to do—curl up under this quilt and go to sleep . . .

He has a daughter your age, Daddy sits on the edge of the bed, speaking softly. I'm sleepy. It takes me time to wake up to the day. On the chair Shlomi's cowboy costume awaits me. A very fine one; his mother made it for him. Do we have to go? I try to bargain. I can't go there dressed up. Daddy takes off his glasses, looks at them from a distance, nods. Me too? You're a big girl now, Daddy puts his glasses on, looks at me. How old was I then. Eleven. He has a daughter your age, says Daddy, and now she's an orphan. I'm an orphan too, I sit up in bed, hug my knees over the quilt. Daddy looks at me without saying a word. Why are you sad, I ask. Daddy is silent. He wasn't part of our family! I am suddenly alarmed. Daddy shakes his head. But it's Purim today, I am almost begging. Loya—Daddy stands up. His tone makes it clear that it's impossible to refuse. The costume looks at me from the chair: blue trousers with leather patches on the knees, checked shirt, waistcoat made of real suede, even a little neckerchief. And a black cardboard hat. And a belt with a holster. And the revolver. A pop gun that looks just like a real revolver. Then the revolver, just the revolver, I want to ask, but Daddy has already left the room. I decide to stick it between my panties and trousers, under my sweater. We travel to Tel Aviv. A bus and a wait and another bus. What about Davidi? I ask. He can't come, whispers Daddy, glancing at the other passengers as if he has just disclosed a military secret. We get off and walk. Children in Purim costumes—Dutch girls, Spanish girls, clowns, soldiers, Arabs, billboards, Queen Esthers—walk past in groups or hand in hand with their mothers, the streets are festive, decorated for the Purim parade, and I walk next to Daddy, feeling a happy little flutter around the revolver under my sweater, will we stay for the parade afterwards, I tug his hand, we'll see, Daddy is so tense that I ask again, he's not from our family? No. We're coming closer to the crowds and Daddy holds my hand so he won't lose me, so what's his name, I ask suspiciously, something won't let me rest, Kastner, Israel Kastner, says Daddy, trying to clear a way through, the one you argued about all the time? I demand in surprise—the vociferous arguments were always about people who died thousands of years ago, and now suddenly—how did he die? I ask, even though all that's left of Daddy is an arm pulling me behind him, a shoulder and half a back, was he old? I am determined to make him stop, turn to face me, people are beginning to pay attention, someone above me says shhhhhh child, and a woman cries, he was murdered, murdered, murdered? Daddy is hedged in by the crowd, he stands still, people behind me, in front of me, stretch their heads in one direction, quiet, attentive, into a handkerchief the woman who said murdered, murdered, cries quietly, she has a blue number on her arm, but they, I know from the neighborhood, say murderers or Nazis about everything. All the people begin to move, us too, and suddenly they stop; what happened, what happened, the hearse got a puncture, the words pass like a rustle, they won't even let him be buried like a human being, and again we start to move, where did they put the coffin, in the bus, what bus, the mourners' bus, and again we stop and stand among people listening to words rising in the distance, some of them are crying, was he someone important? I tug at Daddy's hand, giving rise to an angry, offended shhhh! and decide to concentrate on the hands of the watch on Daddy's wrist; the Purim parade is due to begin in an hour and fifteen minutes, an hour and five minutes, fifty minutes, forty minutes, half an hour, we'll make it, we'll make it—the crowd begins to unravel, to disperse, us too, the streets are full of children, rattles, mothers, masks, look, I tug at Daddy's hand, he drags his feet, dazed, Dad-dy! I pull his hand hard, he looks at me, look! I pull the revolver out from under my sweater, I too, like all the others, am a child with a parent at the Purim parade, what luck that this funeral happened, otherwise we wouldn't be here, look, I brandish the revolver, shoot into the air, Daddy recoils as if he's been shot, snatches the revolver from my hand with a sudden, hard movement, and throws it into a nearby litter bin—because I cheated, I'm sure, I swallow my tears, grit my teeth, so what, I don't get to celebrate Purim, I'm an orphan too, I push my hands into my pockets, I bought that revolver with all my Hanukkah money, he shouldn't have thrown it away, I'll never talk to him again, until he apologizes I won't talk to him, all around us people are celebrating, cats are eating toffee apples, little soldiers are opening their mouths wide for candy floss, mothers take out handkerchiefs, wet them with spit, wipe their offspring's mouths, nobody from that funeral is to be seen, only Daddy and I make our way through the crowds streaming in the opposite direction, towards the Purim parade, if he's as furious as I am we'll never speak to each other again—

How was that whole story sucked into a black hole, wiped out as if it had never happened? I am in your room, on your bed, above me airplanes of balsa and painted cardboard, even if you were alive you wouldn't be able to tell me what exactly happened there, that story was confined to our corner—but Ora's mother might know something; she never misses an important funeral—I get up, get dressed, comb my hair, put on a bit of makeup, Ora's on holiday, I don't phone to tell her I'm coming, what did we do when nobody had a phone at home, we got up, we walked around, we scraped our shoes on the doormat, we rang the bell and waited for it to open. Ora's gate is open, ten steps and I'm on the threshold. Behind the door angry words, Motik and the radio in a vociferous duet—I ring the bell, produce immediate silence behind the door, apart from the radio, very loud, excited, but unclear, it's impossible to understand a word in the uproar, not behind the door, switch it off already, switch it off! Is that Ora's voice, hard to guess from behind the door which is suddenly opened by an Ora as white as a sheet, her face—the face of catastrophe.

"What happened?"

In the background Vered, Udi, Motik—

"Didn't you hear the news?"

"No—"

I go inside without an invitation, since none is forthcoming—

"There was a massacre!" Ora lights herself a cigarette. In the middle of the day. In the middle of the living room. Her hands are shaking.

"There was what?" I look at them: Vered, Udi, Motik. Sitting on the sofa. Stunned. Ora crosses the living room, opens the window, flicks the ash outside—"Where?"

"Where do you think," Udi, in uniform, says bitterly, "Hebron!"

"How many Jews were murdered?" I ask, thinking of you.

"Not Jews—Arabs!" Vered stands up, goes to the television, switches it on and produces noise and snowflakes on a black background. "Shit!"

"Some settler maniac took an M16 and sprayed all the worshipers in the tomb of the Patriarchs"—Udi stood up, stretched his legs—"there goes my leave. I'll be called back to base at any minute—"

"Muslim worshipers?" I can't believe it.

Ora nods.

"How many were murdered?"

"They don't know the exact number yet . . ." Motik goes up to the television, turns it off, turns on the radio—seventy-four according to Muslim sources, says the newscaster, about forty according to the IDF spokesman—

The radio, the telephone, Udi: "It's the army, I knew it—" Motik: "I'll take you to the train station—" Ora: "I'm going crazy, I'm going crazy, I'm going crazy"—Vered: "Why are you going crazy, it was predictable!" And Ora's mother is suddenly here, in the middle of the living room—"I came to tell you to switch on the radio, but I see there's no need—"

"You're listening to the news?" Ora scolds her, why? "Loya, excuse me, but I—" She's on her way there already. "I'm sorry, come this evening." She accompanies me to the front door—

"It's all right, I only dropped in—"

"Loya. Come this evening. Come and sleep over. Don't stay there alone in the house—now I have to go and see how my father is—my mother—"

"I only dropped in to ask her if she was at Kastner's funeral—"

"What?" Ora closes a strong hand around my wrist. Exactly like her mother forty years ago. "Don't dare let that name cross your lips," she says in her mother's Hebrew, looking at me with her mother's eyes, "not in front of her; promise me—"

"Scout's honor." I try to make her smile and succeed in producing a spasm. "And come this evening. Come and sleep over. Who knows what's going to happen now—"

I return to find Amitai at the door.

"Ho, here you are—" I can hear a transistor blaring from the awning. The plot is deserted; all the women have fled—Amitai rubs his hands. "Well, are you coming to help me pick the strawberries?"

"Me?"

"Why not, it's not brain surgery; massacre or no massacre, if we don't pick them the whole lot will go down the drain." He turns to the plot. "Go and put on something more comfortable to work in; look what a lovely day it is, fuck it—"

For five hours I squat like a frog, groping between the leaves to see which strawberries are ripe for picking and which can wait, and a stream of voices pour from Amitai's transistor in the shed onto the field; I don't catch everything. The reception is poor, the wind keeps changing, I move further away in the direction of the citrus grove—but what I do catch sounds terrible—and no less terrible than the massacre itself is the good cheer of the murderer's friends—*L'chaim*, Jews, a merry Purim, Jews, gladness and joy—

In the evening I return to Ora's, thereby preventing Amitai from sleeping over, in the living room, on the sofa, with his revolver, wasn't that terrorist enough for me? Ora opens the door, encloses me in an embrace as if I've come to a wake. Motik is in the living room, glued to the news, he barely nods a greeting. I sit beside them to see what's on the television that was finally repaired, the technician came in the afternoon, we thought he wouldn't come, you know, an Arab from Jaffa. After five minutes I feel nauseous. I can't stand it. The news cuts like knives. It's impossible to believe and impossible not to believe. "I just can't take it in—" whispers Ora, her face cupped in her hands, "and a doctor on top of it." "Doctor Baruch Goldstein," Motik stands up, looks around, "go know what someone like that has in his head—"

"Hel-lo everybody!" Yinon bursts in cheerfully, bouncing a ball. "Why are you all sitting around as if you're in mourning?" He bounces the ball, whirling around himself. "At long last someone stuck it to them good and proper!" He stops, smiles, waits to see how we will react. "Yinon!" Ora rebukes him as if he's a pupil who's just thrown a piece of chalk at her. "Kahane lives!" Yinon makes a V for victory sign, broadens his smile. "Hi Ilil, hi Dad, long live Baruch Goldstein—" "Yinon!!" Ora gets up and moves towards him, in a minute she'll tell him to go to the principal's office— "Yinon!" The boy mimics her, backs away, passing the ball from hand to hand, effervescent as soda water. "Tomorrow," he provokes, "I'm going to the barber and getting my head shaved—" "Don't you dare!" Ora raises her voice. "There's no democracy." Yinon grins at me as if we're on the same side. "They," he turns his curls towards his parents, "are liberals until I begin telling them my opinions . . . I'm for Kahane!" He challenges them, apparently confident that in my presence they won't dare—what? What will they do to him already? At this moment Ora's father comes into the room, confused, blinking in the light. "Baruch Goldstein—" he gropes in the air as if hoping or fearing to encounter the bearer of this name here, in the living room. "Daddy—Daddy, sit down." Ora hurries to lead him to the rocking chair. "Motik, get a glass of water—" Motik hurries to the kitchen. "Yinon, go and see what Granny's doing—" "Come, come," Ora's father beckons Yinon. "Sit here *yingeleh* . . . you know who Baruch Goldstein is?" Yinon walks smugly over to his grandfather, bouncing the ball, steadies it at his feet and sits down on it. "Baruch Goldstein is a hero," he says. Motik arrives with the water. Ora's father drinks. His hand shakes violently. Agitation? Parkinson's? "Motik, go and fetch my mother," commands Ora. "Baruch Goldstein is a hero . . ." Ora's father leans his head back, closes his eyes; his face darkens, narrows, nods. "He brought in weapons and the Nazis didn't notice . . ." "Daddy, Daddy!" Ora bends over him, shakes him. "Should I call the doctor?" I ask. "Are you against opinions too?" Yinon on the ball half-turns toward me, then touches his grandfather's knee. "Grandpa's for Baruch Goldstein too—" Ora's father opens his eyes. "A quiet fellow, golden hands—" Ora's mother comes in with Motik behind her. "Why do you let him watch the news?" Ora attacks her mother who advances toward her husband. "So what do you want him to do all day? Where do you want him to live? On the moon? Baruch, what happened?" "Nothing happened, Granny." Yinon gets up, the ball in his hands. "Grandpa's for Baruch Goldstein and because of that Mom thinks he's cuckoo—in a minute she'll phone for an ambulance to wipe the racist opinions out of his head and turn him into a true leftist—" Ora's mother silences him with a dismissive wave of her hand, bends over her husband. Yinon bounces the ball outside, singing in time to the bouncing *A hero was he, he set me free—*

Ora wrings her hands. "You see," she says to her mother's back. "What am I to see?" Mechora turns to face her. "Does Daddy need the news? Can't he be spared such things? If you want to hear the news—come here!" Ora pushes her hand into her pocket, takes out a crumpled packet of cigarettes, pulls one out, looks for matches. "You're still smoking!" her mother rebukes her back and Motik bends over Baruch Berger and asks him in a loud whisper if he'd like a cup of tea, and Ora turns to her mother with a lit cigarette. "Loya's been living here for half a year already without any news—" and Mechora, only now aware of my presence, says. "Really?" "Baruch Goldstein," Ora's father mutters from the rocking chair, and Motik goes out to make him a cup of tea and Ora goes up to him. "Daddy," she lays a heavy hand on his shoulder, "you can't possibly support what Baruch Goldstein did." "He worked in the *Beute-Lager* . . ." her father mumbles.

"He's confused—" Ora draws away from him with a sigh and makes for the telephone, crushing her cigarette in the soil of a potted plant. "Loya, let me introduce you," says Motik, and I turn around and see Motik with a cup of tea and behind him another Motik, taller, thinner, darker. "My brother, Avi—" I shake a dry hand, Motik goes up to Baruch with the tea, Ora picks up the receiver, her mother goes up to her. "There's no need, Orinka, there's no need—" "Fill me in?" Avi whispers to me, but Ora overhears, raises her head, the receiver in her hand, "the news is killing my father— now he's sure Baruch Goldstein was in the Vilna Ghetto—" Avi crosses the living room, takes a chair from the dining nook, sets it in front of Ora's father, sits down, and leans toward him. "Hello Baruch—I'm Avi, Motik's brother; you remember me, Mr. Berger?" Ora's father raises bleary eyes to him. The teacup trembles in his hands. "You're the one who traveled to Soviet Russia to look up something in the archives—" Avi nods. "And what did you find?" The teacup trembles violently. Avi reaches out, takes the cup, and puts it down on the little table that Ora hastens to draw up. "Everybody," Ora's father points a bony finger at all of us, "is talking today about Baruch Goldstein . . . a wonderful fellow—he worked in the *Beute-Lager*—" His chin sinks to his chest, he nods his bowed head, "a wonderful fellow, a wonderful person—" He seems intent on persuading his knees. Avi stands up and turns to Ora. "Your father is right. There was a Jew called Baruch Goldstein in the Vilna Ghetto. He lived in the commune in number 12 Strashon Street and worked in the armament repair workshops—he succeeded in smuggling a revolver into the ghetto—" Ora's father raises his head, listening, a radiant smile on his face.

I stay there till eleven o'clock. A little after ten Bilu arrives, surprised to see me there, asks Motik to join the Civil Guard, there are going to be serious clashes here, you heard what happened in Jaffa, and Tikva's Kobi too turns up on the same matter, the Arabs, I'm telling you, until they kill thirty or forty of us they won't stop, they have to settle the score, revenge is in their blood, and I—exhausted by picking the strawberries and no less by the talk, the speculations, the pictures of wild crowds on the television, the arguments—I sink into the armchair and observe everything from an altitude of twenty thousand feet. "Loya's tired—" says Ora and stands up. "I'm going to make you a bed in Gili's room—" but I've had enough, I have to get out of here, go to ground in your lair for a little peace and quiet, a little privacy, a few consecutive hours in the company of loudly arguing people is evidently not for me any more, I stand up, my whole body aches—my back and my legs and even my arms. "No, thanks, I'm going home to sleep. It's okay—" I stand my ground in the face of all the protests, warnings, exhortations. At the door Avi asks, "So you're going to drive home anyway?" "I'm not driving, I'm walking, it's here, not far—" "I'll come with you—" he surprises me and I, too tired to protest, shrug my shoulders; let it be—

We walk down the street. We have to talk about something. "Was there really a person called Baruch Goldstein in the Vilna Ghetto or did you only say so to—" "There was indeed—Baruch Berger is a dear man. How he landed up in the Vilna Ghetto is a long story—" We walk down the street between the light of the lamps and the shadows of the trees. "He was married to some German baroness—" I try to concentrate; Ora's photographs; the castles. The young people in riding breeches. The beauty opening her mouth at the piano to sing or shout—"Where did you get that from—" Avi sounds impatient. "But Mechora—" that conversation with her—venomous, intense—"Oh Motherland, Motherland," sniggers Avi, at least as unenthusiastic about her as I am, an instant ally. "So you're a Holocaust researcher?" Any subject except for what's in the news now. "I'm first of all a historian—" he corrects me without acrimony. "My father was a historian—" I let slip, why, what difference does it make, but we have to talk about something until we get to the end of this not long road. "They thought I was going to be a historian too—" I go on committing suicide, one more street and we'll be there. "I know . . . Ora told me that you always knew all the dates by heart—that you knew Latin, Ugaritic."

He smiles. I can't see his face high up in the dark, but he's smiling. His voice is smiling.

"So how did you become a Holocaust historian—" "So how did you become a flight attendant?" we ask in chorus.

"You first," I try to arrest the erosion. He knows too much about me. What else did Ora tell him? "When we studied history—everybody hated that part—"

"But you didn't study the Holocaust—"

"No, no, they didn't say a word about the Holocaust; I don't know how old you are, but when Ora and I were in high school the Holocaust wasn't history yet—I mean the pogroms, the Cossacks, Chmielnicki, Petlura, in short, the whole of Jewish history from Bar Kokhba on—"

"Precisely because of that—" we're getting closer.

"But nowadays they take high school students on trips to Auschwitz—" I think of Minaleh's son.

"Because of that too—"

We walk in the transparent dark between one street lamp and the next. We'll be there in a minute. His voice sounds like brown corduroy, a little shabby, very comfortable—What does he mean by "because of that too," I wonder, but I'm not about to start asking now, here's the little lane, the gate, the cypress tree—"so you're staying in Davidi's house for the time being?" He knows this too—what's happened to Ora's ability to keep secrets—

"Why 'for the time being'? I'm staying here. Period—" I surprise myself and him. Open the locked door—one hard and one soft and one half-turn, and switch on the light. "Would you like coffee?" The house suddenly looks cold and empty. "You're very tired"—he looks at me attentively. He reminds me a little of Jean-Jacques—in the intense concern, the protectiveness—be careful—be careful—be careful—"and I don't drink coffee—" I feel myself blushing. Did Ora tell him that I don't drink coffee too or does he really— "I'd like to ask you a couple of questions," I suddenly remember, "about that whole Kastner affair—if you're not familiar with the details maybe you could recommend someone I could ask or tell me where to find material—"

"Loya," he puts his hand on my shoulder. A warm hand through my clothes. "We could talk for two weeks about the Kastner affair. Go to sleep now—"

I nod. "But you owe me a story—" We're both standing on the doorstep. "You too—" he whispers to my hair. "Me?" I raise my eyes. He's taller than me by a head and a half. "Why you decided to become a flight attendant—" Oh, that. "Ora didn't tell you?" I can't resist the jab. "Ora doesn't tell a lot—" Avi leans against the doorpost. I lean against the other one. Lucky we're both thin. "So how do you know that this is Davidi's house?" I jab again. An encounter with you, complained Hedva, can sometimes be a lot like an encounter with a hedgehog. "I spoke to him—" Avi surprises me. "When? What about?" I demand in agitation. My tiredness turns into heartburn. "Not now—but I will tell you. I really do owe you a story—" And again a hand on my shoulder in a light, almost impersonal touch, and he walks away.

An unusually hot day. Over the strawberry beds hovers a hot, red smell of boiling strawberry jam. Amitai works opposite me, declaiming in time to his picking, "*Medina hofshit, avoda ivrit.*" A Free State, Jewish Labor. No, the chant during the last years of the British mandate in Palestine was Free Immigration, A Jewish State, "*Aliya hofshit, medina ivrit,*" I correct him and he smirks and says that none of those who arrived in the last free immigration is prepared for work picking strawberries. "They came for Moscow, for Leningrad," he does quite a good imitation of a Russian accent, "and this is *rabota* for *primitivski Israelski*—" Are-you-coming-or-not he woke me this morning by knocking on the shutter from a confusing dream, *Agnosco veteris vestigia flammae*, I know the vestiges of the old flame, and so get up, go out, don't lie in bed like a vegetable, Avi won't phone today or tomorrow either, give him a week at least, no two weeks, get up, go out, the sun's shining, the birds are singing, the transistor is silent. "I'm sick of all the fuss and bother," Amitai announces, and hammers a final nail into the corner of a banner: THE PEOPLE ARE WITH THE GOLAN

HEIGHTS. "You too?" I ask, I've seen a lot of these slogans bellying out from a lot of porch railings in the neighborhood, "We'd have to be crazy to give it back." Amitai picks opposite me, efficient, very fast. "Don't you think so?" I begin to pick. "I don't know, I've never been there." "Are you serious?" his eyes are two slits because of the sun. "You've never been on the Golan Heights?" "No—what have I lost there?" "The defense of Lake Kinneret—" Amitai is no longer opposite me, I can't keep up with him. "Lake Kinneret can go to hell—" I hear myself say, thinking of Nahum, Amitai doesn't react, perhaps he didn't hear and perhaps I was speaking to myself, for the past six months I've been speaking to myself so that I am no longer sure what is said out loud and what isn't, when we are opposite each other again—he's already on the next row, I tell him that there was a man called Baruch Goldstein in the Vilna Ghetto, but Amitai is not impressed. "So what? Open any phone book—every fourth person is called Baruch Goldstein or Shimon Mizrahi or Avi Cohen—"

Avi. Avi. Avi. Avi-what: Avraham? Avshalom? Aviezer? Avishai? Avina-dav? Avinoam?

Everything on earth passes away, everything on earth passes away—the school choir would sing and at this stage the second voice would come in to repeat: *Everything on earth passes away*—but by then the first voice had changed its mind—*Only the melody, only the me-lody, only the me-lody is here to stay*—I knew the words, always, but due to the hoarseness of my voice I wasn't accepted for the choir, and at class parties and ceremonies I sang with my lips moving voicelessly, *Everything on earth passes away*, or the opposite, *And Judah shall dwell for-e-he-ver and Jerusalem from gen-eration to genera-ha-tion*, and sitting around the bonfire on Lag Ba'Omer, on Independence Day, on the last day of school, *Vanya, Vanya, my dear son, take me with you to the war, I'll be a merciful nurse and you'll be a Red commissar*—

In the middle of the bookcase, behind the locked flap, instead of bottles of medicinal brandy and Slivovitz vodka and mirrors multiplying thick-bottomed glasses were stacks of old, very familiar records, a selection from the Red Army choir, Daddy would lean back in the armchair with his eyes half closed, and listen to the singing of the ranks of uniformed men, singing that started in the distance and came closer and closer, growing stronger and stronger, as if a battalion of soldiers were marching and singing and the listener was standing on the roadside, seeing-hearing them advancing, seeing-hearing them gradually receding into Mother Russia—all flat expanses and dead heroes and blonde braided milkmaids, in order to make sure of the translation-on-the-side I would go over to Elhanan's mother, why you need learn Russian, she would ask me in astonishment the first few times, language of goyim, curse them, I want forget, I want you learn me Hebrew, but she agreed to help me anyway, for the cinema, serving me heavy, stomach-turning dishes, because I'm always thin and pale, I eat dense meatballs and sticky noodles and offer Hebrew words in exchange for Russian ones, and Elhanan sometimes comes in and recoils, marvelously handsome but shy, nearly all the girls in the class are in love with him, even Ora, who would never admit it, now married plus four, and Adriana divorced plus two, and Arlozora married plus three, and Yosefa on the way to being divorced with two daughters, and Minaleh dying of cancer called her only son after him, these records too you rescued for me, but I suspect I would have to go to the flea market to find a gramophone to play them—something for decoration with a mute trumpet mouth—

"How's your father?" I ask Ora. Ora sighs. "Even in the Gulf War he didn't react like this—" We're in her kitchen. "Yinon is killing me," she cuts up vegetables for a salad, talks about Udi, about Gili, about Minaleh's son, in the hospital now for tests, what a tragedy, about Arlozora's granddaughter, Arlozora's already starting to work for the council, she says they're going to transform the neighborhood, tear down all the old houses surviving from the fifties and put up high-rise buildings instead, they haven't been to see me yet? Well, everything's frozen now, do I want to stay for supper? "Is Avi coming too?" I don't even try to control myself, "No, why should he come, hasn't he got a home?" and I feel a stab, a home means what; a wife, children, or just a rented apartment in Ramat-Aviv? "What's Avi short for?" I risk, Ora throws me a quick look over her shoulder. "Avi-chai—Avichai and Mordechai—they're twins, you know." She adds lemon to the salad. "Did he change his surname to Gadot as well?" I ask her back. I'll phone him—"They all changed it together. From Gerstein to Gadot—" "How many brothers are there?" I try to sound less eager. "Four—" Ora doesn't notice, she's tearing up lettuce for a new salad. "Avichai and Mordechai and Haimka and Menahem; every Passover Seder is a project." She sets the table. "So should I set a place for you?" "You said I should talk to him," I continue my attempts at concealment; it's unbelievable, I whisper to Hedva in my head, I'm trying to hide it from Ora—"We said you should talk to him? When?" Ora opens a cabinet, takes out plates, thinking about something else. "After they caught that terrorist in the basement—" I remind her. She raises tired eyes to me. "Oh . . . right . . . but he was out of the country then . . ." "Can you give me his phone number?" I'm sweating. She's thinking about something else. She won't notice anything. She won't know. She sends me to the family phone book in the living room, yes, the little brown one, next to the phone, there's a pen and paper next to it, I open the book, find the number, return to the kitchen. "Didn't you find any paper?" Ora glances at my empty hands, smiles wearily. "I forgot that you remember everything by heart." "Only what interests me—" I mean to tell her about Kastner's funeral that surfaced after years of total obliteration, but she stops me before I can begin:

"Loya, Avi's married—"

"So?"

"I only wanted you to know—" Ora blushes.

At this moment Motik enters the kitchen. "Hi Loya, you've got regards from Avi—he said he would give you a ring—"

I look at Ora.

I won.

"Maybe you want buy Haman Ears." Morgenstern-the-grocer's pushes a flat cardboard box holding the triangular poppy-seed cookies strewn with icing sugar toward me. "They for next to nothing. Nobody in mood—" The cookies look archaeological but I buy half a kilo anyway. "This very good! Very good!" the-grocer's assures me. "Nobody in mood now because of all this troubles—that why this left over—" She hands me the bag. "But you always in good mood." She hates me. "You young, you pretty, you don't read newsespapers—"

Did the phone ring? No, but I almost fall. I really have to do something about this floor. A new tile has risen here—when I stand on it it wobbles, transmits a muffled pulse of the earth at work, somewhere down there at the center of the planet liquid fire is seething, sometimes driving a blazing vein to the top of a lopped-off mountain, spilling over the edge, dark, thick, embroidered with flashes of brilliant, living fire—

Tikva comes over. "Are you waiting for someone to phone?" She notices straightaway. I deny it. "Purim's over—but I brought you a treat anyway—" she reveals golden pastry roses, glistening with oil and honey. "The Rose of Jacob," she explains, "it's only the Ashkenazis who eat ears on Purim—here, taste. More delicious and more beautiful—"

Delicious—I'm not at all sure. But beautiful—yes; I break the curled-in shape with sticky fingers, remembering, how could I not remember, that it's like a rose—it's like a rose, Brenda said, I've never seen it, I said, then it's time you did, she said, what are you afraid of, it's only a body, your body, which in fifty years time will be earth, I jabbed, is there anything disgusting about earth? She smiled almost like the school nurse before a shot, Brenda, my last and definitely final love, try, she urged me, what can happen, this is something you haven't tried yet, so try it, perhaps this is the right kind of love for you, you've got nothing to lose—only to learn something more about life and about yourself, she promised and kept her promise—but did you learn anything, she came back to it at the airport. She insisted on accompanying me to my flight. We sat in a cafe, she with her back to the window, me with my face to the window, the runways, the planes waiting to take off. Did you learn anything? She laid the palm of her hand on the back of my hand. I nodded. I was afraid to talk. The roof of my mouth was full of tears. I looked at the airplanes. Swiss Air. British Airways. Alitalia. El Al. I knew that she was looking at me with round blue eyes bright in a full, fresh, almost beaming face.—Loya?—I don't look at her but I see her, soft auburn curls, shining skin, painted lips, a warm, padded nest without a single angle—Loya?—she shakes my hand, she wants me to look at her, she doesn't understand that I see her even when my eyes are on the planes like one picture superimposed on another, like a mistake in a photograph—

My mistake, Brenda. And your error. But did you learn anything? That partings hurt more when there is no anger or resentment or complaint against the person parted from, and nor is there any benefit accompanying the parting except for the freedom which becomes more and more, over the years, like armor. Don't touch me. Don't touch me. I wonder if it still grows around here—a plant that closed its petals in alarm at the slightest touch, *Don't-touch-me* we called it, but we touched it again as soon as it calmed down in order to make sure that it still worked, that we still had it in our power to startle a flower and make it clench—

I wander around the house, but the telephone is silent. A museum in memory of the forest fighters—your word for the partisans—was supposed to be established here, what made you change your mind, decide to turn the house and withering citrus grove into a lasso to bring me back to this place on the verge of exhaustion, I know that today, to gamble that this time I would stay, even buy a new hammock to tie to the jacaranda trees, plant a few proletarian flowers, learn to recognize birds and become acquainted with time passing in its appointed order—morning—noon—afternoon—evening—night, start sleeping at night again, sense the seasons change to the accompaniment of constant quarrels between the light and the cold and the heat and the winds—

I wander around the house, but the telephone is silent. In your work room potsherds, ancient maps, books, pages of notes, a terrible, lost war, who has the strength to live among ruins all his life? In Nahum's room, model airplanes. Photograph albums packed with friends, aerial views, a few letters, childhood books—only I pass through life with the minimum: after every affair—suddenly this desire to be rid of everything—letters, notes, postcards, small souvenirs, a few pieces of jewelry, snapshots together—to be light again to fly—and I collect everything in a big envelope into which I put a few pebbles or bits of gravel as well: the memories of Jean-Jacques sank into the Danube, the days with Eliot drowned in the Tiber and dear Brenda disappeared into the Seine. The parting in the water was gentle, conciliatory. Three times I stood on great European bridges and looked at the water of a river—opaque glass tiles, greenish-gray, matte-shiny-matte—and let go of the envelope. Only in Paris a passing Israeli tourist remarked, "Hello—you dropped something," was surprised to find that I understood, "It's all right," I said, and he waved his hand and hurried on his way. The envelope with its love floated on the water for a moment, was soaked up, and sank. Do fish eat paper? Perhaps, in years to come, a poor fisherman will catch a fish in his net, and his wife will find a pearl in its guts. From me, Madam. As a free gift. Once, twice, three times, I returned to those bridges. I stood in the same place. I looked at the water—a brown-gray ripple of never-ending movement, knowing that it was the same bridge, but not the same water, and I too was not who I had been when I let the envelope fall, everything flows and changes, even the past keeps changing as my distance from the point of origin grows greater— who took this photograph? Daddy next to our kitchen table, a cup of tea in his hand. Don't stir things up, he said in a voice that brooked no argument when I tried to ask him—what? What did I try to ask. Gone. A hole torn in my memory. Lost. Kaput. And again Daddy in an unidentified European city, at his side a woman, blurred, she must have moved while the photograph was taken, and here's a very young Davidi against the background of a forest, next to a big woman—a brave Soviet partisan, no doubt, proudly holding a submachine gun, and again an unidentified woman, bending over a baby in a stroller, who's the baby, impossible to tell, they're all alike with pompommed hats on their heads—

I wander around the house, only your room is still locked. Isn't it time to open it too? What will I find there apart from a double bed for one man, an old bureau, a clothes closet, a lamp—where's the key to your room, here it is, what can already happen, I insert it in the keyhole—just a minute—it's the phone, the phone's ringing—

I hurry to the living room.

"Hello?" Tikva's plate is next to the telephone. I tear into—why?—a golden star dripping with oil and honey—

"Loya? It's Avi. How are you—"

"Okay." My lips are sweet.

"Bon appetit—" Avi notices. "What are you eating?" The voice is warm, smiling. Without any lessons in manners.

"A Rose of Jacob—"

"Purim's already over—"

"Hmm-hmm"

"A terrible Purim." His voice is serious, measured. A historian's voice.

"You owe me a story—" I dare to remind him.

"That's why I'm calling—can you come to the university next Thursday? At eleven, quarter past—you can? Great. We'll sit in the little restaurant next to the entrance—"

Super decent. Super protected. Super married. So what. So what. I pounce on my Hungarian cosmetics that have been unemployed all these months, clean my skin, smear on a mask, wait for it to dry, peel it off, smear again, wait with eyes closed under cottonwool soaked in ice water, and I thought it was all over, I'd reached the great plateau, that from now on to the horizon there would be no mountain, no challenge, no tree, no spring, no brown gazelle or golden lion, a safe, flat space, like Daddy, like Davidi, I saw it happen, the way it could happen, life without honey or stings,

I've been through enough and from now on no leaf will stir, no bird will sing, I'm that cypress tree, an old bachelor turning into a skeleton under the flurry of the bougainvillea, but wait a minute—on Thursday before noon, in a little restaurant at the entrance to the campus, a terrible, terrible Purim, half the country is in shock, but look at Yinon, and, begging the difference, look at me. Look at me—

HOT, HOTTER, BURNING

One crystal April morning when the world—new line—*was washed in light of pristine purity*—here I've forgotten something—and now brackets (*it was no doubt just such an early morn*—new line—*when Abraham led Isaac to the mount*)—new line—*my mother rose, and prayed, and*—what comes next; I find a seat in the bus, on my way to meet someone cautious and perhaps already half in love, an agreeable tension building up inside me every time the bus stops—no, I won't be late—in any case I'm early—how everything has changed here. Expanded. The floors have been paved with pagan white marble, already dazzling, what will it be like in summer—

And this is the cafe/restaurant—trying to be dim but flooded with bright sunlight. Avi? He's here, ten minutes early too, sitting and reading a book, flooded with slanting shafts of light full of dancing crumbs of air. "What a sunny day" are the words I choose to open with, and he raises his eyes, smiles. "Spring is in the air—did you get here without any problems?" I nod, he orders real orange juice for both of us. "Will you join me?" and when it arrives, he suggests something to eat. "Have you eaten already?" He is astonished at my refusal, it doesn't occur to him that on a morning of such pristine light, eating is impossible—"Then you'll pardon me if I—" he beckons the waitress, requests breakfast, if it's still available, she smiles, it's obvious she's doing him a favor, she knows him, he always turns up just before lunchtime and asks for breakfast, killing two birds with one stone. Use your eyes and you won't be bored, Jean-Jacques said to me when I complained about French meals, four hours at the table in order to eat!

Observe the people eating, you have no idea how much you can learn from it, how they hold their fork, what they do with the knife, how quickly they chew and swallow, where they put the napkin, you can practice in the air too, and now, Avi—who has no idea how much I have learned from observing thousands of eaters—innocently devours an omelet and salad and a buttered roll, clearly hungry, eating in order to satisfy his hunger, to fill a hole and go on to the next thing—

"Another glass of juice for you? Good, bring another two glasses and clear the table please—" he smiles at the waitress without patronizing her, smiles at me, sets his elbows on the table, now there is only sun on it and two glasses full of dense orange and one flashing saltcellar—

"You're here because of me—" he looks into my eyes with light brown, almost green eyes, smiling to himself more than at me.

"Well yes, I came to hear a story." I don't understand what he's getting at.

"That's the story. It's because of me that you're here, in Israel—" He clasps his hands, leans towards me as if about to whisper a secret to me.

"I'm here because of the will—" I begin, feeling the anger mounting in my throat, this is not what I expected—

"I had a long talk with Davidi a few months before he died—we spoke about you too—a few days later he phoned to tell me that he had decided to change his will—to leave everything to you on condition that you came here—" Avi smiles.

"So are you responsible for the bit about the pyxis too?" I'm sure he isn't, but I ask anyway. To let him know that he doesn't know everything.

"About the what?" I was right. He's perplexed. "No, I don't know anything about that—it's between you and him, I presume—" and he doesn't ask. Two points in his favor. I'm still waiting for the story.

"Why did you talk to Davidi in the first place?"

"Not only to him—I spent three years making the rounds of your neighborhood and recording anyone who was prepared to tell me what happened to him in the period of the Holocaust—I crossed-checked testimonies, but—"

"But—?"

"There are as many versions as there are people—that is to say—basically it's the same story—but the details—you have an interesting life story too—"

"Me?" What's he trying to hint at? He bends over his briefcase, takes out a thin bundle of cards held together with a rubber ring. And a fountain pen from his shirt pocket. He isn't in love. Not even on the way to being . . . Another big mistake on my part. Time to give it a rest—

"Let's make it simple." He writes at the top of a card Loya Kaplan, 1946. "Leah," I correct him. He raises surprised eyes to me, raises his eyebrows, crosses out Loya, writes in Leah. "You were born in Venice—" He knows that too.

"Did Ora tell you?"

"Not Ora, Davidi. And also Gedalya Horovitz—"

"Look," panic rises in my throat—I want it to be clear—"my parents weren't in the Holocaust—"

Avi breathes a sigh, as if he's been through all this before. He moves away from me, leans back in his chair.

"When you say weren't in the Holocaust, what exactly do you mean?"

"They weren't in the camps—they weren't in Auschwitz—they didn't have blue numbers on their arms like Mrs. Morgenstern from the grocery and that madman who lived in the shipping crate and Hasia Horovitz and Minaleh's mother—"

"Ora's father doesn't have a blue number on his arm either—"

For a moment I'm taken aback. Because it's true. And because I never noticed. And because in my foolishness I imagined that anyone who didn't have a blue number—

"In your age group—" Avi turns the cards over in his hands, avoiding my eyes. "It wasn't spoken about—" he gives me a safety net. He waits for a minute. Then he tries again. "Do you know where your parents were between 1940 and 1945?"

"My father's a native of Prague. Most of the time he was in Prague—Prague wasn't destroyed—"

Sometimes, before the movie, on this or that anniversary of the end of the war, they screened documentaries in flickering black-and-white showing tanks heavily moving, cannons shooting screen-searing flashes, recoiling backwards, the facades of buildings collapsing in inexplicable slow motion, tall flames and water hoses and the silhouettes of firemen and cities in ruins and broken-winged airplanes tail-spinning in explosions of fire, lucky for me that I was born later, I shrink in my seat next to Daddy, exempt from translation duties, these movies have a soundtrack in stern Hebrew, was Prague destroyed like that too, I whisper to Daddy, his head moves from side to side in the flickering light of the flames on the screen, what luck for him, I think, feeling protected, this luck, I'm sure, passes from generation to generation like the right appearance, fair skin, blue eyes, life-saving fair hair—

"But at some stage he was deported to Theresienstadt—" Avi says with absolute conviction.

"You mean Terezin?—He was there for a year or two—but it wasn't a concentration camp—it was a kind of ghetto for VIPs—they put on concerts and plays there and they had football teams—" I remembered something to that effect.

"And your mother?" Avi looks at me closely.

"She was a communist—" The rumors, a persistent buzzing, suddenly words in my mouth.

"Was she in Terezin too?"

I shrug my shoulders. Maybe. Maybe not. I have no idea.

"I believe my parents met after the war, in Italy—" It's not exactly an answer, but it's what I have to offer. It's logical.

"And Davidi?" Avi changes the subject. Maybe he senses my discomfort.

"Davidi was with the partisans." This is much easier for me. "He fought the Nazis—"

"Did your father tell you what he did in Terezin?"

"No, not really. A sentence here and there. He worked in the library there—they had a huge library there—over 60,000 books—"

Avi nods. Waits for the continuation. But there is no continuation. They had concerts there, they put on plays, I've already said that.

"And about the deportations—"

"What deportations?"

Avi bows his head. The sun glitters in his hair, once evidently abundant, now sparse, thready. He shakes his head as if disagreeing with the table.

"Your father presented you with a . . . very partial picture—"

"My father was as honest as the day is long—" I raise my voice. Avi leans back. Folds his hands.

"It isn't a question of honesty—" he says finally in a measured tone.

"My father was a very reticent person—he could talk to me for hours about some Roman emperor, but about himself—nothing—nada—when I asked him he would say 'Don't stir'—"

"Don't stir?"

I stir the orange juice left in my glass with the straw, illustrating the way the sediment rose to the surface. "*Why hast thou disquieted me to bring me up . . .*"

Avi nods.

"Yes—I know—he didn't tell you about Davidi, I suppose—"

"What I know is that Davidi was Daddy's student at the University of Prague—he came to Prague from some small town—Banská Bystrica, if I'm not mistaken—"

Avi nods. "The center of the rebellion," he says.

"What rebellion?" The only rebellion I'd ever heard of was the one in the Warsaw Ghetto.

"The Slovak rebellion—"

Everything more or less figures and also fits the dramatis personae; Daddy sitting in the library in the VIP ghetto while Davidi fought with the Slovakian partisans. And maybe that's what stood between them like a shadow for over twenty years—

"Five months after Davidi arrived in Theresienstadt—" Avi begins.

"Davidi wasn't in Terezin!" I protest. Avi leans toward me, his elbows on the table. Glances at me briefly. Bows his head, moves the saltcellar a centimeter forward, a centimeter to the left, as if moving a rook on a chess board. I wait. He lets go of the saltcellar, raises his head. He bites his lower lip.

"Davidi arrived there in April '42—" his eyes are green-brown, narrowed, penetrating. "In September '42 he was sent from there in a transport to Treblinka—"

"To Treblinka?" That name, annoying, grotesque. With a "ka" at the end, like an affectionate suffix. Like Kalinka, like Orinka, like Loyinka—

"Twenty transports left Theresienstadt for Treblinka—" Avi leans on his elbows and forearms, invading my half of the table. "And then to Auschwitz—" I can smell the omelet from his mouth.

"From Treblinka to Auschwitz?" I move away, lean against the back of my chair.

"From Treblinka nobody went anywhere—" Avi bows his head to his forearms crossed on the table, shakes his head, breathes an impatient sigh. "Treblinka was an extermination camp—"

"Like Auschwitz?" my voice is hoarse.

"Like Auschwitz-Birkenau—part of Auschwitz was a concentration camp . . . do you know the difference between a concentration camp and an extermination camp?"

He leans backward, folds his arms, hugs his elbows with his hands. The sun has already moved away from our table. The saltcellar has gone out. The glasses of orange juice are empty.

"I can imagine—" he has to bend over to hear me.

I'm thirsty.

"But the blue number on the arm—" Davidi didn't have one. I'm certain.

"Was actually a sign of hope." Avi tightens his lips. "Anyone who got a number got an extension—sometimes a week, sometimes a month—some people even lasted a year—"

"In Treblinka?"

"No, in Auschwitz—"

"And in Treblinka there weren't any survivors?" So how did Davidi? How did Davidi? What story is he trying to tell me?

"Only a few hundred—most of the survivors escaped in the first months and afterwards during the revolt that broke out there in '43—Davidi managed to escape after eight months and return—but that's really a long story—to Banska Bystrica—"

"And in Treblinka were there gas chambers—crematoria—" No. He'll say no, because if there were, then how did Davidi, how did Davidi—

"Gas chambers, yes. Crematoria like there were in Auschwitz-Birkenau, no. In Treblinka they burned the bodies in open pits—"

"Who burned them—"

"Small groups of prisoners who were kept alive for this purpose until—"

Wood burns, flesh burns, fat burns very well—your voice loud and hoarse, your laughter malevolent—and Daddy puts his arm around your shoulders, leads you to and fro, trying to calm you—

"Davidi too—?" my voice jars.

Avi gives me a long look, as if trying to assess what the effect of his words will be. His nod is barely perceptible—

"And how come my father didn't—how come my father didn't land up in—" my eyes are burning. My head is boiling.

"I thought perhaps you could tell me—I imagine it was a matter of luck. Or maybe connections. Perhaps he was classed as a 'Prominent A'—do you know where he studied? In Berlin? Maybe he had connections with professors who became Nazi sympathizers after Hitler's rise to power—"

The waitress comes up with two glasses of boiling water and a pale wooden box full of teabags, which she sets on the table with a click. Avi chooses mint tea, tears a sachet of sugar and another one and a third one too; the grains fall to the bottom of the glass in a slow drift. He inserts a teaspoon—stirs—the spoon rings against the sides of the glass—the grains become transparent, turn into gossamer threads in gold-green water—in a few seconds they'll disappear without a trace—Avi goes on stirring in silence. Waiting for me to react?

"Such things happened—" he says in the end, his eyes on the glass.

I begin to drink. I sip hot, very hot, boiling hot, I don't care, I take another sip, choke—burst out coughing—spit the boiling water onto the back of my hand—

Avi—

The waitress—

A napkin wrapped around ice cubes on the burn on the back of my hand—

"Are you all right?" Avi holds the ice cubes on my hand.

"Did you talk to Davidi about my father too?" I recover my composure.

"Yes, but he didn't know too much. He was sent to Treblinka—and your father—"

"Remained in Terezin until the end of the war—" Suddenly I remember. "He said something about a typhus epidemic that broke out there immediately after the liberation—"

"Yes—" Avi glances at his watch, looks at me. "Listen—it's enough for today. I'm going to drive you home now—don't say no. You look as if you're going to faint. Let's go—we'll carry on another day—"

Avi drives slowly, giving me sidelong glances every couple of minutes. Outside a blazing sun; light raging in the windowpanes, the chrome trim of the cars, the vestiges of shallow puddles. I left my sunglasses in the cafe—my eyes are burning—a familiar nausea churning above my diaphragm—

"Listen . . . I'm sorry." Avi stammers slightly. Another two points in his favor. He isn't made of wood. "I had no idea that you had so little . . . But of course, you didn't spend much time in Israel over the past twenty years—"

"What's that got to do with it?" I don't mean to, but I sound angry. I haven't got the strength for a Zionist speech. I feel sick.

"In recent years a lot of material has been published here—a lot of memoirs—interviews—television programs—" He stops at a red light, takes advantage of the opportunity to examine my face. "How do you feel?"

"The sun—it's driving me crazy—it's drilling into my head—" I close my eyes, but the sun skewers my eyelids, sends veins of fire to my ears, my throat, when will we get there, I need to lie down immediately in the kind dank darkness as in a moist black shroud wrapped around a body dug up from the grave into the harsh light in order to preserve the moistures of its life—

This morning has turned against me: when I set out, the sun shone, the mimosa bloomed in hundreds of tiny suns on the roadside, gold danced in the air, and I—*Carpe diem* I said to myself, seize the day—

"Here?" Avi had already turned into the neighborhood. "Left and right—" I guide him to what is more and more evidently the noise of sawing—Avi stops the car at the beginning of the path between your garden and the one next door and goes to see what's happening—"They're chopping down your ficus tree—"

If my head hadn't been boiling I would have burst out like you; What, what, by what right—for years that ficus has been growing gloriously here—no, you wouldn't have said ficus—Absalom tree, you called it—but my head—the nausea—and now my knees are trembling too—how am I going to get out of the car—how am I going to walk into the terrible noise—

"I'm not leaving you here," Avi decides for me. "I have to get back to the university—" he drives slowly. "I'm taking you to Ora's—Ora's not at home but Mechora's there—I'll tell her you're not feeling well—so she won't nag you—"

When I wake up I'm in a strange room. How did I get there? Supported by Avi—he whispers to Ora's mother—she brings me a glass of water, hands me a pill, "one of Baruch's—I have never needed such things—but I'm made of iron." Judging by the color of the stripes between the slats of the blinds it's already evening. I try to get up—something falls to the floor—the sound of approaching footsteps—

"Loya?" it's Ora, filling the doorway.

"Yes . . . I woke up—" I try to sit up. I feel dizzy.

"You gave us a scare—" Ora enters the room, "Avi's already called three times to ask how you are—what happened?"

"I had a huge migraine—"

"Are you having your period?"

The phone saves me from having to say no, not for the past three years—Motik answers from somewhere in the living room, "yes, I think she's woken up" and "just a minute, I'll go and check." He knocks on the half-open door. "Loya? Do you want to prove to Avi that you're alive?" and gives me the phone.

"Loya?" His pleasant voice instantly takes me back years. Because this morning happened years ago. Where am I now and where's the Loya who climbed onto the bus on a fine spring day on her way to meet someone cautious and perhaps already a little bit in love—

"Yes, how are you?" I respond stupidly.

"How am I? How are you! How's your head?"

"My head? On its way back to its place, I think—" and I suddenly remember the ficus—the Absalom tree being chopped down by a screaming electric saw—

"Listen—after you feel a bit better—if you want any help—" Guilty feelings. Guilty feelings. I can sense them from miles away.

"Tell me—is there a way of checking—finding out—from when to when my father was in Terezin—and perhaps also if my mother was there—"

"No problem—all I have to do is pick up the phone to Kibbutz Givat Haim-Ihud—they have a museum and archives there—all I have to know is the full name and date of birth—"

"Avi—" Ora removes the receiver gently from my hand. "Perhaps you should wait to investigate all this family history until Loya feels better? At the moment she looks green." She listens to him with her head bowed and looks at me. "Okay" she says. And again. "Okay. Okay. All right. Good-bye—" And to me: "Avi will call you when he has answers—" But I didn't give him any details, I remember, reassured; very good—I didn't give him any details—

All week long I try to rescue what remains of the ficus tree. Phone calls to Advocate Betzer, the local council, the offices of the Nature Protection Society, the "Beautiful Land Of Israel" movement, the Environment Ministry—I didn't know there were so many green addresses and that none of them actually had anything to do.

"Loya?" Arlozora had already started working in the council. "Stop making a fuss. Davidi planted a ficus whose roots spread to the neighbors' plot. Now they have to level the land. To dig foundations. They're putting up a four-story building, and that ficus is in the way—the most we can do is uproot it and try to fit it into the Soldiers' Memorial Park—yes, behind the new center—listen—I'm sending you a landscape gardener—"

You should have seen those bulldozers. Perhaps it was in order not to let them attack your house that you left it to me, you hoped I would arrive on the scene like the goddess Anat, that I would fight the people of the seashore and strike the populace of the sunrise, that I would drive away captives with my club and the foe with my bowstring, glean knee-deep in warrior blood, neck-deep in the gore of soldiers—I never understood what exactly the Ugaritic poets meant, but it was nearly as beautiful as the Bible and also very similar to the Bible and easy as the Bible to learn by heart—

I stand outside and watch them crushing the honeysuckle hedge, trampling the newly planted pansies and petunias, breaking the Jerusalem stone flagstones of the garden path in order to reach the remaining stumps of the ficus and dig among its roots and pull up a large lump of earth and a crippled trunk with half a crest—and all at once to open up a view of the lot from which the neighbors' house has been razed and which is full of builders and surveyors—"I don't know if it will take," the landscape gardener says to me. She's very tanned. She wears an old straw hat. "Pity they didn't think of it before—a tree like that—" They raise the tree onto a kind of platform with a crane. I remain standing opposite the gaping pit with torn roots sticking out of its walls. I wonder if the roots behave like tails—if they go on living afterwards, twitching for a little longer—if this strong root which ran under the floor and raised the tiles will calm down now—suffocated for lack of light and air—

"Fill it up, level the ground—" Amitai scolds the workers, "don't leave an open grave here—" They fill the pit with the earth removed from it—earth the color of reddish clay—and add another layer the color of bitter chocolate—

"Now you can make yourself a proper garden," says Amitai. "Most flowers like the sun—and the season's just right—"

But I go back inside with a feeling of defeat. I begin to understand why you hate bulldozers—

The dates. We never celebrated Davidi's birthday, or Daddy's, Nahum's we stopped celebrating after his bar mitzvah, mine too, although Ora remembered, brought me little gifts—where can I find your birth dates—the Missing Relatives Department gave up the ghost a long time ago—

Perhaps in your room—

You were in Terezin—but you never said a word about it; you were deported to Treblinka—how were you saved from the gas chambers? And Nahum's mother—where was she? And . . . for God's sake, what's her name? I don't even know her name—you kept so much hidden. And perhaps—you were waiting for me to ask. But I didn't ask. And Nahum; did he know? Didn't he know? During the Eichmann trial he was training to be a pilot. You traveled there every day. Daddy too—but he worked in Jerusalem—one evening you came over to our house—Daddy was already back—you were very upset—Daddy poured you a shot of Slivovitz—I stood in the door to my room with a pencil and an eraser—you were stopping me from concentrating: I had to draw a map of central Europe and you were arguing in agitated Czech, spitting Lowenstein and Edelstein and Murmelstein and Epstein like sparks from a stone—the eraser slipped from my hand, rolled between your feet—Excuse me, just a minute, sorry—I pushed your ankle politely aside in order to reach the eraser and encountered something hard. Have you got a revolver in your sock? I asked in alarm, you didn't answer, you turned on your heel and rushed out wildly—

Two weeks later I plucked up the courage to ask Daddy what the quarrel was about. An old argument, he waved his hand in front of his eyes as if to chase away a cloud.

"Are you bad friends forever?" I tried to make it sound ridiculous, but in my heart of hearts I feared that it was true, Davidi had stopped popping in for "five minutes" and staying for hours, standing next to the front door, only consenting to come in after being urged—but not for supper!—sitting down, accepting tea and Marie biscuits—Davidi refuses to let the past rest in peace, said Daddy, and I asked, the Eichmann trial or Bar Kokhba? Because there were bitter arguments between you on both subjects, but Daddy only shook his head and refused to add another word. When Nahum came home on leave from his course I asked him if he knew anything about the new quarrel, but he didn't know either. Or perhaps he knew and didn't want to tell me—I was "too young"—

Between me and the building site they put up a partition of gray boards. Beyond it I can hear the cement mixer and the workers shouting at each other; in Arabic. At night I lock up well, drag up a chair and push the top under the door handle, make sure that the telephone is within reach. Yesterday I slipped the bread knife under my pillow—

The covered pit gleams in the sun like a big scar; not a leaf sprouts from that soil. Black soil. Dead. Only the sun shines on it with a kind of spiteful glee. I won't make another garden—

The noise and the sudden light have chased the birds away; there is no Caesar, no woodpecker, no Dubček. Perhaps they have all moved with the Abasalom tree to the fallen soldiers Memorial Park. The French waiters too, the Polish yentas, the executioners—all gone. Only the Mafia aren't afraid of anyone; black and arrogant they glitter in the sun, cursing in Italian—

Passover comes very early this year, I hear in the-grocer's, and at home I am greeted by the ringing of the telephone—Avi—Avi—Avi—and I still haven't found out when all the dead were born—

"What are you doing for the Seder?"—it's Tikva.

"I don't know yet—" It's hard for me to hide my disappointment. My relief.

"Then you're coming to us!" Tikva decides for me because all-Israel-are-responsible-for-one-another-and-interfere-in-each-other's-lives-and-don't-let-you-breathe—

Passover is early this year? Perhaps that's why there's no smell from the citrus grove yet and the pomegranate tree is bare and not a tree but a kind of fountain of twigs in which the sunset becomes entangled for a few moments every evening—I take all your books out onto the picnic blanket spread on the grass; perhaps an old document, a passport photo will fall out of one of them—here they all are, Canaanites and Sidonites and ancient Hebrews, next to books about Ugaritic rituals, about Bar Kokhba and his friends and about the Roman emperors out to get him, and here's our old friend Hannibal as well—and behind this wall of books is another one— it's Daddy's!—Ranke and Burckhardt and Mommsen, kept for me even though they're written in German, and here's Collingwood and Croce, and also more ancient friends, Plutarch and Polybius and Livy and Thucydides, and I open them all, bus tickets apparently used as bookmarks fall out of a few of them, a small entrance ticket to a Hanukkah party—please keep your seat sir and desist from creating disturbances—a newspaper cutting—HEAR OH ISRAEL! *That which we feared has come upon us. The greatest national catastrophe in history has befallen us!* BLOOD FOR BLOOD! NATION FOR NATION! REVENGE AND REDEMPTION! AND IF NOT NOW— THEN WHEN? THE HASMONEAN COVENANT—I shake another book and am rewarded with a lottery ticket—a ration coupon—a New Year greeting card sprinkled with silver from a colleague—a yellowing newspaper cutting from *Davar* November 1952, *Zionists and Israelis desiring to be citizens of two motherlands have understood that in one motherland they are free . . . whereas over there, in that other motherland, in the kingdom of the Cominform they are enslaved a priori*—I don't remember reading *Davar* at home, why did you see fit to keep this cutting precisely, and here's another one, from *Haaretz* this time, it too from November 1952, what happened then, *The Israeli public demands that they return to the bosom of their people . . . as a mother demands the return of her sons. Will they let their mother's pleas go unanswered?* What pathos and what Hebrew—and here's another cutting—from what newspaper? Not clear, in the margins, in your handwriting, you note "from the debate in the Knesset"—most of it is faded, your underlining for emphasis only makes it more difficult to read, *Our nation is blessed with a long memory—it will never forget*—but what is no longer clear, *We will stand unflinching behind* what, *There is a nemesis in history*, who is the Knesset member familiar with the term, *they have learned that there is no plural of "motherland." A nation does not have two motherlands, just as a man does not have two birth mothers*, why did it preoccupy you, and here, this too is underlined *the Slanksy-Clementis gang of spies and traitors*—wasn't it connected to some kind of trial? From a volume of Polybius—there is no better way for men to improve themselves than by learning from the past—more newspaper cuttings fall, *Al Hamishmar* from March 1953, *The progressive world mourns the death of Stalin*—yes, I remember—*the captain and the general—a mighty and unique phenomenon in the history of the world*—but why did you keep these cuttings—in agreement? In disagreement? Out of a wish to investigate one day the Israeli march of folly, or perhaps, like Herodotus, here he is, among the translations from the Greek historians by Dr. Alexander Shor—like Herodotus simply to preserve from decay the remembrance of the extraordinary deeds of men—and here—here—how glad I am to see them!—the four little volumes of Mommsen's *History of Rome*, and what falls out of volume two, a cutting from *Davar* circled with a fountain pen—*An unknown person threw a stone at the Czech legation in Tel Aviv—a windowpane shattered—a clerk in the legation saw the perpetrator running away*—Davidi? It was Davidi! I'm almost positive—if only I knew what was behind all this—this incident too happened in November 1952—good, in the meantime I'm trying to find a document—a certificate—the copy of a license—something—but there's nothing—another invitation to a Hanukkah party, a railway ticket, a few wedding invitations—I open the books to the sun, to let it evaporate the smell of pickled time from their pages, go back inside, open the windows, fill them with bedclothes and pillows—an early spring cleaning for Passover, and all the germs of darkness will be burned by the fire of the sun, the house will be aired, recuperate—why haven't I done it up to now—and maybe I'll get in a painter—in the rusty mailbox there was an official letter from the local council waiting for me, they're coming to check if your house is worthy to be left standing—go on, let them come, there's a hardware store in the new center, there I'll be able to get plaster to fill in the cracks and a spatula—what did you call it—*mamreah? matiah?*—a smearer? A plasterer?—and a broad paintbrush and whitewash smelling of moist cleanliness—go on, let them come—I didn't manage to save the tree—but the house will be spick and span and ready as an army base for the CO's inspection—they don't know who they're dealing with—

"Are you spring cleaning for Passover?" Adriana laughs at me from the entrance to her boutique when she sees me with the paint and paintbrush. "Come in for a minute, I've just received some fantastic stuff from Milan—"

I go in to take a look, maybe I'll buy myself something new to wear, spring is in the air. "Where are you for the Seder?" asks Adriana between one dress and the next and I shrug my shoulders. "Try this one on." She hands me a discreet creation in beige. "I'm getting away from here," she informs me through the changing booth curtain. "I'm sending the girls to London and taking a cruise on the love boat—" I emerge in the dress. "Oh no!" Adriana wrings her hands. "Take it off, take it off, take it off, that color is terrible for you, it adds ten years at least to your age, no, you need something much brighter—try this one—" I return to the booth to get undressed and put on something burgundy, and in the meantime she invites me to join her on the cruise, maybe there's still room, she'll talk to her travel agent, no? Definitely not?

"Aren't you the energetic one?" Amitai helps himself to mineral water and sits down on the sheet-covered sofa to watch me battling with a high-up crack, sandpapering the banks, wetting them, like the man at the hardware store told me—waiting a minute—and now filling the bed of the Nile with the special white crack filler—

"You're wasting your time." Amitai stretches out his legs, pleased with himself, he wouldn't dream of offering help, not he, he has no such airs and graces. "In a few months you'll have a crack somewhere else—the earth here is hard at work . . . this whole house is standing on chicken legs." He wobbles a floor tile with the toe of his shoe. "What got into you all of a sudden?" "It's Passover isn't it?" This is the best way I can think of to shut him up, but he has pronouncements on this subject too: "I said long ago that it's in the genes of the women here—as soon as Passover approaches—religious or not—they start scrubbing and airing closets and painting walls—" "What's wrong with that?" I ask from the top of the ladder. "I didn't say there was anything wrong with it—why shouldn't you work a little—I'm a feminist—" and at that moment the phone rings. Oh no. He picks it up. "Yes? Yes. Who wants her? No she isn't here—" I climb down the ladder and snatch the receiver from his hand, "Hello?" "Loya?" It's Ora. Only Ora. "Who's the idiot who answered the phone? Your peasant? Send him back to the farm—" Amitai looks at me inquisitively, and I wave him good-bye and send him on his way, go, go already. "He's gone," I say, ready to listen. But Ora has no special news to impart. "I just wanted to know if you have anywhere to go for the Seder . . . I'm drawing up the guest list now, yes, this year it's at my place—who's coming? As of now, apart from all of us, Menahem and his new wife and Avi—" "Avi?" "Yes, and maybe Gadi, Vered's boyfriend, too—" "So count me in as well," I interrupt her. Avi. Avi. Avi. "Great." Ora sounds genuinely pleased. Only afterwards I remember Tikva—did I promise her? No, I didn't promise. So that's okay. I'm going to Ora for the Seder. Wearing the burgundy dress sold to me by Adriana. I need new shoes. A haircut. And a rinse. And until then I'll open everything up to the sun. And I'll buy a new rug for Nahum's room. I saw something in light blue—only your room's left—if they come to check they'll make me open it too—who knows what's in it—maybe a black crack from top to bottom—

Should I open it? What will I find already? Your big bed made, perhaps, calm at last, and what else? Photographs? Documents? Clothes? Leather boots from your time in the *partizanka*? You wanted me to come back here. Miss Loya Kaplan herself, she and not a representative, she and not a party acting on her behalf or standing in for her, she herself in person—Advocate Betzer read the preamble to the will aloud to me—when did he dictate it to you, I inquired from America, I was on vacation, taking the opportunity to wander around Boston with Hedva, a nice, aristocratic, university town, you'll like it, you'll be my neighbor, Hedva was full of plans and practical advice, and it was there the phone call reached me after a weeks-long search, is he dead?—was the first question I asked when it turned out to be a lawyer from Tel Aviv, talking about a will which depended only on me to take effect, is he dead? When did he die? Six weeks ago, the answer crossed the ocean quickly, but the information was not taken in, it was impossible to nullify you, for a quarter of a century I hadn't seen you, for fourteen years—ever since Nahum's death—I hadn't spoken to you, and nevertheless you were always there, that is to say here, in this house, charm and rage and iron-silver curls and blazing silver eyes, Daddy too was there for a few years after he died, brown and bald and quiet, years passed before my memory became hollow of him like the dead in Herculaneum—white plaster accurate and false—horrifyingly real—but nevertheless dead white, as if made from the cold materials of the moon, an induction center of the dead—I saw those plaster-of-Paris dead—none of them thought his death was upon him—like Daddy in the library—Friday. Saturday. Sunday—

Sometimes you would come in dreams; strange, not yourself. Once you were the corpse in Rembrandt's *Anatomy Lesson*—suddenly lifting your head—Eliot used to write down his dreams as soon as he woke up, before they evaporated in the morning light—I was too lazy; I told him, sometimes—after a few months more than the dream itself I remembered the words in which the dream was caught like a flimsy scarf in a thorn bush— the earth works, memory works and changes, the dead too are not idle, but you were alive and I knew that the minute I wanted to I could land right in the middle of your glittering anger, which was, if I may be permitted to say so now, a kind of love—

When did he dictate this will to you? I inquired over sea and ocean, a month before he died, were you at his side in the final moments? I was angry that I hadn't been informed, but how was I to be found, I was on vacation, I left no tracks, who exactly could I complain to, more or less, said the lawyer, what do you mean, more or less? I let my anger escape, I went to the geriatric hospital and spoke to him in the presence of two witnesses—don't worry, everything's legal, he was completely lucid, he only went into a coma the next day—what were his last words? What wouldn't I give to know—Giordano Bruno, on the stake, said to a peasant woman adding twigs to the bonfire of his death *O, sancta simplicitas*, but Advocate Betzer couldn't remember, why should I lie to you, he talked about all kinds of things, Goethe said *Light, more light*, perhaps you might remember anyway, I pressed him, I can't be sure of the exact words, *I have no enemies*, Ivan the Terrible said on his deathbed to the confessor priest who asked him to forgive his enemies, *I killed them all*, why was it important to him for me to come? That's quite obvious, isn't it? But he didn't make it a condition that I stay in Israel, *My troubles*, said Marie Antoinette a moment before mounting the guillotine, *are now ending, yours are only beginning*. No, I convinced him there was no point in that, you can come and sell up and take the money and run—excuse me? It's just an expression, like in the movies, oh yes, right, you don't recall anything else, *God will forgive me*, said Voltaire, *it's his profession*—

Open it. Whatever is behind the door can't do anyone any harm. And neither can you—even the consolation that you are gradually turning into phosphates and carbonates, breaking up into the elements, rising in the roots, climbing up the trunk, turning into light saturated leaves, bathing in the rain, in brief, returning to this world in a plant incarnation, you didn't leave me, it cost a fortune, this madness, the lawyer told me, flying the body to Cyprus, returning the box with the ashes, in the meantime in the pyxis, is it a test and if so of what—

Telephone. This time it's Avi. I'm sure—

"Loya? How are you."

"Better; but I still haven't found documents with dates of birth anywhere here—"

"Pity—" Avi sounds genuinely disappointed. An investigator who sees his prey slipping away from him? "But there's still a way—even if you only know the approximate dates, you can sit in the Theresienstadt Memorial Museum and check—they have lists of everyone who was sent to the ghetto there, when they arrived and when they left—"

"Tell me—those lists—how reliable are they?"

"They're extremely accurate—"

"The Germans listed every Jew who came and went—"

"The Jews did—"

"The Jews?"

"They had a registration department in the Aeltestenrat—"

"Aeltestenrat—is that like Judenrat—?"

"Yes—"

"There was someone here on the block who they said was in the Judenrat—" the memories pounced. The words escaped from me, "Once they wrote on the wall of his porch: Traitor! Murderer!"

"Loya—"

"And Hershkowitz Get-lost from the haberdashers," I'm talking like a burst dam—memories and words all at once. "they called him 'Kapo' behind his back, he had a blue number on his arm, and there was someone who lived in a shipping crate—he didn't want to move into a house, we used to throw gravel at him from a distance and run around the crate—after the Eichmann trial they found him hanging in Abramson's orange grove—"

"Loya—"

"But nobody talked about it, they didn't talk about it at all, except for Minaleh—she told real horror stories—"

"Yes, Ora told me about the trip to Jerusalem—"

"The trip to Jerusalem?"

"At the end of the third grade—"

Nobody related to it afterwards, nobody talked about it, we ourselves didn't want to remember what had gotten into us—the whole class with the homeroom teacher Drora and Bilu's mother and Dina's mother who's a nurse and one father with a gun—Elhanan's father—we shouldn't have gotten onto the truck—Minaleh didn't want to get on and Elhanan's father picked her up and swung her through the air and sat her on the bench and Yosefa pleaded, me too, and Arlozora and Ruthie, Ora climbed up by herself, but I was borne aloft for a moment, I spread out my arms, I was given a full-circle spin perhaps because I was the shortest and lightest, and I landed, too soon, on the front end of the bench and squeezed my way in between the boys' knees and the girls' knees, and reached Ora who made room for me between her and Minaleh and in a few minutes we were already singing "Our Driver's a Jolly Good Fellow" and "Our Truck is Big and Gray, It will Take Us Far Away" and the truck drove and on every turn we slanted between shrieks of laughter and stop pushing and what can I do they fell on top of me, and a bag of fruit toffees passed from hand to hand, go on, take one, and in the middle of all this and who wants to drink and what's the time and how far have we come I hear next to me a kind of high-pitched, continuous wail, barely audible but growing louder, why are you crying, Ora leans over my knees to Minaleh, but she doesn't stop, her fists in her eyes, she cries harder, Bilu's mother makes her way to her, tries to get her to talk, offers her a banana, asks her if she feels sick, if she wants to throw up, if the driver should stop the truck, never mind, it happens, maybe a little water from the canteen or a little hot tea from the thermos, but Minaleh cries and cries, children far from us fall silent, whisper to each other, what's wrong with her, why is she crying, and the crying grows louder, Minaleh opens a pink mouth wide, shouts something in the middle of her crying, her eyes are covered with her fists, Minaleh, look at me, look at me for a minute, Bilu's mother has seated herself on the opposite bench, the boys made room for her, she puts out her hands to take hold of Mina-leh's wrists, grips them, tries to expose Minaleh's eyes, but Minaleh begins to hit out around her, to scream at the top of her voice, you want to make children into sausages! Kapo! You're a kapo! She screams at Bilu's mother, she hits her, you want to make children into sausages! They're taking us to a sausage factory! And the terrible crying infects Arlozora and Yosefa and Dina and Ruhama and Adriana and Sarka, a boy at the end of the bench yells, stamp and shout! Stamp and shout! Make them stop the truck! And he starts to stamp on the floor of the truck with his hiking boots, and Ora makes her way to the window at the back of the driver's cabin and bangs on it with her fists, stop, stop, stop, and the truck slows down and stops at the side of the road between deserted hills, and the teacher Drora gets out of the cabin and Elhanan's father and Bilu's mother together take Minaleh off the truck, crying loudly, kicking, resisting with all her strength as if she is being led to the slaughter, the rest of us are silent, stunned by the stopping of the truck, from its heights we look at Minaleh between three adults, one of them the nurse who offers her something to drink, and Minaleh resists with all her might, turning her head away, pursing her lips as if she is being offered poison, she is still crying but more quietly, she is trem-bling violently, the truck driver gets down too, comes around to the back of the truck, he has a huge black moustache, what's going on here, he asks, and Elhanan's father hands him the Czech gun and turns to us in a pleas-ant voice—come, children, get down for a bit, I'm sure some of you need to pee—you can go over there, behind the bushes—and he holds up his hands to help us down, Minaleh is already whimpering softly, exhausted, they carry her to the cabin—we surround the truck and look around: a narrow road between high hills made of big rocks and small trees—look children, says Elhanan's father—this is Bab-el-Wad—

"Loya? Are you there? Okay, then I'll see you at Ora's, at the Seder—"

"I don't know if I'm coming to Ora's Seder," I demur. Suddenly I've lost the desire. Or the strength.

"But Ora told me you were coming—" he protests. He cares—

"You know how many years I haven't been to a Seder?"

"Then maybe you should—precisely for that reason—" Is he trying to persuade me?

"We'll see—we'll see—" I'm under no obligation; I'm not a relation, not a member of the family. I'm truly free. A single orphan—

"Ora will be very disappointed if you don't come—" Yes, he's trying to persuade me!

"She'll get over it, don't worry—" I'm treading a fine line here. What exactly do I want?

"Aren't you good friends? I understood from Ora that—wait till you meet Loya—you know how many times I've heard her say that—"

"When? A quarter of a century ago? We were very good friends when we were small—but since then—each of us turned in her own direction," I quote Mechora's malicious prediction.

"That's a pity." Avi's voice is suitably sad. A silence. I wait. He has something else to say. He hesitates. I wait. "My best friend fell in the Yom Kippur War." He falls silent. The rest is clear. If he were alive today, they would still be friends—or perhaps the opposite; if he were alive today, who knows—

"Maybe I will come to Ora's—" I wonder aloud, and make up my mind in silence. Yes, I will go. In my new burgundy dress. And I'll find a hairdresser to give me a decent haircut and a rinse and a manicure because my nails have been ruined by the sandpapering and painting—I'll make myself as beautiful as I can. And then we'll see.

The moon is full. The roundest moon of the year—exactly in the middle of the month, exactly in the middle of the year; the neighborhood is bathed in the fragrance of orange blossom and full of parked cars. Guests step out with covered pots or flowers or big baking tins glittering in aluminum foil—in my hand is a stiff cardboard box holding two bottles of Yarden wine, the bestest what is, said the-grocer's, and all the best and happy holiday to you. I also bought two packets of luxury matzo from her—one with eggs, and one with apple juice—that's something I haven't yet tasted; I wonder if they've succeeded in improving the taste of desert dust—

On the pavement outside Ora and Motik's villa three big cars are parked slantwise. The kitchen window is open and full of light and voices. I feel as if I'm pulsating; my ears are roaring as if I'm holding a conch shell to them. I ring the bell with a cold finger. "Loya! Look how beautiful she is!" Ora, in the kind of black dress Polish mothers wear to important weddings, is really glad to see me. "Yinon—here's your girlfriend—"

Yinon—completely bald except for a strange crest—wearing baggy pants and a black T-shirt printed with two horrified silver skulls and the name of the rock band Metallica dripping silver—smiles at me, takes the wine, "We could open a bar here with all this wine—do you know how to mix cocktails?" And I'm already in the living room filled with a long table gleaming with long-legged glasses and little glass bowls and all kinds of Haggadoth and festive people like a wreath around it—Ora's mother lines up the salt-cellars with the bowls of horseradish and the dishes of *haroseth*, her father sits dazed in a corner, Vered, Gilad, and Udi are laughing at something, they barely nod their heads in greeting, Motik is talking to a tall man with a wild mop of curls accompanied by a pretty woman, a few children come in, go out, the archaeological grandmother is here too, already seated at the table, ready to start, she waves at me, remembers me, the only one missing is Avi, Avi on his own? We'll have to wait and see—

Avi arrives. Backslaps, handshakes, a little kiss for the great-grandmother, a quick glance at me, "So you came after all?" and it isn't clear if he's glad or just surprised. "Avi, you're sitting there—" Ora at the end of the table, distances him from me, dispatches everyone to his place in the tone of a sergeant-major: "Motik—you're there, Mother, you're here with Daddy, Vered, you're next to Loya—" Vered breaks off a piece of matzo, dips it in the *haroseth*, eats it. "I adore my granny's *haroseth*," she smirks at Ora's look of rebuke. "Can you tell me who everybody is?" I whisper to her. "Us you know—" she replies with her mouth full of *haroseth* and matzo, "and that's my uncle Menahem over there with his glamorous wife and his new children—Aner and Hatzav and Klil—Klil's the girl—and next to him my uncle Avi—my father's twin as you can see," her voice is that of a tour guide at Madame Tussaud's museum. "Doesn't he have a family?" I dare to ask—very casual, almost joking, taking part in her game. "He has a family in the process of breaking up—his wife—Nehama—didn't want to come back to Israel from America—his sons—he has two—Hagai and Omri—are making millions in Silicon Valley." "Shhhh . . ." Ora hisses at us, sitting up straight in her chair, clapping her hands. "We're beginning! We're beginning!!" Vered breaks another matzo, nibbles it, leans towards me to continue the whispering: "My mother can't stand her." "Who?" I whisper back. "Nehama—even though she's actually nice—a bit stingy, but apart from that nice," Vered throws a defiant look at Ora who is already absorbed in the Haggadah, they're arguing about the Four Questions, Yinon refuses, passes the honor on to Klil, "you're the youngest." "Poor thing." He bends over me with the jug for hand washing. "You see, a boy takes the jug around and the women also wash their hands, that's what happens when your mother is a school principal, what, you didn't know, you're really not up to date with the news," says Vered. "What kind of people give their daughter the name of a plastic blind factory?" whispers Yinon as he hands us the towel hanging on his arm to dry the tips of our fingers. "It's Klil with a kaf, you idiot," hisses Vered, drawing the dish of *haroseth* towards her and cramming the sweet paste into her mouth—if she isn't careful she'll look like her mother in a few years. "Vered!" Ora scolds from the other end of the table. "Never mind, Orinka, never mind, I prepared a lot, there are still two jars full in the refrigerator." Mechora stands up, goes to the kitchen, and returns with two dishes heaped with pinkish-gray mountains. "Good for Granny," cries Udi and Gilad laughs, there are parties here, I sense, Mechora and her grandchildren against Ora, Motik and Vered against Ora, Avi and Ora's father are whispering, the Yekke grandmother has nodded off, who is determined to hold this Seder apart from Ora who perhaps invited me to have someone on her side, she shushes, she scolds, she hands out reading parts, Menahem supports her, but his beautiful wife—Claudine—tugs at his sleeve, interferes. "It's a pity Nehama's not here—she's got a fantastic sense of humor—when she's at the Seder we don't stop laughing," whispers Vered, "but my mother can't stand her—" she drinks her wine, "not now? Okay, what's the difference—in three minutes time—Mom drives me crazy with all these rules—as if there's anyone religious in this house—it's all a show." "Why can't your mother stand her?" I'm determined to find out everything. "Don't you know the story?" Vered polishes off the *haroseth* with a teaspoon. "Mom was in love with Avi—she only married my father on the rebound—" I look up and survey the people seated around the table with new eyes. True? False? Now we're eating hard-boiled eggs dipped in salt water. "Because when the children of Israel crossed the Red Sea, the water came up to their balls," says Yinon, succeeding in making his little cousins blush—a few months after Eliot began wearing a yarmulke his rabbi invited us to a Seder. We arrived by car. The whole Seder was conducted in English and in Hebrew with a Yiddish pronunciation—this is the last time, I announced to Eliot, I'll never take part in this circus again, but here I am, and the woman who was once my best friend is dishing up anemic chicken soup with four matzo-meal dumplings per serving—

"Sorry—they're not up to scratch," Udi lays down his spoon.

"You should have let granny make them this year too, Mom," Gilad agrees.

"Stones for the intifada!" shouts Yinon as one hard dumpling jumps out from under his spoon and lands on the tablecloth. Mechora smiles modestly. Ora tightens her lips.

"They're delicious—" lies the pretty woman at the end of the table. She still wants to please everybody—

"I give her the precise recipe—" says Mechora between one sip and the next; she has banished her dumplings to the edge of the plate. "But the soup is very good—"

"Granny made the soup—" Yinon winks at me from the other side of the table. Avi, sitting next to him, appears detached from the scene. He inclines his head, almost bends over Ora's father, listens to him, whispers to him. The phone rings. Yinon rushes to pick it up. He seems disappointed. "Avi—it's for you!"

Avi gets up with a creak of his chair. Stands with his back to the table. Listens more than talks. Who phones in the middle of the Seder—his wife?

"That must be Nehama," says Claudine. Motik exchanges a look with Ora. Avi is still on the phone.

"From the United States?" Ora finds it hard to believe. She serves the next course—a roast with potatoes and sweet carrots. Everybody eats without complaints, except for me, I'm not hungry anymore—

Avi returns to the table with a worried face.

"How is Nehama?" ventures Claudine.

"Are you crazy?" Vered laughs on my right. "You think Nehama would talk on the phone for fifteen minutes from America?"

"Who was it?" asks Motik whose plate is already empty. Like Avi, he eats fast.

"Paul—" Avi bends over his plate.

"My uncle," Vered volunteers, "collects testimonies from Holocaust survivors—he leaves people a calling card—If you remember anything please give me a call—like Inspector Colombo—"

"It isn't funny, Vered," Ora warns in the distance.

"Of course it isn't funny! One day." Vered leans over to make eye contact with Avi, "someone will kill himself because of everything you reminded him to remember—"

Avi raises his head from his plate. Our eyes meet. A big black butterfly descends from my throat to my heart.

"In ten, fifteen years there won't be anyone to remember—" his voice is quiet.

"But why pester people? Why send them back to hell?" Vered speaks almost like Ora in the debates for and against the Military Government, for and against capital punishment for terrorists—with the same passion, the same intuition—

"I don't force anyone to talk—" Avi says to her and includes me too in that intense brown-green look.

"You don't know what went on here last Passover—" Vered turns to me. "We celebrated the fiftieth anniversary of the Warsaw Ghetto uprising—"

"What did Paul want?" Menahem is curious. Pouring oil on troubled waters too. The good brother, apparently.

"What did he want? Nothing—" Avi pushes his plate away. "The Seder night reminded him of the whole Lederer affair—"

"What affair?" Yinon accompanies his question with a gesture, upsets his wineglass.

"Salt! Put on salt!" Mechora is already on her feet energetically salting the pink stain spreading over the tablecloth.

"It's nothing," says Ora from her place. "I don't remember a single Seder when the tablecloth wasn't ruined—"

We go on to the compote.

"What's the story about Lederer—" Yinon insists.

"On the Seder night exactly fifty years ago he escaped from—" Avi begins but Motik stops him: "Not now, Avi, for God's sake, not now—"

Ora's father has fallen asleep. The grandmother on my left has been snoring gently for the past fifteen minutes. Gilad tastes the compote, gets up and announces that he's going out. Udi says that he is too, in ten minutes time. Menahem and Claudine's children are sitting in front of the television in Ora and Motik's bedroom, Klil's fallen asleep, announces Claudine after going to find out the meaning of the sudden silence in the bedroom. Ora fights for the continuation of the Seder against everyone else. Even Mechora is nodding at her post. Motik collects matzo crumbs with a moistened finger, Vered stores the dishes in the dishwasher, Avi stares at the wall. "*Had-gad-ya*, only one kid," Ora sings in a thick, used voice, and I want to cry.

Avi accompanies me home. On the doorstep Ora stops us for a moment, wants to say something, changes her mind. Streets bathed in a plaster light and a compound smell of orange blossom and gasoline from the cars parked with two wheels on the pavements, if we want to walk side by side we have to walk in the middle of the street—

"What's the story about Lederer—" I say in order to make a crack in his silence.

"Vitezslav Lederer was an officer in the Czech army and a member of the underground organization led by Colonel Weidmann until he was arrested and sent to Theresienstadt—"

"Lederer was in Terezin?" My interest is aroused.

"He was sent there from the Little Fort—they gave him a job in the fire brigade, but it didn't save him from the transports. In December '43 he was sent with another five thousand people to the family camp in Birkenau—there was a Czech family camp in Birkenau then—" Avi sighs. Falls silent for a moment. "In March of '44, after the prisoners who had arrived in the family camp six months before that were exterminated, Lederer realized that this was what was in store for his transport too and he decided to escape. He was assisted by an SS officer, a Volksdeutsch by the name of Viktor Pestek, who was in love with a beautiful girl from the family camp and promised to save her and her mother and needed someone to help him in this project. Pestek put out feelers to a number of prisoners—they suspected it was a trap—but Lederer decided to take the risk. On the night of the Seder they left the camp from the gate, with Lederer disguised as an SS officer, and Pestek posing as his adjutant—they got on a train from Cracow, when it stopped they stowed away on an express train and got off at Prague—"

"It sounds like a third-rate Hollywood movie," I say disbelievingly.

"And that's not the end—" Avi's voice is bitter-dry. "Lederer returned to Theresienstadt and smuggled in weapon parts—only when a rumor spread that there was an armed partisan roaming around the ghetto he left and rejoined the underground. He took part in the Slovak rebellion; Davidi met him in Banska Bystrica—"

"Davidi?" I stop in the middle of the street. A slow car approaches. Hoots. Avi grips my elbow, leads me to the verge of the pavement. "Did he survive the war?" "Yes—" we're approaching your house. "And he was awarded a medal for heroism—"

"Is he still alive? Is he in Israel?" I'll find him.

"No—he died at the end of the seventies." We're already at the gate. In the absence of the ficus the cypress tree stands out; a dark stalagmite against the background of a metal sky, Lot's wife stretching out a long arm, leaning on a fence bulging under the weight of her cloak—

We are both on the path blue in the moonlight. The trunks of the palms make a black colonnade—"Just a minute—" I stop on the step. "Kastner—doesn't he belong to the whole story of Terezin—"

"He belongs on the margins—" Avi puts up his hand to scratch his neck. "Kastner appeared in the Theresienstadt Ghetto in May '45, a few days before the liberation—he apparently succeeded in persuading the Nazis not to exterminate the Jews remaining in the ghetto—"

"Apparently?"

"According to him—in everything concerning the Kastner affair," he shifts his weight from his heels to his toes, "not everything is closed and not everything is clear and unambiguous—"

"Did my father owe him his life—?" I interrupt him.

"Very possibly." Avi sighs and begins walking backward. If the ficus were still planted there I would have been able to say to him, beware, that tree has roots like the piercing serpent and the crooked serpent, in a minute you'll stumble on one of them—what happened between our last meeting and this one; he got scared / Nehama phoned and talked to him for half an hour from the United States / Ora hauled him over the coals / nothing happened on the last meeting—"Okay—good night then—or would you like to—" For a moment it occurs to me to invite him in.

"Good night—" He didn't hear because he'd moved away? He heard and chose to ignore it? He walks backwards, facing me, waves with a limp hand, a bent arm, like a child told to wave good-bye to the auntie embarking on the ship—

I stretch my hand inside and switch on the light. He disappears. You can't see from light into darkness—after the holiday I'll go there, I decide.

On my own. I saw it with my own eyes when I hitched a ride to Giora's kibbutz, a blatant orange sign announcing in the heart of the Land of Israel: THERESIENSTADT—

SCORCHED

The windows are open and over the strawberry beds which have reverted to being earth (the season's over, said Amitai, we'll let the earth rest a bit before we sow again) the fragrance of the lost orange grove rises from an incipient heatwave, hesitant, striped with bands of wind, taking me back to a snowbound night in New York, the crew stuck in the airport playing Battleships, Country-Town, landing up with Definitions, define pilot, define flight attendant, define nebula, love, in one word or as few as possible, define El Al, define Israel, heatwaves and the smell-of-orange-blossom, said Shai, the steward, and Hedva added sand, heatwaves, and the smell-of-orange-blossom, and Ahikam, the pilot, added hummus, sand, heatwaves, and the smell-of-orange-blossom, and Dudu the navigator protested, demanding that we stick to the rules of the game, what's wrong with home, heat, and hummus, that's the whole story in a nutshell—

The windows are open. Those in your room too, Davidi. I opened it at last. Most of it's a bed. On either side a chest of drawers. On the right hand one an enormous old radio. One window, facing west, in it the jacarandas, still bare, behind them the hibiscus hedge—and the south window opens to the plowed strawberry plot at the end of which the trees of the citrus grove join the earth to a no longer clear sky, smoky from this morning—

Passover—and after the end of the holiday and a week of eating matzo Tikva's brother drives specially to Jaffa to buy pita bread and returns with a huge pile and the smell fills the house and the garden and even wafts into Brigade, now Cypress Street, and after the holiday—a week's break, and Memorial Day to remind everyone that the hourglass of the year has already been turned over and from now on it is trickling to its end, hot, hotter, very hot, soon we'll get end-of-term reports, soon we'll be allowed to go to Tel Aviv and spend the whole night and come back in the morning, hoarse as after the annual school trip, sooty with *kartoshkes*, giving off a smell of scorching and sea sand and tiredness that can't be slept off, that has to be dragged along for a few days longer (burning eyes, heartburn, slightly dazed, slightly spaced-out) until it fades—

An opaque spring, spring with a patina of heat-haze diluted by faint, barely perceptible depression, what's wrong with you, eat yogurt, lots of yogurt, says Adriana, it's good for the skin and good for the soul, and honey, honey too, on the grocery counter two battalions of memorial candles are lined up in ranks of six—a battalion of tin, a battalion of glass, something new—people come in, buy two or three, go out, come back, "Some people buys ten," says the-grocer's "or twenty, or thirty, one for everybody that gone in their family, one customer buyed sixty-five, yogurt you can have as much as you like, but for honey come on Rosh Hashanah—"

At last I succeeded in finding a station that coughs less on your radio—the green eye in the middle of the fabric forehead blinks—the tail of a melody with a bitter Greek taste—pity it's over—a song begins about the kitchen door which is still locked, when will the war end, this question remains open, and now the well-starched voice produced in honor of catastrophes, why are they so festive, I once asked Eliot, we were eating in the living room opposite the television which was showing commercials for funeral parlors, the mourners were wearing dinner jackets, the women little black dresses, their faces veiled in femme-fatale tulle, and the undertakers glided around them, elegant, discreet, waiters serving up death, who are they trying to impress, God or the departed, I suddenly remembered the fat woman coming up to me with an unsheathed razor to slit my throat, no, she's aiming lower, at the neck of my blouse, it's the *kriyah*, the ritual rending of the garment, Ora's mother grips my elbow throughout the funeral service, and after it, eat something, you must eat, how can you eat watching that, I asked Eliot, if we don't eat—we'll die, he smiled, he was right, "And where is he now?" asks Adriana, the two of us are sitting in her kitchen. "He's an insurance agent with some firm in Jerusalem—" "What, he's here?" "I wouldn't call it 'here'—he's become completely ultra-Orthodox: yarmulke, beard, earlocks, four fringes—he's probably married by now with three hundred children—" "What do you say, there, it'll be ready in forty minutes, no, don't switch it off, I need it to be on for these programs even though I can't look at them." On the television screen a gray forest of Nazi helmets marching, snow, shots, more snow, I go back to the kitchen, on the corner of the table is a newspaper with a photograph of a woman sitting on railway tracks without sleepers leading to a kind of hut with a chimney and under the picture in white letters on a black background "The Children's Hut" and underneath that in huge black letters IN THE SHADOW OF THE CHIMNEYS—when he was a child, Daddy told me, he believed that if he touched a chimney sweep it would bring him luck, why aren't there chimney sweeps here, I said regretfully, Are there chimneys here? My father educated me by the Socratic method; questions instead of answers—a woman sitting next to the remains of the children's hut in the family camp in Auschwitz, I read, so they're not railway tracks but strips of concrete, two sides of a very long rectangle, once there were walls growing from them, and between the walls, above what is now trampled grass—"Do you want that newspaper? Go on, take it, I don't have the strength to read those things any more." Adriana sits down opposite me. "You remember when nobody talked about it?" I nod. "Except for Minaleh—"Adriana turns her head to the oven. "This lasagna is for them—they've brought her back home—" She suppresses a sigh. "There's nothing more to be done. At least let her die in peace—" "Does she know?" Adriana nods. "Everyone knows. They're getting used to the idea—the truth is, they're already in mourning now." "Terrible—" I shudder. To die at once: a fireflower opening to the sky—without preparations-farewells-tubes-deathbeds—without seeing it coming and bending over you and cupping your chin in fingers made of bones—"Terrible, but—" Adriana disagrees, "when it descends on you all of a sudden—remember what happened to you when your father died?"

At this moment the girls file in to cheers of "Lasagna for supper—you can smell it from miles away—when will it be ready?"

"Good morning Loya." Avi doesn't wait for my good morning in return, he's obviously in a hurry, calling only to tell me that this evening they're showing Lanzmann's *Shoah* on television, "If you haven't seen it you really should—it's a film of testimonies. You don't have a television set? What do you say—then go to Ora's—I told her to see it too—teachers in Israel should see a movie like that—"

And that's it. Good-bye—good-bye.

Horses of the heart, go back to your stables.

And at midday, Ora.

"Loya? I've just got back from school—Avi called . . . so are you coming this evening? Good, because I haven't got the strength to see it alone and Motik and the children will probably want to watch Channel 2, if at all— what's on there? Some American kitsch—but I want to see Lanzmann— hang on a minute—Mother? What? I can't hear you—I'm talking on the phone now—what? What did they say on the radio? Oh my God—a bomb in Afula? Did you hear? Put on the radio—and come this evening—yes—"

The radio in your room gives details from the scene—seven dead—dozens of burn wounds—a suicide bombing marking forty days after the massacre in Hebron—ambulance sirens—then whistles, grunts, the dry coughing of an old instrument—I switch stations, hit it angrily on the head and hear with sudden clarity—Death to the Arabs! Death to the Arabs! And screams in the background, weeping—and again noises from which rise rhythmic cries of Rabin is a traitor! Rabin is a trai- and a long whine followed by absolute silence. It hasn't been so quiet around here for a long time. A power cut? No, the lights are working. What then. I go outside and discover: the building site behind the boards is silent. All the workers have gone. I stand on the scar in the ground and peek; the cement mixer is still. There's nobody there except for someone coming closer—

"They left," he says, "heard the news and picked up their heels—went back to their villages—I told them who do you think's gonna harm you here, this is a quiet neighborhood, cultured people, this isn't Afula here or Migdal Ha-emek, lawyers and doctors live here, and then one of them goes, Goldstein was a doctor too and look what he did—" He comes closer—not young, unshaved, smoking a cigarette—"You live here? Pleased to meet you. I'm the guard. You were surprised by the quiet I bet. They made us a Holocaust on Holocaust Day. If anyone asks tell them the guard went home. A person can go crazy with the news—I haven't got the strength for it, believe me—I buy the paper and all I read is the sports—this a country that devours its inhabitants, just like it says in the Bible—"

In Ora's kitchen a flickering, pale yellow glow rises from the sink. "You still put them in the sink—" I comment. "So they won't burn the house down," Ora quotes herself quoting her mother forty years ago. "It's just begun," she leads me into the living room, and I, who came ready for blurred black-and-white with squeaky mouse voices, see a screen full of rich generous green—fresh forest green and juicy grass—silver green of a river and banks and a rowing boat gliding and a sweet song—

"Is this it?" "Yes, this is it, sit down, sit here—" A man with soft curls, a child's face, sings in a melodious voice, falls silent, draws in his lips—and again—draws in his lips, as if he wants to swallow his song, sad, stunned, walks down a dirt track, a forest on his right, no sound but for his steps, his stifled sigh, brief cough—his eyes stare—he stops. Looks. Nods. Stands facing the grass and sees other things—gas vans—ovens—bodies—the flames reached the sky, demonstrates with a jerky upward gesture, *Zum himmel*? asks an invisible voice, *Yo*, he's talking Yiddish, this place was always quiet—nobody screamed—green pastures—trees—river—a wooded hill—on top of it a church—a white spire, red tiled roof—everything denies his story—another survivor smiles without stopping with teeth not his own, Is it good to talk about it? he is asked, No, not good, he replies, *nischt gut*. For me it's not good, and a woman's voice translates his Yiddish into French, ask him why he smiles all the time, the French is repeated in Yiddish, what do you want, says the survivor, for me to cry?

A very beautiful young woman, black hair, black eyes, "She reminds me of you," I whisper to Ora. "A hundred years ago," she dismisses-acquiesces, the young woman says, Father was very quiet, it was hard for me to reach him, she speaks in my name, in my place, it was only when I grew up a little that I had the strength to confront him and extract a little and a little more—the camera pans over her father's face against the background of a fresh forest clearing—stumps of trees—scorched earth—big stones and blue mountains in the distance, you could say it resembles Ponary, he says, only there there were no stones, there the forest was thicker, and now we are among tall trees, green grass, three little people going for a walk in the forest—do people hunt in the Sobibor forest, inquires Lanzmann in French translated into Polish answered in Polish and translated into French and appearing at the bottom of the screen in Hebrew and English subtitles—the camera revels in a view of heavy blue-green forests as far as the eye can see, yes, this is the magic of our forests, says the Polish voice, they planted three- or four-year-old trees here to cover up the traces, a tree screen? Lanzmann is ironic, but irony apparently fails to cross the language barrier—

And again the face of the smiling survivor, what did he do when he unloaded the gassing vans, what could he do, he cried, his eyes fill with tears—his mouth trembles, its corners droop, tighten—on the third day he saw his wife and children, he laid his wife in the pit and he wanted them to shoot him too, but the Germans said that he was still strong enough to work—Was it very cold? Lanzmann's voice insists on the details, digs into the details, they buried them, five-six layers, arranged them like sardines head-to-foot, the forest clearing is flat, yellowing grass, spotted with snow, no trace of a pit, or of the dead, did they remove the bodies and burn all the Vilna Jews, Lanzmann perseveres, these are the previous survivors, behind them the beautiful daughter, smoking, my wrist hurts, it's Ora gripping it, staring, I discovered my mother and three sisters among the dead, says her father—my father too, whispers Ora, how did you recognize them, Lanzmann presses cruelly, they were in good condition—they were in the ground for four months—it was winter—the survivor's face is melancholy but far from tears, on his sunburned forehead are three horizontal lines, the older corpses had completely disintegrated, there are ninety thousand bodies here, the head of the Gestapo in Vilna told us, and not a sign of them must remain—and in truth there are no signs, the forest grows, the snow falls, the people are silent or fall silent or say little, against the background of a bridge and a river sits a bronzed, bearded, spruce man in a spotless shirt, describing fantastic flames in every possible shade, and suddenly one of us got up—he was an opera singer in Warsaw—and began to sing a song we didn't know—*Eli, Eli*, My God, My God, he began in Hebrew, went on in German, why hast thou forsaken us—and we are back with the singing survivor with the child's face, walking in the meadow, stopping, looking around, poking with the toe of his shoe, they threw the powder of the ground-up bones into the stream and it was swept away on the current—the stream opens into a wide river, gleaming like silk, all silver and pink and peach—

Sudden sounds of traffic—a bluish street—a bus coming towards us—the town of Auschwitz. Were there any Jews in Auschwitz? A plump-cheeked, silver-haired, bespectacled Polish woman, delighted with all the attention, yes, eighty percent of the population, she says, and does she know what happened to the Jews of Auschwitz? I think they all finished up in the camp, she smiles in satisfaction—Were there Jews in Włodawa? Yes, there was a beautiful synagogue, Włodawa was a Jewish town, and what did people think when all the Jews of Włodawa were deported to Sobibor? They were sent there to die, but they themselves knew that it was the end for them, quite a large crowd answers eagerly—were there Jews in Kolo?—a little village rotting in the rain, more Jews than Poles, they collected them in the synagogue, they killed the ones who couldn't walk, they led them to the train to Chelmno, the testimony of a black-haired Pole, not all Poles are blond, with a dimple in his chin—

A chestnut horse with a star on its forehead pulls a wagon loaded with hay. Perched on top, a peasant in a red shirt, small nose, mighty jaw, now in close-up, in his farmyard, peasant arms crossed on a swollen, beefy red belly, it was here, he saw it, certainly he did, it was in his field, the train passed here, where it passes now, a slow freight train, violet-gray beyond the trees not far away, you could see everything from the first row in the balcony? The sarcasm doesn't cross the language barrier; of course, replies red-belly, it was clear they were going to kill them, but it wasn't clear how, were they concerned about the fate of the Jews? Lanzmann inquires innocently, the peasant pulls a face, as if to say, "certainly not, what an idea," speaks in a rapid flow, with hand gestures, okay, what he's saying is this, the translator hesitates, making sure she has it right, when I cut my finger—he doesn't feel any pain, the Jews from other countries arrived in Pullman cars, wearing furs, you could see the women in the windows, combing their hair, getting ready—the peasant mimics them with a glee he makes no attempt to hide—they didn't know for what, but he knew, he showed them, like this, and he slides his finger over his thick neck pleased with himself and also with what was done to them, his three neighbors—lined cheeks, clamped jaws, sunken fox-eyes, wearing cloth caps—testify that they heard horrible screams, and did it bother them? inquires Lanzmann by means of his translator, yes, at first, later on they got used to it, you can get used to anything, right? The sarcasm doesn't come across, because the man replies with a ye-es which implies that it's self-evident, obvious, and what do the houses say, the streets, the trees, the geese, the mud, the farmyards, all shrouded in eternal grayness, we're back with red-belly, describing with relish how the Ukrainians killed the Jews jabbering in their railcars ra-ra-ra-ra-rara, what is la-la-la-la-la says the startled Lanzmann, ra-ra-ra-ra-rara is an imitation of their language, they made a noise, and the Ukrainians—they wanted quiet, does he speak Jewish? asks Lanzmann innocently, the fat man's "n-o-o" is accompanied by a gesture of disgust—

A train driver stands next to his locomotive with his head bowed and a melancholy expression on his face, as if standing to attention in a memorial service, why is he sad, inquires Lanzmann, because he saw people being taken to their deaths, he replies as it wasn't him who transported them two-three times a week for a year and a half into the depths of Treblinka—interior: Lanzmann and the train driver—without a cap, with spectacles—because they are bending over a map. On the wall behind them a big cross and on it Jesus far too small for the size of his cross. Did the engine pull the cars behind it or push them? Lanzmann digs for details, pushed, replies the train driver emphatically, and a train going backwards fills the screen—

A gray house—a tiled roof—three windows—a green yard—a fence. Four benches. Railway tracks. Is it all the same as it was in '42? On the bench Lanzmann, the translator, the stationmaster, balding, wearing a terra-cotta sweater, leaning on a cane, no, it's a long, thin branch, here, he raises the branch, there was a fence that reached to here, another fence reached to the trees over there—Am I standing now in the area of the camp? Lanzmann seems incredulous, ordinary green grass, sunshine, a railway line, *Tak . . . tak . . .* yes, yes . . . the stationmaster's voice is lilting as a storyteller's. So this is the Polish part—and over here—death, Lanzmann pretends incomprehension, the Pole nods, confirms, an orange hen walks through the grass, a small sign, black-on-white SOBIBOR, the platform began here, Lanzmann points at his shoes, *Tak . . . tak . . .* This is the exact track? He, the stationmaster, and the translator are standing on the sleepers, *Tak*, exactly the same tracks, nothing is changed, here they set down the victims destined for extermination? *Tak . . .* Did they arrive in passenger cars? A warm sunny day, the camera lingers on the forests—forests as far as the eye can see—rich, green to blue—Were there beautiful days like this then too? Lanzmann does not refrain from irony. To my regret, replies the stationmaster, there were even more beautiful days—

A sudden noise of traffic—New York. In fluent but stiff-cornered English, like my father's, a black-haired survivor with a sardonic smile describes the transports he saw on their arrival at Auschwitz. Two hundred at least. And the lights. And the SS men and the dogs. *Schnell-schnell*—and the blows. And sometimes—a sense of humor: "Good morning madam,"

"How nice of you to come"—within a short space of time the platform is cleared—not a trace remains—the movie returns to this obsessively, not a trace remains, not of the arrivals, not of their belongings, not of their deaths, the murder passed like a knife through water and the world closed, unscarred, suitcases were left, with names written on them in white—Saul Freitach, Singer Leon, Kurt Willinger, Pasternak—What's going on, where are all the people, asked Richard, today on the balcony in Basle against the background of a bridge and river, I couldn't believe it, the barber from Holon says too, what happened to all the people, we asked, Don't you know? Everybody's put to death by gas—

Franz Suchomel is filmed with a hidden camera, appearing on the screen like a blue ghost; You're an important eyewitness, Lanzmann flatters-presses, perhaps you can explain to us what it was like in Treblinka? It was a hot August, the earth moved on top of the bodies because of the gases, it was hell, complains the ex-SS guard, and the stink—dreadful, you could smell it from kilometers away! From kilometers? Lanzmann clarifies for the sake of all those who will soon claim that they didn't see, didn't hear, didn't smell. From ki-lo-me-ters! The murderer emphasizes, speaks of a surplus of murdered people, a surplus of bodies, what could they do, they brought in an expert from Belz—

Snow falls on a gray wall, at its feet wreathes. The execution wall in Auschwitz. A soft, emotional voice, the voice of a survivor of five exterminations of the Sonderkommando in Auschwitz, white-shirted, tanned, his dark eyes sunken and stricken, relates how he was sent by an SS officer to stir the bodies—

I never started with the big questions, Raul Hilberg, historian, in a blue-and-white checked shirt, hair combed back, speaks quietly: the left eyebrow rises high above his spectacle frames, the left corner of his mouth twitches when he is silent—I preferred to relate to the small details in order, with their help, to build a picture that would constitute a description, if not an explanation—they took almost everything from the reservoirs of the past—he sums up—the decrees, the administrative measures, the propaganda, even the caricatures—it was only the final solution that they had to invent—

Auschwitz; brown-beige brick buildings glisten in the rain like asphalt, like the windowsills, the roofs, the barbed-wire fences, the famous entrance that everyone watching the movie is now traveling towards, entering—suddenly it transpires that the shape of the arch is specially designed to swallow up trains—and rain, thin rain, horses clicking their hooves on asphalt which has a leaden sheen, villages rotting in the interminable rain, here, it happened here, in the yard, in the church, they brought them in trains, trains, blue-gray trains traveling though the rain-lands, old freight trains operating on coal, you can see the coal, glittering in the rain, shining with a black light, the engine driver leaning out of the locomotive window, looking back at the train cars as if to make sure that not a single one is missing, passing a slow finger across his throat as his train approaches the sign which appears after the public bathrooms and a bit of lawn a bench and potted plants—*Treblinka*—

A soft dirt track in a wooded landscape, then sleepers without rails, in a low shot like a row of tombstones, and groups of gray stones, pale gray, dark gray, pointed stones, like groups of people turned into pillars of stone, like Lot's wife hundreds of times over, there are some blackish ones too and some with a brownish tinge, some are golden—or is that the sun again—the camera zooms in on a dark honey-colored stone—*Czestochowa*—a survivor from that city against the background of the Tel Aviv-Jaffa sea talks rounded, almost Italian English, his gaze stares into his memories, but his mouth, look at the mouth, I was taught by Jean-Jacques who kept his own story to himself, the mouth says everything, people don't know that they have to watch their mouths, Mrs. Mickelsohn's mouth twists viciously when she remembers with affection her German youth in Chelmno, she loved adventures, what were her impressions of the place? Primitive and more than primitive, she accompanies her words with a dismissive wave of her hand, what does she mean, wonders Lanzmann, the sanitary facilities were a ca-tas-tro-phe—there were no toilets at all—

Chelmno. The singing survivor with the childish face in the town square, behind the church, surrounded by people, most of them older than he is, old women in headkerchiefs on this side and that, today is a holiday, the Virgin Mary's birthday, are they glad to see him amongst them, asks Lanzmann, very glad, they chorus in reply, a woman behind his shoulder in a red headscarf recounts, he sang, his legs were in chains, and he was so thin, ready to be put in his coffin, the survivor listens, nods with his mouth closed in a thin line, his hands hold each other, and around him they recount, yes, they do remember, they brought them in trucks by day and by night, the trucks stopped here, next to the church door, yes, they knew that they were death trucks, it was impossible not to know, the survivor smokes with his cupped hand covering his mouth, the Jews called on Jesus, on Mary, on God, the testimony stops, almost swept up in the procession streaming out of the church door—banners, priests, little girls dressed in white scattering rose petals—continues in the same place, the survivor in the center, withdrawn into himself, his hands in his pockets, his mouth a silent line, why did it happen to the Jews? Lanzmann wonders, because they were rich, the people gathered around have no hesitation, they are full of very good reasons, because they sentenced the innocent Jesus to death, explains a bald, bespectacled, sharp-nosed man, stepping forward with his hand held out like a pistol in front of him, and the crowd nods and the woman in the red headscarf steps forward too, her whole body sways as she recites from the New Testament—

Forest. The survivor, with a handsome head of gray, wavy hair, looks around him, his voice speaks as if of its own accord about people thrown into the crematoria while they were still alive, he walks here and there as if searching, bends down, picks something up, cups soil in his fist, squeezes, lets go, goes on walking, when I saw it it didn't affect me, he says in a detached voice, I was only thirteen and that was all I had seen in my life. Corpses . . . in the Lodz Ghetto I saw people walking and falling down dead . . . I thought it was normal . . . if I survive, I thought, I'll want five loaves of bread to eat—that's all—he says returning me to Hasia and

Gedalya Horovitz's wardrobe, full of bread, I can't take any more, I stand up, I'm going, Ora is riveted to the screen, wait, it'll be over in a minute, no, I can't—I walk, in the dark, to your house—

I don't turn on the light. I grope in the dark. Open a window. Another window. Lie down in my clothes on the bedcover, see through the windows night, stars hanging between the ribs of the trees, the smell of orange blossom fills the room: the withering citrus grove is blooming—you were in Terezin. From there you were sent to Treblinka—and I, the fool, thought the pyxis was to punish me—perhaps you left something written down here, in this room or in your old suitcase, I can go and get it, they notified me in a registered letter, every day at the police station between nine and one, please bring an identity card. What would you have said about this film, green meadows, forests, villages in the rain, and in the midst of all the juicy green always a red stain—a coat, headscarf, church roof, sweater— every few minutes gray-black trains like giant zippers opening to new silences—you kept everything in your heart or in one of these drawers, I get up, pull out a drawer, the gray dawn light shines on old underwear, rough bundles of men's socks, leather belts snailed around their buckles, another drawer—handkerchiefs, pajamas, long johns, the one below it—a balaclava from the War of Independence, you took part in that too, how could I forget, a round cloth hat, a leather (partisan?) cap, in the right-hand bedside cupboard the drawers are heavier, this one hardly slides out, sticks, a blow returns it to its place, what's in it, postcards, postcards, postcards in my handwriting, for ten years at least I sent them regularly, and you didn't reply, didn't forgive. Perhaps you hoped that this silence would put pressure on me to come back if only to confront you, to quarrel vociferously, "'I will seize it with my right hand / by my mighty long arm / I will smash your crown; / I will make your beard run with blood / the gray hair of your beard with gore.' / 'I know you, O daughter, that you are furious / Among goddesses no scorn is like yours' / you will answer me like El from the seven rooms, from the eight enclosures / 'What do you desire, O Adolescent Anat?'" To know, to know, to know how many postcards I wrote you—this drawer doesn't open all the way—it's really stuck—just a minute—ah!—suddenly it leaps from its rails, falls onto my foot—the gray window is rent by a clear, piercing, familiar Hihihihihi. Dubček? I limp to the window. Just in time to see a flutter of glorious blue. He's here. Back to announce the coming of morning in a fanfare of lament—

I limp to the overturned drawer lying on the pile of spilled postcards. Pick it up. What's this wooden board—did it have a double bottom?—a thin piece of plywood, a false floor, balancing on a hill of everything I wrote to you, and on top of it, on view for all to see, what was hidden beneath it: a medium-sized brown envelope, full of what—documents? Certificates? Letters?—I turn it over and discover your handwriting on it, big, wild—*Loya, open!*

And if I open it—if I open it—I'll grow in an instant to fill the house until my arm sticks out of the window and my foot out of the door and my head raises the roof—or everything will fly around me like a pack of cards—pieces of yellowing paper fall out of the open envelope and scatter roundabout—all that's missing now is a sudden rabbit hurrying past and disappearing down a tunnel that descends to the bowels of the earth seething under your house, and reaches another world—

Old papers, not the same size, scraps of whatever came to hand, on them in faded pen, dulled pencil, in the tiny crowded writing of someone short of paper and nevertheless you can see it's foreign handwriting, more drawn than written, when did you write it, maybe notes from the *partizanka*, maybe from the War of Independence—hard to understand—here, this is clear—*around us people in peaked caps*—and here in pencil *darkness dust and commotion*—and on this scrap—*to abandon the soul to chaos*—these are notes from Treblinka—how did you manage to write them? On a few scraps the date is visible—just a minute—just a minute—the long-tailed 9 is Daddy's, not yours, and the 7 without the line across too—*the number of dead multiplies from day to day*—when is this from—*carrying carcasses to the crematorium*—and here's something in Latin—

Daddy wrote it! Not you—

Good. Not now. Now I'm putting everything back into the envelope—just a minute—there's something else inside it—one—two—three thin letters in gaily-edged air-mail envelopes: one addressed to Dr. Leo Baeck in London, England in Daddy's elegant handwriting, with an Israeli stamp saying Happy Holidays on it, unstamped, this letter was never sent to its address, I wonder why—I tear the side of the envelope, yes, it's Daddy's writing, the letter dated 23.6.55 is written in German, which I always refused to learn and now can't read, Daddy wanted me to learn it, it's an important language, a lot of research was written in German, and Goethe and Schiller and Heine, one day I'll teach you, he promised. How old was I? Nine? Eight? At the beginning of the year, Yossi Kuperstein took out of his schoolbag a pencil case made of pale wood, two tiers with the top tier swiveling on a hinge and a lid on which was painted in lifelike shades of brown and gray the antlered head of a deer in a triple-striped frame of yellow-red-black, and in the long break, after we ate our sandwiches, after the homeroom teacher Tirza left the classroom, we stood around his desk and took turns to spit on his pencil case. Yossi cried, I was sent it, my uncles sent it, but this didn't help him. After we had all spat Ora took the shining pencil-case and to the sound of a loud and general yyyyuuk she dropped it into the litter bin in the corner and hurried to wipe her hands on her handkerchief which to be on the safe side she dropped into the bin as well. I'll never learn German as long as I live! I declared. Daddy said nothing and you were pleased. And now look—

The second letter was enclosed in a mute envelope, without an address, without the name of the sender at the back, without a stamp, it had apparently been left next to a mirror or on a table in a conspicuous place, the receiver must have known who it was from—what's written in it?—what's written in it is in vigorous Czech dated 1.5.51, on the letters round rings, wedges, lines of flying birds, I can read it, of course, Czech is read as it's written, but without understanding a word, a short letter, signed with a big, blatant M, like the alias of a James Bond operator, a tough, unknown woman, there were always hooligans in that house, said Morgenstern-the-grocer's, perhaps I should go and ask her, the third letter is from Switzerland, typed by an unpracticed hand, concluding with *Je mi líto*—that's Czech and that I understand—I'm sorry—and afterwards a signature in unclear writing—

A clue. You kept a clue for me, a lead—not to lead me out but to lead me into a dark labyrinth which who knows how I'll get out of, and why the hell doesn't what comes out of an envelope ever get back into it again—

"Did I wake you up? Sorry—it's already noon and I thought that—did you see *Shoah* yesterday? How did it impress you? Who, Raul Hilberg? I have his book in English, if you want—should I bring it to Ora's for you this evening? I'll come, I always drop in there on Memorial Day—did you hear the news?—that's the way it goes here—good. So I'll see you this evening—"

Yes. No. Yes. No. Yes. No. Yes.

But I'm late. For more than a quarter of a century I've succeeded in always being ready for a pickup, made-up, groomed, taller by twelve centimeters in order to pour coffee and heat up meals at an altitude of forty thousand feet, and now, what have I done since noon except stare at the yellowing scraps laid out on your work table, trying to arrange them in chronological order without which it's impossible to understand processes, to classify them in sub groups according to the type of paper, color of ink, thickness of pencil, here and there a clear date—

But it can wait.

Perhaps something more will become clear to me this evening—

So jeans and running shoes.

In any case there's no chance of anything—

"Come in, come in—" Ora opens the door to a freight train passing by green trees and a blond man in a red jacket walking calmly next to it—Avi sits leaning forward, riveted to the screen—"Hi," I whisper, he nods, looking at the screen, where the Nazi from yesterday says, Treblinka was a little village, and indeed mud, huts, white geese, the camera repeats the path trodden by those who were transported there, stopping on the concrete sleepers, turns and climbs the gentle slope of the hill to the gas chambers in whose place now stands a monument of huge, gray, uneven stones, split through the middle into a deep crack of darkness, perhaps the gate of mercy a moment before it closes, perhaps the tablets of the law which have turned into two chimneys, they reached it in a tunnel, explains the Nazi, still blue and spectral, how wide was the tunnel, Lanzmann demands to know, and the women—why didn't they beat them, what was the reason for this humanity? In any case they were going to die! Incredible, but the Nazi is stunned by this indecent proposal, however he recovers immediately and confesses in a confidential voice: At the entrance to the gas chambers they beat them too . . .

The pale blue interior of a barbershop. The man in the barber's chair with a lemon-yellow gown and curly silver-iron hair almost like yours—but yours was wilder, more mane-like—the barber who sat yesterday with the Mediterranean Sea at his back cuts and talks, the sound of the scissors can be clearly heard, his English is rounded, his movements are rounded, he slides gently over the customer's curly head, a good barber, he obviously enjoys his work, he cuts, circles the customer, describes how the women arrived, naked, how he and his fellows had to cut their hair, what did you feel then, presses Lanzmann, when you're working among corpses you have no feelings, replies the barber, my friend saw his wife and her sister coming in—his narrow lips stick out and are sucked in, stick out and are sucked in as if what wants to burst out will not burst out, he wipes his face with a little towel, turns his back, comes back, licks his lower lip, go on Abe, pleads Lanzmann, but he shakes his head, it's too hard, his mouth trembles, tears flood his eyes, it was impossible to tell them it was their final hour, he says in the end, the SS were standing behind us, all we could do was hug them, try to stay with them a minute longer—the camera returns to the honeycombed stone of Czestochowa—standing out among the rest—

It was very important for none of us to say anything that would cause panic, says the black-haired man with the ironic eyes, good-looking, surprisingly young. "That's Walter Rosenberg," whispers Avi, although the subtitles say Rudolf Vrba, "he escaped from Auschwitz a few days after

Lederer," if anyone had hinted to them where they had come to they would have shot him behind the train, and the soft voice of the survivor from the Sonderkommando describes the deception, the quiet filing into the disrobing room, the camera moves slowly over a cross section of a hall full of plaster statues of people getting undressed, still innocent, still not guessing what awaits them in the next room, to which the camera now moves, focusing on distorted crushed plaster bodies trying to climb over each other on the walls, to the ceiling, moves away a little to reveal in the center of the terrible crush an empty circle under the hole in the ceiling, that's where they introduced the gas, explains the soft voice of the person who removed the bodies entangled with each other like a lump of basalt, there was no point in telling the truth to someone who had already crossed the threshold, he recalls a woman from Bialystock who had been told by an acquaintance and who told others and was severely tortured until she gave up the name of the acquaintance; he was thrown alive into the flames and she was gassed—none of those she had managed to warn believed her—

I go outside to get a breath of air, return to the eerie blue of the hidden camera shots, this time it's Walter Stier, ex-chief of the Sondertransport, thin mouth, thin nose, skin stretched tight over a skull face, the person responsible for the special trains never saw a train, had never budged from his desk, people called them trains for criminals, he explains, I was only a clerk, only a little clerk, mocks Lanzmann, but he misses the mockery, agrees absolutely, absolutely, a little clerk, and when did you nevertheless find out, insists Lanzmann who introduced himself as Dr. Sorel, and the blue clerk stammers, *also* . . . there were rumors, *och ja*, there were rumors here and there towards the end of the war, did it come as a surprise to you? asks Lanzmann-Sorel, certainly, *wahrlich*, with a shake of his head for emphasis, that camp . . . what was its name . . . that belonged to the Oppeln district . . . Auschwitz, he remembers at last, and the Polish population, did they know? Lanzmann asks innocently, *ach so, Doktor Sorel*, the clerk responds eagerly, they were nearby, they heard, they saw, and they shouldn't have kept silent . . .

I stand up. My head is splitting. My eyes are burning. Ora and Avi are welded to the screen. I go to the kitchen to get a glass of water. When I return the historian Hilberg is holding in his hand a non secret document—an order for a special train which reached at least eight addressees—a long train—50 cars—departed from Radom on 30 September at 4.18 hours, arrived in Treblinka at 11.24 on the following day—at 15.59 it had already left—empty—to collect victims from the next ghetto where it arrived at 3 A.M. and set out again for Treblinka full—we're still talking about the same train—Hilberg's finger wanders over the document, counting the full trains—we're talking about 10,000 Jews per one special train, more than 10,000! protests Lanzmann sitting opposite him. Let's be conservative, Hilberg is ironic, tightens his lips, this is the original document which the original official held in his hand—he holds the printed page in both hands—this is an historic exhibit; all that's left—the dead are gone—

He raises his eyes. His lower lip juts out accusingly—

"I'm going." I stand up. My head is full of hammers. My eyes are burning.

Ora and Avi don't turn to look at me. Across the television screen the trains go on passing.

RED WALL

I don't know if I have succeeded in arranging everything according to the necessary order in which all history proceeds, the order dictated by Kronos, the god of time, first things first, last things last, but I hope that I will nevertheless be able to tour your *Terra incognita*, to understand, perhaps, the *Alethestate prophasis*, the true motive for your "don't stir" look, once, twice, three times and *Sapienti sat!* a word to the wise. I asked no more—what did you intend to do with these pages—burn them? Why didn't you burn them? You had more than twenty years—or perhaps to write this chronicle up into history, *sine ira et studio*, without favor or anger, to recount what happened as it happened, *res gestae ut gesta*, to preserve, like Herodotus, the memory of what the barbarians did, and like Polybius, without calling, heaven forbid, on the gods—

You see? I remember. I can see you—*tristissimus hominis*, saddest of men—looking around you curiously, addicted to observation, gathering facts, sights, rumors—

And let providence take care of the meaning—

The first pages are torn from a writing pad, written with a fountain pen in the legible hand of someone who has time and who has and will have paper and only—what; Depression? Suspicion? Restraint?—and perhaps quiet protest—your kind of protest—poker-faced—blank eyed—impose this dry brevity on your stiff, slightly awkward Hebrew.

It begins *in medias res*—

19.11.39
My pupil was hurt in a demonstration. I visited her home. In courage she is the teacher and I the pupil. Many are fleeing. A difficult talk with M.

28.12.39
It is forbidden to attend the theater, restaurants, public parks. Statues of Moses and Maharal have been removed from their places. And what will they do with the Altneushul? And the Hebrew-letter clock that counts time backwards? A harsh argument whether the time has not come to leave. Our servant returned to her village.

20.3.40
The lawyer K. has separated from his non-Jewish wife to protect her from harm. Conversation with M. about it. It is possible we may obtain an exit permit for Holland. My neighbor relates: they refused to transport his wife to the hospital in the ambulance.

30.7.40

France too has fallen. Bad news from Poland. *Relato refero*, I relate what I have heard: They intend to gather all the Jews in Madagascar—where is Madagascar? In the Indian Ocean. There are mountains and forests and much rain and plantations of coffee and sugar and tobacco. The irony of history—the Germans will supply a Zionist solution to the Jewish question: they will gather them all in one place, teach them manual labor. Some of my students are happy. I diminish their happiness: And will the French colonialists and the local inhabitants sit idly by and wait for millions of Jews to arrive and squeeze them out?

28.11.40

News of the sinking of the "Patria" but no names of those drowned on her. For an hour a day the Jews are permitted to shop, but there is nothing in the shops. M. will buy from the Czechs for the family of my pupil who have also been residing with us for three months . . .

20.12.40

A letter from G. in Palestine: he arrived there five months ago. There is no work, no place to stay, the heat is hard and the language is hard. He regrets having gone there.

25.12.40

It is forbidden to breed pigeons, to visit the barber, to fly the flag of the Reich. Is there a Jew dismayed by this prohibition?

2.1.41

Yesterday after the festive meal M. informed me of her departure. She cannot tolerate life in "this overcrowded Jewishness" etc. She took her clothes and her jewels. The dog Max she left me. For a long time he lay at the door in deep dejection.

You got up and left him—perhaps this is what he tried to spare me—and perhaps the vein of anti-Semitism that he suddenly discovered in you, beating under your skin, conducting blood to your heart—he was sent to Terezin, you remained in Prague—until he returned, very thin, probably already bald, and offered to take up from where you left off—did he forgive you? Or did he prefer to return to what was familiar, afraid of new passions, of changes, feeling that his life was already lost anyway, wanting above all tranquility without any surprises—and you—because of what: pangs of conscience? Feelings of guilt? Love?—Is there any love in your story?— Ready to travel to Italy with him, to give birth to me, even to adopt the motherless Nahum until Davidi came home from all the wars, to emigrate to Israel and one year later—a great silence: no tombstone, no grave, no anniversary, not even death, she's gone, he said to me about you, where did she go, far away, when will she come back, in the autumn and afterwards in the winter and afterwards in the spring, next year, when you're big—

8.2.41

My pupil is polishing floors in the Jewish Hospital. I am teaching high school pupils since my work in the University of Prague was terminated. Their hearts are not in learning. Every lesson—a big political argument. The Communists believe in the equality of nations. The assimilationists say, "We are Czechs," and the Zionists ridicule them both.

18.4.41

Yugoslavia has been defeated. The net has closed, the fish are boiling inside it. The telephone is prohibited. Many are living under assumed names until the troubles are at an end. D. thinks that being concentrated together will return us to a situation like the ghetto. He has left Prague, taken a room in the home of his Communist friend in the country. The father of my pupil who lives with us says to his daughters: This is no time for heroism. Now is the time to appear dead. The wild beast will come, sniff, and go away.

10.6.41

The sister of my pupil and her friend have "dived in" among the people of the land. Their appearance is good, their eyes are blue. From the newspaper: A Doctor of Philosophy is growing chickens in America. A Professor of History has opened a coffee house in Mexico. The owner of a factory is making cheese in Chile.

20.9.41

The Middle Ages have returned—every Jew from the age of six must wear the "Jewish Star" on his heart. A great argument among my students—to wear the badge or not? It is forbidden to leave your home. The words of the President—the Czechs are with the Germans in their war. Perhaps he hopes in his heart for their defeat at the hands of General Winter. Heard: Jews were beaten in Brno and Ostrava.

22.9 . . .

Musical instruments, gramophones, dogs are prohibited.

26.9.41

In the evening M. came to take Max. She saw the Jewish star on the breast of my coat. She said nothing. The dog welcomed her with great joy, licked her hands, waved his tail, and went with her willingly. If Professor Pavel and Professor Vasco and Dr. Vaclav will not greet me—how should I complain of a dog?

It's a pity you didn't tell me, you know. I wouldn't have nagged you for a dog from the end of the fifth to the end of the eighth grade, just a little one, a cute little puppy, I'll wash it, I'll take it for walks, I'll remember to feed it—

4.10.41

The Jewish New Year. From my childhood I have not celebrated this festival. People say: in eight months time the Protektorat will be "cleaned" of

282

Jews. The Reds are defeated. In Brno youths were hanged for not wearing the Jewish star. The President has been put in jail.

15.10.41
The "cleaning" has begun. An expulsion order has been published against five thousand Jews signed by the Police Commissioner. A number of my students summoned for transportation will not go. What will they do if they fail to appear?

30.10.41
This is what they will do: they arrested two officials in charge of the registration department. Heard today—they drowned escaping from the penal colony. It is said: those summoned traveled by train to Poland. Perhaps they will concentrate all the Jews there, turn Poland into Madagascar.

3.11.41
Prague—a cauldron of rumors. It is said: in Poland they collect Jews in wooden houses and set them on fire.

29.11.41
Heard: fourteen members of "Hehalutz" who attempted to cross the Slovakian border were caught and killed by hanging. D. came from B. Someone betrayed them, he says. He has not yet sewn a Jewish star on his heart. He still has hopes of "diving." His Communist friends will help him.

1.12.41
The sister of my pupil came in secret, bringing food and greens. She says—for five thousand crowns it is possible to purchase a work permit. You only have to remove the yellow star. My pupil refuses: now she works in a charity kitchen for the hungry. From there she brought the rumor: they intend to concentrate all the Jews in one town in the Protektorat and an advance guard from the Zionists have already set out to prepare the place.

The student P. tells me of a translator of Kafka into Czech, a Christian woman, who put a Jewish star on her clothes, and called on all Czechs to follow her example. The father of my pupil asked—and where is that heroine now? And where are all the Czechs wearing the star? This year has taught me: not all the Czechs love Jews. Many were happy to receive the plundered property. Perhaps it would be for the best if they concentrated all the Jews in one town until the war ends. The brother of my pupil says: It will not be a Jewish town they build, but a trap. His father says: What is the point of arguing? They will not ask us. We shall go *nolens volens*. Whether we wish to or not.

15.12.41

People run hither and thither like mice in a trap—seeking gloves, a flashlight, batteries, a winter coat, ointments, candles. They buy "black." Gallows humor abounds: A knock on the door of the Cohen family at midnight: "Gestapo! Open at once!" "Thank God, we were afraid it was the messengers of the Jewish community organization at the door!"

1.1.42

D. brought a Communist newspaper from the fifteenth of October, 1941. "One of the latest crimes of the civilized Germans is the deportation of our Jewish citizens to Poland"—if this is true and not war propaganda the intention is clear: concentration, concentration, concentration. I would not be surprised if Terezin is only a station on the way to Poland. They will make Poland the "Land of the Jews" and all of Germanized Europe "Judenrein." Perhaps the Nazis think: Polish hatred will consume the Jews, and our hands will be clean.

20.1.42

D. quoting a railway worker: In the middle of January several hundred of the Jews arriving at Terezin were sent to Poland . . .

29.1.42

In the middle of the night a messenger of the Jewish community knocked at the door, presented an order to go to the Exhibition Palace, to bring all personal documents, passport, money, jewels, ration cards, a list of all the property remaining in the apartment, the key of the house.

1.2.42

Among D.'s friends is a young Communist "Mischling," a nurse in the military hospital in Terezin, where she also has her home. According to her: the number of Jews assembled in Terezin is already greater than that of the Czech residents. The Jews are all crowded into army barracks. Contact between the Jews and the Czechs is not allowed. It is said that in January they hanged a few Jews who wrote letters to their families.

What is "Mischling"? A spy? A double agent? An underground name? A pet name?

3.2.42

M. came. She brought jam and asked for my signature on a document of divorce. Our suitcases are open, all the time things are added, removed. I am taking my books, much writing paper, many pens. M. observes my preparations with an ironic eye: "Can you no longer wait until you are the first historian of the last ghetto?" Perhaps she is right. She promised to await me "at six after the war." My ring is still on her finger.

Here the pages torn from the letter pad, the clear handwriting in a fine fountain pen, come to an end, from now on the pages are nothing more than random scraps of paper, torn envelopes, squared pages from an accounts ledger, gray packing paper, all written in faded pencil, in a small, cramped hand—

I read slowly, deciphering. From now on I am not sure of the sequence. What is clear: my maminka—your M.—really did stay in Prague to wait for you like the good soldier Švejk, until six after the war, but what motivated her to sail with you to the land of the blazing sun simply to burn here for a year and something, to cry behind glass doors with a pattern of frost flowers—

10.2.42

Terezin. "Sudeten" barracks. The train traveled about three hours. At Bohusovice the cars were opened—Jews in peaked caps, Czech gendarmes, and SS men waiting. The cold below zero. Suitcases and invalids taken by wagons. The healthy walked to Terezin in threes. After three hours we saw the red wall. We entered each with his number around his neck, like cattle. The little town has not changed much since I visited it with my history students. Its streets straight, crossing at right angles, their length about five hundred meters. In the Hohenelbe hospital the assassin Gabrilo Princep died of tuberculosis . . . the streets are empty. Where are all those who came before us? A man from the ghetto police whispers to me—they were ordered to remain in their rooms to prevent contraband.

11.2.42

In the basement of the "Kavalier" barracks dust and darkness and commotion. They open our luggage and take everything—smoking equipment, cameras, soap. The brother of my pupil does not rest. His two friends from the Ghettowache rescued some pages and a few pencils. A Communist acquaintance of D., Eng. P., got us out of there quickly. My pupil was sent to the "Dresden" barracks. Her father and brother are with me in the "Sudeten" barracks, abode of the ghetto pioneers. The entrance is guarded by a Czech gendarme and one of the ghetto guards. There are no beds, only sawdust mattresses on the cold floor. No table, cupboard, chair. The Aeltestenrat is located in the "Magdeburg" barracks which has horses' heads on its gate.

17.2.42

For the meager food we wait in a long line. In the end we hold out our bowls and food coupons and receive cold cumin soup. It is raining. The water falls into the food.

?...2

It is permitted to write one postcard a month in print letters in the German language. It is forbidden to speak ill of the place. I write to M. I am well, but sorely miss the company of my good friend Mister Hleb.

I remember you polishing off five-six slices of bread at a meal, bread—*hleb* in Russian—with nothing on it, just plain bread, advising, almost urging me, too, to eat with bread, plenty of bread, concerned, you hardly eat any bread—

?42

I am working in a "Hundertschaft." Pushing a black hearse with fine pillars topped with "crowns." The "dead"—potatoes or loaves of bread. On the right and the left of the wagon pushers there are guards from the ghetto police to protect us from the hungry. More death wagons pass noisily with their wooden wheels over the eroded streets, carrying suitcases or books and also dead people covered with thin paper to the morg...

5.3.42?

My pupil comes to sweep the floor in the "Sudeten" barracks. Only in this way can she exchange words with her father, with her brother. She looks thin and ill. She regrets not removing the Jewish star as her sister recommended. When she has completed her work I go out with her to the entrance of the barracks, try to restore her good spirits. The ramparts on the walls are growing grass... and the smell of spring is in the air. If you raise your eyes to the north you will see blue lead mountains higher than the wall, like hope—not very near but not so far...

8.3.42

Today we carried dead bodies in the hearse. Next to the room of the dead we saw a short, broad man doing the work of a pathologist. The rulers wish to know the cause of death of the dead because they fear plagues. When we came out of the morgue the brother of my pupil told me that this man is the hangman who hanged the Jewish youths last January. A Jewish man? Yes, certainly. Here everything is done by Jews . . .

10.3.42

In the night we were visited by emissaries from "Magdeburg," the home of the Aeltestenrat, bearing strips of paper. The "block elder" takes the long narrow papers, reads the names written on them, goes to the sleeping men, awakens them to their fate. Who will rest in the ghetto and who will move on is determined by the "Poland Committee." Each of its members fights for his dear ones to leave them in the ghetto. Eng. P. gave my name with the thirty names of "his people" to be protected from transportation. But tonight the father of my pupil was called. I helped him to pack his few clothes and I lent him a book. He promised me that he would write from the new place. Perhaps it is better than this place . . . he has much family in Poland. He hopes to meet them. He left a letter in my hands for my pupil, when

. . . 42

It is said that soon another transportation will depart. Many rumors (bunkes) pass from mouth to ear, speculations of fear and hope, but only the rumor of transportation is proven true. A number of people from Mandler's "Circus" have been seen here: they collected Jews with a harsh hand from many villages to send to Terezin, and at the end they too fell into the same trap. At the "Order of the Day" there was jubilation because the food allocated to each person was increased: bread—from 347 gr. to 372 gr. (but beans were reduced from 24 gr. to 4 gr. . . .).

18.3.42

Another transportation departed. People say: they traveled in carriages for cattle. The old, sick, and children were sent. A rumor: a new ghetto is being set up in Moravia.

20.3.42

Before every transportation many people assemble in the corridor and in front of the door of office 85a in the Magdeburg barracks, crying, pleading, groveling. Everybody knows favoritism is shown to the young and the Zionists. Some people call Magdeburg "The Castle"—*Das Schloss*—after the book by Kafka. Like there, on the way to the "Master of the Castle" bureaucracy, "vitamin P," black market.

27.3.42

A small transportation arrived from Prague with the wives of the dignitaries, straight to Magdeburg. They were not arrested and robbed at the "Schleusse." They brought with them good furniture, fine china, beautiful carpets, food. A deep gulf is growing between the "Ministers of the Castle" and the "plebs." My neighbor went to prison for two days for spoiling the honor of a member of the Ghettowache.

Transportation is obviously "transport." What remains a mystery is that "my pupil" of yours to whom you don't even refer by her initial—let me guess: it was because of her that my mother remained in Prague—young, dark, attractive—perhaps she looked like Ora—here she is again—without a date—"My pupil will go with other women to work in the forest"—what was there between you?—what could there have been? Here, on this piece of paper—"Men separate from women. Only the Aeltestenrat stay with their families. The Magdeburg sentry gave me"—here some pages are evidently missing because the continuation is on different, squared paper, written in a soft, very faded pencil—a jump straight to May—

1.5.42

On the Communist holiday my bygone student D. arrived. He came straight from the "Schleusse" to the "Sudeten" barracks. He appears well but his anger is great. He brought a big parcel for me sent by M. from Prague, but everything was plundered in the Schleusse.

What is Schleusse? Something connected to a key, apparently—lock-up? Reception depot? Detention? Induction center?

10.5.42

Another transportation left—this is not a ghetto but a way station. Bunkes abound here and no one knows how much is true and how much fear. Some are even happy to leave—anywhere is better than the ghetto . . . Spring has come. The sun sends its warm rays and the old folks sit in the yards and pluck the lice from their clothes . . . People fight the situation with jokes: Every poodle in Terezin says that in Prague it was a Saint Bernard dog.

18.5.42

The camp Commandant abolished the big ghetto police (two hundred and fifty policemen) and put a small one in its place (fifty men). The jokers say: They reduced the police because there are no more criminals in the land. The pessimists say: They reduced the police because the rulers fear their power. Today I took the exceedingly old in the hearse for disinfection. The old are as thin as paper. Their food is the poorest in the ghetto . . . Boys and girls go out every morning to cultivate gardens outside the walls, they make schleussen with potatoes or a lettuce. The workers in the kitchen and bakery too make schleussen with the food and the guards . . . schleussen from the confiscated luggage of the arrivals. Many people who came here are in a situation where they are compelled to do things against their principles.

?5.42

According to D.: There is no room to bury the many dead—they are going to build a big crematorium—they have requested builders to build it. He gave his name . . . his friend came to the ghetto in secret. She crossed the street at night from the side of the Terezin gentiles to the side of the Terezin Jews in great danger to her life. In the morning she went to the sickroom for old people, but they would not allow her to work until she gave her name. She gave her name. They promised her that nurses would not be called up for transportation . . . From M. no sign or parcel . . . because . . .

26.5.42

It is said—exceedingly old Jews will be coming from the Reich . . . perhaps a sign that the end is near. There is no longer a German newspaper on the streets . . . three days ago a transportation left. Many of the belongings of those who went remained here. My neighbor says, they will give them new, strong clothes. D. asked me for books about Bar Kokhba . . . for his friend who returned from Palestine in disappointment only to fall into the trap of Terezin. After the end he will search for traces of the great revolt in the ancient land. An interesting psychological process: people "cross over" the walls by thinking of their past or their future. In the present— "überleben"—they survive.

30.5.42

A conspiracy to assassinate the Reichsprotektor . . . they are hunting the conspirators. Many people have been arrested. D. is anxious for the fate of his Communist friends.

5.6.42

The enemy flag at half mast. The "Pasha" died of his wounds. We hear: in Prague they have killed many writers and professors among my colleagues. The irony of history: here, in the hunger, the crowding, the filth, with the lice, I am more safe than my colleagues remaining in the capital of the land.

13.6.42

My neighbor was taken to work three days past and last night he returned, without a word to say. Today he told me that they were driven to a burning village . . . they ordered them to dig a big pit and throw tens of men . . . murdered . . . into it . . . at the end they shot two dogs too and threw them into the pit on the murdered men . . . my neighbor and others from Terezin worked without rest and without food, around them drunken SS men. At the last they sent the goats, the sheep, the geese in a procession to Terezin. They spared their lives until they mount the table of the SS here . . .

16.6.42
Everyone was called to come out into the yards and say to whom a jacket, a bicycle, a satchel belonged. One old woman asked to see the satchel up close . . . : How old are you? She replied: Eighty-two. He said to her: Jews live too long . . .

?
A transportation left. They sent strong young people. D. says: the rulers want to weaken the ghetto for fear of revolt or conspiracy . . . but my neighbor P. sees it as a good sign: if they are sending strong young Jews to work in Germany it is because all the German youths are employed in the war in the east.

20.6.42
Jews arrived from Cologne. They say that the whole city is destroyed by English bombs. They regard their surroundings with a resentful eye—they were promised a convalescent spa town with lawns—and what do they see: three-storied beds, lice, no hygiene, hunger, noise. Czech Jews understand their German but pretend to be deaf. I heard some of them say to the new arrivals: In order to make room for you our friends were sent from Terezin to the East. *Relato refero*: in Prague they are shooting and killing people in the streets. No sign of life from M.

27.6.42
Terezin is "Gentile-rein." The family of the friend of D. too (the father—Czech, the dead mother Jewish, the second wife of the father—Czech)

have left the town. Only her half-brother works as a gendarme at the gate. In some days time it will be permitted to walk in the streets, except for the market square, the Victoria Hotel, the parks . . . And the road that leads to Prague. Heard: thousands of Jews were killed in . . . nice. K. received a postcard from her brother who left with a transportation on the fifteenth of January . . . "It is hard—but the hardship can be overcome to the end."

7.7.42

. . . Permitted to walk in the streets until nine hours in the evening . . . the streets are full of people. People who have not seen one another for a long time embrace, are amazed, make jokes: How elegant you look. It is warm and pleasant outside. I met my pupil. She has returned from her work in the forests. Her face is beautiful, bronzed from the sun. Her life now is good—she is friends with a supplies man. *Ubi bene ibi patria*. Wherever I am content is my fatherland. She also takes from the post parcels of three women sent away from Terezin with the transportations. These days she is working in the vegetable garden. She gave me half a lemon. Very sour.

I can hear a muffled tenderness in your voice, almost a caress, when you pronounce the words "my pupil"—you call the rest of your students "my students"—don't stir things up. Don't stir, because if you stir you will discover *angius in herba*, a snake in the grass—your dry, formal Hebrew covers like the scab on a wound, but my mouth tastes as sour as if I have just bitten into that lemon given to you by "your pupil"—the next page is particularly big—where did you get it from; did she give it to you with the lemon?

12.7.42

Thousands of old people from the Reich, from Vienna fill the streets . . . Gray-haired old women with black hats, black gloves, and walking sticks with silver knobs. Many of those from the Reich wear ski caps that resemble the caps of the Nazis. I walk in the streets, observe the faces of the assembled Jews—the Jews resemble the gentiles of their countries more than they resemble each other. Only a minority are Semitic types with "almond eyes" and big noses. Some of the Reich Jews say: If only the Führer knew the truth about our hard lives—he would never agree to the treatment we receive here. Among them are war heroes who bear medals for fighting with distinction for Germany in previous wars. Among them are well-known professors such as my acquaintance Prof. Philippson from the University of Bonn.

The date is blurred—but apparently from 42
According to the friend of D. that works as a nurse in the "Kavalier" barracks: two sisters of Dr. Sigmund Freud arrived. Their age is over eighty . . . My work now: pushing books in the hearse to L304. Those bound for the east left their books here. *Habet sua fata libelli.* Books have a fate of their own.

The date is blurred, also the opening lines
. . . parasols to protect from the sun. At the entrance to the latrine stands an old usher . . . the lost who do not remember where they live. A sign . . . with a death skull, "Beware, disinfection by poisonous gas!" On the walls signs in red and black paint—garbage, urinal, cleanliness-order-comradeship.

1.8.42
Order of the day no.185: Many reports of theft have reached the Aeltesten-rat. The punishment of the thieves—jail, reduced rations, confiscation of belongings, public disgrace. Anyone catching a thief will hand him over to the "Ordnungswache." If not—he will be punished along with the thief.

3.8.42
The number of the dead is very great . . . the year of their birth is no longer written next to their names. The heat, the lice, the filth brings people out to sleep in the yards. Notice of another transportation to leave tomorrow. Three people have committed suicide. One stood on the window sill in the Cavalry barracks and jumped from the second floor head down. He fell at my feet and his head split. The loaves of bread fell from the

hearse onto the mud of the street. The men of the Ghettowache hurried to put to flight the crowd gathering around the bread and the death. The bread we loaded onto the wagon, the dead man was carried by his hands and feet. On my return with blood on the hems of my trousers, I met my pupil, her face white. The ribbon of death in her hand—she has been called up for transportation. *Stat sua cuique dies.* The day of his death awaits every man.

You are gloating at her downfall? The man as bald as a brown egg whose eyes are expressionless behind thick glasses and who never—in hardly any circumstances—raises his voice—

5.8.42

My pupil was saved from the transportation at the last minute at the hands of her friend. She is not the only one to sleep with an important man in the ghetto to save her life. She has no property other than her beauty. From the mouth of the friend of D.: Dead old people lie next to old people who will soon die. Young girls from the "Heim" who come to help flee after their first dead. Today she handed me the *novissima verba*: the last words she wrote down from the mouths of the dying. "I have not eaten strudel for a long time," "Search the cellar," "I am going to a better world," "Regards to my son in Mexico."

13.8.42

G. is helping me to sort the many books left behind by those sent on the transportations. G. is a zoologist . . . he says—this ghetto is one big laboratory for observing the behaviour of many people in a small cage—boot-lickers, opportunists, egoists, gangsters, power lovers, status seekers. In short: "The Chosen People." Charitable souls—*corvo quoque rarior albo.* Even rarer than a white crow. Order of the day 124: One birth, one hundred and ten deaths.

17.8.42

From the mouth of the friend of D.: The sisters of Kafka too have arrived in the ghetto. Last night I met the younger sister, Mrs. David, divorced from her Christian husband, she came to be here with her people. Their daughters she left with him . . . but . . .

30.8.42

The friend of D. is pregnant. It is forbidden to perform an abortion of the fetus. Pregnant women are sent on the transportations to the east. D. wants to marry her, but he is afraid: his work on the construction of the crematorium is completed—he may be sent East as a "Specialist" in this work and his young wife they will send with him—what to do? In the ghetto it is impossible to be a giver of good advice. One day they promise unification of families—the next day they send the husband East, and leave the wife here.

3.9.42

Mrs. Polak, the elder sister of Kafka, has received a transportation order. Mrs. David went to people of culture and pleaded with them, but she found no help.

11.9.42

The Jewish New Year. The Aeltestenrat offers good wishes, thanks the workers for their loyal work, calls all residents to maintain iron discipline. They have opened Potemkin shops. It becomes known—Mrs. Trude Herzl-Neumann is also here. A beautiful woman, her mind is disturbed. She reminds the Zionists of her famous father, but they will not help her due to an old quarrel with her husband (who has already been separated from her for years . . .)

17.9.42

Announcement by the Ghetto Commandant: Engineer Leo Hess is accused of conspiring with Aryans outside the ghetto and of contraband in food. He is expelled from the Aeltestenrat and will be sent on a special transportation to the east.

20.9.42

In the evening I was called by the room elder: You have a visitor. On the threshold stood my pupil. Her protector is a friend of Engineer Hess who was sent East on the "Special transportation." Now both she and her friend have received transportation orders. Do I have a book to while away the hours of a long journey? I gave her a forbidden book, *Beware of Pity* by Stefan Zweig. My pupil is optimistic. It may not be so very bad in the east. Perhaps she will find her father. She promised to write me of her fate.

21.9.42

The Day of Atonement. Some fast and some eat, they say: All year we fast and suffer. Today too a big transportation left with old Jews from the Reich. After the end we will have a nation of the young alone, without fathers, without mothers, without grandparents. A nation without tradition, starting from zero . . .

. . . ?42

Reorganization of the ghetto: headed by Dr. Loewenstein, a highly decorated war veteran, head of the Jewish Police in Minsk. They brought him to make order in the Czech disorder.

27.9.42

In the Order of the Day: an expert in making artificial flies for fishing is wanted. The construction of the crematorium is completed. The work of D. now—to carry carcasses from the central morgue in the city walls to the crematorium. He says there are about two hundred dead a day. The ashes are to be placed in boxes with the name of the dead in a "columbarium." I say to him: You have much work. They will not send you away. You will be able to marry your friend . . . I see that I have grown hard in my heart . . .

Here is the columbarium—indeed a vault for the ashes of the dead and not a dovecote, Davidi, and here you are: carrying corpses from the central morgue to the crematorium. You have a lot of work, your ex-lecturer in the history of Western Civilization writes here, and as long as two hundred people a day die here—you will not be sent away . . . so how did you land up in Treblinka anyway—did they stop dying in Terezin? And what happened to that nurse? And how is it that not a word—not ever—perhaps the explanation is here, right in front of my eyes. "I have grown hard in my heart." Both Daddy and you. And you couldn't get rid of the stone—or otherwise: you didn't want Nahum and me to grow stonyhearted too—

3.10.42

Mala avis: They have changed the Aeltestenrat—Edelstein is still the head, but in place of the Czech dignitaries they have put Jewish dignitaries from Berlin and Vienna. Much anger among the Czechs. *Divide et impera.*

6.10.42

At night I was awoken by the messenger, he gave me the ribbon of death with my name on it. If the Vitamin P does not avail—I will leave on the transportation departing on the eighth of October—

7.10.42

Prof. Utitz saw me among the crowds pushing in the "Castle" and promised—we will do whatever is in our power to do. It will help you if you have hidden gold or tobacco . . .

9.10.42

Much commotion, pushing, weeping. I handed in my work card, ration card. They wrote the letters Bu in white paint on my suitcase. The porters carry the luggage of the deportees on wagons to the Bohusovice station. The exits from the "Hamburg" barracks, our place of assembly, to the ghetto are guarded by men of the Ghettowache. Suddenly Dr. R., the SS doctor, came into a little room. They call me to go to him. I give him the letter from Professor Philippson and also a ring with a small diamond, my mother's ring, which my student sewed into the lapel of my coat before we left Prague . . . The doctor read the letter from the professor, took the ring, said, do not leave this room. I remained in his little room until midnight. Behind the door a great commotion. Then running feet, shouts, "Schnell, schnell Jew-pigs" . . . Afterwards silent as the grave . . . At dawn a guard from the Ghettowache escorted me with another five people rescued from this transportation for one reason or another to our quarters . . . The streets were empty as on the day of our arrival. All the people were shut in their quarters until all those going East had departed.

13.10.42
I went to the "Kavalier" barracks to ask the friend of D. his whereabouts. She looked at me as if seeing the face of a dead man. D. was on the reserves of the Bu transportation; the Vitamin P which rescued me—sent him on my place. Next to my name Dr. R. wrote: "Not eligible for deportation." This protects me for the moment . . .

Achilles and Patroclus, Aeneas and Achates, Alexander and Hephaestion? No, more than that, far more than that, a teacher and his student who was sent "on his place" to hell—now everything is clear: your limitless patience with him—your arm around him—the gentle tone—the sudden anxiety: Loya, why don't you go over to see how Davidi is—the responsibility: to watch him so that he wouldn't—wouldn't what—and also that boiling bitterness—let me guess; you would not have given me this chronicle to read; you wouldn't have wanted me to know—but Davidi wanted it—Davidi brought me here to place this document in my hands—

7.10.42
. . . Doctors and nurses too have been taken for transportation . . . M. begged me to put in an application for marriage. Her brother the guard at

the gate heard from a railwayman: in one of the cattle carriages which took the Bu transportation he saw written in chalk: Three o'clock. Warsaw. No food no water . . .

Another M.? A slip of the pen? A coincidence? Or much simpler—short for "Mischling"—

27.10.42
A great commotion. Many people did not present themselves for transfer By. The rulers forbade leaving the barracks, forbade shining torches, canceled all lectures and meetings.

10.42
Every place is searched, every person is counted. They are hunting those in hiding . . . for the first time since the inception of the ghetto some one hundred people did not come to the transportation. Many are waiting to see if the hiders will succeed. It is said that large numbers escaped the walls, reached Prague, and "dived."

30.10.42
MALA AVIS: Most of those who did not present themselves for the transport have been caught . . . We have received a date for our marriage . . .

11.42
We signed a grotesque document: the couple agree to share their lives, help each other in all circumstances, go together everywhere. The couple swear to undergo a legal marriage at the first possible moment. I broke a paper cone with my foot and that was the end of the ceremony. "My wife" returned to her quarters in "Hamburg." I to mine in "Sudeten."

More complicated than I thought—and perhaps more simple—almost symmetrical—Davidi was sent "on your place" to Treblinka, and you married his "Mischling" "in his place" in order to protect her (and her fetus?) from the next "transportations"—

25.11.42
They opened the library (L304) the director—Prof. Utitz. I will arrange the books in boxes and carry them in hearses to the elders of the buildings. Belletristics for the young, Zionistics—for the members of HeHalutz, Maccabi et cetera, classics—for the old, damaged books—for the sick. Yesterday they celebrated one year since the establishment of the ghetto . . . the Aeltestenrat requests all residents of the ghetto to maintain loyalty and discipline.

8.12.42
It is possible to sit in the coffeehouse for two hours, drink pseudocoffee, listen to jazz. There are no more transportations. Perhaps the end is near. General Winter is fighting the Germans in the East . . . the pregnancy of "my wife" is hardly evident. Her work with the sick can no longer give her protection. Her friend organized work in the "Hamburg" kitchen for her . . . Her gendarme half-brother smuggles vegetables for her to eat. No sign from my pupil. No sign from D.

3.1.43
The Christian New Year. We celebrated with a small branch of a tree which her brother gave us. We stood in the street in great cold and saw Jewish police marching in the Nazi goosestep . . . The postal workers made merry in Sylvester celebrations with food robbed from parcels not their own.

16.1.43
Cold to make teeth chatter. The rulers visited the houses of the prominents and ordered for the apartments to be expanded . . . I bring books for these dignitaries too. For my friend Prof. Philippson the great geographer, for Prof. Emile Klein—international celebrity and big snob, for the songstress

Henriette Beck, highly decorated for her singing to German soldiers in the last war, for the granddaughter of the banker of Bismark, for the grandson of Baron Hirsch, for the head of the government of Saxony—*Sic transit gloria mundi*—

31.1.43

The rulers have made Dr. Epstein from Berlin the Jewish Elder and degraded Edelstein the Czech Zionist to the rank of his deputy . . . Dr. Kahn arrived from Prague. They have abolished the Zentralstelle there. Our isolation from the world is being completed.

5.2.43

A long conversation with the Revered Dr. Leo Baeck. He visited Palestine in 1935. His impression: the Jews and the Arabs live as good neighbors . . . he came to Terezin with the new Judenaeltester. Here he volunteered for work since he was not obliged due to his age (70 years) and his status (Prominent A). The scoundrel Mandler, owner of the "Zirkus," also arrived in the ghetto, received Prominent A for his great help in rounding up Jews and their property. A number of young men beat him energetically. Now he is in the hospital. The nurses refused to nurse him. (Evidence of M.)

Rabbi Leo Baeck? The one you wrote the letter to in London? After so many years? Actually—why so many? Not so many: from the time you wrote this to the time you wrote the letter you didn't send only twelve years passed—

10.2.43

Heard: a big quarrel in the "Jewish council"—Dr. Kahn refuses to accept any position in the council. He said to Edelstein, "They are the arm—you are the fingers."

The date is blurred. So are a couple of lines. I guess that it comes here—
Typhus. Giving the hand in greeting is forbidden. A superior German

doctor has come. The deputy post office director was arrested for theft. Perhaps M. sent me a parcel and here I was robbed. Conversation with Prof. P. who arrived from Prague two weeks ago—he could not believe his ears that the Registration Department would provide names for those going east on the transportations . . . Why should we do the work of our haters, he asks. He will yet become accustomed to the situation.

15.2.43

"My wife" gave birth in her room in "Hamburg." She did not go to the hospital for fear of the typhus and lest they gave the name of the infant for registration . . . Her friends among the nurses helped her . . . The son is small but healthy. No news from his father.

15.2.43?

Mazel tov, Nahum!—on your identity card it says Czechoslovakia, and I always assumed, for some reason, that it was in Prague. Another few scraps of paper will bring the news of the death of your mother and also clarify how you survived—the gendarme uncle?—and perhaps an almost impossible combination of luck and circumstances and connections and "vitamin P"—it's so strange, you know—your father was sent instead of mine to Treblinka, my mother brought you up instead of your mother—if you had lived you could have told me more about her than I know—for me she is only a pale echo, a collage of memories and fragments of black-and-white movies on the wall of the meeting hall in summer, a Soviet nurse crowned with a blonde braid like a halo, enterprising and energetic, suddenly looking at the window—weeping soundlessly—when all the little candles danced with their mothers at Hanukkah I danced with Malka the teacher, where's your mother? the other children asked me at the end of the party and Ora rushed to my defense, her mother went on a trip, when's she coming back? Yosefa doesn't believe it, in the long vacation, I weakly repeat the lie, lie, lie, why did she go for such a long time, asks Minaleh in a kind of complaint, seeming on my side, actually against me, she went abroad, Ora comes to my rescue, stands behind me, taller than me by half a head, firm, warm, a wall, so your mother's some *yoredet* from Israel, chants Arlozora, around us a group has gathered, Bilu and Elhanan and Hezi and Zvika and Dina and Dudik and Ruthie and Nitzhia, Your mother's a *yoredet*, Minaleh—a white cheese dumpling studded with cherry lips—your mother's a *yoredet*, and I, to save her, to save me from the disgrace, announce in a cracked voice, she didn't go abroad—she went further than abroad! And Elhanan snorts contemptuously and turns his back on this nonsense, but the others believe it, they stare at me in silence, children, what are you doing there? Come along, help yourselves to refreshments, we have doughnuts, Malka the teacher's voice rises above us sweet and cheerful, and some of them hurry off to the tables arranged in a horseshoe shape parallel to the classroom walls, but a few remain to hear the sentence passed by Minaleh, who swells a little as she proclaims: Further than abroad—that means dead—

Memory: sometimes it hides like a sinew of grass running under the earth and sometimes like a pipe buried in the wall, gurgling, growling, sticking out the bent finger of a faucet inside which is darkness and beyond which what is waiting there for us to allow it to emerge into the light, a glass snake writhing and spraying chips of silver and gathered quickly into the mouth of the sink in order to be imprisoned in another pipe, because nothing is ever lost, not the water, not the rain, not the clouds, not the light of the sun, not even what existed thousands of years ago, you see, here's the market and these are the houses and here's a street and there's a street and the bathhouse, you see it, from the top of the hill you can see the whole town, but the minute you go down to it it breaks up again into a stone here and a stone there and sun and dust—

My mother isn't dead, I try to save my honor. Minaleh pouts. At the age of eight she is already no mean expert in death. She is very sure of herself. Your mother is so dead, she accompanies her words with little nods of her head that say is so—is so—is so, your mother's dead and the Nazis made her into soap—

On the night of the Passover Seder we eat rolls. But everybody eats matzo, I complain. I like matzo. The next day they send me to get some matzo from Hasia. Just for me. In the meantime there's the *haroseth* Hasia sent. Spread it on the roll, it's very good—but the round roll suddenly looks to me like soap and my mouth clamps shut.

Where's my mother?

I couldn't have asked a more terrible question. Davidi stands up. Daddy coughs hard. Nahum looks at me, looks at Daddy, looks at him, suddenly it seems that he's in charge here, he opens his mouth to answer, but Davidi lays an archaeological hand on his head to silence him.

Is that one of the Passover questions?—his voice is scorched. His eyes—two slits of boiling silver.

Minaleh said thatthenazismadeherintosoap—I whisper in one breath.

What?

Davidi is already on his way to them to make a scandal in the middle of the Passover Seder. Daddy gets up, tries to stop him, but he pushes, shoves, rushes out, almost running, and Daddy hanging onto his sleeve is dragged behind him halfway down the garden path—Nahum and I hurry to the door, but everything's black, wait, Nahum goes back inside, turns off the lights, and the garden emerges out of the darkness, black and gray shadows tremble in a blue mist, the hose pipe draws a giant tin S on the lawn and on either side Daddy and you stand and hiss at each other in a black, whistling-rasping language, Czech, Nahum whispers to me, what are they saying, I ask, but Nahum shakes his head, not understanding, or understanding and not wanting to say or just wanting me to shut up and let him listen—

The gate slams.

Daddy comes back to us heavy with sorrow, tries to smile—come children, let's return to the table—but it's impossible to go on eating—he sits down and we stand on either side of him, waiting, and suddenly as if he has taken a decision, he turns back the white tablecloth and pulls out the table drawer and takes out a pen and the little shopping-list pad and writes on the first page in beautiful, carefully shaped figures, 1939–1945, can you read, Loya? Yes, between those years was the Second World War. He tears out the page and puts it in the middle of the table under the saltcellar, and you were born in—? He waits to hear it from me, 27 July 1946 I say, he writes, before the war or after it? He peers at me, I am insulted, after it! I say, and he tears out the page, puts it a little closer to us, weighs it down with the water jug, writes down a new date 5.1.50 what happened then? We came to Israel, Nahum knows, and stayed in Haifa—when Davidi isn't there he blooms, sure of himself, smiling—and we saw Phoenician ships in the harbor, I try to join the party, but on Daddy's forehead three surprise-lines rise, Phoenician? I peek at Nahum, who if not him showed them to me, and Nahum confirms with a firm nod of his chin, yes, we saw them, even though it's clear as daylight to him too that this is childish nonsense, do you know when the Phoenicians lived? Daddy actually sounds relieved, he writes a big 0, tears it out, sends me to push the date under the horserad-ish, this is the date of the birth of Jesus, this is the beginning of the Chris-tian era, he explains as he writes down a new date, beautiful as a painting, 333, tears it out, gets up himself to push it under the napkin-holder we made in handwork class in school, B.C. of course, he says walking, here Alexander of Macedon conquered the land of Israel, and here—he walks around the table, places on Davidi's abandoned plate 814, B.C. of course, here Karthadshat in other words Carthage was founded—he puts a fork on it so it won't fly away—it was founded by the Phoenicians; they came from Tyre, from Sidon—and Hannibal? I ask. Daddy is surprised, he didn't tell me about him, Hannibal crossed the Alps here, he writes down 218, B.C. of course, sends me to put the page between the napkin holder and the horse-radish and to weigh it down with a glass, and Judah Maccabee? Pay atten-tion Loya, Daddy writes 161, B.C. of course, Nahum and I chorus, here he was killed, I already know that I must place it closer to us than Hannibal's campaign, and Bar Kokhba, demands Nahum, Bar Kokhba? Daddy glances at him and writes 132—A.D. he preempts our refrain, bending down and placing the page between the birth of Jesus and the Second World War, weighing it down with a wineglass, and what comes between them? I ask, the bitter Diaspora, replies Nahum, Daddy looks at him amused, almost smiling, but he does not refute the description, he writes down another pair of dates, what will he do when the pad is finished, 1950–1951, tears it out, then we lived in Haifa, where should I put it? He asks us and Nahum and I point almost in unison at the glass next to him, it was then that you stood on the balcony? Daddy looks at me—at him—at me, yes, we both nod, and you could see Phoenician ships? Socratic as usual, he points his chin at the table, Nahum and I measure the distance of years between the page under the glass close to us and the page lying on Davidi's abandoned plate on the other side of the table, between us and it Bar Kokhba, Jesus, Antiochus, Hannibal, Alexander of Macedon, and more, there were more, the table was full of torn-out pad pages fluttering in the breeze blowing through the window steeped in the fragrance of orange blossom, consoling, I yawn, tired? Daddy looks at me and writes 2.9.45, this is the last date, he promises, Nahum doesn't know it either, Daddy taps it with the tip of his pen, spots it with blue dots, here the Allies finally defeated the Nazis, and when were you born, Loya? Before or after? I am very tired, leaning on the table, no longer sure of the right answer, after, Nahum whispers to me, after, I whisper after him, and therefore the Nazis couldn't have killed your mother, Daddy turns to me, but my eyes are almost closing, they beat them and killed them all, I hear Nahum say, No! a voice cries behind us, I wake up immediately, it's Davidi, he's back, he approaches our historical table, most of the murderers are still walking around free—

17.3.43
The daughter of Theodore Herzl is dead . . . a conversation with Mrs. David: Prof. Utitz studied with her brother the writer in the German Gymnasia in Altstaedter Ring. If her brother had lived, says Mrs. David, he

would have been today in Palestine. He studied Hebrew too . . . After the pogrom in November 1920 he said: People who remain in a place where they are hated and persecuted, resemble cockroaches whom all poisonous chemicals will not succeed in banishing from the bathroom—

20.3.43

The typhus grows more severe. We try to find a way to get the infant out. Four people who did not wait long enough after their rooms were disinfected with Zyklon gas against fleas died. Another spring has come . . . young people play football in the Dresden yard.

25.3.43

Today I gave the "parcel" to its uncle. We wait on news in great nervousness.

30.3.43

The sign has come! The parcel arrived safely at its destination . . . to see the operetta *The Ghetto Girl*. After the performance I was approached by the head of the police, he asked my opinion whether the play had helped to reduce the bad opinion of the Ghetto Police . . . Why does he care about my opinion?

He heard that I am writing the history of the ghetto—my secret is safe with him—he will give me writing paper too—it is only important that I see the picture from the correct perspective—that I tell the truth without beautification and without blackening. Ever since he came to the police he has fought against the theft of food and the unequal distribution of food, therefore those who profited from the plunder slander him.

But the following entries are not written on superior paper—did you refuse the deal offered by the head of the police?

8.4.43

Forbidden to go out, forbidden to illuminate. The reason—six people escaped from Terezin! And why not us, says M. She yearns for her infant.

She has already rebuked her fellow workers in the kitchen for stealing the common food and they have already warned her: One more word—and her name will be given for the next transportation!

M. again: Mina? Mila? Malinka? Maryusha? Marta? Marina? Masha? Mona? Magda? And perhaps—Milena—like the name of my *maminka* waiting for you in Prague until six o'clock after the war—

Here there are a few illegible scraps—the next entry is written on the inside of a torn envelope—

. . . 43
Three people were arrested for stealing potatoes . . . great anger against the head of police for asking the railway workers to give up their extra rations in favor of the old and sick. Sport on the bastion—whoever climbs up there sees a little bit of freedom—trees and pasture and geese and vegetable gardens. M. has returned to her work with the sick in the "Vrchlabi" barracks . . .

28.6.43
They cleaned the bank, polished the windows in honor of a visit by journalists from the Reich. They came, they saw the houses of the prominents, talked a little with acquaintances. I saw the play *The Grave* with the actress Sanova . . .

23.7.43
They have changed the names of the streets to "poetic" names: Ocean Street, Park Street, Tower Street, South Street, Train Street, et cetera. The intention of the rulers is clear: to beautify their evil acts before the end . . . They fear the judgment of the nations. Their fear will protect us from their wickedness.

2.8.43

Urgent order: to leave the "Sudeten" barracks in 24 hours. My new address—Hanover. Bodenbach and Zeughaus are also to be evacuated—much speculation about the purpose of these measures. The more optimistic say: they will house important Germans here to protect themselves from the allies. The heat is too much to bear . . . people are abrased.

10.8.43

A new order—to register the name of every youth from age 14 to old men of 60 for a big work transportation . . . many register gladly. They are sick of the heat, the crowding, the fleas . . . Heard: they are building huts outside the walls, in "Kreta."

15.8.43

Heard: a postcard from those sent to Poland reached Prague: "We eat like Yom Kippur, sleep like Sukkoth, dress like Purim." The joke is too neat to be true.

19.8.43

. . . the head of police has been overthrown from his post. Many of the policemen have been registered for transportation . . . pretext for the act—they will set up a new ghetto in the east.

23.8.43

From the mouth of M.: the sister of the writer Kafka and other nurses and doctors have been sent to the huts outside the walls. It is said—Jewish orphans from Poland will be brought there. Sense of humor of the rulers: they registered all the soft-handed for the work transportation.

26.8.43

From the mouth of my neighbor Z.: they ordered the kitchen workers to prepare food for one thousand five hundred people . . . to the cattle carriages in Train Street . . . to leave the place. From the corner of a window in "Hamburg" he looked out and saw the SS open the locked carriages: hundreds of thin children with big heads burst from the carriages and devoured the food like madmen . . . they returned them to the train and locked the carriages. Are these the orphans of Poland?

29.8.43

From the mouth of a worker in the health department: they brought the thin children to the disinfection station under SS guard . . . forbidden to talk to them. The children did not want to take off their clothes and enter the showers . . . they screamed—Gas! Gas! People complain here that we are hungry—but the sight of the orphans of Poland made him realize how severe is the damage which terrible hunger can do to body and soul.

7.9.43

A transportation of five thousand left. Among those leaving Janowitz, members of Aufbaukommando 1, the Ordnungswache, the sportsman P. Hirsch, Dr. Weiss from the Kripo (criminal police). It is said: this is the clearest proof that they are making a new ghetto in the east.

20.9.43

Germans have come to stay in Terez . . . Not allowed to open windows in the barracks facing to . . . Heard: the orphans in the wooden houses outside the walls came from the Bialystok Ghetto. They will stay here until they recover from their hunger and the agitation of their minds, and then they will all be sent to Palestine in exchange for German prisoners.

. . . 43

The orphans left for Palestine, they and their counselors and the doctors and nurses looking after them. The irony of history: Kafka made an application to be accepted in a commune (kibbutz) in the Land of Israel and was rejected by his Jewish-Israeli brothers because of his sickness and "soft-handedness"—and his sister who divorced her Christian husband and came to the ghetto to be with her people—was sent by the Nazis to the Land of Israel . . . Heard: the orphans were given new clothes, without the Jewish star . . . in place of the orphans a few hundred Jews from Denmark were brought to the wooden houses. They served them a fine meal, gave them . . . to smoke. Their king protects them here too. Why should the Nazis regard the opinion of the king of a small weak country? Everything shows that the end is near.

30.10.43

M. came to stay with me in the kumbalek . . . good news from the "parcel," but she is anxious lest . . . after the end—

What's a "kumbalek"? Eight months have passed since the baby—Nahum—was born and his mother is still alive—she didn't die in childbirth, or soon afterwards—perhaps she was deported to Treblinka or Auschwitz and in the meantime she moved in to live with you—where? How? What as?

11.11.43

They held a big census—everyone from young to old marched out of the gates, five to a row, street after street from six hours in the morning. At ten hours the meadow was full of tens of thousands . . . Czech gendarmes with their guns stood all around the people, and SS men passed between the ranks on motorcycles . . . the commandant on a big black horse. They counted and counted again—the minions of the scoundrel Mandler pass between the ranks, wearing white caps like cooks, helping to count the Jews. A cold day and fog. Many *bunkes*—Zionists escaped, communists escaped, Christians escaped with the help of Czechs, the rulers do not know how many escaped and how many remained. We stood there until darkness. Old people swooned on their places . . . rain . . . escended. Suddenly a voice was heard: Back to Terezin—and everyone hurried into the ghetto like sheep.

12.11.43

Why do the Germans concern themselves with a few more Jews in their net? Chaos frightens them to death. They are lovers of order. In a state of order it is easy to control crowds. Anyone who helps them to keep order—works against the interest of his people.

13.11.43

They arrested Edelstein! It is said: because he mixed the count of the dead and the living . . .

16.12.43

Another big transportation. It is said—Edelstein and his family too are among those departing, also many young people, children, consumptives. The new ghetto will be established in Neuberun . . .

25.12.43

The people departed—the books remained; 10,800 Hebrew books, 10,930 Jewish and Zionist books, 5300 belletrist, 3000 Klassiker, 1300 historical, 600 ancient languages and more. A postcard arrived from the "Septembrists": "Life continues as usual. We are often visited by Mister Malakhamaved." *Malak Hamaved*, the Angel of Death. We too could write them the same thing: Mister Malakhamaved is much seen in the Kavalier, Genie, Jaeger barracks.

15.2.44

Today is one year since the birth of the child. His mother says, he is already walking, already saying a few words. Most of her friends have departed on the transportations. Those remaining were removed from "Hamburg," in their place Jews from Holland . . . the Danes receive fat parcels from their compatriots. Already there are young girls who favor them for margarine.

1.3.44

They removed the wooden fence around the market square and planted more than a thousand roses . . . painted the bank, the post office, the fire brigade, the library. In "Sokolovna" they are making a fine library with a big reading room . . .

8.3.44

The birthday of our President Masaryk. From yesterday it is no longer obligatory to greet the rulers by removal of hats. Names are changed: no longer ghetto Terezin, but "Jewish resettlement territory." No longer "order of the day" but "announcements of the autonomous administration." No longer Judenaeltester but "his honor the mayor" . . . different words create a different reality. I would not be astonished if after the end they say: there was no ghetto, there were no dead. It is all Jewish propaganda . . .

20.3.44

Spring has come. They plant flowers, grass . . . they sent fifty lunatics eastward to "clean" Terezin of unaesthetic elements.

27.3.44

The library will move to L514. It is heard: a postcard was received from a "Septembrist." He wrote "Sophie is very close." His brother says—there is no woman among their family or acquaintances called "Sophie," but *sofi* is Hebrew for "my end."

4.4.44

We transport the books in hearses to Sokolovna. They are making a wooden hut for a band in the market square . . . Yesterday I was shown a postcard from Birkenau. Its date—25.3.44: "I am well. If you come here, don't travel by car. You had better walk by foot." There was a big argument about these words. The most logical interpretation: the traveler by car—a sign that his strength is exhausted. He who walks on his feet—still has his strength, and will be taken to work outside, in the field . . . My opinion was asked. I said: Only one thing is sure—on 25.3.44 the writer was alive—

20.4.44

They made a dining room for the elderly. They will no longer stand in long lines and eat in sun and rain—

Here the page is torn—then several pages are apparently missing—not a word about Nahum's mother—perhaps she is already dead—perhaps she will die in one of the next entries—

5.5.44

Rumors multiply about the defeat of the Germans. The "Orel" hall was opened with many in attendance . . . the prominents have hung up curtains and pretty pictures. The Danes have been moved into small, nice rooms—

Here too the page is torn—in any case, the situation is improving, you don't write about "transportations"—perhaps it was under the impression of these improved months that you told me your Terezin stories—the plays—the concerts—the lectures—even the musical for children that they put on there—what was it called—Brundibar—I wonder if you will mention it—

15.5.44

The old, the exhausted, the consumptive will be sent east not to spoil the "beauty" of Terezin . . . the friends of P. too left on the transporta . . . oot-ball competitions on the Southern corner of the bastion. Relay race in the streets . . . Who is for life—lives and plays sports, and who is for death departs like a dumb lamb.

30.5.44

From the mouth of the carpenter who is making bookshelves: he was already on the carriage for the transportation East—and he was taken off. Every manual worker is required for the beautification of the town.

7.6.44

Today I was ordered to wash the street. All day people passed me carrying objects—toys, clothes. The sound of the players practicing their playing came from the square full of blooming roses. People who look well and are not thin are invited to dress in their best clothes and walk here and there in the park.

The rest is blurred—look, Nahum: all the material is in my hands and precisely the fate of your mother I am apparently not destined to discover— what did you say to me once? It's impossible to know everything—one thing is almost clear; my father was reunited with my mother only after being liberated from Terezin—in Prague—or perhaps I shall discover that she volunteered to help nurse the victims of the typhus epidemic after the liberation—

15.6.44

Lecture by Rabbi Dr. Baeck: much taken from Dilthey . . . much from Hermann Cohen. The essential principle in writing history—to find the meaning of events and prove their obedience to laws . . . I have seen many events in Terezin and the one law common to them all was already stated by Polybius: There is no animal so wicked and cruel as man.

Here too what follows is almost effaced, impossible to read—interesting; you hardly ever mention names—protecting people? Seeing them only as incidental illustrations of general laws? But a few names recur—this rabbi you have already mentioned once—in your letter to him do you continue to the argument about laws and events and the historical conclusions to be drawn from the subjection or nonsubjection of events to laws—

Perhaps I'll ask Avi to—

In clear writing, on good paper—

24.6.44

Yesterday the visit came. Four from the Red Cross and the Camp Commandant and his men in civilian dress. A great day for the "mayor" Dr. Epstein: he wore a suit, a top hat, he rode in a car, an SS man drove him, opened the door for him. The orchestra played in the square, the flowers gave off their scent, people walked here and there, children played in the play garden. From the hearses the bread was unloaded by hands in white gloves. Sport competitions were held . . . the visit lasted from eleven to seven hours in the evening. The visitors went to the Denmarkians. The Denmarkians sat in their beautified rooms, complained of their distress and requested . . . books. Today the "Jewish Council" thanks all the residents for the beautification work. The prize—a day of rest today and tomorrow until noon. No one cracked the wall of deception.

12.7.44

Members of the youth administration fired. The dining room closed . . . People with typical Jewish faces wanted for a documentary cinema. A Jewish actor from Berlin, Kurt Gerron, will be the "direktor."

16.7.44

Week in memory of Theodore Herzl. Lectures, community singing, dances of pioneers ("hora"). I heard Dr. Kahn speak. His words were not optimistic, but he concluded with "The People of Israel live" . . . Why do the rulers allow such a nationalist demonstration? The optimists: because the end is near. The pessimists: because our end is near. The cynics: everything is a cinema. Did you not see Kurt Gerron in the audience, looking for a "Jewish but photogenic face"?

30.7.44

Heard: they arrested the painters. Gerron and his group walk about the town, photographing children at play, youths at work in the park. There are people who hear the thunder of cannons in their sleep.

15.8.44

I work now in the bakery. For the first time since my arrival in Terezin I eat my fill of bread and also bring for M. in my clothes. M. refuses to taste the stolen bread.

20.8.44

Aeroplanes in the sky over Terezin, loud sirens . . . all the people hide in their houses. The streets are empty—but the heart is full of hope.

22.8.44

I have been returned to hunger among the books. Today the people of the "actuality" cinema came to the library. Like anthropologists they record on celluloid the life of a dying tribe disappearing from the world . . .

10.9.44

Heard: Slovak partisans fought the Germans in Slovakia. In the Warsaw Ghetto Jews fought the Germans and killed many . . . English parachutists came down in Paris . . . Soviet cannons in Bratislava. There is no knowing how much of truth and how much of impatience is in the rumors of the last days before the end.

23.9.44

It is announced: a big transportation will leave to set up a labor camp next to Dresden. At the head—Otto Zucker. Only young men will go. Their wives and their children will remain in the ghetto . . . a good postal connection is promised.

28.9.44

It is announced: all the women desiring to go with their husbands to the new labor camp are to hand in their names. Young Mrs. Fritzi Zucker said that the ruler Guenther gave her "the word of a German" that as soon as she arrives she will meet her husband. She took eight suitcases with her.

3.10.44

Big transportations left with the dignitaries of the ghetto—Zucker, Redlich, Schliesser . . . a nurse who works with M. told her that she asked Rabbi Leo Baeck what to do—her husband went with the last transportation. Should she give her name to go too? The rabbi said: it is written in our Torah, it is not good that the man be alone. She gave her name and in two more days she will leave for the east . . .

8.10.44

Many transportations leave every day: on them—doctors, nurses, children, their educators, the actors and musicians . . . the optimists say: they take the best to make another "exemplary ghetto." The pessimists: before the end they will take all the Jews with them into the pit of their grave.

23.11.44

Snow wraps the ghetto in a white shroud. We are ordered to transfer our living quarters. M. goes to stay with her patients. I am moved to Magdeburg, the abode of the prominents . . . I share a room with two others only, professors, their Christian wives outside (Prague, Ostrava). Prof. Gottholz takes a walk in the snow. He has a good coat. Prof. Hermann heats the stove with coal, toasts thin bread, plasters it with sardines. Prof. Gottholz returns from the snow and removes one apple from his pocket. Prof. Hermann divides it with a knife into three. The first apple I have eaten since my coming here.

28.11.44

M. is working in the crematorium with other women and children. They pass jars with the ashes of the dead from hand to hand to a vehicle which drives to the river and pours the ashes in the water. They strengthen their hearts with macabre laughter: Look, it's my uncle! No, my aunt. A sharp conversation about the sardines she brought from her work as a "bonus." She too is helping the interests of the rulers—to erase every trace of the dead that died in Terezin from sickness and hunger and broken hearts and broken spirits.

11.2.45

A transportation left for Switzerland! Fine carriages arrived at the Terezin railway . . . the passengers received sweets, jam, vitamins for the journey. The Slovaks who came to Terezin from Sered mock the passengers: they will not be the first to arrive at Auschwitz in fine carriages and leave through the chimney—they tell horror stories from second and third hand. There is no eyewitness. Atrocity propaganda, like in the first World War.

26.2.45

All the workers from Zossen returned. Transportations of people of mixed race (Mischlinge) arrived from Prague.

So "Mischling" is a person of mixed race? And what does that mean exactly? Half-Jewish?

4.4.45

Visit from the Red Cross. The streets scrubbed with water. In the market square the roses are blooming. A white vehicle with a red cross drives around from street to street. Prof. Gottholz says: another transportation is leaving for Switzerland and I leave with it.

15.4.45

The Denmarkians go free on Swedish buses. Their parting photographed for the cinema—hands of happy healthy people waving farewell—this will be the visual evidence of Terezin and its people. Anyone saying otherwise—will be counted a liar . . . says Prof. Hermann. I answer him: But nobody can take our memories. To this Prof. Hermann replies: Time, my dear Herr Prof. Kaplan, time will take everything—health, love, beauty, good friends and bad memories . . . time is the greatest traitor to the human race. In the evening we ate from the good parcels left behind by the Denmarkians.

16.4.45.

To the library came Dr. Murmelstein, a few of the rulers, and a Jew speaking German with a Hungarian accent. The Jew asked Prof. Utitz about the number of readers. The Camp Commandant answered on his place: "Nobody reads—they prefer to wander the streets doing nothing." In the evening I heard from the mouth of A. that the Hungarian Jew informed him that liberation is very close. Who is this Jew? Why does he walk around with Nazis as if he was their boyhood friend? How does he know what they do not know?

Can it be Kastner? You don't write his name—perhaps later—there are still a few scraps left—

18.4.45

A rumor went around that the Germans have already left. People cheered, shouted . . . packed their belongings, went into the streets. The incident came to an end with a speech by the Camp Commandant: "Esteemed gentlemen, the end of the war is very near. Maintain order and quiet for the good of all."

20.4.45

. . . procession of walking skeletons, demented eyes in death skulls . . . torn striped clothes, full of lice. Who are these people? They are evacuees from harsh concentration camps. They are sick, they drag their feet. Tereziners! a man shouts . . . a mother recognized her son and fainted. In the half year since they left here they have changed beyond recognition . . . in the hearse I push them from the disinfection station to the quarantine . . . there are not enough doctors, not enough nurses.

26.4.45

M. went to work with the living dead. Came back like a dead woman. They are not human beings, just hungry wild animals. Suddenly they beat each other to death for the sake of a cube of sugar . . . many are apathetic, stare into space, say not a word. M. asked many of them about Dolohovski, about Mrs. David, about the doctors . . . about my pupil too she asked. To everything she received the reply—"No"—"Kaput"—"better you shouldn't know"—"gone up the chimney"—

30.4.45

Some people complain: Now, that the end is so close, we will all die of the plague brought by the Muselmänner from the death camps! I went and gave my name to work with the sick. Perhaps I will find my pupil among them. "You are signing your death certificate today," said the doctor when I entered the hospital.

1.5.45

There are no beds for everyone. Many lie on thin mattresses, thin as the image of death, wallowing in their excrement . . . not all are from Terezin. There are Greeks and Turks and Poles. They are abrased, shout, "You are worse than the Nazis in Buchenwald!" I ask about my pupil. Nobody knows. A girl pioneer, survivor of the "Septembrists" shouted out loud . . . Was she good? All the good died. Only the sinners remained alive . . . Suddenly, in a corner of the room, curled up like a little mouse, I saw Leah Schechter. She looked at me with glassy eyes. She did not know me even when I called her by name. The doctor said, she has lost her senses, her body too is sick, in a few more days she will die.

Am I named for you, Leah Schechter?

6.5.45

Dr. Murmelstein has resigned. It is said he will stand trial; he went too far in doing the will of his German masters. Rabbi Leo Baeck—the head of Terezin. He announces: Terezin is in the hands of the Red Cross. (A good title for a book.) Anyone leaving risks his life. The war has not yet ended. After the end everyone will be returned to his country. All the SS have disappeared. Only the Camp Commandant remains, rides on his bicycle, locks the gates of the town, puts the keys in his pocket. The people of Terezin look at him—no one does anything. A young man who returned from the death camps tells how they lynched a "kapo" on the day they were liberated. We are not barbarians, says one of the Tereziners who remained in the ghetto. Perhaps it is already time for us to learn this craft too, replies the young man. But nobody moves from his place. And Karl Rahm, commander of the exemplary ghetto Terezin, rides on his bicycle, carrying the keys to the gate of our town in his pocket.

8.5.45

Last night the retreating Germans shot at Terezin. A shell hit the yard of Q704. An old Austrian officer died and a Dutch general was wounded. At nine in the evening the first Russian tank entered—many people ran to it, clapped their hands, sang. M. was sure all the time that the Reds would win the war. The war increased her Communism.

9.5.45

The Red Army arrived! They brought cigarettes, bread, sugar, tea, chocolate. People sit with Soviet soldiers—there are many Jews among them—around campfires, sing, tell. Every Jewish Soviet soldier points his finger to his heart, says, "*Amcha.*"

11.5.45

. . . the gates of the town are open— . . . to go out to the hills, to breathe spring air, to look at the road to Prague full of Wehrmacht soldiers, wounded, in torn uniforms, going to POW camps. People throw stones at them, shout. More refugees from camps arrive at Terezin. The town is full of the sick and infirm . . . I am not allowed any more to go in to see my pupil . . . typhus. Milena too has despaired of finding Dolohovski among the returnees.

Milena? Another Milena? So what—so what—in our class there was another Leah, in the army—another two, in the second flight attendant crew—another one—and wasn't it the name of Kafka's sweetheart too—

25.5.45

The day of our departure from Terezin. We walked on our feet to Bohusovice, from there by train to Prague. From the train we were taken by the father of Milena. We came to the house of her brother and his wife. The child Jan already walks, already talks, calls his aunt "maminka." But all who see him will say: Milena is his mother.

30.6.45

I went to my past home to thank Magda for her parcels. The dog Max knew me, but Magda did not recognize my face. I told her that I was a married man, I married a good woman in the ghetto. Magda removed my ring from her finger and said: I always knew you would return to the Jews. I did not disclose to her that Milena is a "Mischling" for in her heart she is not even half a Jew. She is a Communist, who regards all religions as "opium of the masses."

I returned to the home of Milena's father. Her brother opened the door. I saw Milena sitting, the infant Jan in her arms. Head to head touching. In Terezin we signed a grotesque document that we would make our marriage legal as soon as possible, what was her opinion? Dolohovski would not return if he had not returned up to now, and of the death of Leah Schechter the doctor informed me three days before we left. I am ready to be a good father to the child and a good husband to her. If they do not return me to my old position at the university perhaps we will go to Palestine.

Concluded but not completed, they used to write at the bottom of the last page in children's books, concluded, I used to explain to myself, in other words, finished, but not completed—because after the story in the book the characters went on growing up, got married, had children, made money or lost it or got sick or went to live in another country, for example Palestine—

And all these years—not a word—

Perhaps you waited for me to turn twenty-one, the age at which, in enlightened countries, people inherit a fortune or a castle or a kingdom—did you intend to sit me down in the living room for a "talk"—you did that twice, three times, no more—Loya, come, sit down please—the "please" softening the tone that would not take no for an answer—I want to talk to you, but we didn't talk; you paced the room and spoke to the toes of your shoes, to the carpet, to the skirting tiles, and I sat in the deep armchair, my feet dangling in the air, watching you, from time to time you stop pacing, ask, do you understand? And I always say yes, afraid of disappointing you, afraid of—what. Why didn't I ever try to protest, no, I don't understand anything, explain again, from the beginning, explain as if I was a little girl, because that was the most terrible thing, to be considered a little girl, Loya's a big girl now, you declared from the day I remember, Loya understands, Loya can, you can't cry like a little girl, you scolded me, at the age of four I was already grown-up—how convenient—you didn't have to bring me up— you declared me a big girl from the day that *maminka* Milena left us—why "left"—why that lie—died—you hear?—died. Dead as a doornail. She wrote a letter signed M. and killed herself. And she was buried outside the fence. That's why there's no grave, no memorial, no anniversary, no death—

Perhaps she'll come back next year, you lied, you spoke in that sweet voice, the voice of disaster that tries to drip stinging iodine because it's necessary and blows on it immediately to alleviate the pain, how long is a year, I tried to understand, a year is spring and summer and autumn and winter, you explained, we sat on deck chairs on the porch surrounded by the smell of cypresses and hot dust, and what's it now, I asked, now it's summer and we eat watermelon and grapes and go to the beach, and after that? I asked, after that it's autumn, you said, and in autumn we'll move to a new place and you'll begin to go to kindergarten, and after that? I asked, after that it will be winter, you told me, and what will happen in winter, we'll buy you new boots and we'll go to Davidi and Nahum's orange grove and we'll pick oranges and make them into juice, and after that? I asked, after that it will be spring, the rain will stop and it will be warmer and we'll buy you sandals, and then Maminka will come back? I wouldn't let go, maybe, you dripped iodine, you blew, how many years—three? four?—I counted the seasons summer-autumn-winter-spring, I always began with summer, summer-autumn-winter-spring like love-jealousy-hate-friendship according to which we would add and subtract identical letters from names and guess who loved who, who was jealous of who, summer-autumn-winter-spring, the years began to go faster with time, I don't remember when exactly it became clear to me that she was dead and that even if I nagged you without letting up I wouldn't gain anything but a glassy look and "don't stir—"

You and Dolohovsky-Davidi and Jan-Nahum and Leah-Loya in a small apartment on Mount Carmel and with us one Maminka Milena—Nahum's—mine—that's the secret, Nahum, right? That's the reason why—did you know when we were in Eilat or did you find out afterwards? There's nobody to ask. There's nobody to talk to. It's only me here. The dead—are dead—

Summer, autumn, winter, spring—you made me a calendar of the seasons to hang over my bed, yellow for summer and green for autumn and orange for winter because of the oranges, and sky blue for spring, when I had lived for a decade it was ceremoniously replaced by the felt board with the Latin sayings that every civilized person was supposed to know: *Historia magista vitae*—history is the teacher of life; *Adversus solem ne loquitor*—don't argue with the sun, but *sapere aude*, acquire knowledge without delay, for *nihil est annis velocious*, the years pass quickly, *maxima quaeque ambigua sunt*, great events are so ambiguous, and *nescire autem quid ante quam natus sis acciderit, id est semper esse puerum*—not to know what happened before you were born, is to remain a child forever—

We emerge from the water, clad in black skins. Slowly we peel them off, exposing white skin. Brother and sister? The diving instructor smiles from next to the oxygen balloons. We exchange glances. We don't say yes, we don't protest. We're used to people asking. Brother and sister. Almost. Fifty percent common genes. We could have given birth to a genius or a monster.

ALIVE

A sad smell. The smell of a house without a family—what did I expect? When I walked into the apartment in Rue d'Amsterdam the smell of cooking would surround me like a pack of golden wolves. Jean-Jacques would be in the kitchen, tied to the pâté or the soufflé or in the middle of the gâteau, not even answering my call for fear of alarming whatever was rising on the counter or in the oven, I would cross the living room, stand in the kitchen doorway and see his back—very thin inside whatever he was wearing—the apron strings tied around his waist—he would give me a quick glance over his shoulder, go on stirring, always with a big wooden spoon on a low flame and always without a pause so it wouldn't stick or congeal or burn, the smells, I would say to him, welcome me instead of you, and he would smile—are you hungry?

"Where's the toilet?"

Ten years ago I would never have permitted myself—the first question in a strange man's house?—but I've grown up, grown out of all that. And it's a lost cause anyway. The toilet is clean. But it has a smell too. What of. Of a dank towel and a spray against bad smells, and the soap is dry—cracked—

Avi is waiting for me next to a low table in the middle of the living room with two cups of coffee (was he lying when he said he didn't drink coffee?) and a bought cake. The coffee gives off a fresh smell. "*Hel?*" I ask in Arabic: cardamom? "Heaven," he smiles. Is he trying to be witty? I close my eyes and sip. It tastes, as always, awful.

"What did you find?" Professional interest? Personal? He sits with his legs apart, bending over the coffee.

I take a deep breath.

"My father's diary from the Terezin ghetto," I stop to register the impression. Now he sits up straight, turns his shoulders to me, tilts his head to examine my face. "Written in Hebrew—" I add. His eyebrows rise. His eyes open wide. He almost smiles. I've surprised him. Definitely. In a minute he'll ask me if he can read it—"and also three letters," I make haste to direct him to the purpose of my visit, even though it's obvious that the letters interest him as much as last year's snow. "One in German and two in Czech," I disclose the reason for my presence. "I thought that maybe you could—"

"A diary? An actual diary? With dates?" I knew he would be thrilled by the diary. What wouldn't you have given, Davidi, for Bar Kokhba's diary—

"The letters—" I bring him back to the matter at hand. "One in German and two in Czech—"

"Did you discover anything interesting there?" Avi returns to the diary. Of course. Dying to get his hands on it. Formulating his question carefully, restraining his enthusiasm so I won't clench. Okay, I understand. I can offer him—

"Kafka's sisters came to Terezin—" an impersonal current.

Avi nods. He doesn't seem surprised. He knows from other sources. But let's see if he also knows that—

"Kafka's younger sister was sent from Terezin with a group of orphans to Palestine—"

Avi shakes his head as if refusing to believe this information.

"It's written in the diary! A group of orphans who arrived from Bialystok—they exchanged them for German prisoners—" I feel the anger rising in my throat.

"Yes, I know," says Avi in a tired voice, "except that the orphans and all the people taking care of them didn't come here. They were sent to Auschwitz—" His right hand separates from his left, makes a little gesture upwards; a gesture that says "they went up the chimney"—

"So my father was wrong—"

"He had no way of knowing the truth—" His voice is low to the point of whispering.

"My father had connections—" I enter the minefield.

Avi nods. He doesn't seem surprised.

"He married Davidi's fiancée to protect her from the transports after Davidi was sent—" I pick my way carefully between the mines.

Avi bows his head. As if waiting for the blow.

"But she was a 'Mischling'—" he says quietly to the fingers clasping his knees. Davidi told him!

"Yes, so what!" I am indignant. Like a betrayed wife, I am the last to know—

"So *she* protected him from the transports, and not the other way around—according to the directions given to the registration department in the last year of the ghetto's existence—" Avi stops, tries to measure the impression made on me by his words.

"Whose directions?" My mouth is dry and my voice sounds hoarser than usual; as if I've been smoking all my life.

"The SS—"

"And my father didn't know—?" My lips move and Avi reads them. He shakes his head.

"Presumably not—unless he worked in the registration department or was close to someone who worked there—"

How can I tell. All I have is scraps—

Silence.

"Loya—" Avi puts out his hand to take the letters. "Are these the letters? I can translate from German for you—but Czech—I'll fax them to my assistant—she knows Czech." He looks at me from under knitted brows as if to assess the extent of my disappointment. "I'll tell her it's urgent—"

"It doesn't matter, it isn't urgent—how could it be urgent—those letters are forty years old—" I'm speaking to him, but he's not listening. He's staring at the envelope of the letter addressed to London.

"That letter is addressed to Rabbi Leo Baeck!" he sounds angry. No, disturbed. Perhaps confused. What do I know about him?

"Why does that surprise you so much? My father mentions him in the diary—that rabbi was in Ghetto Terezin—" I say and he nods, agrees—

"But the letter wasn't sent—there's no Post Office stamp on the stamp—" Avi turns the envelope to me. "I wonder when it was written—may I?" He looks at me, I consent with a nod of my chin and he pulls the letter out of the torn envelope, opens it—"It's from 25.6.55—so it's not—"

"Not what?"

"I thought the letter was written after Leo Baeck died and therefore it wasn't sent to him—"

"You know when he died?"

"October '56—"

"In Israel?"

"No, in London—" His eyes are already on the letter. His brows lock his eyes. His mouth is pursed. He goes on to the second page. Returns to the first page. And breathes a long, low, hissing sigh.

"Can I tell you something?" He holds one page of the letter in his right hand, the other in his left, they tremble slightly at the ends of his arms, "Not as a historian—"

I try to catch his eye. But his eyes are on the pages of the letter—

"It's a good thing that he didn't send this letter—"

"Will you please translate what he wrote there to me?" My sharp tone elicits a raised eyebrow and a slight twitch of the corner of his lip.

"You want me to translate it just like this? Here? Because I can—"

"Just like this. Here. Now—"

Avi looks at the page in his right hand. "He wrote it three days after sentence was passed in the Kastner trial—"

"We were at his funeral—" Am I about to tell the story, postpone the translation of the letter?

Avi waits.

"So what does he write—" I didn't mean to betray the impatience in my voice—

Avi puts the pages together, lays them on the low table, rests his elbows on his knees, and starts translating—

To the very esteemed Reverend Doctor Leo Baeck,

Three days ago I sat in hall number two of the building of the Supreme Court of the State of Israel to hear the sentence of the court in the libel case brought by the State of Israel against an addle-brained (or eccentric) old Jew called Malkiel Gruenwald, who accused our acquaintance Dr. Israel Kastner of collaborating with the Nazis. The Judge, Dr. Benjamin Levi ("that should be Halevi," Avi gave me a sidelong look) began to read the verdict at eight in the morning and finished in the late hours of the evening.

Yesterday a journalist friend supplied me with a full copy of the verdict, over two hundred pages long, which he had purchased, like other journalists, from the court secretary for two Israeli lira. Now that I have the full text before me, and I do not have to rely on (or be assisted by) my memory only—I permit myself to translate a number of sentences from the verdict for your eyes.

Most of the Jews from the Transylvanian township of Cluj ("Twenty thousand people—" Avi glances up as he informs me) got onto the trains to Auschwitz-Birkenau ("and here he opens quotation marks," says Avi) "due to their ignorance of the true destination of their journey and because they believed in the false announcement that they were being transferred to a labor camp in Hungary." ("End of quotation," says Avi.) It was the Nazis who ("and here there are quotation marks again; your father is quoting from the verdict") "Spread these false rumors by means of Jewish channels. The Jews of the ghetto would not have believed the Nazi or Hungarian rulers; but they believed their Jewish leaders." ("Here he apparently leaves out some text, there are three dots." Avi turns the page with its elegant handwriting towards me, but without glasses I haven't got a hope of seeing three dots—) "Many Jews could have attempted to cross the border ("between Hungary and Romania—" Avi raises his eyes when he fills in information) despite the not particularly great risk of being caught by the border patrol, but they made no attempt to take the risk because they knew nothing ("or:

they didn't have the faintest idea—" Avi raises his eyebrows) about the danger of extermination awaiting them . . ." ("end of quote, three dots.") Those that knew of the fate awaiting the deportees and did not warn the members of their communities ("and here he quotes again—") "were not sent to Auschwitz with the members of their communities, but were for the most part included in the transport to Bergen-Belsen . . ." ("end of quote, three dots.") The train to Bergen-Belsen with the 1,684 "Prominents" ("the dignitaries," explains Avi. "I know," I say) was the payment ("or the reward . . . or maybe prize—no, not prize. Reward—") that Kastner received from the Nazis for his collaboration with them, which was expressed (or embodied—) mainly in his silence: he knew where the trains were going, he knew what awaited the deportees, and he said nothing. ("And here he quotes from the verdict again—") "But *timeo Danaos et dona ferentes* (Avi looks at me questioningly. "Go on" I say, "that I understand—") by accepting this gift Kastner sold his soul to Satan." ("End of quote." I remember vaguely. Big headlines in the newspapers—but—"Did the judge really say that?" "The judge wrote it in his verdict," Avi answers with his eyes on the bottom of the first page of the letter.)

Unlike your honor (or perhaps as opposed to your honor) I believe neither in God nor in Satan. ("Quite right," I interrupt. Avi looks up at me. A kind of smile hovers around his lips. Then he grows grave and returns to the letter.) But I do believe in the responsibility of someone who sees himself and allows others to see him as a spiritual leader—(Avi goes on to the second page of the letter.)

When your honor was President of the Reich Representation of the Jews in Germany you opposed mass Jewish emigration from Germany since you saw it as capitulation to the tendencies (or perhaps—the plans or the intentions) of the Nazis and abandonment of the magnificent heritage of German Jewry. Your honor was of course a spiritual shepherd, not a prophet. ("He's being sarcastic." Avi raises his eyes. "I can hear," I say.) Later on your honor headed the Reich Association of Jews in Germany. Need I remind your honor of what you yourself told me about the role and functions ("or tasks") of this organization? The preparation of lists of names of Jews for the Gestapo, the delivery of deportation orders to Jewish families, the sending of the Jewish Ordnungsdienst to round up the victims—("Is that true?" I ask. Avi nods, his eyes on the letter) then too your honor and his colleagues in the Jewish leadership were public figures, not prophets.

But during your stay in Ghetto Terezin your honor received information from a first-hand and reliable witness about what was happening in Auschwitz-Birkenau. I am referring to the former officer Vitezslav Lederer ("The one you told me about?" Avi nods, his eyes on the letter) who was deported in December '43, succeeded in escaping from Auschwitz-Birkenau and returned to the ghetto in April '44. From my colleague Berco Dolohovski—he too a former inmate of Terezin—who fought alongside (or shoulder-to-shoulder with) Lederer in the Slovakian revolt I learned that Lederer warned your honor and other members of the Aeltestenrat against these deportations. He told you about the fate of the deportees of September '43 and also that of the previous deportations.

From May '44 to the end of October '44 over twenty-five thousand Terezin inmates were sent to Auschwitz-Birkenau. When they got onto the trains in "Train Street" they believed that they were being sent to a labor camp in Silesia. Not one of the deportees imagined (or guessed) the truth. Your honor knew—and said nothing. Your honor, a very distinguished personage with an international reputation and influential friends in Germany, a Prominent A in Ghetto Terezin, was not sent to his death.

Would your honor please tell me: what is the difference (or the distinction) between yourself and Dr. Kastner, who a judge of the Jerusalem District Court, with a doctorate in jurisprudence from the Berlin University, determined, after a long trial with many witnesses, to have "sold his soul to Satan"?

Except, perhaps, for the fact which nobody denies, that Dr. Kastner succeeded in spite of everything in rescuing 1,684 Jews from the jaws of death?

Former inmate of Terezin
Professor Ota Kaplan
The Hebrew University Jerusalem

Avi's eyes are on the letter trembling slightly between his fingers. I don't know what to say. I am silent. Avi too is silent. He folds the letter, tries to put it back inside the envelope which I had torn carelessly, fails, gives up, hands me the folded letter. I take it from him and put it in my bag.

"No one in the world knows who his father is." In the end I choose to quote the words of Athene to Telemachus son of Odysseus, because what can I say—

Avi stands up and goes to the window, his hands in his pockets.

"Why did you say that it was a good thing he didn't send the letter?" I say to his back.

"Because the knowledge wouldn't have changed the facts—not basically—"

"Just a minute, just a minute—are you trying to tell me, that if Rabbi Baeck had warned the people in Terezin about the transports, they would have gotten onto the trains anyway—?"

"And gone like sheep to the slaughter—" His voice is angry. His hands are deep in his pockets. His eyes stare into the darkness.

"But—according to what my father wrote—there were artisans there, gardeners, engineers—they worked on renovations there, for some reason he called it 'beautification'—they must have had hammers, axes, saws—if they'd known where the trains were going, they could have hidden their tools—they took a suitcase with them—and broken down the doors on the way—jumped off the train—"

Avi still has his back to me, he sways backwards and forwards on his feet, now he shakes his head too—

"It could have saved a few—tens—but not masses—not thousands—"

"How do you know?"

"I don't know—I can only guess with a high degree of probability— look—" He talks as if I'm standing outside, outside the window, his hands in his pockets, only his shoulders move. "All this business about knowing—your father mentions Kastner—precise reports about what was happening in Auschwitz reached Hungary in January '43, March '43, May '43—so turning Kastner into the only person who had his hand on the tap and saying that because he didn't tell us we didn't know and we had no way of knowing is a little . . . you want more than that? In the Vilna Ghetto, the Warsaw Ghetto, the Bialystok Ghetto, members of the underground circulated the facts about the extermination by pamphlets and by word of mouth and that too did not prevent the masses from getting on the trains—there is shocking testimony from Haika Grossman—" Avi goes to the next room, comes back with a thick, gray book in his hand, opens it a little after the middle, reads from it: "Our couriers circulate throughout the ghetto, explaining and exhorting: Jews, don't go willingly . . . Every departure from the ghetto means death in the gas chambers . . . but the wave streams, streams without stopping . . ." His eyes go down to the bottom of the page. "How to explain this mad rush of thousands and tens of thousands into Jorowice Street? . . . In vain we tried to return the Jews to their houses. They did not want to listen to us—" Avi slams the book shut. "So it is very likely that even if they knew where they were taking them—most of them would have gone like sheep to the slaughter—"

He repeats this phrase with a kind of vehemence—

"You said that today it isn't acceptable to use that expression—" I remind him of a casual remark he made at the Passover Seder—

He makes a dismissive gesture with his hand as if continuing a bitter academic debate with invisible opponents. "That expression is completely authentic—" He goes to the next room and returns with a few books. He leafs through a thick, pale, new book. "This is Emanuel Ringelblum, the historian of the Warsaw Ghetto," he finds the right place, reads: "December '42: the Jewish intelligentsia went to the slaughter just as the masses of all the people went, quietly, without protest and without resistance . . ." He puts the book down on the table, glances briefly at the other books, chooses one, thinner, also new, "And this is a diary kept in hiding by an agronomist called Salek Perchodnik who served in the Jewish police." He flips through the pages. "Here—listen: 'All honor and glory to the German genius, only it could have succeeded in stupifying all the people and causing a mass befogging of the senses to such an extent that they assemble of their own good will like sheep to wait for the executioners to come.'" He puts the book down, doesn't come back to sit beside me, paces to the wall, returns. "Today they're trying to round corners—" He stops in front of the window. The window is dark. "But saying there are none so blind as those who don't want to know is too easy." He talks with his back to me. "The only one who suggested an intelligent explanation for the phenomenon is a Dutch historian called Louis de Jong—" Avi turns around, bends over the table, looks for the book, pages through it with his back bent. "Here it is." He straightens up, reads from the book: "It is a historical fact, which can also be explained psychologically: the Nazi extermination camps became a psychological reality to most people—and even that not to the full extent—only after they had ceased to exist, and perhaps precisely for that reason."

He closes the book, hugs it to his chest with his arms crossed.

"The extermination was impossible to take in and comprehend in real time—and therefore people went like sheep to the slaughter and therefore there was also no point in informing the victims—is that what you're saying?"

"It was impossible to comprehend and also impossible to prevent—not on a large scale—" Avi speaks to me from his full height. "And by the way, your father was wrong; Leo Baeck knew about the gassing when he was still in Germany, before he arrived in the ghetto. He decided not to tell even the members of the Aeltestenrat, because he was afraid that the information would get out and spread through the ghetto—"

"And supposing that the information did get out—"

"Leo Baeck was afraid that the Nazis would find out and liquidate the ghetto—"

"And they didn't liquidate it anyway? How many people were left in the end out of all the tens of thousands that were imprisoned there?"

"About eleven thousand people—"

"Including Leo Baeck, of course—"

"And your father, Loya—"

I feel the blood flooding my face. I lean against the back of the sofa. Speak to him with my eyes closed in a cracked voice—

"And nevertheless, explain to me—as somebody who justifies Rabbi Leo Baeck—not as a historian—who the hell gave this rabbi the moral authority to keep information from those being led to death in order to make it easier for their murderers to murder and for them to be murdered? The Lord is our God, the Lord is One?"

Avi is silent. I wait for his answer with closed eyes. I can't open my eyes. His silence is like a stone on my heart.

"I don't judge—history will judge—" he says quietly, speaking to me from the wall.

"What's that supposed to mean—'history will judge'?" I suddenly find within me a voice to shout, I stand up. "Since when can history judge? History is written by people, and people—" My voice breaks. Avi leans against the wall. He looks at me and doesn't say a word. It's not the sea between us, a line from a slender blue book wells up in me, it's the two of us between us.

The pomegranate tree comes weakly into leaf. Through the little leaves its branches are still as thin as bones, each branch turning in its own direction, without a central trunk, without a crest—the bougainvillea is blooming with all its might—the cypress in its claws like a mighty stalagmite in shades of flesh and peach—the sky is clear and high and full of light clouds, moving slowly as if flowing. But after looking for a long time everything changes: the high sky with the clouds sculpted in it stands still as a painted sky. And the cypress, it and the earth at its roots and the earth connected to the earth at its roots, the cypress—it and all its surroundings—is moving. The earth is sailing. I lose my balance and land on the wild flowers—the groundsel, the scorpion tails, the salvia—but beneath the crushed vegetation I can feel the earth: movement, like a leisurely stretching of muscles, heartbeats muffled by great depths, and the sound of distant splashing and bubbling, as if there, in the center of the globe, the drum of a gigantic washing machine is turning, washing molten iron in fire-water—

From the surviving quarter of the flower bed a few pansies look at me, yellow, purple, one crimson—and that dark stain at the heart of them all—

The phone. The phone. What did we do before the advent of the telephone? Ora? Hedva? Adriana? Maybe Avi—that the letters—

"This is the police—" a policewoman's voice chirps.

"Excuse me?"

"The police, miss, the police. You're Miss Loya Kaplan, right? So it was your storeroom that was closed. So they're going to come and open it. Just get your own private lock ready. So it won't stay open and get you into trouble again. And just a minute—the suitcase that they took—you can come and get that too. No, they won't bring it to you. This is the police, miss, not room service. Every day between eight and two—today, too—at the police station in Jabotinsky Street—ask for Sergeant Ben-Shimol or for Sarit—"

And your suitcase comes back to me, sails across the counter towards me. A faded burgundy color, strapped with a shabby leather belt. "Open it," the policeman behind the counter says impatiently. "See that there's nothing missing—" I open the buckle, two metal fasteners jump into my palms when I press them, the suitcase opens—khaki trousers, underwear, a pale gray shirt, a pair of khaki socks, a handkerchief, a squashed leather cap— the partisan cap?—two passports—your face but not your name—and this, what's this, at the bottom of the suitcase a precise cut made by a knife in the shape of three sides of a rectangle—a suitcase with a double bottom, what else, and there, in a stained, rusty envelope, another old letter, in Czech, apparently—"They found it in there," the policeman explains. They opened it and read it too, apparently, we never succeeded in gaining privacy here, Davidi. "Sign here and here and here," the policeman points to the form, and I sign and pack and close the suitcase. "Tomorrow they'll come to open up the shelter for you," announces the policeman after a telephone call, "did you get a good lock?"

But what do I need a lock for when it's so easy to get in through every window, through the porch, since they uprooted the ficus the house has grown more humped, today a big piece of plaster fell from the living-room ceiling and in your room I discovered a crack—a black root branching in the shell of the whitewash—

The phone. The phone. What did we do before the era of the telephone? Ora? Yosefa? Tikva? Maybe Hedva from America? She's gone on holiday and all my boiling stories are waiting for her to get back—and maybe Avi—Avi with the translation of—

"Loya? This is Arlozora from the council." She's talking like a complete stranger. "Listen—we sent you a registered letter—some people are coming to examine the house and see if it has to be pulled down—when will you be at home? Okay. Are you coming to Elhanan's memorial service?"

They're widening the road. Tikva drives with one hand, in her other is the mobile phone, without wanting to I listen to her: "Yes, my soul. Tell him that I need it for tomorrow. Regards from my mother. No, I'm not alone. Loya's with me. Yes, the flight attendant who gave us the Purim costume. Okay then, bye—"

They're widening the road. On the verges—red strawberries displayed in slanting boxes, mountains of oranges. Later on black pails blooming in a rainbow of colors—

"Should we buy flowers?" I take out my purse.

"What are you thinking of?" Tikva strides ahead with me behind her— we're late— "The military cemetery is all flowers. Every soldier has a flower bed on his grave—have you forgotten?"

Paved with Jerusalem stone. Organized in sections according to the wars. There are trees too and benches for those who no longer have the strength to stand. Each grave—a stone pillow and a blanket of low flowers

with here and there an outbreak of cactus or a sudden vase of dead gladiolas. Tikva hurries along the paved path. "There they are!" We are indeed
late, the little group is on the point of dispersing. "And here are Loya and
Tikva," says Ora. The dispersal is halted. Tikva goes up, kisses Elhanan's
parents?—I wouldn't have recognized them—they've shrunk—

"Loya!" Elhanan's mother hugs me with a trembling arm and brushes
my cheek with dry fire.

"Loya—" Elhanan's father crushes my hand in a long grip. Everyone is
looking at us—Bilu and his wife, Ora and Motik, Adriana, Yosefa, Arlozora, Hezi and Dina and Batsheva and Sophie and Herzl and Tikva, here's
Ruthie too, and those must be Elhanan's sisters, Masada and Yodfat, Tikva
embraces them, I shake their hands, twenty-five years have passed and
nobody cries any more, people apparently get used to this too, nobody
knows whether to leave or not, they speak in whispers as if they are afraid
to wake the dead, now Avi confers with Elhanan's parents as if he is a close
friend or a relative, I glance questioningly at Ora. "Avi interviewed them,"
she answers my mute question in a whisper, about the Holocaust, I understand. "He interviewed half your neighborhood," says Motik. Avi hears,
looks up, knows we're talking about him, signals me with a gesture to wait,
I nod. "I understand you're going back with him," Ora's whisper is tense,
biting. "O-ra." I turn to her in a tone that makes her purse her lips. "Are
you representing the Rabbinate or what—" Apparently there was more
than a drop of truth in Vered's story. I turn my back on Ora, say good-bye
to Tikva and follow in Avi's long strides. It's almost dark in the parking
lot. The cars crunch the gravel, dazzle for a moment with their headlights,
turn, leave—

"Were you in love with him too?" Avi leans over to start the car. I can't
see his face.

"With who?"

"Fasten your seat belt." He straightens up. "Two days ago a policeman
caught me and I had to pay a four hundred shekel fine—" he starts the car.
"With Elhanan—were you in love with Elhanan too?"

"I was in love with Saul Tchernichowsky—"

Avi snorts. Perhaps he doesn't believe me. I can't read him. He's hot/cold close/far. We merge into the night traffic.

"Your letters haven't come back yet—" Avi drives carefully, talks to me without looking at me.

"You won't believe it, but I have another Czech letter for you—they found it in Davidi's old suitcase—the police—the case had a double bottom—"

"A proper detective movie—" Avi passes the car in front of us, hoots, he still doesn't look at me. Is he trying to be funny? "Is it from the fifties too?"

"Actually, no," I say almost aggressively. "It's from '68—February '68—"

"Put it in my briefcase—on the back seat—I'll fax it as well—in a day or two, at the most a week—we'll solve all the mysteries for you—"

Clearly he attaches no importance to Czech letters from '68. That's not history—it's almost journalism—

He turns on the radio to the news headlines: the condition of the wounded in the terrorist attack—

"Ora gave me hell," he says after the news. Both hands on the wheel.

"Because of me?" I know.

"Because of me—" his face is illuminated by the headlamps of the cars opposite us, carved out of the darkness, and extinguished again. Could I love him?

"I can't get used to it," I produce in the end. "I lived in Paris for years and nobody had anything to say to me except for *bonjour*—"

"I know." His face thaws. "We lived in the U.S. for two years . . ."

"And here—"

"A small country with a moustache—"

"With what?"

"Never mind, it's a line from a popular song—" He stops with a screeching of brakes. "Last station—"

We've arrived. I open the door. We are both bathed in yellow light.

"Loya?"

"Yes?"

He is silent. Both hands on the steering wheel. His gaze is focused on the windshield as if he is still driving. I wait.

"I'll wait here until I see you go inside," he finally says.

"That's okay. I'm not afraid—you can go—" I get out of the car.

"I'll wait," he says in a resigned voice.

"Then please switch off the lights—"

"Don't you want me to light the way for you?" Avi sticks his head out of the window.

"It prevents me from seeing the stars—"

In the sky of the garden without the ficus the wounded shoulder of Orion, the heroic hunter, flickers. Orion himself—the glittering head, the slanting belt, the sword—are lost. But his dog is still with us, and the twins born from a swan's egg, Castor and Pollux, and not far from them crouches a lion of darkness, a bright star on its nape, a bright star at the tip of its tail, and between the two, an ominous orange star—Mars the god of war right in the middle of my garden—

"Are they all in the right place?" Avi calls from the car.

"Almost—" I leave him with the stars outside and go inside: Greetings your majesty the house, Greetings my dear daughter, where have you been and what have you seen, I've been to the cemetery and now I'm here, opening the fridge to get a drink, flooded by a white light of the dead, drinking from the bottle, closing the fridge, groping in the dark, almost stumbling, another tile dancing under my feet, they uprooted the ficus but its roots are still barking under the floor, greetings your majesty the house, greetings my dear dead, greetings Davidi, greetings Nahum, Hasia, Elhanan, Daddy, Mother. Where have you been and what have you been doing all these years—

On the corner of Rimon Street and Rakefet Street is a notice board of rough wood in a rustic style: Classes in dances of the sixties—cha-cha-cha, rumba, samba, twist—a three-level villa for sale, owners going abroad, serious buyers only—bicycle good as new bargain offer, next to the public is invited to attend a memorial ceremony for the fallen in the battles of Israel to take place in the school yard on Monday at 10.45, and in the right-hand corner, in the round letters of a teacher's handwriting *You are requested to come in white shirts*—a sudden wind blows my hair about and lifts the bottoms of the notices—nothing really sticks to this rough wood; what's underneath them? Qualified beautician. Flute lessons. Pedigree Rottweiler puppies for sale. And underneath the announcement of the memorial ceremony another one just the same, no, but very similar, the same format, the same print, Holocaust Martyrs and Heroes Day, the memorial ceremony will take place on—here the two are stuck together, but in the corner, in the same pedagogic handwriting, the same request—*in white shirts*—

The light is soft. The trees are very green. The cypress bleeds bougainvillea. It's quiet behind the fence. The Arab workers never came back to build the four-storied building for Russian emigrants who can buy butter and milk at the grocer's in Russian. The engineers from the council came. They walked around the rooms, they looked, took notes. A black velvet mafioso curses me in clear Italian. What do you want, am I responsible for what happens here? The plot beyond the palms is already plowed up. All that remains of the strawberries are dirty polyethylene shrouds lying in a heap next to the little awning like the placenta of a giant whale that was born here and immediately swallowed up by the earth—the orange grove at the end of the plot is gradually drying up. Advocate Betzer called, said that he was sending a buyer. For the orange grove. As for the house—he understands, he doesn't need more than a hint, he's an old fox already—I'm not going to sell. My account of the experts taking notes makes him extremely nervous. I need to make up my mind about what to do with the ashes, otherwise he won't be able to transfer the ownership—but soon—if they decide to pull down the house I'll get a lot less—it's true that the house in itself is worth almost nothing—but that's the way things are—that's the way things are. What would have happened if that wasn't the way things were, if they were different. If I had stayed here: I would have married Elhanan and been widowed at the age of twenty-three. A second possibility—I would have wandered around the country burned by the sun and hoarse from the dust, brushing dirt off Roman mosaic floors, a single woman with a big straw hat and a cat. A third possibility—I would have married Shlomi, become a professor of ancient languages. We would have had two sons and a daughter. One of the sons would have fallen in one of the wars—or: I would have stayed here—and one day—Giora—

The old radio suddenly came back to life. The green eye in its forehead flickers, translates the sound into a Cyclops light. Daddy's scraps of paper are on the right hand chest of drawers—I don't go back to them but they're here, looking at me with letter-eyes. *We're both from the same village*—sings the radio, and the green eye flickers, *I walk through a green field,* it sings, *and you're buried on the other side of the fence,* a beautiful, poignant song, once they would have said who wrote the lyrics, who composed the music, but now people apparently know, one song follows straight on to the next, *the heat of July–August was very heavy then,* the singer stifles a sob, stifles a scream, steaming with feelings of guilt *I go to dance with dead soldiers in my heart, evening falls on a burning horizon,* we sang that to the accompaniment of a melancholy accordion on Memorial Day before the siren that always sounded at exactly eleven o'clock and was nevertheless alarming, beginning dreadfully and tailing off like a real alert, *this melody can never be stopped,* claims the radio over and over again, but I switch it off—

Urgent. Special delivery by motorcycle. The structure is dangerous for habitation—to be demolished—are they crazy? Advocate Betzer isn't in his office. He's at a memorial service. Yes, his cousin fell in Lebanon. Arlozora at the council says that it's a mistake, but have a heart, not today, you know what, bring the letter to the ceremony, aren't you coming to the ceremony at the school? Come, bring it, I'll be there, I'll sort it out for you, but not today, not this week—next week—

The light is steamy, viscous. A guard in the uniform of a security company with a walkie-talkie and a gun opens the schoolyard gate. "Are you for the ceremony?" I nod. "Since when do they have armed guards here?" "For years already, don't you know? And now—what do they say—how much the more so. The parents are willing to pay to have a vehicle from the security company stand here all day, and me, it's only today that I'm standing guard here at the gate, because of the ceremony, usually I walk around the yard and at the back every hour, half-hour to check—what? Do I know, for bombs, terrorists, believe me, I've been guarding here for four years and what have I found? Sweaters and sandwiches that the kids here throw away, these rich kids, their mommies make them sandwiches and they throw them out and go and buy junk at the kiosk, no, they're not allowed out, but they climb over the fence, no problem, I'm telling you if terrorists wanted to take over this school they wouldn't have a problem, this fence is a joke, and me, what can I do, call for help on the radio-transmitter is all, that's my real weapon—" he tightens his grip on the instrument and whoooooooiiiii—the siren—close—deafening—far more terrible than at home—a few in the distance join in like weeping, one infecting the other, I'm already standing to attention, the guard as well, three mothers and an old man freeze on the opposite pavement, the siren straightens out and goes on, even, incessant, until your deafened ears almost start accepting it, growing accustomed to its presence here in the air, necessary to breath and life as oxygen, a mixture of metal and electricity, a bitter and continuous presence, filling your mouth and nose going down your windpipe—but now comes the descent, the terrible sinking wail that tears a hole in your stomach, and in the distance the others are added to it like an echo of an echo of an echo, the guard moves first, I wait a little longer, for the frozen mothers to move, and now the mother with the baby bends down to lift her baby out of the carriage, he's crying, and another mother hurries up to the gate. "The ceremony has already begun—" she almost pants, "can you let me in?" "Me? No, I don't have a key, there's a guard, wait a minute, where's the guard—" The guard emerges from the booth almost at a run, in an outstretched hand he holds a transistor radio far from his body as if it were a yellow scorpion, as if he wanted us to take it from him, to hear, to listen—another bomb's gone off—in Hadera—

Ora's in the living room, bending over the radio.

"Have you heard?"

"What else did they say?"

"Six dead—thirty wounded—eighteen of them soldiers—they've just finished removing the bodies—" she switches off the radio, straightens up. "I'm going to phone everyone—" She says not to me but to Motik who comes in from the garden, Avi behind him, "this is no time for a party—"

"Ora, wait, Ora—" Motik in short pants, sweating, speckled with bits of grass, just finished preparing the garden for the occasion, goes up to her, Avi, already festive, signals me with his hand—the letters are ready? I'll give them to you in a minute? Be patient—?

"What wait? What else should we wait for? I'm calling and cancelling!" Ora is already picking up the phone, paging through the family phone book with her other hand.

"But what are we going to do with all the stuff we bought? Never mind the drinks, but what about the meat—I've already thawed it—and in this heat—" Motik sounds flabbergasted, insulted. He puts out his hand—to take hold of the telephone receiver? To take hold of Ora's hand holding the receiver? Ora looks around, sees us looking at them—

"What's up?" Yinon comes in a white, sweaty shirt. "Hi Ilil, hi Avi, hi parents, what happened, who's dead—"

"Yinon!" Ora puts down the phone.

"Your mother wants to cancel the party tonight—" Motik tries to get the youngest son on his side.

"Yeah!" Yinon cheers. "Then I'll take all the steaks to the gang—" The Indian tuft of hair on his shaven head doesn't make him look ugly—on the contrary—it adds an exotic touch—"Every Independence Day they have a party here and sing songs from the old-age home." He smiles at me.

346

"I don't think you should cancel," Mechora's voice rasps from the kitchen door, "even during the period of the Holocaust people celebrated Purim here with fancy dress and masks and treats, correct or not, Avi—"

"Mother, leave me alone with the Holocaust—" Ora picks up the phone again. Her chin is thrust forward, stretching her double chin, imitating with a considerable measure of success the face of thirty-five years ago, the Ora of *No pasaran*, she'll phone, she'll cancel, she won't allow there to be mourning in the six homes of the murdered while here, in her private garden, people celebrated with steaks and beer—"What's Adriana's number?" she asks herself or maybe the air that has become crowded with the entry of Gilad and Vered—

"If you cancel the Independence celebration it will be a victory for those who hate us," her mother pronounces.

"Death to the Arabs! Death to the Arabs!" yells Yinon, waving both fists in all directions, until Vered grabs hold of one of them.

"Stop that, idiot—and go and take a shower—you stink!"

"Stink? I stink? Excuse me—excuse me—excuse me—excuse me for living—excuse me for having opinions—I stink of opinions that are out of bounds in this commune—" He bows, smiles, winks at me, leaves the room, returns. "Is there any hot water in this house?"

"Come with me, grandson, come and bathe in Grandmother's house, there's always hot water in Grandmother's house—" Ora's mother takes him by the wrist and leads him out of the room, raising his arm in the air, like a referee announcing the winner in a boxing match.

"That child is proof that your production line is out of whack," says Vered to her parents. "You should have stopped screwing after the first three—"

"Will the demonstration please disperse?" Ora picks up the phone again, Gilad whispers to Vered, "You went too far," Avi comes up to me, whispers "The letters came"—"Translated?" "Only two. She hasn't had time for the third yet. I told her that if she finished by this evening she could fax it to Ora's—"

"We could just cancel the sing-along," Motik implores Ora, looks at us. Avi looks at Ora. Nods. Ora gives in. She sits down in the armchair. Bows her head. Her dyed hair is painfully sparse. She is defeated. Gilad goes out to check Mechora's dripping faucet, Vered explains to me that it's no light matter for her father to give up the sing-along, he waits for it all year, he has slides with the words of all the songs before the state was established, Avi promises to bring me the translated letters in the evening, reminds Ora that a fax might come for him, not for him, for Loya—

I take a shower with the door open, and the green-eyed radio sings at the top of its voice to reach me through the needles of water with *Bab-el-wad, remember our names for ever*, going on to *There were nights I'll remember to the day I die*, imploring, I'm already drying myself, *Let it be, please let it be*, going barefoot to lower the volume in order not to disturb the rest of the neighbors even though I haven't seen a single neighbor since I returned or heard this request over the radio, perhaps everyone is deaf *under the Mediterranean skies and it costs us, it costs us so much*, complains the singer, and in a completely different tone, full of little bursts of energy, *parted in the middle, parted at the side, heads shampooed every one*, just like me, ready to get dressed in what, black trousers, black shirt, narrow gilt belt, and sandals, in this heat only sandals, but where are they and where am I on the eve of Independence Day in the obligatory blue pants and white shirt almost torn between the one pushing ahead in front of me and the one dragging behind me—trying not to let go—to maintain—with arms stretched to breaking point—our human chain in the crowd pressing around the entertainment platform—what's going on there now—who can see—only the loudspeakers pouring down on us *I Zachariah ben Ezra* in a melodious Yemenite voice, and the crowds, and the shoving, and someone steps on my foot, hey mister, mister, *I was born here! My children were born here!* your radio declares in a self-satisfied song, and now—for the fireworks! And the crowding in the darkness is like a dense wave and don't push, stop that, stop pushing, it's impossible to breathe here, look, look at the sky, a golden palm tree opens, chrysanthemums of blue light explode, turn into crystal chandeliers fading into spiders of smoke slowly swept along in the wind, and that's the end, no, not yet, it can't be, the best hasn't been yet, they always save the best for the end, and tonight will there or won't there be fireworks, tomorrow the IDF will hold a display of ships from the navy on the Tel Aviv beach and helicopters from the air force will demonstrate a rescue operation and *today I'm still alive, I'm still alive-live-live.*

Ora's back garden is full of darkness and people and the faint light from paper bags half full of sand with a memorial candle stuck in each one, it was Adriana's idea, it's safer and the light lasts for hours too, yes—but, but what—who is that? Loya? You're here in Israel? What, didn't you see her at Tikva's on Sukkoth, no, I wasn't here on Sukkoth, who is that, Behira? How is it possible to see anything here, Ora's made it dark as Egypt here, never mind you'll get used to it in a minute, look how lovely it is, what lovely—it's like a graveyard here, who's in charge of the meat? The man of the house, where is he? Over there, in the corner, under that yellow star, Arcturus? Whatever, in any case it belongs to the constellation of Bootes, the Bear-keeper, how far away is it? Arcturus? Thirty-two light-years from here, what's that for us, hey, Hezi, all we have to do is get into the Volvo and drive, there's no need for you to drive to it—it's getting closer to us at a speed of five kilometers a second, what do you say, come on people, leave the politics, come and listen to the science fiction, so when is the collision due, Professor, who says there's going to be a collision—there's more of a probability that it will die first, who'll die, that star, it's already old, you're kidding, no, you can see by the color, okay show us a young star now, okay, look to the side of Arcturus, there—see? That's Regulus, it's a young star, and that yellow one? That's Asad Australis, we said no politics, listen people, guess what, Asad's right on top of us, I'm not kidding, ask Netzach, why on earth is a star called Asad, Asad in Arabic means lion, look look, where's Asad? There, over the salads, who's going to help Motik with the meat, you made it so dark here, come on, sit down, get used to it, you can see the stars, who's that? Avi, Ora's brother-in-law, do your stuff Netzach, tell us, how far is this Asad from here, 346 light-years, how much is a light-year, a lot . . . maybe it's easier to think about it like this—the light that we see at this moment left that star 346 years ago, Loya, where's Loya, go on, tell us what happened 346 years ago from today, the Chmielnicki massacres, Shabbetai Zevi, the Peace of Westphalia, okay, okay, that's enough, are you trying to say that the light we see now left that star when the Cossacks were raping the mothers of the mothers of the mothers of our grandmothers' mothers? He's saying more than that, I intervene, he's saying that perhaps that star is already dead, kaput, nonexistent, so how can we see it? In the same way as we hear the sonic boom after the supersonic aircraft has disappeared from view, I use Nahum, my dead brother's, image, but it doesn't convince them, is she pulling our leg, Netzach? I wouldn't have used that image, but on principle she's right; it may be that the whole disposition of stars that we see at this moment no longer exists, what we see now isn't what's there now but what was there—what we see now is history, I intervene again, someone nearly falls over me, who is it? Dubi, I almost stepped on you in this dark, whose idea was it, is it in aid of the slides for the sing-along, there isn't going to be a sing-along tonight, why not, because of the bomb in Hadera, that's why, who wants to drink? What is it? Kinley, okay, hand it over, is Minaleh here? Not yet, how is she, not good, she couldn't make it to Elhanan's memorial service, she must be in bad shape then. It's not only the cancer, it's all these terror attacks too, last week in Afula, today Hadera, the day after tomorrow our community center will go up in smoke, no—the next bomb will be in Jerusalem, who said that? Arlozora's husband, he's an Arabist—the next attack will be in Jerusalem, the confident voice repeats, or in Tel Aviv, in a central place, the Mann Auditorium, Dizengoff Center—why not Givatayim or Holon? Because they think in symbols; Hadera—the symbol of early Zionist settlement, Afula—the capital of the Emek, they want to show us that they can hit at the heart of the consensus. The spleen of the Green Line, you mean? I'm not joking, who wants a steak in pita? Ah, what a smell—who said spleen? Have you ever tasted a calf's spleen? Here's Minaleh, come and sit here, how are you—and you? I am about to descend on a steak in pita—

we've lost our appetite, the two of them—Avi and what's your name?—
Aldema—sit there and decide where the next bomb's going to go off, who's
that, Motik? Here, take, eat, you want a few chips? Ora, bring the chips!
What can I give you, Minaleh, nothing, out of the question, you must have
something, how about salads—someone, bring a plate with samples, what
salads are there? I don't know, everyone brought something, who's next
to the salad bar? Tell us what's there—Greek salad and Turkish salad and
Russian salad and French lettuce salad—a real melting pot, pass a plate to
Minaleh, here, here, Ora, nobody can see a thing in this darkness, guess
who's here, hello, say something, greetings all! Who is it? It's not Shlomi
Horovitz? Welcome Shlomami, welcome to the punished land, how long
do you intend staying in our terrorized country, only five days? What a
pity, you won't be here for the bomb in Dizengoff Center or when the
Knesseth goes up in smoke—don't worry, I'll see it on CNN, isn't that how
we saw the Gulf War? As far as the Gulf War is concerned—we have news
for you Shlomami, you see that star over there? It's Sadam, not Sadam, idiot, it's Asad, Asad-Sadam-Arafat—all the Arabs are the same, all the stars
are the same, sit down Shlomi, sit there, hello Shlomi, I say, Loya? You're
still here? He gives me a clumsy hug, the arms of the chairs are between
us. So are you back for good? Let's find somewhere with more light, I want
to see you, we stand up, go inside the house, the light's on in the kitchen,
Avi's there, making coffee—

There's no need to introduce them. "How's your father?" asks Avi. "On
and off," says Shlomi, even in the lethal neon light he is a very attractive
man, tanned, well preserved from the top of his curly head (beige with
strands of silver) to the tips of his fingernails, a professor of Yiddish in a
New Jersey college, who would have believed it, skinny, sniffling Shlomi,
married plus two, looking at me with an American smile, but I can read
the disappointment in his eyes—I've put on weight, aged—"You look
good," he lies. "You too," I say truthfully. "Do you want the letters now? I
have them here—" Avi leaves the kitchen, returns after I've explained what
it's about to Shlomi, hands me two closed envelopes. No, they didn't come

by fax, his assistant had to drop by his office at the university and she left them there—

"You want to read them here? Now?" he says in surprise.

"I have no secrets from Shlomi," I smile and open the first envelope.

Avi observes us from the doorway. Jealous? I hope so. I look directly at him. He understands. Leaves without a word—

Opposite me, a meter away, Shlomi's beautiful eyes. He rests his chin on his fist. Examines me. "When we were kids I had a crush on you—" I smile. Take the two pages—original and translation—out of the envelope—

1.5.50

My dears—

When you find this letter you'll understand that I won't be coming home from the May Day demonstration. I intend going to Kfar Masaryk and joining the comrades returning to Czechoslovakia. I wouldn't have left if I hadn't been sure that you will be good fathers and give Loya and Jan more than I am capable of giving. I couldn't choose between you or remain in your country which is, unfortunately, the only option you see as possible at the moment; I don't blame you. If not for the war, you too would have seen that the Zionist state serves the interests of American imperialism, that it's cultivating favoritism and corruption—after everything that happened with Berco, it should have been clear even to you, that the Zionists are continuing here with the same vitamin P methods that ruled Terezin!

But there is no point in repeating our barren arguments—

I hope that in a few years time one of you, at least, will sober up from the Zionist intoxication and return to Czechoslovakia. And bring our son/daughter with him.

I'll try to write to you as soon as I have a permanent address.

Keep the children out of your terrible sun—

M.

My mouth is very dry. I look up at Shlomi.

"It's a farewell letter from my mother—she went back to Czechoslovakia—she didn't die—"

"Who told you that she was dead?" Shlomi sounds horrified.

"They said that she was 'gone'—you know—that's what they said then about the ones who died: 'gone in the Holocaust'—'gone up the chimney'"—I feel as if I'm choking. My hands, I discover, are gagging my mouth, my thumbs are digging into my throat—

"Drink, Loya—drink—" Shlomi is at my side, holding a cold glass close to the back of my hand. I put out my hand to take the glass. My hand is shaking.

"Take a deep breath—" Shlomi is translating from English, "and let go—let it go—" I take a sip. I can't drink any more.

"Shlomi—I have a mother—" I hold the letter out to him. He sits down opposite me, reads intently. Raises eyes the color of smoke.

"Loya—this letter is from 1950—"

"But she could still be alive—no? Your father is still alive, Elhanan's parents are still alive, Ora's parents—even Motik's and Avi's grandmother—"

"Do you have a more recent letter from her?" Shlomi leans towards me with a gentle expression that suddenly reminds me of his mother.

"I have another letter—" I open the second letter, even though I know, I'm certain, it's not hers, not from her—

4.5.53

My dear Ota,

I am writing to you at Milena's request. I don't know when this letter will reach you, because it will be sent via Switzerland. I met Milena two weeks ago in Prague, and although she didn't remember me I remembered her and stopped to ask her what she was doing in Czechoslovakia, and how you were doing over there in that hot Palestine. Milena looked very tired and frightened. She didn't want to talk in the street. In the end she agreed to walk in a small park where amidst the shouts of the children and the barking of the dogs she told me that immediately after her return she was arrested by the police for her connections with a couple of Zionists. She was released after grueling interrogations that lasted for a year and a half. But she is afraid of being arrested again, she feels that she is being followed wherever she goes, she doesn't dare write a letter to Israel because she is afraid that it might serve as a pretext to arrest her again. She asked me to write to you and Mr. Dolohovski and tell you that she is working in her profession, that she is managing, and to give her love to her son and daughter. In the meantime she asked you not to try to get in touch with her—times are not easy—and any such attempt is liable to get her into trouble again. She promised to write to you as soon as "the skies are blue again." I add that I am married to a mining engineer and that we have two healthy, handsome sons. I hope we meet again one day—

"Max's mother."

"Shlomi—" I say with my eyes closed.

"Should I make you a strong cup of coffee?"

"All right—"

"Was the letter from your mother?"

"No—according to the signature it seems to be from my father's first wife—their dog's name was Max—"

"And what does she write?"

"That my mother was arrested—she was detained for a year and a half—my father would have called it 'the irony of history'—she left Israel for the sake of Communism and was arrested in Czechoslovakia because of Zionism—"

"Listen—" Shlomi gives me the coffee and stands behind me, massaging my hunched shoulders. "Remembering the Prague trials and all that business—there's probably only a minimal chance that your mother is still alive—"

I can't breathe.

I stand up. "Shlomi—let's go outside—"

We return to *the tanks set out on creaking tracks* in Motik's loud and melodious voice, so they're having the sing-along anyway, *nevertheless and in spite of everything, Eretz Eretz Eretz Israel*, after the neon light in the kitchen I'm almost blind, where's Ora, I have to tell her, she was sitting between Minaleh and Adriana but in the darkness singing *the two of us are from the same village* where is she, there, there, hands of darkness reach out to me, be careful here, you can't see where you're going, no, I can't see yet, only masses of swaying darkness, singing fervently, who decided to go ahead anyway, *he didn't know her name*, they sing, but *that braid went with him all the way*, where's Ora, there, at the end, on the deck chair, next to Minaleh, yes, I see her, I reach the place, Ora is singing in a hoarse voice, Minaleh too, Ora? I bend down to her, I haven't got a chance, when they begin to sing along it's almost like synagogue, it's impossible to stop, impossible to interfere, if you don't know the words then hum with your mouth closed, if you can't sing in tune then move your lips and shut up, Ora, I shake her shoulder, my face close to hers, I have a mother, I want to tell her, I'm flying to Prague to look for her, I suddenly know, but Ora hisses at me *Ss-samsons foxes*, where did they dig these songs up from, someone says to someone else as they walk past us, I pull up a stool, sit down at Ora's feet, "Ora, Ora, listen here for a minute, the letters—" "Can't it wait, Loya—" She stops singing to say these four words to me and rejoins the foxes.

I stand up. An appetizing smell, strong, devouring, rises from the fat burning into smoke and dimming the stars. I go there. Avi is standing next to the embers, his one hand turning over the meat, in the other a pita stuffed full to bursting, he takes a bite, talks to me with his mouth full. "Well Loya—have you solved all the riddles yet?" "Almost," I reply, starting only now to feel a kind of joy, I have a mother made of steel, she went back into the lion's jaws, she was arrested, interrogated, released. "What do you have to offer me?" I ask Avi. "Steak, chops, sausages, hamburger." "Give me a small hamburger." "Hold this for me." Avi hands me his pita, picks up a new one from the table behind him, slits it open with a knife. "Should I put in hummus? Tahini? Coleslaw? Pickled cucumber? Aren't you going to tell me what you discovered in the letters?" "Everything!" I'm hungry, I could devour the whole world, and Avi is quick, efficient, hands me a pregnant pita, "Take a napkin from over there, it's going to start dripping in a second." I take a big bite, nothing has tasted so good in a long time, this week, this very week I'm flying to Prague, I'm more and more certain, and I'll take the pyxis with your ashes to her, what do you say, *a year has already passed*, they sing behind me, *in our fields we hardly felt the times go by*, and somebody who hasn't got the patience to wait for *love sanctified by blood* stands up and proclaims, enough, enough of these laments, Memorial Day is over, Independence Day has begun, and some people protest, but there was a terror attack, and others give him their support, he's right, today's supposed to be a celebration, Motik, let's have some optimistic song from the old days, and Motik obliges with *It is no legend my friends, It is no legend my friends*, and people join in with singing and clapping, but the song is not completed, it peters out in an argument, how come we gave them back Sinai, we're suckers, idiots, so what do you want, I want security, that's what I want, just wait, soon they'll give back the Golan and the West Bank too, no they won't, sure they will, didn't you hear Peres? Didn't you hear Rabin? I'm telling you, that Rabin, one day somebody will murder him, what are you talking about, I did reserve duty in the territories, I heard the settlers—believe me, Baruch Goldstein's next to God as far as they're concerned, so what do you suggest? Enough, people, enough politics for today, enough, this is a holiday, who wants coffee who wants tea, the cakes are out of this world, Adriana gets up, a tall silhouette, holds out fingers of darkness on which she counts, Yosefa—what do you want to drink? Bilu—you said tea. Anat—nothing? Motik? Ruthie? Batsheva? Netzach? Arlozora? Here, take my hand too, says Hezi, volunteering his fingers, Yossi? Aldema? Shlomi? Ora? Ora? But Ora stands up, call an ambulance someone, Minaleh isn't feeling well, and Hezi's voice, I have a cell phone, what's the number, and the sound of the dialing, what's the address here? Yes, it's urgent, it's very urgent—just a minute—here's her husband—where's Yudah—

Quarter past four in the morning. A pearly light blackens the jagged leaves of the palms, covers the polyethylene shrouds with a milky sheen. Heeheeheeee—Dubček passes before my eyes with his whinnying lament, and the two executioners reply with deliberate coughs. I still don't know what's written in the letter from '68—but as long as nobody has notified me of your death, you're alive and kicking. And I can talk to you—

We've never talked, you and I.

What could I have said to you up to the age of four—Maminka, look, Maminka, it hurts, Maminka, drink? Once I fell and cut my knee. You took care of me with a sure but unconsoling hand—iodine—gauze—band-aid. I still have the scar. Here, look. I don't remember your face. Only your hands—very quick, efficient—freckled—in what language did I talk to you—Czech? It's gone, nothing's left. Only rarely something twitches, a word escapes from the uninterrupted darkness—

If you hadn't run away, who would you have chosen? There's no way of knowing. They're all dead. The only ones left are you and me—they never told me a word about you. They only said that you'd gone—and you really had gone—maybe that was their way of being angry about your going—to take you off the agenda—to imprison you in a fortified silence—not to allow you to be a possibility in my life—don't ask me about Nahum—I don't know how much he knew, how much he wanted to know—but none of them even asked me—What were you. Who were you. I have to go back to Daddy's notes, pick out all the sentences referring to M.—neither of them married another woman in your place—even though Daddy had someone in Jerusalem in the last years of his life—I didn't know—I saw her at the funeral—she came to condole with me afterwards—but I—you should have seen me—they called in a nurse—a doctor—the police—Davidi—Dolohovski to you—Berco, is that what you called him, he was faithful to you until his last breath—so what do I know—what I know is that he didn't want to let me sell up—leave—if I'd known that you were an option, would

I have found a way of reaching you? They brought me up as a motherless child. They didn't give me a choice—they simply presented me with a fait accompli—but who had a choice in this story?—they too were presented with a fait accompli—only you, you chose—you chose to come to Israel—you chose to go back—where is my motherland it says in the Czech national anthem, did they arrest you again there, stand you in front of a firing squad, and you, refusing a blindfold, looked straight into the barrels of the guns and sang the *Internationale*?

No, not yet.

We've only just met, you can't die on me yet.

I'm sitting on Davidi's bed now. From the open window you can see a plowed plot and at the end of it, between the ground and the sky, the dense, dark embroidery of an orange grove. It's dying, but on the threshold of death it sends me a pungent reminder of the fragrance that it is still capable of producing in a heatwave—what will they do with it?—they'll send in the bulldozers—like with my and Daddy's house—to this day I haven't gone to that street to see what has grown up on its ruins—Yosefa told me that they built a Mediterranean-style villa there—Daddy's notes are on the right-hand chest of drawers. The wind from the grove is ruffling the pages—in a minute early and late will be mixed up again—I have to bring something heavier to weigh them down—here—from the Biedermeier—the iron Anat—

If I'd known you were alive, maybe I wouldn't have stood up and smashed up and sold up and left the country, like you, in fact, but how could I have been like you, if I didn't know anything about you—

The light is still very faint. I'm cold—but it's only tiredness, I didn't sleep all night—I'm cold—you hear—even though you'll tell me that it isn't cold here, the winter isn't winter, the forest isn't forest, the mountains aren't mountains, everything is shallow and miserable—except for the imperial sun that skewers us with bayonets of fire at five o'clock in the morning—

The light is increasing, and the birds with it. In our garden we have executioners, mafiosi, Polish yentas, and one brightly colored bird, very like Dubček in profile, which wakes me up every morning—did you get to see the Prague Spring? Or were you dying in a hunger strike—and perhaps you were crushed under the Soviet tanks when you went out again to demonstrate—to protest—just and militant—the goddess Anat, suddenly it's clear who it came from, and Davidi, all those years, looked at me and saw you—

Listen. Today is the Independence Day of the Zionist state—you probably haven't changed your mind about it—I can only go to Shai Oved's travel agency tomorrow to book a flight to Prague—there are direct flights now—in a few hours I'll be able to be near you—to find out your address, to wander around Terezin, to discover the house you lived in—to try and discover where the barracks Daddy wrote about were, where the railway tracks passed, where the hospital you worked in was—where your grave is—I won't be surprised if you too, like Davidi, chose to turn into ashes and ground bones—I'll bring you the pyxis—I'll put it on your grave or stand it next to your urn—you'll be like Abelard and Héloïse—not to your taste?—but the dead, Maminka, have no right to speak; as long as you were alive you did what you liked—now it's my turn—

The phone. At six in the morning? Must be a wrong number. I don't pick it up. And again, the phone. Maybe it's Hedva back from her vacation—wait till she hears what I've got to tell her—

"Loya?"

"Ora? What happened?"

"Did I wake you? I'm sorry but—listen—I'm calling from the hospital—Minaleh passed away half an hour ago—Yudah collapsed—their son doesn't know yet—and all the arrangements have to be made—"

"I'm coming—where will you meet me?"

"In the entrance hall—next to the hotel—next to that little mall—there's a taxi rank there—you can't miss it—"

The taxi drives in the growing light, in the empty streets. I sit with eyes burning from sleeplessness, full to overflowing with a heavy liquid which I don't know whether to call sadness or oppression or anger and impatience, Minaleh's dead, Minaleh's dead, only a few hours ago I passed her a glass of mineral water and now she's a corpse, never a close friend, not loved, but if childhood is the mosaic of a face—she, perhaps, is the pupil of the eye, the little black stone—

Ora is waiting for me outside the entrance hall. Her face is gray. Her eyes are swollen. Her sparse hair sticks out in stiff strands—I hurry to her and she envelops me—big, warm, soft, smelling of smoke and Chanel No. 5, she closes her arms around my shoulders and shakes. She doesn't cry.

After the arrangements—Motik? Ora's father didn't feel well—he drove him to Ichilov—with Mechora, of course—Avi's with them—the two of us sit on a wooden bench in an inner garden enclosed between concrete walls and patients' windows. Ora drinks coffee from the machine. The half-risen sun of her eyes is lost in pink swelling, surrounded by gray rings. "Elhanan has to be told—he went out with friends to the Palmachim beach—we have to decide when to hold the funeral—did you know that her mother is still alive?" Her eyes wander over a few shade plants, a bed of gravel, concrete. I look at her. "Don't you want to call and find out how your father is?—there's a pay phone over there—" Ora shakes her head, points to the cell phone sticking out of her bag. "Vered will let me know—" "Aren't you worried—" I put out feelers. "My father's eighty-five years old." Ora stares at the gravel. "You have to die of something sometime—" "And your mother?" I meant to ask how old she was. "My mother will never die—" Ora suddenly fights dry sobs, coughs, the coffee splashes from her cup onto her trousers. I take the cup and wait for her to finish coughing. She takes a tissue out of her bag, blows her nose noisily, looks for another one—

"Loya—" she looks up at me as if she's seeing me for the first time—"I completely forgot," she holds out a folded piece of paper. "It came by fax—it's for you—"

"Did you read it?" I take the paper from her hand. Ora's eyes round in astonishment, almost in insult—she's the only one I believe wouldn't have even given it a glance—which doesn't make things any easier for me at this moment—

I stare at the fax. Your death awaits me, folded into three. But not yet—

"Aren't you going to read it?" Ora has recovered. Now she leans over, her elbows on her knees, peers at me with her head on one side.

"I'll read it at home—" I put it into my shoulder bag.

Yudah's brother Zvika has relieved us of the additional procedures. We go up one floor to find out how Yudah is doing. He's sleeping. Hanoch, Zvika's son, has driven to the Palmachim beach on his motorbike to tell Elhanan the news—Ora and I drive home in her car. Grandpa's sleeping, Vered informs her on the cell phone. "She's a wonderful girl," says Ora, "what would I do without her?" She drives slowly, knowing that she's tired, not focused, and perhaps simply trying to postpone getting home as long as possible—Avi will bring Mechora back in her car—Vered will stay with her grandfather—

She doesn't ask me about the letters—her present is full of fresh troubles. "Thanks for coming—" She scrapes up a smile for me from one of the dark corners of her anxieties and lets me off at Rosemary Street. "I'll let you know about the funeral—" "I probably won't be here—I'm flying to Prague—" I hasten to inform her so there won't be any surprises or misunderstandings. Ora narrows her eyes. Her mouth purses. "Can't it wait?" she asks in a teacher's disapproving tone. "No, it can't—" Ora sighs and shakes her head in her mother's tsk-tsk-tsk movement, "I'll let you know anyway—" she leaves me a loophole—

She drives away—

And now for your death.

Who is notifying us of it? Max's mother again? Max died long ago—even Argos, Odysseus's dog, died after twenty years—

25.2.68

Dear Berco,

Last week I was released from prison after serving a term of fifteen years for attempting to overthrow the regime. But now new winds are blowing and I am taking the opportunity to send you a sign of life. A few letters from the friends at Kfar Masaryk were waiting for me with Ota's first wife and also your letter notifying me of Ota's death. I am very sorry. He deserved a more loving wife, a better life.

How are Loya and Jan? I would like to see them, to get to know them, to talk to them. Could you come here, the three of you, or, if you don't want to, only the son and daughter? To the daughter I can offer a home, and if not motherhood—I don't deceive myself—then close friendship—or so I hope—

I beg you to prepare them before the meeting. And me too—send me photographs, tell me about them, what they like, what they do, if they are already married—I'll send a picture of myself in a few months' time, when I look better—I don't want to frighten them—

I have come back to live at my old address in Terezin. I couldn't stand Prague—the noise, the traffic, the crowds—after so many years in jail I need quiet, familiar surroundings—and Terezin has remained almost as it was before the war—

And how are you, my dear Berco? I expect you are married and have more children. I would be happy to meet them too.

Milena Hruzova

The old address? On the envelope. Avi had the envelope, and he gave it to his assistant—Avi is at the university, or at Ora's, or already at home—don't worry, I'll find you, dead or alive.

And afterwards we'll see.

There's still a bus to convey the passengers to the plane. We are greeted by young flight attendants—their smiles are almost natural, but their eyes wander off into space. I have a window seat, in front of the wing, a tall man sits down next to me, cursing from the word go—he has no room for his legs—I turn my head to the window. The sun explodes in the scratched pane into a chrysanthemum of light—the flight attendants move down the aisle, closing the baggage compartments with a pleasant and decisive click, their lowered eyes checking for loose seat belts. Another minute and another minute—and the plane shakes with rage, gathers strength to take off, starts to travel down the runway, slow, waddling, but its flight is already rumbling in its belly; I can feel it in my feet, straining to trap it, to lift it into the blue—fly, metal, I repeat my invocation, fly metal, against all the forces of gravity, fly—and again I've missed the miraculous moment of detachment, the plane slants, the green fields gradually recede, the roads grow narrower, the automobiles smaller, the houses are arranged in crescent shapes or horseshoe shapes, the solar collectors on the roofs shoot diamonds, and here are the dunes, the great lace of the sea, the green water with its secret glints of hoarded gold, and already the sky turns gray and fuzzy—from this height you can see that the haze is man-made—only above it is the atmosphere pure blue, growing bluer all the time, offering groves of white clouds and in the distance—a mighty anvil of cumulonimbus made of pure white marble and azure blue—Breakfast? No thank you, I can't, but when the flight attendant returns the man sitting next to me says to her, "Bring the lady breakfast, she's changed her mind," smiles at my astonishment. "You don't mind if I eat what you don't want?" "Be my guest," I reply, accept the offered tray with a suitable expression, pass it to him. "Everything's for dwarfs here," he complains, "the chairs, the food—" He rips the aluminum paper impatiently and bolts down the hot mushroom omelet almost without chewing, reminding me of Eliot, a meter ninety-one smiling with innocent-looking dimples at my meter sixty, the love between us takes us both by surprise—before me he had only very tall, athletic women—he too was once a basketball player—on our third date he showed me pictures of himself taken a decade ago, when his whole height was taut and muscular, look, he urged, look at that body, as if trying to persuade me that what I saw in bed was only a regrettable accident, a temporary mishap, he never forgave himself for putting on weight, but as for me—I actually rather liked the comfortable chubbiness, the years had been good to him, I thought, it was a good thing that he had grown fat, less in love with himself, less conceited, better fit for love—what didn't he try—vegetarianism and seaweed pills and the fit-for-life diet and Weight Watchers and acupuncture—and each time he would lose ten or twenty kilos and go back to his bad old ways, send everything to hell, choose a gourmet restaurant and polish off impressive amounts of food with relish and enthusiasm, telling me that I eat like a bird, while I pass him whatever I can't possibly get down, not even a crumb, and he devours, wipes his plate clean, he never looked happier than before a feast and during a feast and after a feast, from the moment of decision, choosing the restaurant, reserving a table on the phone, wondering what to wear, entering the dim space full of candles and noiseless waiters, the knowledgeable conversation with the waiter, the rubbing of hands and beaming expression of a child opening a present—after eating he might suggest driving to some observation point to see the spectacle of the night lights, taking in a midnight movie—for lovemaking he had neither the strength nor the desire, and he would envelop me in a soft embrace and fall asleep contentedly until the next day—when he would climb onto the scales and hate himself—don't let me! he would request, almost demand of me. I only tried once to comply with his request, to persuade him not to go out, to make do with an omelet and a vegetable salad, "A roll for the lady, too," says the bear next to me to the passing flight attendant, but he was angry with me, demanded that I love him as he was. I, for example, was twenty centimeters too short for his taste, what to do, nobody's perfect—put everything on the table, said Hedva, you've been eating yourself up for at least a year—and I chose a setting of gray velvet curtains and ivory tablecloths and tall candles in silver candlesticks in order to ask Eliot what was going to happen with us. I'm already thirty-nine—I reminded him and hated myself. I couldn't believe that I was already thirty-nine. And I love you, Eliot smiled with his mouth closed; he didn't realize that it was a terminal conversation. Don't you like it? After polishing off half the food on his plate he noticed that I hadn't touched mine. No I don't, I said in a tone that froze the laden fork halfway to his mouth. Can we postpone whatever it is to after the meal? I nodded because I was afraid I would raise my voice or throw my wine, like in the movies, in his face. I sat opposite him and watched him eat, steadily, dedicatedly, almost like the bear next to me, nothing can spoil the appetite of such people, I wished he'd choke on it, but Eliot went on eating, I'm going to powder my nose, I announced and I stood up and took my bag and went to the toilet, and there, in the vast mirror I saw a sour little Loya, how much do you really want to go back to that pig eating himself to death, I asked myself and I knew the answer, I'm simply not going back, I leave the toilets, pass through the cloak-room, take my coat, and go out into the night—hail a cab—on the flight to Israel I was in a wonderful mood. After two days in the Avia Hotel I flew to Paris. Don't you think you should explain to him? Hedva asked me over Turkey. I shrugged my shoulders. He told you he loves you, she reminded me over Greece. I was heating up the coffee and she the rolls. You don't know Canadian-Americans, I said to her. And nevertheless I considered—to write? Explain? Maybe apologize and—? I continued the for-and-against on the banks of the Seine too. It was a fine day and the water gleamed like molten jade, and the houses on the opposite bank were blurred in a film of light. His complacency—his self-satisfaction—his hedonism—his independence—everything that had been in his favor four years ago turned against him—"Thanks," says the bear in the seat next to me, offering me a swollen hand. "Yehuda Levitsky." "Pleased to meet you." "I didn't get your name?" He leans toward me. "I didn't say it—" I turn my face to the window—

What's in the window? The sea. Chips of light and lines of light on a semitransparent jelly-like blue and on it an island, a relief of brown velvet surrounded by a ribbon of pale sand and an exquisite frame of purple and turquoise. A miniature ship draws two lines of an opening and receding train. The anvil of the cumulonimbus is already closer, pure and solid, casting a tender blue shadow on itself—

And I journey on—fly through the sky—no longer there and not yet here—have you ever flown, Maminka?—I wouldn't be surprised if not—if only I'd known you were alive I could have—no. Stop it—stop it—don't develop expectations—next to me the bear is snoring with his mouth open—a flight attendant passes—she doesn't even give me a glance—a different generation—different flight attendants—none of them would have taken any notice of Jean-Jacques, damp with the perspiration of fear, pale, his eyes terrified, none of them would have smiled to promise that this plane won't fall, I give you my word, his lips quivered, I was afraid he would burst into tears, but three years later I knew he wouldn't. I sat on the edge of my suitcase, a meter from the door. You have another ten hours before the flight, grumbled Jean-Jacques sulkily, he always knew when I was supposed to take off, when I was supposed to land, his anxiety tightened around me like a lasso, I'll find something to do until then, you don't need to worry about me. You? Jean-Jacques folded his arms, there's no need to worry about you, you're like an alley cat, you always land on your feet, go, go, go, his voice became venomous and I decided not to leave bitten. I stood up and lifted the suitcase. Shalom, I said in Hebrew. Shalom, he mimicked me mockingly and opened the door with a flourish. I left— Loya! His voice clenched around me, but I didn't turn my head back. I waved my hand in something between good-bye and leave-me-alone and hurried down the stairs and into the street and into the Metro and got off close to Notre Dame and gave myself a leisurely walk along the Seine and I saw the long tourist boats on the gray-brown water and I wondered from which of them Alterman was cast into the water, *for falsely were you torn from me and truth is my return to thee*, perhaps all these years I belonged to Giora and Jean-Jacques was nothing but a dead-end alley, a mistake in navigation, a slip—

I walked along the bank of the Seine swinging my light case, feeling free, feeling the energy accumulating in the center of my body like the rumbling of the plane before it takes off, leaving behind me like the shell of an egg everything that closed and blocked and believed that I was this and not that, that I was incorrigible. "Something to drink?" the flight attendant whispers so as not to wake the bear. "Grapefruit juice," I request, she doesn't have grapefruit, maybe orange, okay, whatever, she pours, hands me the glass and her eyes are already on the next seat, I return to the window, a wooded land, juicy, green, tiny hamlets on hill slopes, valleys divided into rectangles of green fields, brown fields, a winding stream—one minute silver, the next blue—a cloud casts a round-edged shadow like a huge, dark anemone, I didn't know what to do with you, Nahum said to me after we took off to fly back, you did very well, I assured him, I did the only thing I know that can help, he smiled, it's impossible to be depressed when you're flying, he dived into the desert landscape—shades of camel, gravel, limestone, hazy light, an exposed land, all teeth, nails, big knee bones, from time to time a crowding together of palms like a frightened herd, their fronds like knives, and more and more dirty beige, a dry, wrinkled land, gray-veined, with pigmentation spots, growing whiter all the time, steaming hellish smells of sulfur and potash, becoming mineral, all stalagmites and congealed clouds and giant nibbled mushrooms and monsters of salt and sirocco, glittering with sudden daggers in the sun, breathing hot vapours, Sodom and Gomorrah, Nahum shouts over his shoulder, tilting the plane, the land slants, even the lake coming into view violet-turquoise azure tips to the side, people only get depressed on land! shouts Nahum, a herd of black goats in the dusty glare, a carbon shepherd, can we keep on going north? I shake Nahum by the shoulder and Nahum shakes his head, why not? I yell, there's a border, have you forgotten the map? He tilts the plane, turns sharply southwest, no, I haven't forgotten the witch's face invading us from the east, the poking nose of Latrun, the sunken, toothless mouth of the Jerusalem corridor with half the capital stuck inside its maw, the jutting pitted chin of the Judean desert, Beersheba, shouts Nahum over gray apartment blocks in a camel-colored desert, a few goats, a few black tents with pointed corners like bats' wings, Nahum turns northwest, making rocky hills, a road, cars tilt towards us, are you afraid? No, no, I'm not afraid, I'm full of a wild joy, I know now what I'm going to do—anything so as to look down on everything from a height of a few thousand feet—we're landing in a minute, shouts Nahum, in the window only the hazy blue of sky and the shining blue of sea—how will we land if there's nothing to land on—"It's over, thank God—" The bear wakes up. The plane descends to the downy clouds. Already the damp gray European light surrounds us, it's summer and outside it's seventeen degrees and drizzling, the captain informs us, *Welcome back*—how does the first poem in the book of poems by Bialik go?—*Welcome back pretty bird, from the lands of the sun to my window*—

EPILOGUE

A fine, quiet rain, in a dimmed world, only the wet roads gleaming and the leaves on the trees—a low blanket of clouds and a depressing, uniform gray light, easy on the eye, don't know if it's seven in the morning, or one in the afternoon—

In the Tourist Bureau next to Vaclav Avenue—Vaclavski Namesti, they call it, Vaclav Square, even though it's a broad, double avenue, with a crowded rectangle of flowers in its center, gradually rising to a little hill surmounted by a bronze saint on a bronze horse, behind them the palace of the National Museum—in the Tourist Bureau I am informed that no, there's no train, what have they done with the tracks, but there is a bus, several times a day, departing from the Florenc station, it's advisable to get there early and buy a ticket at the ticket booth, the journey only lasts an hour, and a hotel, yes there's a hotel there—the Park Hotel in Machova Street—I can sleep there if I like, and if not, there's a reasonable hotel not far from Florenc bus station—Hotel AXA—the helpful clerk writes it down for me—

The bus station is small and dilapidated; narrow platforms with no roofs—dejected people waiting in the rain, dressed in the style of the fifties—most of them haven't got umbrellas—they simply hunch their shoulders—waiting under cloth caps opposite a long brick wall—most of the platforms are almost empty, only for Terezin a small line collects: a few heavy women carrying baskets—three men in cloth caps—three armed with cameras—Israelis—a grandfather, father, and son, talking to each other in excited Hebrew—I avert my face—trying to ignore them—not to give myself away—they can't guess: my fair hair turns me into a local—although the local girls are very tall, more Scandinavian than Slavic, many of them beautiful—

The bus is a pleasant surprise; its windows are large, through them, after the suburban outskirts of Prague, fields, white flowers, trees, an occasional house, sometimes a tiny hamlet or little village, a few passengers get off, everything is obsolete, faded or peeling, this is Eastern Europe after all, the houses—no more than two stories—painted ocher or banana, shutterless, their elongated windows muffled in flimsy, milky drapes, light, they lack light, the bus goes on to more fields, a flat, fertile, chilled land, the sun after the drizzle a cold yellow, illuminating this bright green that spreads to the edge of the road, there's no earth exposed, everything is bursting at the seams with green, green grass, the Israelis are getting ready, the grandfather shifts on his seat, peers through the window in suspense, if they're getting off then so am I. "Is this the little fort?" the grandson asks, "Yes," his father answers, "and from there we'll go to Terezin on foot." They get off and I sit down again, one more stop—the bus enters the village—stops next to a big house painted banana and caramel—it's the municipality and it's here—

First of all to get rid of my suitcase—the pyxis weighs a ton—lucky they didn't stop me at the airport—where's Park Hotel, I ask a young woman in English, she understands but answers in Czech, here, close by, I understand, I follow her finger straight ahead and right to Machova Street, before my eyes, at the end of the street, the wall: yellowish, reddish brown bricks three or four meters high, and beyond them very clear, very close— you can put out your hand and touch them—bony blue mountains—are these the lead mountains, Daddy? I go on walking, the street is straight as a ruler, behind me too—I turn to look behind me—at a distance of five or six minutes walk—the wall—the town is so small—almost empty— the houses one or two stories, attached to each other, painted in vain in the colors of light, faded yellow, mustard, ocher, pale egg-yolk, pink that's known better days, a tiny town, moldy as an archeological chocolate box, on my left now a dank, dark park, its trees tall, dense, black trunks rising out of muddy mire, on my right the Park Hotel, yes, there is a room free, the reception clerk speaks a right-angled English, the toilet is at the end of the corridor, she examines me, wondering whether I am one of the tourists who come here specially to see where—there's a museum, she indicates tourist leaflets, in English, in Hebrew, THE TEREZIN GHETTO MUSEUM above a photograph of a gigantic gray stone Menorah planted on a pale lawn sprouting little headstones, the same size, maybe triangular, against the background of a rustic white house, with poplars behind it—the folded leaflet opens to disclose a numbered map with an index—I glance at it—try to get my bearings—where am I at this moment—Machova Street—where's Machova Street—where's the park named after Bedrich Smetana, from whom we stole our national anthem—the map seems straightforward enough: a rectangular town, divided into right-angled rectangles and squares, only its circumference sprouts protuberances—half-octagons—pentagons—triangles—at its center is a large rectangular square surrounded by little circles—maybe they're trees—the person who drew them dreaming of orange groves—is this the park I saw on the other side of the road—"Can I help you?" the reception clerk inquires at my puzzled look—"I can't see where we are— where's Park Hotel—where's Machova Street?"—the reception clerk turns my map around to face her, draws a red circle around number 15 and fills in the street between it and Brunnenpark on the map with the name Machova—but that's not what it says on the map—well, yes, the names have been changed a number of times since then, this map isn't a map of the present town, that is to say of the town yes, the blocks are the same, and the streets too, and the parks, but they changed the names, here, you see, Machova Street was Langestrasse, and here, the museum, she makes haste to circle in red the black spot with the number 1 printed on it in white, filling in the street the map calls Hauptstrasse with the name Komenskeho, on the park to the north of it—Stadtpark—she writes Jan Hus—him I know, dean of the philosophical faculty, 1401, rector of the University of Prague, 1409, vehement opponent of the selling of indulgences, betrayed by the Emperor, tried by a church council, burned at the stake on the sixth of July, 1415, his disciples fortified themselves on a hill near Prague, which they called Mount Tabor, all the world is one little village—at the center of the map, in the middle of the rectangular public park, among the circles of the orange trees, the reception clerk writes with her red pen the initials, apparently, of Czechoslovakian Socialist Army Square, right, I get the idea, thank you, I pull the map towards me, understanding in a flash that my problem is solved, no need to dig in the archives—if such a thing exists here at all—or rummage in creaking drawers in order to find a map from those days, right here, in this tourist brochure, is all the information I require, no need to ask anyone, and now I see Seestrasse, at the bottom of the map, very close to here, straight and first turn to the right and the second street on the left, three or four minutes walk from Park Hotel, in other words number 15, with the red ring around it, which was, I read below in Hebrew, the canteen and living quarters of the camp staff and the men of the SS Komandantu—"Is there another hotel here?" I ask. No, of course there isn't, this is a very small town, almost a kibbutz—

So what should I do first—maybe the museum—it's open till six—I almost flee from what was once the living quarters of the SS—how did I land up here of all places—I'll have to sleep here—No, there are no more buses back to Prague today, *to ye škoda*, too bad, I understand, what to do—one night—and tomorrow I won't be—if you could keep going for a good few years then one night won't kill me—here's the museum, a solid building, its lower windows arched, upper ones rectangular, their frames a pleasant ocher against the background of its yellow walls, around it a dark barred fence, the front door stylized, above it an arch with bars in the shape of an open fan, above it, supported by two massive pillars, a gray architrave emblazoned with the Hebrew word in black letters Yizkor—

The steps are broad, easy—once young boys ran here—now it's all full of pictures—drawings—most of them show terrible overcrowding, the twitching movements of abrased people, you called it, yes, I think I can taste a hint, but only when I succeed in forgetting the spacious, well-lit museum hall, drowning in the pictures, portraits of people with prominent Adam's apples and Dubček faces, shriveled women with wild hair, if you're still living here, *maminka*, perhaps you look like this old woman— or that one—a few old clothes with the yellow patch—the star of the Jews, in your words, did you call it that in order to reverse the humiliating decree, next to them two dark suitcases with the transport number written on them in white paint, very like your suitcase, Davidi, but all old suitcases look alike, on the left a list of the people being transported printed on an old typewriter on folio paper one page and then another trapped in a thin ring binder, *ma'avar*, you called the transports, because in Hebrew it apparently sounded less dreadful to you, less real, like a curse word in a foreign language that doesn't burn the mouth, *kibinyamat* or *pizdamat* or *psiakrew cholera jasna*, pictures of people leaving, huddled lines, bowed under heavy bundles, brows without faces, bowed people waiting for food with bowls dangling from their hands, distant people getting into the cattle trucks, huge bundles on their backs, at the forefront of the picture an SS officer from behind, riding breeches, black boots, his hands on his hips, and here a transport coming in, people spilling from the train, looming over them an SS officer, erect in a long coat, his hands in his pockets, legs apart, and here's a theater ticket with a *Sitzplatz*, a seat, a Hebrew-Czech pocket dictionary—flea, bedbug, shift duty, bark tea, secret police, economic police, food for the fastidious—unbelievable, an entrance ticket to the Passover Seder, 1945, bring a spoon and good spirits, and here is one of the decorated carts you wrote about, full of crouching people or bundles, hard to tell, and a room for "prominents," only two beds, checked blankets, crockery hanging from the shelf, a program for *The Marriage of Figaro* printed, apparently, on the same typewriter that printed the list of the transportees, but decorated with arabesques and angels—

I've had enough, I leave, maybe I'll have a look around the town, find the sea-street or the lake-street, from here too it's very close, straight and left, ten minutes walk tops, but I tag along behind the Israeli trio I meet outside the museum, the grandfather, son, and grandson, no, he's the son-in-law, the daughter didn't come, she didn't want to, I gather from their conversation, they're going to see the reconstruction of an inmates' room in the Magdeburg barracks, where the offices of the Jewish "Council of Elders" were located, I keep behind them, in the arched entrance is a tourist shop selling brochures in several languages, tapes, music composed in the ghetto, books on the subject, most of them in German, there's nobody there but what's there to steal? I follow the trio up the stairs, the vaulted roofs like hands rounded to protect, to lull, the stairs are low, easy to climb, the corridors open many windows onto a paved inner courtyard, two bicycle-pushing cloth caps set their mounts between the iron hoops of a parking contraption, sit down on a wooden bench, I return to the corridor, at the end a fat woman in a uniform points wordlessly to an open door where a thick rope prevents entry into the reconstructed room—three tiers of bunks, shelves everywhere, suitcases, hanging clothes, eating utensils, everything crowded, dark, but exploited with a shrewd, Švejkian efficiency, determined to survive. Impossible to go in, of course, impossible, what would happen if every visitor went in and tried to see what it was like to sleep on a bunk where it was impossible to sit up, what it was like to try to reach the suitcase under the pillow, it's so crowded even without people filling the space with bodies and breath and voices and complaints, the three Israelis and I crowd together in the entrance and already there's no room for anyone else to see, they go downstairs, arguing about whether I'm an Israeli or not, I go down behind them, but turn south, from here too you can get to the sea-street or the lake-street, walking along the Hamburg barracks, where you lived *maminka* until the Dutch arrived, here on the left is an opening in the wall, there are railway tracks sunk in the road, built by the inmates of the ghetto to accelerate the transports, the map explains, and if I walk down the road leading outside I shall see, sunk into the double wall opening on this side and that, the morgue on the right and the columbarium on the left—here the wall is almost black, the arched entrances distempered a new, glaring white, calling to the tourist to peep into the poterna—the dark tunnel between the inner and outer wall—this is the place to put the pyxis, in this empty columbarium, but no, it will attract attention, someone will come and pick it up, no, I go out following the arrow on the map to the Jewish cemetery and the crematorium, a big parking lot surrounded by flowering shrubs, a wide path between gigantic poplars, making a sound like the sea, at the end of it the lawn in the tourist brochures with the scattered tombstones and the gray stone menorah, and the white rustic house with the poplars behind it is the crematorium that you built. It's still open. I go inside behind a few American teenagers. The smell almost repulses me, the sooty interior still smells of burning wood, of kerosene, four open iron furnaces, the ashes still at the bottom, the teenagers light memorial candles, I refrain, we don't light candles or believe in pagan superstitions, perhaps I'll bring you here, empty you into one of the furnaces when nobody's looking, why couldn't you die and stay still under a tombstone—Betzer's articled clerk argued with the customs, paid, drove straight to the military cemetery on Mount Herzl to scatter you on Nahum's flower bed, but left me half, only on condition that I found a place for your ashes would I receive my inheritance. I won't do it! I raised my voice, I tried to argue, but Advocate Betzer said, you can decide to scatter them in his garden, what's the problem, believe me, I've seen wills that are a lot worse, you don't have to look after a retarded son until the day he dies, you don't have to cherish thirty Angora cats or wait on two bulldogs hand and foot as if they were princes from the British royal family, just make up your mind, and do it quickly because the local council—the day after Minaleh's funeral the phone calls flew back and forth, twice I postponed the flight and in the meantime Yigal Mossinsohn died, Jacqueline Kennedy Onassis died, Haim Bar-Lev died, Avner Hezkiyahu died, the stars, Adriana was sure of it, the stars were against us, and I decided to go and find a place for you without waiting any longer— maybe this is the place? The trouble is that there are a number of superintendents here following me with suspicious looks—"What did they do with the ashes?" I ask, they explain that they threw them into the river, right, Daddy wrote about it, is the river far? Not far, maybe there, I go out to inspect the terrain, there's a road, grass, flowers, moist, rich soil, it's already evening but the sky's light, the dank smell leads me there, yes, here's the river bank, next to a weeping willow a little tombstone, here, on the silken water to let you sink, fifty years later to join the other dead, what do you say, *for we must needs die, and are as water spilt on the ground that cannot be gathered up again*, so what do you want, why are you so stubborn, Daddy decided to donate his body to science but didn't make the arrangements in time and died suddenly and received a religious funeral and Nahum said Kaddish and you grumbled and protested and tried to disrupt the funeral rites and swore that nobody was going to bury you like that, nobody was going to mumble verses thanking God over your body, you'd had nothing to do with Him for years, so what will you do, asked Nahum and you promised him that you would find some other arrangement; you kept your promise; the other arrangement is me—

I return to Terezin before it gets really dark. Dim lamps light the streets— better lit is the doorway of something between a grocery store and a kiosk, a little cluster of drunks gathered around it, giving off a smell of beer, I can't read the map properly in the lamplight, I ask them the way to Park Hotel, they argue among themselves, *na-prav, na-levo*, to the right, to the left, I'll find it on my own, I go on walking straight ahead, apparently I miss the turning, take a left too late, no, it's not here, it can't be here, the wall's already in front of me, I have to turn right, there's a better lamp here, okay, where's the map, I'm in . . . Seestrasse—here, in one of these little houses you lived—tomorrow—tomorrow morning I'll come back to find out if somebody knows something about you, but not this evening—not now—now I have to go back to the hotel—I have to take a shower—it's already nine o'clock—no, I have time—I can still walk around a bit—the sky is light, only the town is dark—what's this here across the road—the "Sudeten" barracks—here you were brought with your student's father and her brother, ask me, Daddy, I remember, a large, angular building, with identical arched doors giving onto an inner court-yard where a few battered old cars are waiting to be fixed, the Sudeten is a garage today, what is marked on the map as E1 is now called *Náměstí Dukelských Hrdinů*, it's a worldwide hobby, apparently, to change names, to confuse the enemy, to hide the old price tag with a new one, to ex-purgate, like our Talmudic sages did to Judas Maccabaeus, not a word about him, and hardly a word about Bar Kokhba either, who told me if not you, Davidi, and you too changed your name—I return to the street of the lake or the sea, a relatively broad street, it has pavements, benches, trees, it doesn't rate a number on the map, ergo—it had no SS or Czech gendarmes or torture dungeons or storerooms for confiscated baggage, just little houses, I can sit on this bench, even lie down on it, it isn't cold, I could sleep all night here, they won't put me on a charge for going AWOL in the ex-SS hotel—there—my bag will be my pillow. Let them think I'm drunk—who knows me here. The leaves of the trees flicker above me in a cool chiaroscuro and the silence is interrupted only by a brief burst of laughter. I'll sleep here—what the hell—

Someone shakes my shoulder. A representative of the law. Speaks to me in Czech. *Rosumíte mi? Rosumíte mi?* Do you understand me? It's already broad daylight. I slept like a log. *Nerozumím, nerozumím,* I draw up from the depths—I don't understand—he understands me, switches to German, *nerozumím, nerozumím*, I repeat the refrain, *mluvíte anglicky?*—a sudden memory surfaces, *trochu*, he smiles, realizing that I'm a tourist, he speaks a little English, what luck, I'm looking for a woman who lives here, I rummage in my bag, pull the note on which I wrote down your address from my purse, but the policeman doesn't know, doesn't understand, he only repeats the word *zakázáno*, forbidden, it's forbidden to sleep in the street, apparently, *je mi líto*, I'm sorry, he decides to let me off, leads me behind him—to the police station? No, to show me that from here to the museum is straight ahead, I've already been there, *vrely dík*, thank you very much, he lets me go and I retrace my steps—the garage mechanics are already coming to work, sending me looks of who are you, what are you doing here, it's a small place, everybody knows everybody else, I pluck up courage, approach a sympathetic character, "*Můžete mi pomoci?*" can you help me, the forgotten language resurfaces in small, essential chunks, "*Bydli tu Paní Kaplan?*" Does Mrs. Fanny Kaplan live here? I venture, he pulls the corners of his mouth down, "Kaplanova?" I correct myself, one of his mates comes up, a good-looking blond youth, black-toothed, smelling of beer at eight in the morning, an old woman, how do you say an old woman in Czech? "*Babicka*," I try, they look at me blankly, now another man comes up, "*Mluvíte anglicky?*" I take a chance, he smiles in embarrassment, the three of them look at each other, shrug their shoulders, despairing of me, turn back to their work in the "Sudeten" barracks. What do I do now? What I would do at home, knock on a door and ask, it isn't New York here, ask, they'll answer you, if they understand, if they know, I turn to the houses stuck to one another, only the color of the walls and the pattern of the curtains show that inside they're divided into separate apartments, a door opens, a heavy old woman, her hair gathered into a bun, leads out a little dog that has seen better days, she'll surely know, she's from those times, "*Pani, pani, prosím . . .*" but she doesn't turn her head, maybe she's deaf, which leaves me with no alternative but to go into the courtyard and knock on one of the doors. Which one? There are several. It's a small courtyard, with a pail and a bicycle and a ladder and a tin tub and an old boiler and a cat, but the doors are splendid, solid wood, carved as if they were at least the portals to a state bank, a government office, a love palace—a new coat of paint and you could send them straight to Paris, I try to see if there are names, no, there are no names on the doors, so what door should I knock on, I choose the least magnificent, one, two, three, and—

No response. I am emboldened and knock again, loudly. I clench my fist and bang—the inhabitants haven't gone on a Caribbean cruise after all—a neighbor opens the door opposite—"*Co si přejete?*" What do you want, she asks me in a hard voice, a short, shrunken woman, her face furrowed with wrinkles, her scant hair betraying the fact that she was once blonde, her hands roped with veins, she approaches me with her chin up, a faint moustache on her upper lip—"*Co je to?*" What is this, she demands to know, "this" apparently meaning me, how to explain to her that I'm looking for someone who knew Paní Kaplanova, just a minute, maybe she reverted to her old name, Paní Hruzova, how do you say I'm looking for, damn it, "Paní Hruzova," I say, "Paní Hruzova," she comes closer, now she's right next to me, wearing an old floral house dress and a brown cardigan, the apparel of an East European refugee, ugly and practical, "Paní Hruzova," I repeat, breathing into her face, her eyes are blue, filmed with age, "Paní Hruzova," I insist, maybe she's deaf too, maybe slow-witted, maybe she's just trying to remember, "*Jak se jmenujete,*" she wants to know what my name is, she's completely senile, "*Ja turistsa,*" I explain, "*turista from Israel*"—her face clenches in anxiety, she takes two steps backward, "*Odkud?*" she asks in a hoarse voice, in a minute she'll chase me away, "Israel—" I turn away, how to tell her that I came especially to, what the hell, my whole body hurts, I haven't got the energy to go on breaking my teeth on the splinters of Czech filling my mouth, "My *matka*—you understand? You don't understand—anyway *matka* in Hebrew is a bat—people play *matkot* on the beach—click-clock!" I imitate the sound of the bat hitting the ball, accompanied by a swing of my arm, she stares at me—"But what am I talking to you for—you know Paní Do-lohovski? Davidi? Hruzova? Good—we've tried all the possibilities—have a wonderful day *babicka*—" I turn to go, but she grips my arm with stiff fingers, looks at me as if I am about to steal something from her and starts to shout—not at me, at the lady with the dog returning from her walk, she hangs onto me and shouts at her, perhaps telling her to call the police, the little dog barks at me loudly, every bark lifts him a few centi-meters off the ground, perhaps he's getting ready to bite, another neigh-bor opens her door, the one where I knocked and got no response, house-coat, rollers in her hair, stout, cigarette in one hand, looks on with inter-est, I try to free myself, but I haven't got a hope, all three old women pounce on me, surround me, grab me, they want to rob me, *pomoc*! Help! How much money have I got in my purse, the first old woman pulls me by the sleeve and the other two push me from behind so that we all burst inside in one bunch, a tiny parlor, dark brown, heavy furniture, plastic gladiolas in a cut glass vase, they seat me on a hard chair, what do they want, the first old woman lets go of me at last, the owner of the dog seats her opposite me, the dog stays outside, she stands behind her, the smoker behind me as if to make sure that I don't escape, they consult each other above our heads, "*pás*," they chorus, what's *pás*, a mispronunciation of the English "peace" or a pass, like in the army, I don't believe it, maybe they're three madwomen, "*pás*," they point to the shoulder bag hugged to my body, just a minute, perhaps it's short for passport, I pull out my pass-port, put it on the table between me and the first old woman, who gives me hard, penetrating looks, waiting for them to open it, the wrong way around of course, they reach the end, realize that it's the beginning, stare at my ten-year-old photograph, approach the one sitting opposite me, apparently the intellectual of the group, indeed, she asks for *brýle*, glasses, I know even before the dog owner brings them from the adjacent room, hands them to her, she puts them on and sternly inspects my passport, old habits die hard, perhaps this is the way she behaved when she was in the KGB. "Loya Kaplan," she reads my name slowly, I nod, my passport trembles in her hands, "Lo-ya Kap-lan," she repeats, her mouth bubbles, her lips pout and purse, trembling at the corners, and pout again, as if something is about to burst out but is suppressed, swallowed, she chews my name in, okay, enough is enough, the interrogation is over, I stand up, hold out my hand for my passport, if she doesn't give it up willingly I'll snatch it from her hand, how much strength can she have, "*prosím,*" please, I say in a tough voice, but she shakes her head in alarm, waves her glasses at me, "*prosím, prosím,*" the familiar iron "r" comes not from her mouth but from the mouth of her neighbor stationed behind her, who also stretches out her hand to me, says something very long, very excited, in which the word Israel keeps on coming up, okay, the Holy Land, I understand, the old woman behind me presses her hand on my shoulder to make me sit down again, I sit down but go on stretching out a demanding hand for my passport trembling in the hands of the mistress of the house, still chewing tears or anger or both, and the one behind her points at her and says while waving her finger from her head to mine, "Hruzova, Paní Hruzova," what is she talking about, now she points at the balding head of the mistress of the house who is still holding my passport, it's not possible, it's simply not possible—"*Maminka?*" I can feel my lips trembling, the old woman stands up, is she my mother, the height's the same, the hair once blonde, very straight, the blue eyes, now she's coming to embrace me, circumventing the little table, pushing the neighbor aside, shall I stand up to meet her, but my knees are turned to water, my feet are frozen, my mouth dry, she makes a sign with her hand, a kind of just-hang-on or you'll-see-soon or wait-a-minute, "*Počkejte chvíli,*" the dog owner confirms my third conjecture, Pani Hrozova goes into the next room, followed by the dog owner, it could definitely be a coincidence—if the name is as common as Kaplan or Davidi—and perhaps she's my aunt, the wife of that gendarme who smuggled baby Nahum out, I try to get up, but the fat neighbor's hands are heavy on my shoulders, "*počkejte, počkejte,*" wait, wait, it's not every day that a drama like this comes their way here, the two of them return together, the old woman has a photograph album in her hands, I breathe a sigh of relief, she removes the fat woman stationed behind me with her hands on my shoulders from her place, passes the album over my head and sets it on the table, her meager breasts brushing against my hair, opens it, her arms over my shoulders, I have to bow my head, her chin rests on my head, a crooked finger hits an old, grayish snapshot, hiding it from me, the fat woman with the rollers, opposite me now, protests, bends down and removes the pointing hand and exposes to my eyes a photograph of myself I don't remember—I never had my hair done like that either—from behind me, behind my back, the old woman says something, her hands abandon the photograph, are gathered up from the table, trap my face in cold talon fingers, she talks and the neighbor looking from my trapped face to the photograph nods, yes, very like, my mother sobs dryly into my hair, my head between her hands, afterwards my shoulders, her grip is spastic, painful, like the grip of the dead on a last letter, on a flag, sometimes you have to actually break their fingers, she leans on me from behind, the back of the chair between my back and her stomach, her head weighing on my head, I can't see her face, nor can I turn to face her, I'm between the chair and the table and she's behind me, the neighbor watching the spectacle moves from her place, pulling the chair against which she has been leaning her stomach with her, dragging it up to the woman weeping on my head, reaching out and seating her next to me— and still I cannot see her face—she buries it in a big man's handkerchief—When she looks at me the tears are already behind her: the rims of her eyes are red, the tip of her nose is red, but she peers at me curiously, eager to know everything about me, now, immediately, forty-four years in five minutes. She leans an elbow on the table, her cheek on her hand, looking at me with one eye almost like a hoopoe bird, in a moment she will turn her other eye towards me, her other hand cuffing my wrist, she asks me something, but what, "*Sprechen sie Deutsch*?" the neighbor asks, I shake my head, and the old woman tightens her grip and repeats her questions, "*můj syn, můj syn*," my son, I hazard a guess, she's asking about Nahum. "*Dead*," I say in English, "*muerto*" I add in Spanish, "*toit*" maybe it's like in Yiddish, "*kaput*"—she understands, her grip on my wrist tightens, her lips pout to stop the tears, purse, and pout again, "*kdy*?" she finally asks, when, I make a sign with my free hand to ask for a pen, the fat woman with the rollers hurries to bring a little pad and a pencil, I write down 5.3.1980, and immediately regret it, there was no war in that year and how can I explain his death to her, her head is tilted to the side, almost parallel to her shoulder, and she demands answers, am I my brother's keeper, mommy, he died in an airplane accident, fell into the Sea of Galilee, don't look at me like that, there's a whole squadron down there, "*accident*," I say, hoping that she understands a few words in English, she purses her mouth, nods stiffly, goes on asking about *syn, dcera*, son, daughter, apparently she wants to know if I'm married, if she has grandchildren, no, I shake my head, and now she asks about Dolohovski, I write the date of his death down on the little pad, 5.8.93, I say "*kaput*" twice, to be on the safe side, she nods, she understands, quick on the uptake, looks at me with a hungry, aggressive gaze, as if she wants to suck all the information about me and my life out of me, but has no means of doing so. How did I fail to notice the neighbor with the dog, going out and coming back again, the dog in her arms, so he wouldn't, heaven forbid, miss the excitement, behind them a young woman, apparently her granddaughter, speaking basic English, glad of a chance to practice, to explain to me that yes, this is my mother, she was rearrested at the end of '68, and only released in 1990, she was in hospital for two years, but now she's all right, she came back to live in her family home, she even wanted to go to Israel, she always talked about having a son and a daughter there, but she didn't have the money for the trip, the young woman speaks, faltering a little, searching for words, accompanying her speech with gestures to fill in what's missing, my mother watches her with an eagle eye, occasionally interrupting the translation, protesting, so she does understand something, when the translation satisfies her she nods vigorously, my wrist still trapped in her hand, and in the meantime the table fills with homemade jams, cheese, salami, sausages in a brown gravy, they pour me a cup of coffee, cut a fresh poppy-seed cake, the photograph album is removed, the table is cleared, the woman with the rollers administers a light slap to the freckled back of her hand to make her let go of me, you see, now there's room, she says, apparently, my mother lets go of my wrist, but leaves a red mark on the skin, sees it, snickers in embarrassment, tries to rub it off, to stroke me, her palm is coarse as sandpaper, her friend banishes the gesture from the table, to make room for black bread, dense country bread with a sour smell, "*chléb*," I try to please her with what I remember, "*mléko*," I point to the milk, "*palačinky*," because the dog owner has brought pancakes too, my mother nods, confirms, begins to drink her coffee before the neighbors pull up chairs to join the feast, she's the queen here, that's obvious, the granddaughter hurried out to bring an extra chair from her grandmother's house, there's only four chairs here—

The five of us sit squeezed together around the round table; I am no less hungry than the woman sitting opposite me. Squeezed in between us is the translator—a tall, athletic, pretty young girl with bronzed skin and auburn hair—now she eats too, also the dog, a Pekingese, I think, thrusts his squashed face into the circle and gets his share, my mother eats and talks rapidly, chokes, coughs, the woman with the rollers gets up quickly to pat her on the back, should I have done it, perhaps, but I can't move, my knees have given up the ghost, how I'm going to leave here I have no idea, my mother starts talking again, she doesn't wait for a translation, the young girl between us glances at me, she can't keep up with the pace, understands too, like me, that it's more important for the speaker to speak than to be understood. I eat, occasionally raising my head and nodding, so she'll think I understand, I imagine she's telling me about her life history, perhaps about her long imprisonment, twice over, perhaps about the time in the ghetto, perhaps about her decision to leave on the first of May, I try to catch key words, coordinates, but this language is like no other, and she's still talking, the neighbors crowded elbow to elbow shift uneasily in their chairs, what is she saying, I whisper to our translator, she hesitates, looks around, searching for the right words to sum up the nonstop flow into a sentence or two, in the end she shrugs her shoulders, I understand, imprisonment and then imprisonment again, how many years was this woman in prison, from 1950 to '68, from '68 to '90, forty years, not counting Terezin and the two years in hospital, I smile at her but she glares at me, now she keeps repeating "Israel," am I getting a lecture, presumably so, the neighbor with the rollers stands up, strokes her shoulder in a mollifying movement, trying to calm her down, opens the dresser in the corner, takes out a bottle of Slivovitz, pours it into five different glasses—"*na zdraví!*"—I fetched my suitcase from the hotel. Tonight I'm sleeping at her place. The moment she opens the door I recognize the smell filling the little apartment, the smell of old mold to which is now added that of potatoes and cabbage, she's standing at the stove and cooking, wearing an old tracksuit, over it a knitted cardigan, she's very thin, she smiles at me and talks, gestures towards the other room, I push the suitcase there, how dark it is in her house, this is the bedroom, a high bed dominates it, pregnant with pillows and quilts, and next to it an army cot—canvas on crossed legs—I put my suitcase with the pyxis on it—don't worry, Davidi, I'm not leaving you here—

I want to take a shower. How do you say to take a shower—I return to the kitchenette—a little cooking alcove separated from the parlor by a dresser—and try to explain by pantomime, scrubbing my clothes with a clenched fist, raising a hand with spread fingers over my head and saying tshhhhhhh, does she understand? I'm not sure, her eyes are on the pots and with her hand she makes a dismissive gesture, "*neteče horká voda*," she says, she didn't understand what I want, "*douche, touche, doucha, shower . . .*" I try, but she repeats "*neteče horká voda*" almost angrily, I decide not to ask any more, I'll simply go to the shower and turn on the water, a miniature bathroom, the toilet separated from the shower by a white plastic curtain with a pattern of bluebells, the toilet lid is covered with synthetic blue fur, the shelf below the little mirror is blue too, everything very clean, betraying a bourgeois aspiration, like the plastic gladiolas in the cut glass vase now moved to the window sill, here the dank smell is almost suffocating, as if the river is gurgling and rising, dark and viscous, in all the pipes, in the arteries of the faded electricity, I get undressed, pile my clothes on top of the toilet lid, open the hot water tap, needles of frozen glass burst out of the shower head in the ceiling, shatter into stinging splinters at my feet, I'd forgotten how cold the water can be abroad, but I opened the hot water, I wait and wait, "*neteče horká voda*"—she's standing in the door and contemplating my nakedness, there's no hot water, the penny drops at last, damn it all, there's no hot water and she's standing and contemplating my nakedness, her hand on her hip, abruptly I enter the stream of icy water—the cold is truly alarming—I'll have a heart attack here—my pulse is racing—where does she keep the soap, here it is, a broken old piece, I turn the water off, try to soap myself, her hand draws the bluebell curtain aside and she stands there, looking at me with an amused smile, "*to nevade, to nevade*," never mind, she says to me, after everything she's been through what have I got to complain about, and she turns around and returns to the kitchen, no point in asking her for a hair dryer, and a towel, how do you say towel, but she's left me a grayish towel on top of my clothes, I make haste to dry myself, go to the room, take a comfortable tracksuit and slippers out of my suitcase, so she won't feel as if a capitalist relative has come to visit her—

The two of us, face to face. Is this what I'll look like in thirty years' time? Her face seamed with wrinkles, her eyes pink-rimmed like Nahum's, her hair straight, a dirty yellow, tied back in a kind of skinny rat's tail, revealing a pink scalp—"All these years I thought that you were dead," I say to her, she nods, now I'm the one doing the talking and she's listening, her eyes fixed on me, but what does she understand, "I thought you were dead," I say to her, "how could you go off and leave two small children like that," I call her to account, "and for what?" I tell her about

Nahum and me in Eilat, I have to get it out once and for all, and who's to blame if not you, I conclude and she nods, agreeing with everything I have to tell, to tell, to tell, I tell her about Daddy, about Davidi, about the will, enjoying her patient silence until I notice that her head's bobbing, she's fallen asleep—

I clear the dishes off the table. The meal was heavy, sticky, too salty. I wash up with cold water in the little sink. Go back to the parlor. Still sleeping. You have a mother, I say to myself, contemplating her, able to see the likeness between us, and actually finding it off-putting, almost repellent—she sleeps with her head sagging to her chest, her hands folded, snoring faintly, and I sit opposite her and try to feel something flow—warmth—closeness—compassion—tenderness—but there's nothing—I'm dry, shrivelled up, rolled into myself like an old parchment scroll, it's only in telenovelas and American soap operas that mothers and daughters who haven't seen each other for forty-four years fall on each other's necks, kiss, cry, caress, become best friends in five minutes, go out together shopping—cooking—the mother teaches the daughter how much salt to put in and how much flour and to take the eggs out of the fridge an hour before beating them, the daughter takes the mother to a movie from the forties—they both visit some grave or other—a father or lover or little sister who died young—and put flowers on the grave— they go to the zoo together, to a cafe, meet my mother, the daughter says to her friends—she shifts in her seat—in a minute she'll wake up—and I—what will I say to her—I thought I would find a grave or an urn with ashes, but here you are, thin but alive, independent, cooking for yourself, shopping, washing, bossing the neighbors, you can go on like this for another twenty years—so what shall we do? Bring you to Israel? Leave you here?

In the evening the neighbors return with reinforcements—another neighbor woman with her husband and daughter—she speaks English quite well—and again we all sit around the table—it opens out—it's a meter longer than before—they moved the dresser, the sofa too—Paní

Hruzova spread a festive, embroidered tablecloth—it's easier for me to think of her as Paní Hruzova—the conversation flows in Czech. The neighbors' daughter—thirtysomething—talks to me in English, is excited to hear that I was a flight attendant, she wanted to be one too, once, Paní Hruzova, she tells me about my mother as if she were a local attraction, gets a government pension, this is the moment to put out feelers, to sneak a fantastic possibility into the conversation, I thought of bringing her to live with me in Israel, I say, why should you, Antka shoots a glance at the national heroine, what does she lack for here, and over there in Israel it's so hot, and dangerous, wars all the time, and she's not young any more, Paní Hruzova, how old are you, she asks my mother who's stirring the salad, translates her answer to me, seventy-five, would you like to go with your daughter to Israel? She glances at me as if to say, I'm only asking to show you I was right, there you are, listen to the answer, God forbid, she says, no, she's not going anywhere, this is the house she was born in and this is the house she'll die in, Antka translates almost simultaneously for my benefit, but she hopes you'll come to visit her more often—

The guests leave. My first and last night with my mother. She switches on the light—a naked electric bulb—in the bedroom, takes bedclothes out of the heavy wardrobe—makes up my bed on the army cot—and I stand idle and look around me. In one wall a window overlooking the inner court. On another a large framed photograph—I go closer to make sure that it's not Daddy and not Davidi, it's a strange man; her father? Her brother? Another lover? The man is bespectacled, sharp, aged between forty and fifty; she sees me looking, tries to explain who it is, but I can't understand. Above her bed is a small iron cross—I stretch out my hand to it—is it hers? Has she become religious?—She notices my gesture, smiles, nods, says something, I don't understand—

Now she's in bed and I'm on the stretcher. She looks at me over the mountainous featherbed, takes her teeth out of her mouth and ages abruptly by twenty years. She puts them in a glass half-full of water on the chest standing between us. "*Dobrou noc,*" she says, smiling a witch's smile. "*Lilah tov,*" I wish her good night in Hebrew, and to my surprise she responds "*Lilah tov,*" and switches off the light and sentences us to darkness.

Dark dark dark dark. The stretcher creaks horribly underneath me—the blanket allocated me—a heavy woolen blanket smelling of naphthalene, the air around me is thick, dank, the sounds of the night are different, she sighs—in her sleep? Not in her sleep?—turns over, sighs again, coughs, I forgot how awful it is to sleep with somebody else in the room, she breathes deeply, and what if she dies on me here in the night because of all the excitement, nonsense, she's made of iron, this woman, she'll sleep tonight like a baby and wake up tomorrow like new—and only I'll put my back out for good; yesterday on the bench—today on a stretcher—I—

Fell asleep like a stone in mighty waters.

The first thing I see is the milky window. Morning. Morning already. Where am I? It takes me a minute to interrogate the walls. The cross has been removed—when?—no doubt because of me. She's not stupid or senile—she's not in her bed—where is she—what's the time—a quarter past ten, I don't believe it—I really did sleep like a stone—but in the window the light looks more like six, half seven—Daddy sometimes used that expression—maybe a word-for-word translation from the Czech—where is she?

From the kitchen comes a soft hiss of gas, water bubbling in an old kettle, she's wearing a shabby quilted robe, working silently, chopping up, stirring something, "*Dobré ráno,*" I surprise her, she turns around, smiles, her teeth, thank God, are in her mouth, "*Boker tov,*" she says in Hebrew, suddenly filling me with alarm, she's going to want me to stay here, teach her Hebrew, in six months she'll learn the language, come home with me, my gift for languages apparently comes from her, what else comes from her, what difference does it make, in any case it's a lost cause, I sit down to eat, struggling with *palačinky* swimming in a pool of butter so as not to hurt her feelings, feeling as if I've swallowed concrete—

Afterwards we go out into the street. She tries to explain something to me about her time in the ghetto, consults the map in my hand, leads me to the Vrchlabi barracks where the central hospital was situated, she worked there, I know, but she doesn't know that I know, or perhaps she thinks that Daddy told me, why not, she leads me to Prazska Street—presumably Prague—stops at the corner of Prazska and Komenskeho, points to a building and says "*knihovna*," I have no idea what she means, the map here is mute, we walk south, pass the park named after Smetana, turn right, the wall is already in front of us, she points to a blocked up arched opening in the wall, says, "Gas, gas," presumably meaning something else, there were no gas chambers in Terezin, now we return to the street of the lake, walk past her house, turn left in the direction of the main square, she points to a big junk shop, we go in, old china dishes, chamber pots, blackened silver spoons, military medals, threadbare velvet cloths with gold tassels that have gone green, a baby's bottle, a punctured football, suitcases with straps around them, presiding over the goods a red-faced giant who exchanges a few words with her in German, it isn't clear to me why we have come in here, according to the map a cafe was opened here in December, 1942, people sat here drinking a murky beverage and listening to an excellent jazz ensemble, here, instead of all this pathetic junk, records without jackets, corsets, binoculars blind in one eye, third-hand towels and tablecloths, a bronze teaspoon, sailor buttons, I leave the national heroine with the Nazi and go outside, turn back in the direction of her apartment, in half an hour the bus stops here and I'm not staying even one day longer—

The day is dull. The sky low, layer upon layer of gray clouds filtering a sour, unchanging sunlight. She accompanies me to the bus stop. If I read her correctly, she's relieved I'm leaving—perhaps she was afraid I would choose to stay and sleep on the army cot next to her or insist on taking her back with me—this time she's wearing a narrow blue skirt, a pink blouse, clothes from the sixties but the height of elegance for her, I drag the trolley behind me, the pyxis inside my suitcase, we're going home, Davidi, I'm not leaving you here—

From the dog-owning neighbor's house we called the AXA Hotel in Prague and I took a room for three nights, until the next direct flight to Tel Aviv—perhaps I'll tour Prague—Prague is very beautiful, Daddy once told me, even more beautiful than Paris—

We stand at the bus stop next to a leafy tree. She glances at her watch—an old men's watch—perhaps it belonged to the bespectacled man in the photograph on the wall of her bedroom—she raises her eyes and gives me a smile of it'll be here soon, you needn't worry, you're not staying here, I smile back at her, the silence between us is embarrassing, but we don't have a common language, and if we had, what would she say to me, she's trying to give me something now, rummaging in her bag, perhaps she's only taking out a handkerchief or cigarettes, no, she takes out an envelope, another letter? No, the envelope is heavy, it holds something that isn't paper, a piece of jewelry, perhaps a brooch, I start to tear the flap of the envelope, but she—how strong she is—grips my hand, preventing me, later, I understand, when I'm by myself, when she's not there, okay, here comes the bus, before me a middle-aged man gets in, a young boy, then me, a brief, stiff embrace in parting, and I'm already on the bus, paying the driver and going inside to choose a seat, the bus starts to move and I see her so small next to the enormous tree, waving with her right hand, turning to go—

She doesn't even wait for the bus to leave the station—

I turn my head to see more—but the tree hides—then the houses—the bus turns, we're already in another street—already on the main road—it's not Terezin any more—

And she didn't even give me a single kiss.

Nor did I give her one.

Now let's see what she did give me. The envelope is heavy, it contains a round flat object, apparently a brooch or a medallion, no, it's an old medal, her medal for heroism, apparently, brown, almost black, on one side an inscription in Czech, on the other a relief of what, I angle it opposite the light and discover three glorious heroes in the Soviet style, if she was awarded a medal how come they put her in prison, perhaps that's what she was trying to explain to me and I didn't understand, I can ask Avi as soon as I get back, he can ask his assistant, she can ask her father, an ex-prisoner of Zion, all the world is one small village, here are the three Israelis too, "Shalom," I surprise them, no, the son turns to his father with a triumphant look, "I told you she's an Israeli"—

Not far from the bus station is the AXA Hotel: the lobby's tiny, not even the big mirror can deceive the eye, the lift is old, leading to my room is a long, gloomy corridor, straight and then sharp left then straight ahead and sharp left again, the long narrow lobby showed no evidence of these intestines, a dark khaki carpet, dim lamps, an occasional rectangular window, covered with a flimsy curtain letting in a depressing gray light, overlooking, I draw one of the curtains aside, another building, very close, here's my room, it's tiny, the bed is squeezed into the angle between the walls, the window looks onto a low roof and above it a building, not a scrap of sky, I feel I have no air to breathe but I'll be all right in a minute, the bathroom's clean, I've been in worse places, I hope they have hot water here, I'm going to have a good scrub and then lie down to sleep—

Sleep? How can I sleep, I'm almost suffocating, I'm burning up, I have no air, I need to go to the bathroom, my stomach's in a turmoil, I'm in a cold sweat, I must have caught a bug, what to do, drink, first of all drink a lot, but the water tastes of sickness, of nausea, and that window—I'll ask them to change my room, and in the meantime I'll sleep, and again I wake up, neither night nor day, the sheet around me is damp and crumpled, and my neck—my neck's stiff—I can barely turn my head—maybe a hot shower, boiling hot, will thaw the muscles cramped on her army cot—and if that doesn't help—I'll have to call a doctor—how the hell do I ring reception—

Two weeks in a hospital in Prague. What did I have? To this minute they're not sure, perhaps meningitis and perhaps not, the main thing is it's over, the tests are all okay, you can get on a plane, when you get home go and see your doctor—

On the plane I find my seat and sleep like a stone. A flight attendant wakes me after the landing. "Do you feel all right?" I nod, join the rest of the passengers on the bus shuttling us to passport control—with cramped muscles I drag myself to the taxi rank, fall onto the back seat, ask for the block, all I want is to be home, the light in the windows is molten fire, the driver turns his head, asks if I want to go via the new intersection or by the old road, no, because you know some people prefer the old road, it's longer but there are less traffic jams, so it works out shorter in the end, you have to think about the time too, not only the distance counts, who am I to argue with an Israeli cab driver, I say, "Take the old road," and change my mind three minutes later, "no, you know what, go to Hadera"—the driver turns a dark head crowed with thick gray hair—"Hadera? That's the opposite direction . . ."—"I know, go to Hadera." I try to sound decisive and sink into the seat, the heat is sickening, a blazing wind is blowing through the window. "Could you put the air-conditioning on please?" The driver laughs, "What do you think, if I had it I wouldn't put it on? It's kaput, lady, kaput, yesterday they promised to bring me a new one," he peers at me in the mirror. "Are you hot?—Never mind, how did people live here before they invented air-conditioning, mother and father and five children in one tin hut in the transit camp and believe me, we didn't complain like they do today, my kids won't walk one yard by foot, Daddy take me here, bring me there, they won't even go by bike, they're hot, they're cold, I'm telling you, if we were like them in the forties we wouldn't have stood a chance, we wouldn't have had a state today, but the people were different then—my father, your father, made us a state—and now we can't live without air-conditioning, isn't that so?" He drives calmly, talks, glances at me from time to time, "If you like we can stop and I'll buy you a cold drink—on me—because of not having air-conditioning—you look to me like you're really hot, just say the word and I'll stop, your face is red like fire, what can I tell you, the Ashkenazis, living here isn't for them—"

he glances at me in the mirror, cocks his head, smiles. "Don't call me a racist, but hand on my heart, you little immigrants, you *vuzvuzim*—this place isn't for you, the sun kills you and you don't know how to talk to the Arabs—believe me, the best thing would be if we had a Sephardi Prime Minister, then there'll be peace, not a minute before . . ." I sink further into the seat, in a minute I'll evaporate—open my eyes to "Lady, lady, what's wrong with you?" and a small bottle of mineral water, we're parked next to open stalls selling fruit, sunflower seeds, teddy bears, wicker furniture. "We've arrived in Hadera," the driver's standing outside the car, the door's open, he's drinking Cola standing up, "drink, drink, now tell me where in Hadera you want to go." I look around, no, it's not here, it's further north. "Drive further north," I request, the driver wipes his mouth and gets back in the car, "Further north? Where further north? The Palyam junction? Or Akiva? The Binyamina junction?" "Or Akiva!" I hazard a guess, it makes sense, he came ashore not far from Caesarea, was caught, sat in jail for a few years, was tortured to death. I sit up tensely, "Drive slowly," searching, everything has changed so much but nevertheless, the curve of a ridge, a ruin, no, I can't recognize it. "This is Or Akiva!" the driver announces, already, so close? "Should I turn in?" I nod. He turns west, drives along a tarred road, no, this isn't it, and the trees lining it too, no, so where was it, we enter a built up area very reminiscent of the State, two-story apartment blocks, neglected yards, torn newspapers and empty plastic bottles blown about in the wind coming from the sea, I don't re-member all these buildings, and there, what's that over there, grassy sand dunes at the end of the street, "What's that over there?" "Over there? The new Haifa-Tel Aviv road—the autostrada"—"So we can't get to the sea from here?" "We'll find the sea soon enough"—he gives me a twinkling look, challenged, turns the wheel, "just tell me where you want to go—the meter's ticking," he drives comfortably, slows down, sticks his head out of the window, asks one of the residents the way to the sea, straight ahead and right, they reply, and he drives, the buildings change, snow-white vil-las, an open two-lane road. "This here's the new Or Akiva," he explains, "once I thought of buying a villa here—ask me why—" but I don't ask, I sit on the edge of the seat, the wind from the sea is salty, soothing, soon I'll see, soon we'll be there, but no, we're in—what's this? Caesarea? We're already in Caesarea? Cars cram the parking lot, tourist buses, the reconstructed moat, white in the light. "Drive a little further, a little further—" I request and he goes on driving slowly, "This is already Kibbutz Sdot-Yam," he announces, "Hannah Szenes' kibbutz," I say, knowing that it wasn't here, but it was somewhere near here, the driver stops the cab in a parking lot. "There's a way down to the sea there—" he points to a little tourist building at the side of which there is indeed a path descending to the sea, "go down there—I'll wait here, I'm not going anywhere—"

I go down to the sea along a path sunk between artificial hills held in a kind of plastic netting, with a fleshy creeping plant peeping through its diamond-shaped gaps, it will have purple flowers, I know, and here's the sea, here's the sea, silver crests savagely torn apart, between them blue-green dulling for a second and immediately flashing into a chain of daggers, one moment a patina under white skies and the next segments of hard light and a glaze on top of deep water ceaselessly moving, sending me shallow, transparent waves, frothing to the narrow strip of beach widening to the south, hemmed in by giant smokestacks, and to the north, very close, a few limestone rocks clinging to the remains of a wall—here? Was it here? Once we could climb from here, run down the slope of the remains of the Roman amphitheater, Nahum already charging up the seats again, you two behind him, and only I on the stage below, alone, cupping my hands to my mouth to test the acoustics—Do you hear me? Do you hear me? But now they've built a concentration-camp fence here; concrete pillars bent like hooks, barbed wire between them, all that's missing are watch towers, dogs, stop it, stop it, look at the sea—here's the sea—much bigger from here, broader, hammered flat, all flickering tin, catching fire, melting, dying down, from there the wind comes to salt my face, and there's the horizon and here's a ship? I can't see, the horizon is a fiery thread, I climb down, holding onto the jagged bits of rock growing out of a few broken down rows of hewn stones eroded by the sea and the wind, here, here was the city of Bethar, here the blood flowed from the grilles and embrasures, rushing down and rolling the stones of this wall out to sea to a distance of four miles, a mighty city, hundreds of thousands of inhabitants, Bar Kokhba's Tel Aviv, twenty-four thousand warriors set out from it to conquer Caesarea, but were routed in battle, the city was destroyed and the sand and the sea finished the job: even the ruins are lost, *etiam periere ruinae.*

I'll leave you here—in the Bethar of the ancient maps—among the broken bits of marble—would you believe it?—after all these years they still peep from the sand, planed and smoothed by the sea, looking like bits of soap, next to them potsherds, still rough to the touch, but if there was ever anything on them—a name or engraving or relief—it's all been eroded, obliterated, lost, among the few shells here's a little lump of copper, an arrowhead warped and corroded, a war was fought here, without the shadow of a doubt, here Elazar ben Harsom anchored his ships—double agent = informer (?) you asked in big green letters in the margins of your notes, and perhaps Bar Kokhba's relation, ally and rival—Bar Kokhba killed him (?) you didn't believe it, the Talmudic version!! you rejected it aggressively, yes, this is the place—I return to the waiting taxi, signal the driver, a little longer, take the pyxis out of the suitcase and go down to the sea again; the sea—rippling silver muscles and sinews of green fire—the sky above it black with light—with my eyes closed I open the pyxis and tilt it and scatter your remains to the winds—

When I return to the taxi, the driver is drumming on the steering wheel and singing to himself: "*A modest man was Rabbi Akiva, a shepherd was he in the fields.*" He sees me and smiles at me. "Are you done?" I nod, and sit down with my feet outside the door, trying to scrape off the muck sticking to my shoes, "Leave it, it doesn't matter—tomorrow I'm going to clean the car," he turns to face me but suddenly his radio—"Yes, Akiva here—yes, I hear—I hear you—are we off?"—He turns to get my consent, starts the car and moves out of the parking lot, "You know who Rabbi Akiva was?" He starts driving back the way we came, "*Kol de'avid Rahmana—l'tov avid,*" he quotes the Aramaic, pleased with himself but without taking his eyes off the road. "That's something that is," he turns right, "everything God does—he does for the good," he glances at me in the mirror, his eyes black olives, twinkling: "Everything is for the good!—even when we think, what a rotten deal, why is he doing this to us, why do we deserve it—he means it for the good, you understand what I'm saying? In the end we see too that everything works out for the good—isn't that so?" I lean back in the seat, feel obliged to protest, "I don't altogether agree with that approach," I choose a low profile, I'm utterly exhausted. "Let me give you an example," the taxi driver is full of renewed energy, ready and willing to embark on a theological debate, "take this fare of yours—I didn't want to take it—I thought, she'll want Tel Aviv, and to tell the truth, I don't go to Tel Aviv—it doesn't pay, not with all those traffic jams and that—I didn't want to take you—I wanted to change with Moshe—but then again—I said to myself, it's your turn, take her, I took you, and see how much we've already got on the meter—" he shows me—342 lit up in red, "the truth? I had a feeling about you—the minute we started driving I saw you were looking for somewhere, and me—I've got a sense—" the radio interrupts him, he responds only with "yes," "no," and "I heard you," and makes haste to get back to his lecture: "'*Things concealed from human beings—Rabbi Akiva revealed*'—and I—why did I want a house in Or Akiva? Because me, I'm called Akiva—after my grandfather's grandfather, of blessed and righteous memory, and this grandfather—not Akiva, his grandson—he taught me Talmud—every morning before school, he put some verse in my mouth, '*Lovely is man created in the image*'—you understand? It means the image of God—" "Perhaps we could retouch God from the picture—" I ask, there's a limit to what I'm prepared to swallow during the miles stretching from here to my house—"Retouch? What do you mean, retouch?" he peers over his shoulder at me, turns back to the wheel, "Erase—cut out—" I say from a parched palate, "remove him from the picture—" I hope this will shut him up, but he raises his shoulders, "Ahaaa . . . you're one of those secular yuppie types, believe me, it doesn't frighten me, I'm secular too, you see, no skullcap, but what's that got to do with God, everybody believes in God, and if anybody tells you he doesn't, don't believe him, he's lying, believe me, once I took this professor to Jerusalem, a man with brains, he told me that even Einstein believed in God—you don't believe?" he examines my face in the mirror, "You don't believe—it's up to you—'*All is foreseen but free choice is given*'—where do you want to go now? Where you wanted to go in the beginning? It'll take us longer now, you want to go via the new intersection or take the old road? No, because you know, some people prefer the old road in peak hours, every day there's more traffic on the roads, the whole country's blocked, choked—"

It's nearly evening. The sky's transparent, greenish. The trees—carbon-copy silhouettes. My head's burning. If I don't drink soon I'll die. "Left," I direct the driver impatiently, "and here right stop here—that's it—" "Four hundred and fifty-seven!" he announces triumphantly. "Before or after the common era?" I ask—"Whatever you like, lady, the tip's optional—" "If it's B.C. it comes out at the beginning of the Second Temple—" I get out of the taxi, hand him five hundred shekel, "that's okay. Keep the change"— and shalom-shalom, and thankyou-thankyou—and "If you ever want a trip like that again, no problem, here's my card, just give me a ring, I'll take you to Eilat via Metulla—"

So, I've arrived, the suitcase is a lot lighter, but it's pitch dark, why aren't the street lamps on, and what's this, what's this here in the garden, on the scar in the ground a huge tractor, with a giant shovel sticking out in front of it, yes, it's a tractor, the street lamp blinks and goes on, spills yellow light on it, who the hell put a tractor in my garden, I hurry to the house, but it's boarded up with criss-crossed planks, there's a note or letter nailed to them with a big nail, a notice from the council, but how can I read it in the dark, maybe if I stand under the street lamp, but first to drink, first of all to drink, I hurry to the garden faucet, disconnect the hose from its mouth and turn its head which responds easily, it's grown used to me, but its mouth isn't even damp, not even a single drop is hiding in its throat, it's absolutely dry, arid iron, and its head turns easily, turns on empty until it sticks and I hear the sound the pipes make at the end of the water khkhkhrrrrrrrrr—

TRANSLATOR'S NOTES

p. 13   KaKaL: Keren Kayement LeIsrael, the Jewish National Fund; TAR-SAT: the Hebrew year 1909, when the city of Tel Aviv was established; MALAL: Moshe Leib Lilienblum, Hebrew writer; YALAG: Yehuda Leib Gordon, Hebrew poet.

p. 15   Fourteenth Street . . . avenge his blood: The Hebrew letters *He, Yod, Dalet* are an acronym for "May the Lord avenge his blood," and may also mean "the fourteenth," with the letters *Yod* and *Dalet* used as numerals.

p. 31   *Loyot ma'aseh morad*: The meaning is obscure; the King James Bible gives "certain additions made of thin work," and the Cambridge and Oxford New English Bible gives "fillets of hammered work of spiral design"; *loya* is generally held to be a guilloche, or spiral design.

p. 92   Palmach: Striking force of the Hagana, precursor of the IDF before the establishment of the state.

p. 123   *Po: Nes gadol haya po* (There was a great miracle here), the words written around the four sides of the dreidel, with *Po* meaning "here."

p. 125   Bar Kokhba: The reference is to the bonfires lit on the holiday of Lag Ba'Omer to symbolize the smoke signals sent by the fighters in the revolt led by Bar Kokhba against the Romans.

p. 126   Bar Koziva: Derogatory turn given to the name Bar Koseva based on a punning allusion to the Hebrew *kazav*—a lie.

p. 139   "With the mole I struggled from darkness, stubborn and under a spell" and "My every thought besieged you—the hairs of my head upright": From the poem "The Mole" by Nathan Alterman, translated by Robert Friend.

p. 160   A trial: The Slansky trial held in Prague in 1952, first of a series of anti-Semitic show trials in which prominent Jewish Communist leaders such as Rudolf Slansky were accused of conspiracy against the state and connections with the Zionist movement, which was accused of espionage and subversion in the Communist countries. Mordechai Oren, a left-wing politician and Israeli citizen, was one of the people arrested during these trials, in the course of which hundreds of Czech Jews were sent to jail or forced labor camps.

p. 167   "Sticking the Knife": A game in which a circle drawn in damp soil is divided between the participants by means of a knife thrown at the perimeter.

p. 213   Israel Kastner: Rudolf (Israel) Kastner, 1906–1957, Zionist leader in Romania and Hungary, after World War II emigrated to Israel, where he was accused in 1953 by Malkiel Guenwald of having collaborated with the Nazis during the war. In the slander case against Gruenwald which followed most of his allegations were accepted by the judge. The verdict of the lower court was later quashed on appeal, but by then Kastner was no longer alive, having been assassinated in Tel Aviv on March 3, 1957.

p. 217　Kehane: Rabbi Meir Kahane, leader of the "Kach" party in Israel banned for racist incitement against the Arabs, assassinated in New York in 1990.

p. 230　*One crystal April morning . . . and prayed, and*: The lines quoted here are from the poem "Parting" by Haim Nahman Bialak, translated by Ruth Nevo.

p. 240　You hoped I would . . . neck-deep in the gore of soldiers: Based on the translation by Mark Smith of "Anat's Battle" in *Ugaritic Narrative Poetry, the Baal Cycle.*

p. 272　" 'I will seize it with my right hand . . . 'What do you desire, O Adolescent Anat?' ": Based on "Anat's Journey to and Audience with El," translated by Mark Smith in *Ugaritic Narrative Poetry, The Baal Cycle.*

p. 279　Maharal: Rabbi Yehuda Loew of Prague, a sixteenth-century sage to whom legend ascribes the creation of the golem, a clay figure which came to life.

p. 336　*For falsely were you torn from me and truth is my return to thee*: From the cycle "Joy of the Poor" by Hebrew poet Nathan Alterman.

HEBREW LITERATURE SERIES

The Hebrew Literature Series at Dalkey Archive Press makes available major works of Hebrew-language literature in English translation. Featuring exceptional authors at the forefront of Hebrew letters, the series aims to introduce the rich intellectual and aesthetic diversity of contemporary Hebrew writing and culture to English-language readers.

This series is published in collaboration with the Institute for the Translation of Hebrew Literature, at www.ithl.org.il. Thanks are also due to the Office of Cultural Affairs at the Consulate General of Israel, NY, for their support.

GABRIELA AVIGUR-ROTEM was born in Buenos Aires, Argentina in 1946 and came to Israel in 1950. She holds a degree in Hebrew and English literature. She has taught literature at the high-school level and directed writing workshops at Haifa and Ben Gurion Universities. She now works as an editor at Haifa University Publishing House. *Heatwave and Crazy Birds* is her second novel.

DALYA BILU lives in Jerusalem and has been awarded a number of prizes for her translation work, including the Israeli Ministry of Culture Prize for Translation, and the Jewish Book Council Award for Hebrew-English Translation.

Petros Abatzoglou, *What Does Mrs. Freeman Want?*
Michal Ajvaz, *The Golden Age.*
The Other City.
Pierre Albert-Birot, *Grabinoulor.*
Yuz Aleshkovsky, *Kangaroo.*
Felipe Alfau, *Chromos.*
Locos.
Ivan Ângelo, *The Celebration.*
The Tower of Glass.
David Antin, *Talking.*
António Lobo Antunes, *Knowledge of Hell.*
Alain Arias-Misson, *Theatre of Incest.*
Iftikhar Arif and Waqas Khwaja, eds., *Modern Poetry of Pakistan.*
John Ashbery and James Schuyler, *A Nest of Ninnies.*
Gabriela Avigur-Rotem, *Heatwave and Crazy Birds.*
Heimrad Bäcker, *transcript.*
Djuna Barnes, *Ladies Almanack.*
Ryder.
John Barth, *LETTERS.*
Sabbatical.
Donald Barthelme, *The King.*
Paradise.
Svetislav Basara, *Chinese Letter.*
René Belletto, *Dying.*
Mark Binelli, *Sacco and Vanzetti Must Die!*
Andrei Bitov, *Pushkin House.*
Andrej Blatnik, *You Do Understand.*
Louis Paul Boon, *Chapel Road.*
My Little War.
Summer in Termuren.
Roger Boylan, *Killoyle.*
Ignácio de Loyola Brandão, *Anonymous Celebrity.*
The Good-Bye Angel.
Teeth under the Sun.
Zero.
Bonnie Bremser, *Troia: Mexican Memoirs.*
Christine Brooke-Rose, *Amalgamemnon.*
Brigid Brophy, *In Transit.*
Meredith Brosnan, *Mr. Dynamite.*
Gerald L. Bruns, *Modern Poetry and the Idea of Language.*
Evgeny Bunimovich and J. Kates, eds., *Contemporary Russian Poetry: An Anthology.*
Gabrielle Burton, *Heartbreak Hotel.*
Michel Butor, *Degrees.*
Mobile.
Portrait of the Artist as a Young Ape.
G. Cabrera Infante, *Infante's Inferno.*
Three Trapped Tigers.
Julieta Campos, *The Fear of Losing Eurydice.*
Anne Carson, *Eros the Bittersweet.*
Orly Castel-Bloom, *Dolly City.*
Camilo José Cela, *Christ versus Arizona.*
The Family of Pascual Duarte.
The Hive.
Louis-Ferdinand Céline, *Castle to Castle.*
Conversations with Professor Y.
London Bridge.
Normance.

North.
Rigadoon.
Hugo Charteris, *The Tide Is Right.*
Jerome Charyn, *The Tar Baby.*
Eric Chevillard, *Demolishing Nisard.*
Marc Cholodenko, *Mordechai Schamz.*
Joshua Cohen, *Witz.*
Emily Holmes Coleman, *The Shutter of Snow.*
Robert Coover, *A Night at the Movies.*
Stanley Crawford, *Log of the S.S. The Mrs Unguentine.*
Some Instructions to My Wife.
Robert Creeley, *Collected Prose.*
René Crevel, *Putting My Foot in It.*
Ralph Cusack, *Cadenza.*
Susan Daitch, *L.C.*
Storytown.
Nicholas Delbanco, *The Count of Concord.*
Sherbrookes.
Nigel Dennis, *Cards of Identity.*
Peter Dimock, *A Short Rhetoric for Leaving the Family.*
Ariel Dorfman, *Konfidenz.*
Coleman Dowell, *The Houses of Children.*
Island People.
Too Much Flesh and Jabez.
Arkadii Dragomoshchenko, *Dust.*
Rikki Ducornet, *The Complete Butcher's Tales.*
The Fountains of Neptune.
The Jade Cabinet.
The One Marvelous Thing.
Phosphor in Dreamland.
The Stain.
The Word "Desire."
William Eastlake, *The Bamboo Bed.*
Castle Keep.
Lyric of the Circle Heart.
Jean Echenoz, *Chopin's Move.*
Stanley Elkin, *A Bad Man.*
Boswell: A Modern Comedy.
Criers and Kibitzers, Kibitzers and Criers.
The Dick Gibson Show.
The Franchiser.
George Mills.
The Living End.
The MacGuffin.
The Magic Kingdom.
Mrs. Ted Bliss.
The Rabbi of Lud.
Van Gogh's Room at Arles.
Annie Ernaux, *Cleaned Out.*
Lauren Fairbanks, *Muzzle Thyself.*
Sister Carrie.
Leslie A. Fiedler, *Love and Death in the American Novel.*
Juan Filloy, *Op Oloop.*
Gustave Flaubert, *Bouvard and Pécuchet.*
Kass Fleisher, *Talking out of School.*
Ford Madox Ford, *The March of Literature.*
Jon Fosse, *Aliss at the Fire.*
Melancholy.
Max Frisch, *I'm Not Stiller.*
Man in the Holocene.

FOR A FULL LIST OF PUBLICATIONS, VISIT:
www.dalkeyarchive.com

SELECTED DALKEY ARCHIVE PAPERBACKS

FOR A FULL LIST OF PUBLICATIONS, VISIT:
www.dalkeyarchive.com

SELECTED DALKEY ARCHIVE PAPERBACKS

ARNO SCHMIDT, *Collected Novellas.*
Collected Stories.
Nobodaddy's Children.
Two Novels.
ASAF SCHURR, *Motti.*
CHRISTINE SCHUTT, *Nightwork.*
GAIL SCOTT, *My Paris.*
DAMION SEARLS, *What We Were Doing*
and Where We Were Going.
JUNE AKERS SEESE,
Is This What Other Women Feel Too?
What Waiting Really Means.
BERNARD SHARE, *Inish.*
Transit.
AURELIE SHEEHAN,
Jack Kerouac Is Pregnant.
VIKTOR SHKLOVSKY, *Bowstring.*
Knight's Move.
A Sentimental Journey:
Memoirs 1917–1922.
Energy of Delusion: A Book on Plot.
Literature and Cinematography.
Theory of Prose.
Third Factory.
Zoo, or Letters Not about Love.
CLAUDE SIMON, *The Invitation.*
PIERRE SINIAC, *The Collaborators.*
JOSEF ŠKVORECKÝ, *The Engineer of*
Human Souls.
GILBERT SORRENTINO,
Aberration of Starlight.
Blue Pastoral.
Crystal Vision.
Imaginative Qualities of Actual
Things.
Mulligan Stew.
Pack of Lies.
Red the Fiend.
The Sky Changes.
Something Said.
Splendide-Hôtel.
Steelwork.
Under the Shadow.
W. M. SPACKMAN,
The Complete Fiction.
ANDRZEJ STASIUK, *Fado.*
GERTRUDE STEIN,
Lucy Church Amiably.
The Making of Americans.
A Novel of Thank You.
LARS SVENDSEN, *A Philosophy of Evil.*
PIOTR SZEWC, *Annihilation.*
GONÇALO M. TAVARES, *Jerusalem.*
Learning to Pray in the Age of
Technology.
LUCIAN DAN TEODOROVICI,
Our Circus Presents . . .
STEFAN THEMERSON, *Hobson's Island.*
The Mystery of the Sardine.
Tom Harris.
JOHN TOOMEY, *Sleepwalker.*
JEAN-PHILIPPE TOUSSAINT,
The Bathroom.
Camera.
Monsieur.
Running Away.
Self-Portrait Abroad.
Television.
DUMITRU TSEPENEAG,
Hotel Europa.

The Necessary Marriage.
Pigeon Post.
Vain Art of the Fugue.
ESTHER TUSQUETS, *Stranded.*
DUBRAVKA UGRESIC,
Lend Me Your Character.
Thank You for Not Reading.
MATI UNT, *Brecht at Night.*
Diary of a Blood Donor.
Things in the Night.
ÁLVARO URIBE AND OLIVIA SEARS, EDS.,
Best of Contemporary Mexican
Fiction.
ELOY URROZ, *Friction.*
The Obstacles.
LUISA VALENZUELA, *Dark Desires and*
the Others.
He Who Searches.
MARJA-LIISA VARTIO,
The Parson's Widow.
PAUL VERHAEGHEN, *Omega Minor.*
BORIS VIAN, *Heartsnatcher.*
LLORENÇ VILLALONGA, *The Dolls' Room.*
ORNELA VORPSI, *The Country Where No*
One Ever Dies.
AUSTRYN WAINHOUSE, *Hedyphagetica.*
PAUL WEST,
Words for a Deaf Daughter & Gala.
CURTIS WHITE,
America's Magic Mountain.
The Idea of Home.
Memories of My Father Watching TV.
Monstrous Possibility: An Invitation
to Literary Politics.
Requiem.
DIANE WILLIAMS, *Excitability:*
Selected Stories.
Romancer Erector.
DOUGLAS WOOLF, *Wall to Wall.*
Ya! & John-Juan.
JAY WRIGHT, *Polynomials and Pollen.*
The Presentable Art of Reading
Absence.
PHILIP WYLIE, *Generation of Vipers.*
MARGUERITE YOUNG, *Angel in the Forest.*
Miss MacIntosh, My Darling.
REYOUNG, *Unbabbling.*
VLADO ŽABOT, *The Succubus.*
ZORAN ŽIVKOVIĆ, *Hidden Camera.*
LOUIS ZUKOFSKY, *Collected Fiction.*
SCOTT ZWIREN, *God Head.*
